Laurie Ellingham li... Essex border with her tw... cockerpoo Rodney. She has a... Psychology and a background in public ~~relations~~, but her main love is writing and disappearing into the fictional wor... ... ...ge coffee and ... ...) to hand.

HQ

An imprint of HarperCollins*Publishers* Ltd.
1 London Bridge Street
London SE1 9GF

This edition 2017

1
First published in Great Britain by
HQ, an imprint of HarperCollins*Publishers* Ltd. 2017

ISBN: PB: 9780008211479

Printed and bound by
CPI Group (UK) Ltd, Croydon, CRO 4YY

one endless summer

Laurie Ellingham

For Andy

PART I

CHAPTER 1

Day 1

Lizzie

The sweet unnatural fragrance of hairspray and deodorant clung to the air in the windowless dressing room. The scents clawed at the back of Lizzie's throat. She drew in a shallow breath and stared into the camera. 'My name is Lizzie Appleton, I'm twenty-nine years old, and I have three months to live.'

Lizzie's words hung in the silence, bringing the enormity of her situation crashing down on her, and with it a fusion of colours that blurred the edges of her vision; blobs of reds and blues floating next to purples and yellows as if she was looking down the barrel of a kaleidoscope. Her head began to pound. What was she doing? Three months. 90 days. It wasn't enough.

'That was great, Lizzie.' Caroline clasped her hands together from behind the camera tripod. 'Let's try it one more time with a bit more feeling, OK?' Caroline pushed her glasses further up her thin nose as she bent over to watch Lizzie through the small, digital screen poking out from one side of the camera. 'Remember that this is for the advert, so we *really* need to grab the viewers' attention.'

'More feeling? Are you serious?' Lizzie asked, pulling at the black wool of her dress where it prickled her skin and wondering, not the first time, how it had come to this.

'Just think of something that makes you sad,' Caroline said with her usual pursed lip smile.

'Because dying isn't sad enough?' Lizzie narrowed her dark-blue eyes and waited for the documentary producer to squirm inside her grey trouser suit. The producer had been an almost-permanent fixture in Lizzie's life for the past seven days, and Lizzie was looking forward to saying goodbye to her at the airport in a few hours' time. In the meantime, any payback Lizzie could give for the hours of listening to Caroline's voice – which was always a notch higher than it needed to be as she encouraged and chided all in one breath – was worth it. *Smile, but not at the camera. Be yourself, but without that sarcasm of yours. Wear comfortable clothes, but be presentable.*

But Caroline didn't squirm or flinch. Instead, she pushed her glasses onto the top of her nest of dark curls and returned the stare. 'The sooner we get this done, the sooner I'll be out of your way.'

Lizzie sighed. After their week together, her sarcasm no longer seemed to goad the producer. Lizzie tried to focus; she squared her shoulders, fixed her gaze on the camera, and stared at her reflection in the circular glass of the lens: the button nose and high cheek bones she'd inherited from her mother; the dark-blue eyes; and brown hair of her father, now cut short to accommodate the bare patch at the nape of her neck – a parting gift from the radiotherapy.

The throbbing in her head intensified. Images of her parents from the previous evening bombarded her thoughts. The shaking hand of her father, Peter, and the watery-grey eyes of her mother, Evelyn, which had begged the words her mum had been unable to voice: *Don't go, Lizzie. Stay here with us.*

Both her parents looked ten years older than their sixty-one years, and had the lines on their faces of people who'd spent so much of their lives worrying. She'd done that to them. An ache spread across her chest. They deserved so much better than the hand they'd been dealt. But, then again, so did she.

'Ready?' Caroline asked, pulling her glasses back into place and brushing off an imaginary fleck of lint from her jacket.

Lizzie nodded. 'My name is Lizzie Appleton, I'm twenty-nine years old, and I have three months to live.'

'How does it make you feel?'

Lizzie's eyes shot to Caroline. 'I didn't know you were going to ask me that. We ... we haven't practised that one.'

'I didn't want you to practise it,' Caroline said, raising her perfectly shaped eyebrows. 'I want to know how you feel. The viewers will want to know – how does it feel to know you only have three months to live?'

Panic swept through her body. What was she supposed to say? What did people want to hear?

'It's a mixture,' she said, making herself look into the camera once more. Her voice sounded echoey and strange over the drumming of her heartbeat in her ears. 'Relief and fear.'

Carline lifted her hand and drew circles with her index finger. 'Keep going,' she mouthed.

Lizzie thought of *Little Women*, and Beth giving her dying speech to Jo. She'd read the book once, maybe twice, but it was the film Lizzie was thinking of. Claire Danes and her shaking voice telling Winona Ryder that she was doing something first for once. She was the one having the adventure. If Lizzie could remember that speech, then maybe she could say that, but her mind blanked.

'There's a relief in knowing you're going to die. Well, there is for me anyway,' Lizzie said after a pause. 'I've been dodging death all my life. I've survived brain tumours I wasn't supposed to survive. It's felt kind of like I've been on borrowed time, and now that time is up. But I don't have to waste another second of my life in a hospital, or a waiting room. I don't have to have any more treatments. I can live my life, and there's a relief in that.

'But if you're asking me what it feels like to know that I'm never going to see another Christmas. That the trees are going to blossom this year, and I'm not going to see it. I'm never going to look out of another window and see a world of white and think it's a late snowstorm, before realising it's blossom flying off the trees. Or what it feels like to know that my brother is going to be competing in the next Olympics –' Lizzie's voice cracked, she swallowed hard '– the actual Olympics, and I'm not going to be there cheering him on. That fills me with a fear beyond words. So, I'm trying very hard not to think about that, and just to focus on the first part. The relief that I can live my life.'

Lizzie stopped talking and tried to smile. She glanced at Caroline and wished she'd been able to remember the speech in *Little Women*, rather than the jumble of confusion she'd just spoken. If Caroline asked her to do it again, she'd have to think of something better to say.

'That was perfect, Lizzie, well done,' Caroline said, flicking a switch on the camera and stepping out from behind the tripod.

Lizzie sighed and slouched against the back of the chair.

'Now onto the breakfast interview,' Caroline continued. 'In a few minutes, you'll be called into the studio and positioned on the sofa with Samantha and Jaddi. Try to remember some of the answers we've practised, and, I know I've said this before, but I'm going to say it again anyway – please don't be sarcastic. It really doesn't play well on camera.'

'You do know it's not exact, don't you?' Lizzie asked. 'I might live longer. I might live three and a half months, or maybe even five.' Who was she trying to convince? Caroline, or herself?

Caroline exhaled through the small gap in her front teeth, creating a low whistling noise. The sound reminded Lizzie of the times she was little, sitting in the dips of the sand dunes near her house on the Suffolk coast, cushioned between her mum and dad, and Aaron just a bundle of blankets on her mum's lap. The wind had howled around the dunes and the North Sea had smashed on the shore below them.

Long days spent on the beach. Bonfires, barbeques and the sideways glances assessing her. Was she all right? Was she ill? Was that a limp in her run? A tremor in her hand? Followed by the forced cheer and smiles. 'Who needs to go abroad when we have so many treasures on our doorstep?' her mum liked to say in her chirping voice, glossing over the real reason for another year without a holiday – the infection risk, the hospital appointments, the cost. Her father losing his job as an engineer after the weeks, sometimes months, when she'd been in hospital.

Her life was like a large pebble thrown past the waves into the calm of the sea, dropping into the water with a plop and sending the ripples outwards, affecting those closest to her. She'd played along; she'd tried to make it easier for them. She'd always done as she was told, without question or complaint. Until now, anyway.

The whistling stopped and Caroline set her gaze on Lizzie. A decision had been made. 'Ninety days or under would be better.'

A sudden urge to laugh propelled its way up Lizzie's body, like the bubbles in a glass of Prosecco dancing to the top. The sound exploded out of her, alien and unwelcome, rebounding off of the dressing-room walls. 'Well, Caroline, I'll do my best.'

Caroline threw her hands to her mouth and shook her head. 'I'm so sorry, Lizzie, I didn't mean it like that. I just meant from an audience-viewing perspective. Obviously, nobody wants you to die; it's just that the documentary is called *The Girl with Three Months to Live*, and as you are going to ...' Caroline's voice trailed off.

'Ninety days or under would be better,' Lizzie finished for her as the desire to laugh evaporated, leaving a hollow void inside. She'd finally managed to rattle the producer, but had shaken herself up in the process. Lizzie stood up and stepped towards the door. The small room had an oppressive quality, clouding her thoughts so that she couldn't think straight.

Before she could reach it, the door swung open, bringing with it a fresh wave of fragrances: honeysuckle and roses, the scents that surrounded Jaddi like an aura.

Jaddi grinned as she stepped into the dressing room, flashing a row of perfect white teeth. Her sleek black hair brushed the middle of her back and shone under the bright bulbs surrounding the mirror in the centre of the room.

'Did you get what you needed?' Jaddi said.

'Yes. Perfect timing, Jaddi,' Caroline replied. 'I need to check everything is in place for our cameras. Where's Samantha?'

Jaddi stepped in front of the mirror and dabbed a finger along the sheen of gloss on her lips. 'In the toilet throwing up.'

A line formed on Caroline's brow. She caught Jaddi's eye in the reflection of the mirror. 'Is she going to be all right for the interview?'

'Don't worry –' Jaddi smiled '– she'll be fine. She was exactly the same before her final exams at uni, and that assessment-centre thing she did last year, wasn't she, Lizzie? And she aced them.'

'I'll tell the producer to make sure she isn't asked any direct questions, just to be on the safe side,' Caroline said, the crease on her forehead disappearing. 'Stay here and one of the production team will come to collect you in a few minutes.'

Caroline scooped up her leather organiser and smiled at Lizzie and Jaddi.

'You'll do fine this morning. Try to enjoy it.'

'Thanks.' Lizzie smiled. 'Not for this –' she waved her hand around the room '– but for making our dream happen.' The two words didn't seem enough, didn't seem right, either, but she felt like she should say them. 'Thank you.'

Caroline nodded. If Lizzie didn't know better, she would've sworn a tear glistened in the producer's eye. 'My pleasure,' Caroline said, before walking out of the room.

Jaddi turned to Lizzie with another wide grin. 'Ready?'

'No.' Lizzie shook her head and fiddled with the ends of her hair where it tickled the tops of her ears. She wasn't ready. She'd never be ready, for the interview, or for everything after it.

'You'll be fine, Lizzie. It's just two people talking to us on a sofa. It's no big deal.'

'It's OK for you, "Miss Beauty Pageant winner two years running".' She'd meant it to sound funny, but it hadn't. That was one of the problems she'd discovered since her final round of radiotherapy, since Dr Habibi had sat her down and shown her the brain scans: the things she was supposed to find funny, the things other people laughed at with light-hearted ease, washed over her. And yet, she laughed all the time, maybe more than before, but always at inappropriate moments, always a hollow noise echoing in a silent room. It was the same for jokes. She'd lost whatever knack she'd had for telling them. 'Besides, those two people you mentioned are actually famous TV presenters, and you seem to be forgetting all the people who'll be watching.'

'You do realise that I haven't done beauty pageants since I was sixteen?' Jaddi said. 'My mum practically forced me to do them. It was just something to add to my Indian marriage CV.' Jaddi smoothed a wrinkle in her charcoal-grey dress.

Lizzie sighed. 'All I know is that you are so much better at all of this than I am.'

'You'll be fine, I promise. You look lovely, by the way.' Jaddi turned away from the mirror and took Lizzie's hand. 'Your hair really suits you that length.'

A pressure built inside Lizzie. She clamped her fingers around Jaddi's wrist. 'Seriously,' Lizzie said, dropping her voice to a whisper. 'What we're doing is ... is insane.' A brief moment of relief washed over her. Finally, she began to voice the fears that had been haunting her for weeks.

Jaddi pulled her hand out from Lizzie's grip and touched her arm. 'It's a bit late to put the lid back on that can of worms, don't you think? I know it feels out of control, but if you think about it, nothing has really changed. You're worrying about the breakfast interview, that's all.'

'What about Samantha?'

Jaddi's shoulders dropped. For a moment, the bravado her friend wore like perfume was gone. 'You know as well as I do that this was the only way we—'

The door to the dressing room flew open.

'Only way we what?' Samantha asked.

CHAPTER 2

Samantha

Samantha's mobile buzzed in her hand, almost slipping out of her grip as it vibrated against the layer of sweat forming on her palms.

Jaddi mumbled a reply to her question, but Samantha didn't hear the words. The dressing room and her friends fell away as her concentration fixed on the incoming message and its sender.

My flat. 1pm. We're all set xxx

The words so simple, so normal, but there was nothing normal about it.

'Sam? Are you OK?' Lizzie said, tugging Samantha's thoughts back. 'You look sort of pale, honey. Maybe you should sit down.' Lizzie pulled out a stool from under the make-up counter and motioned for Samantha to sit.

Samantha stared at her friends as they waited for her response. She wanted to tell them everything, but how could she? How could she tell them what David, the love of her life, and the only man that had ever made her feel smart and beautiful, had planned for her later that day, when she couldn't contemplate it herself? She forced David and his message to the back of her mind. There were so many other things to worry about before 1pm.

'Why am I the only one being sick?' Samantha asked instead. 'This is national television.' She turned to the mirror, raking her fingers through her limp, blonde hair and pulling a face at her reflection. No amount of make-up could mask the grey sheen that seeped out from every pore. She didn't like having her photo taken let alone being filmed for a documentary for the next three months. And before she even got to that, she had to take part in a television interview, which had an average of 950,000 viewers every day. She'd looked it up at 4am when she'd been unable to sleep. Almost a million people would be watching her, listening to her, judging her. Nausea burnt at the back of her throat. This is their dream, Samantha reminded herself, willing the sickness to pass.

'Hey, don't worry,' Jaddi said, her face appearing behind Samantha's in the mirror. 'It will be over before you know it, and we'll be right there next to you. We're in this together, remember?'

Samantha nodded and fiddled with the fabric clinging to the curve of her hips. 'I should have gone for the green dress,' she said, trying to block the reflection of Jaddi's figure from view. Comparing her curves and wobbly bingo wings to Jaddi's beauty, not to mention Jaddi's svelte figure, was the quickest way into a pit of misery and crash dieting.

Samantha sighed. 'How did I not realise that my dress is the exact same colour as the sofa? No one will see me. I'll be a floating head.'

Lizzie's smiling face appeared behind her in the mirror. 'When,' Lizzie asked, resting her head on Samantha's shoulder, 'are you going to see how gorgeous you are? Not to mention intelligent. You will not be a floating head, you'll be perfect.'

Samantha smiled at Lizzie's pale face and the dark smudges under her eyes. The unfairness of it all washed over her just like the nausea had done an hour ago. Why did it have to be Lizzie? Of all the millions of people in the world who smoked, took drugs, lived life on the edge, who killed, and hurt others, the millions of people that, without question, deserved to die, why did it have to be kind, loving Lizzie going through this? It was a question Samantha had asked herself at least once a day for the past few months, more than once on the nights she couldn't sleep, mulling the question over in her mind with dozens of others she didn't have the answers to.

Jaddi stepped away from the mirror. 'So,' she said, placing her hands on her hips as Samantha and Lizzie turned to face her, 'you know I love you, don't you? We're like family. So you know when I say things, I say them for your own good, right? Well, I need to tell you that the two of you need to pull yourselves together. It's natural to feel nervous, but this is our chance. We've talked about travelling the world since university. I know it's scary, but we can't focus on how we got here or why we're doing it, or it'll make it too hard. We have to live in the here and now.'

Samantha listened for a quiver in Jaddi's voice, any sign of the fear and sadness that clouded Samantha's head, but there wasn't any. Jaddi sounded just like Caroline, forthright and self-assured in a way that only people confident with their own place in the world could be. No amount of education, elocution, or expensive clothes could make a person that way. It was in the way Jaddi and Lizzie were raised, something middle-class that Samantha tried to emulate, but so often failed.

She'd seen the looks from her peers at the Home Office. They knew just by looking at her that she was different. The first-class degree, the hours she spent at her desk long after everyone else had made their way to a back-street pub or home, how she knew parts of the law inside and out; none of it wiped out her upbringing in their eyes.

'It was nine years ago that we first planned this trip,' Jaddi continued. *'Nine years*. That's almost a decade. And we're finally doing it.'

'Easy for you to say,' Samantha said. 'Having a cameraman tagging along is all well and good when you're tall, thin and drop-dead gorgeous. I, personally, don't relish the thought of half of Britain seeing my gigantic bottom climbing up a mountain. Not to mention –' a lump lodged in Samantha's throat forcing her voice into a whisper '– Lizzie's tumour.'

Just then, a woman wearing a headset appeared in the doorway. 'We've gone to adverts. Three minutes and you're on,' she said before disappearing again.

'Was she talking to us?' Samantha turned to Lizzie as wasp-like panic swarmed in her stomach.

'Who else?' Jaddi grinned.

'I … I can't do this. Lizzie, I'm so, so sorry. I've tried to hold it together. I love you so much and I've tried to support you through this …' Samantha could hear the rupture in her voice, but she couldn't stop now. 'You're dying.'

'We're all going to die at some point,' Lizzie shrugged, a weak smile touching her face.

'But not in three months. We can't just up and leave as if everything is normal.' Tears spilled from Samantha's eyes. 'Everything is not normal. What about your parents? They're devastated, we all are. And what if you get ill whilst we're in the middle of nowhere? Then what? We can't go, we just can't.' A sob escaped Samantha's mouth.

Silence grew between them. Samantha tried to read Lizzie's wide-eyed stare, but all she could see was her own fear reflected back in her friend's face. Then Lizzie's gaze turned to Jaddi, causing frustration to surge inside Samantha. Sometimes, just sometimes, she hated how they both deferred to Jaddi, as if they were still standing in the kitchen of their houseshare, total strangers on their first day at university. Jaddi had oozed self-assurance. She'd chosen the pubs they'd gone to, the boys they'd spoken to, the clubs they'd joined. Back then it had seemed as if Jaddi had had a magic wand that could alter the course of their destinies.

Samantha let the thought go. This wasn't another one of Jaddi's daredevil plans. This trip belonged to all of them. It was a shared dream that had kept them going through exams and dissertations, and long days slugging it at work followed by evenings in the dingy one-bed flat they had shared in East London. Their reasons for travelling might be different – Jaddi wanted adventure; Lizzie wanted new experiences; and Samantha had wanted to escape (or she had once anyway) – but the dream was the same and they'd clung to that. Just not like this.

Jaddi stepped towards Samantha and pulled her into a tight embrace. Part of Samantha wanted to push Jaddi away, but she didn't. Jaddi's cool confidence had a way of rubbing off on the people around her, Samantha included. The knots in her stomach began to unravel.

'I'm scared too, Sam. But Lizzie can't stay here waiting for it to happen,' Jaddi said. 'There is so much she hasn't seen or done. There is nothing anyone can do for her here. It shouldn't end like that for anyone, especially not Lizzie.'

Samantha nodded, dabbing her fingers under her eyes in an attempt to wipe away the tears without smearing any more of her make-up. 'I know. I'm sorry, you're right.' She drew in a long breath. 'I'm panicking about this interview, but I'll keep it together.'

Lizzie's arms wrapped around them. 'I don't think I've said thank you to both of you, for doing this with me,' she said. 'I couldn't do it without you.'

'You don't need to say thanks, Lizzie,' Samantha said. 'You know we'd follow you anywhere. Except off a cliff, of course.'

'You two had better not be getting tears on my dress,' Jaddi said a moment later, making them all laugh in a shaky uncertain sort of way and releasing the sadness that hovered over them.

Jaddi squeezed Samantha a little tighter before letting go and spinning on the points of her heels. 'Let's go then.'

CHAPTER 3

Lizzie

Bright white lights on tall metal frames emitted heat like the summer sun, causing a bead of sweat to trickle down Lizzie's back as she stepped into the studio.

Jaddi's hand touched her arm, shepherding her forward quicker than her feet wanted to move.

A dozen people in dirty jeans and baggy T-shirts stood in clusters around screens and laptops, speaking over each other in rushed voices. Wires covered the floor around her feet, held in place by strips of silver tape. They looked like a bed of snakes about to slither over her body and squeeze the breath right out of her.

Like the eye of the storm, the blue sofa sat serenely amidst the wires, equipment and people. The breakfast-show presenters were huddled over a clipboard in two armchairs opposite the sofa. They looked up and smiled as Lizzie approached. Adrenaline pumped through her veins.

When they reached the sofa, Jaddi tugged her arm, pulling Lizzie down next to her. Samantha sat on the other side of Jaddi, her gaze fixed straight ahead as if she was about to be interrogated by MI5, rather than interviewed by Britain's most likable breakfast duo. Guilt stabbed the pit of Lizzie's stomach. Lizzie thought of the pebble dropping into the sea again and the ripples it caused.

'OK, people,' someone shouted from behind her. 'We're back in five, four, three.'

The studio fell silent as if a mute button had been pressed.

'Welcome back to *Channel 6 Breakfast*. I'm Frankie Scott,' the female presenter said, flashing a row of white veneers.

'And I'm Tim Reynolds.'

'We're joined on the sofa now by Lizzie Appleton and her two friends, Jaddi Patel and Samantha Jeffrey,' Frankie said in a mellifluous voice.

Lizzie turned towards the cameras and stared at the screen of writing moving along underneath. She could see Caroline's head just beyond the cameras. The producer gestured a 'don't forget to smile' U-shape with her hands.

'I don't think there can be many people out there who don't know Lizzie's harrowing story. She was diagnosed with a brain tumour three months ago, and after the radiotherapy failed, Lizzie was given the damning news that there was nothing more her doctors could do. With just months to live, Lizzie's lifelong dream to travel the world seemed impossible. Until her best friend and flatmate, Jaddi, created a website and asked for people to donate money for their trip.'

Frankie turned her gaze to the sofa. 'Lizzie, first of all, thank you for joining us.'

Lizzie forced her mouth into a smile. Her heartbeat quickened. 'Thank you for having me.'

'Can you tell us what's been happening since Jaddi first set up the fundraising page?'

Blobs of colour threatened Lizzie's vision again. She blinked until her focus returned, drew in a deep breath and tried to remember the lines she'd practised with

Caroline. 'It's been a whirlwind. Jaddi set up the website overnight. I didn't know anything about it until the next morning, by which time my brother, Aaron, had shared it on Twitter, and things have been pretty crazy ever since.'

'For those at home who don't know,' Tim said, staring into the camera, 'Lizzie's brother is Aaron Appleton, British gymnastics champion, and arguably one of our best hopes for Olympic gold in the next games.'

The mention of Aaron caused an ache to radiate from Lizzie's chest. Her brother had been too young to remember her stays in hospital growing up. He hadn't even been born the first two times. Until recently, Aaron had been oblivious to the burden of waiting. Waiting to hear a diagnosis. Waiting to hear if the treatment had worked. Waiting to see if the tumour would come back.

Aaron had insisted on coming with them for her last hospital appointment. Lizzie had known what Dr Habibi was going to say the moment he'd clipped her CT scans onto the viewing screen and flicked on the light behind it. There it was, the kidney-shaped blob at the base of her brain. No bigger, but no smaller either. Months of treatment wasted. The neurologist had launched straight to the point – 'Unfortunately, the radiotherapy hasn't been successful ...' – but Lizzie had only been half listening. It felt as if she was watching an out-of-control car skidding on ice, spinning straight towards a lamp post on the other side of the road. She gazed at her parents, then at Aaron, powerless to alter the course of the scene unfolding in front of them. The anguish on their faces would haunt her forever.

'I guess he has a lot of followers,' Tim said, dragging Lizzie's thoughts back to the interview.

She nodded and smiled. 'Just a few hundred thousand more than me, I'd say. A lot of his followers shared the link and then the donations started coming in.'

'When I saw the website for the first time, about a month ago,' Tim said, 'it was the helplessness of your situation, Lizzie, that really touched me. The fact that there is just nothing more you can do must be tough to accept. I don't know how I'd cope in your shoes, and from the comments people made when they donated, I'd say I'm not the only one who feels that way. How did it make you feel when the donations began to pour in?' Tim asked.

'I was completely overwhelmed by the kindness and generosity. People we didn't know were giving us money to go backpacking. It didn't seem real. It still doesn't.'

'But it didn't stop there?' Frankie said.

'No, it didn't. The story started appearing in the local news and in some of the national papers. Then Jaddi got a call from a producer at Channel 6, offering to pay for the rest of the trip, if we agreed to be part of a documentary covering the last few months of my life. So here we are. We're all packed and leave for Thailand tonight.'

'That is truly awe-inspiring,' Frankie said, before turning her gaze to Jaddi. 'Jaddi, did you have any idea that your website would become so popular? That you'd be able to fulfil Lizzie's dream?'

Lizzie looked at Jaddi, who grinned back before focusing on Frankie. 'It was a long shot, but I had to do something. When Lizzie came home from the hospital and told me the radiotherapy had failed, I felt so helpless. I guess setting up the page was my way of coping. The fact that we've made it here, is just as Lizzie said ... overwhelming.'

'I remember going to Thailand some years ago,' Tim began, 'and getting a visa was a nightmare. With the speed at which this has all happened, have you found that side of things a problem?'

Jaddi laughed. 'Thankfully, that's not been a problem, Tim. Samantha is the most organised person I've ever met in my life. She even colour codes her socks. She and Caroline have made sure we have all the visas and vaccinations we need.

Samantha's cheeks glowed red, but she managed to smile. 'Well, I have to be organised living with these two.'

Samantha's comment sent a spattering of laughter across the studio.

'Caroline has upgraded our phones so we can access the internet anywhere we have signal,' Jaddi said, turning her head a fraction and staring into the camera. 'So feel free to post messages on our Facebook page and tweet us.'

'So, girls,' Tim said, 'can you tell us and the audience at home a little about yourselves? I gather from the website that you've been good friends for a while?'

Lizzie looked at Jaddi, then Samantha. 'We've been best friends since university.' She smiled. 'Our halls of residence preference forms got lost and we ended up getting put together in a student house.'

For the smallest of moments, the urgency and the fear lifted as Lizzie thought about that first afternoon when they'd dragged their boxes and suitcases into the kitchen and met for the first time, Jaddi, hands on hips, insisting a trip to the nearest pub, and Samantha, picking at her fingers, suggesting they unpack first.

'We moved to London together after university and still live together now,' Jaddi added. 'Samantha works in the Home Office, writing policy documents or something else extremely important that I don't understand. She's the brains behind us. I work in public relations for a confectionary company.'

'So we have a lot of chocolate kicking about,' Samantha chipped in.

Jaddi grinned. 'It never lasts long though, does it? And Lizzie, she ...' Jaddi faltered. The smile remained on her face, but the glow behind it had gone.

Another ripple, Lizzie thought with a pang in her chest. She slipped her hand inside Jaddi's. 'I was working as an office administrator up until last summer,' Lizzie said, 'whilst I figured out what it was that I wanted to do. I'd just started teacher training when I got ill again.'

Tim nodded. 'Can you tell us about your tumour, Lizzie? I must admit I wasn't expecting you to look so well.'

'Thank you.' Caroline's words echoed around her head. *Speak slowly, be clear, no medical jargon.* 'My tumour is called a benign low-grade meningioma, which doesn't mean much, except that it's slow-growing and it's not cancerous. Generally speaking, these tumours are relatively easy to treat with either surgery or radiotherapy, or both. I should know as this is my fourth one. But it's a problem this time because of its position in the brainstem.' Lizzie paused and touched the nape of her neck. Her fingers brushed the prickles of hair that had started to grow back.

Should she describe the radiotherapy? How she'd been bolted to a table by a white mesh mask, the claustrophobia so overwhelming that it had stolen the breath from her lungs. How she'd wanted to scream but couldn't because the mask was fixed so tightly to her face that she couldn't open her mouth. Did people want to hear that? She guessed not.

'The brainstem is the part of my brain which controls my breathing and tells my heart to beat. Any surgery to remove the tumour would destroy the brainstem. Something the tumour will do itself in a few months.'

Frankie touched her ear. 'My producer is telling me that we're almost out of time. So I just have one more question for you, Lizzie. As you mentioned, your story has reached many of the national newspapers. How does it feel to be considered a role model to others suffering with terminal illness?'

Role model? Lizzie pulled in a sharp intake of air and tried not to wince from the explosion of pain in her head. The only answer teetering on the tip of her tongue was the truth. 'I'm not a role model. The truth is that I ...' Her eyes felt drawn to the camera. She stared into the screen and imagined the people sat on their sofas watching her, her parents and Aaron included. 'I feel lucky,' she stammered.

Frankie smiled. 'It's clear this must be very difficult for you to talk about, Lizzie, but I don't think any of our viewers would use the word *lucky* to describe your situation.'

'Oh, I'm very lucky. This is my fourth brain tumour. The first one, when I was three, was removed by surgery. The second one, when I was nine, was shrunk down to the size of a speck of dust. The third, when I was sixteen was also removed. Most of my life has been about having treatments and operations, and scans. Lots and lots of brain scans. But now ... now I've been given the opportunity to live.

'There will be people out there right now, walking down the street, thinking they've got years ahead of them. When *bam*, a bus hits them, and it's over. I've been given a chance to live my dreams. I'll always be grateful for that, and for all of the people who've helped me get here.'

'Well, you might not see yourself as a role model, Lizzie, but you're certainly an inspiration. Good luck on your adventures,' Frankie said, before turning to face the camera. 'The first episode of Lizzie's documentary – *The Girl with Three Months to Live* – will be right here on Channel 6 at nine o'clock this Saturday evening.'

'Now,' Tim began, 'have you ever thought about starting your own business? Up next on the blue sofa, we'll be chatting with entrepreneur, Anne Thornton-Smith, about how to make your business a success, and more.'

'We're out,' a voice shouted from somewhere behind the cameras.

Four women holding make-up pots and hairbrushes rushed forward, crowding around the presenters like fans vying for an autograph.

'Well done, girls,' Caroline said with a smile, ushering them off of the sofa and back to the dressing room.

'Samantha, Jaddi, you've got the day to yourselves. I'll be waiting at Heathrow check-in at six-thirty to introduce you to your cameraman and to say goodbye. Lizzie, we've got some magazine interviews lined up this morning. You'll get a bit of time to yourself this afternoon.'

A caustic remark lingered, but for once Lizzie didn't voice it. The final question from the presenter had staggered her. For weeks she'd been swept along in Jaddi's plans, like a guppy caught in a current, unable to change direction or simply stop, and when she'd been given an opportunity to explain herself, she hadn't taken it. She could no longer blame Jaddi for whatever lay ahead.

CHAPTER 4

Jaddi

Jaddi stepped through the opening in the revolving doors and instantly found herself barricaded between the glass panels as they jolted to a stop.

'It's your backpack,' a man in a rumpled suit said from the other side of the glass. He raised his eyebrows and muttered something under his breath. Jaddi nodded and moved forwards. The automatic doors whirred back into life for a second before dying once again as her foot nudged the glass in front of her. *Bloody hell, why would anyone install revolving doors at an airport?* Jaddi pictured the airport security team, sipping cups of tea on their breaks whilst sniggering at her incompetence.

'You can't touch the doors,' the man she'd trapped shouted, throwing his arms in the air.

Jaddi resisted the urge to give him the finger, flashed an apologetic smile, and twisted her body sideways, taking crab-like steps until the opening into the terminal appeared and she moved into the throng.

Voices, laughter and the distant beat of music echoed around the terminal. The whir of suitcase wheels rattled on the floor as men and women in black suits wheeling miniature cases strode purposefully around her. Groups of people sat in huddles on the floor, their luggage strewn around them as they ate sandwiches and salads out of plastic packets.

A movement from her left caught her eye. As she turned, the wheel of a luggage trolley clipped the side of her ankle sending a searing pain up her leg.

'Sorry, did I get you?' a red-faced man in a dark polo shirt asked before turning away. 'Kids, calm down, *please.*'

'It's fine,' she said, rubbing a spot at the bottom of her combat trousers where the pain had already started to dull.

Jaddi watched the father with the overflowing trolley of suitcases take the path of least resistance through the airport as three young children danced and skipped around his legs.

She should be feeling that child-like buzz. Tomorrow she would be in Thailand, absorbing a culture and a history she'd dreamed about since her eleventh birthday, when her uncle Prem had given her a light-up, plastic globe. She'd loved spinning the sphere on its axis until the greens and blues had blurred into one, then stopping it with a jab and reading the tiny place name under her finger. She would go to bed every night dreaming of adventures and undiscovered lands.

Instead, all she could think about was Suk, and their argument. If she could still call it that. Did it count as a fight if they'd repeated the same words over and over for the past year? It had started with raised voices and accusations, but after so long, and with no resolution in sight, their tones had mellowed.

'We really should get married,' Suk had said, nuzzling her neck as they'd sat behind the black-tinted glass of one of her father's town cars.

'Are we going to do this again, now? When I'm about to get on a plane and leave for three months?' Jaddi touched Suk's leg, hoping to cause a distraction.

'You know it makes sense.' Suk sighed. 'If we leave it much longer then you know our parents will decide for us, and I'll probably end up in India.'

'I've told you, I'm not ready to get married.' Jaddi slipped her hand inside Suk's. The warmth of their touch spread through Jaddi's body. 'Things are great between us right now. Why can't we carry on as we are?'

'Because I'm sick of living with my parents and working for your dad's car service.' Suk shifted away from Jaddi and leaned against the door. 'In case you've forgotten, your family are a lot more relaxed than mine. We've been seeing each other off and on for twelve years. We need to settle down before one of our families find out. Unless this is just a game to you?'

Frustration and hurt wound through Jaddi. 'How can you even suggest that? Do you know how hard it is for me to lie to Lizzie and Samantha? They are my best friends; they deserve my honesty. Instead they think I hook up with a different guy every week, when really I'm seeing you. I'm the one that wants to tell them. Come with me now if you don't believe me. We can still keep it a secret from our families, but wouldn't it be nice to be a proper couple—'

'Don't speak like that,' Suk cut in. 'Don't even think it. No one can know. If we tell even one person, our families will find out. Marriage is the only way to decide our future for ourselves.'

'I have to go, I'm late as it is,' Jaddi said, staring into Suk's dark eyes. Her heartbeat ramped up a notch. One lie on top of another. What would happen when the three months were up? Jaddi shook her head; she couldn't think like that. This had been her idea, and she had to make it worth it. Live in the here and now, that's what she'd said to Lizzie and Samantha, and that's what she had to do.

'Here,' Jaddi said, holding out her door keys, 'take these.'

'Why?' Suk asked.

'I don't know, just have them. Our flat is going to be sitting empty for three months. I'll probably just lose them if I drag them around in my backpack with me.'

Suk nodded. 'Will you ... promise me you won't ... you know.'

Jaddi laughed, her smile widening as a rush of love covered her fears. 'I've been with someone else once, Suk. Once, in twelve years. I was away at uni. We'd had a huge fight and you'd broken up with me, remember? You really should come and meet Samantha. She'll tell you how drunk I was that night.'

'Why would Samantha—'

'Because she never lets me forget it, and the fact that he was someone she liked.' Jaddi shook her head. 'I love you, that's what matters. I always have, and no one will get in the way of that.'

She slid across the smooth leather seats towards Suk until their bodies touched. They kissed, tentative and slow as the remnants of their fight hung between them, then faster as desire took hold. Jaddi could still feel the pressure of Suk's lips on hers as she weaved through the terminal.

Jaddi caught sight of Samantha, shifting from foot to foot, by the check-in desk. Samantha had yet to shake the blanched pallor from the breakfast interview.

Had she pushed Lizzie and Sam too far this time?

Lizzie's eyes caught hers and she waved. Pushing the thought aside, Jaddi bounced towards them with a wide grin. She'd get a drink into Samantha after take-off; that would cheer her up.

'Here she is,' Samantha said. 'I told you she'd be late.'

Jaddi laughed. 'Of course I'm late. I'm always late.'

Lizzie leant forward and pulled Jaddi into a tight embrace. 'I thought for a minute you might not make it,' she said in a quiet voice. Jaddi drew back as the pinch of Lizzie's nails dug into her back.

'I'm here now,' Jaddi said, staring into Lizzie's wide, blue eyes and willing her to relax. Tomorrow they would be in Thailand and it would all be worth it. It had to be.

'Jaddi,' Caroline said from behind her. 'Now that you're here, I'd like to introduce you to the cameraman.' Jaddi let go of Lizzie and spun around.

'Ouch,' Samantha cried out as Jaddi's backpack caught her arm. 'Watch it.'

'Sorry, Sam, are you OK?' Jaddi shrugged her backpack away from her shoulders and dropped it to the floor before she could do anymore damage.

Samantha rolled her eyes as she rubbed at her arm. 'I'm fine,' she said, the hint of a smile twitching on her lips.

'Jaddi,' Caroline said, 'I'd like you to meet Sherlock. He'll be your cameraman for the next three months.'

'Sherlock?' Jaddi turned to face the man towering over Caroline. He was tall, with cropped, brown hair, cut short to a bristly number one and almost enough dark stubble on his face to be considered a beard. The arms protruding from his navy T-shirt weren't the toned biceps of someone who spent hours in the gym, but his shoulders were broad and muscular.

'Ben Holmes,' he said, pushing his black-framed glasses closer to his eyes before offering a hand to Jaddi. 'Sherlock is a nickname.'

'It's nice to meet you.' She grinned as his hand wrapped around hers.

'I was just explaining to the others that you'll need to tell me whenever you plan to go anywhere. Even if it's the middle of the night and you decide to go out for a bottle of water, I need to know,' he said.

Jaddi nodded. 'Yep, sure. No problem.'

Lizzie mumbled something inaudible under her breath, causing Ben to glance at her with narrowed eyes before directing his focus back to Jaddi. Jaddi had the distinct impression that she'd just walked into the middle of an argument between Lizzie and their new travel companion.

'Here's your microphone pack,' he said, holding a small, black box with a wire wrapped around it. 'The battery clips on your waistband at the back, and the lavalier – this bit,' he said, tapping the small, black head, 'clips onto your collar or the top of your vest. I've got a monitor which will tell me when the batteries are running low, and I'll swap them when necessary.

'All you need to do is wear it and make sure it's switched on at *all* times.' He flicked a switch on the side of the box and handed it to Jaddi. 'Starting now.'

'Great, thanks, Ben,' she said with a another grin, taking the microphone. 'Or do you prefer Sherlock?'

'Ben's fine,' he said, already unzipping a side pocket on a large leather holdall hooked over his shoulder. 'I've also got a smaller camera here for you to take, Lizzie,' he said. 'For your video diaries. Apart from mine, it's the only camera we're taking with us, so please look after it.'

'What video diaries?' Lizzie asked, ignoring the object in Ben's outstretched hand.

Ben turned to Caroline and raised his eyebrows. 'You haven't told her?'

'I'm sure I mentioned it,' Caroline said with an airy laugh. 'It's not a big deal, Lizzie. We thought you could do a video diary before you go to sleep each night. Just a few minutes talking about your day and how you feel. A way to get the audience into your head and make them feel part of your journey.'

'The camera has Bluetooth and Wi-Fi,' Ben said. 'Once you've pressed 'save' it will automatically send the file to my laptop. If we're not in a signal area, I'll take the camera and load the video manually. Then I'll edit it, along with the other footage, and send it on to the Channel 6 studio.'

'We're breaking ground in documentary-making here,' Caroline said. 'Due to the ... er ... sensitive timeframe and current media coverage surrounding you, Lizzie, we'll be airing your travels weekly, as they happen.'

'Well, if you're breaking ground,' Lizzie said, her tone biting, 'then by all means, yes, I'd be more than happy to share my inner most feelings with the world.' Lizzie grabbed the camera and dropped it into her satchel.

'Look—' Ben said, glaring at Lizzie.

'Shall we go then?' Jaddi flashed a smile at Ben and hooked an arm around Lizzie. He would learn soon enough to let Lizzie's sarcasm wash over him. The last thing they needed was to start their trip with a falling-out.

'Are you all right with this?' Jaddi asked Lizzie, as they scooped up their backpacks.

Lizzie shrugged. 'It doesn't feel like I have a choice. I just want it be us, that's all.'

'I second that,' Samantha said, moving closer. 'How can we be ourselves with a cameraman tagging along?'

'It will be us. We'll get used to the camera in no time, that's what they always say on those reality shows, but look, we're in this together. If you don't want to do it, if you want to go home, figure something else out, then say the word and we can.'

Jaddi could sense Caroline's panic as she hovered behind them and willed the producer not to jump in. This had to be Lizzie's choice.

'Promise it'll feel like it's just us?' Lizzie asked, pulling her lower lip between her teeth.

'I promise.' Jaddi smiled, wrapping her arms around them both and dipping her head forward. She hoped it was a promise she could keep. Lizzie and Samantha did the same, their three foreheads touching. They stayed like that for several seconds, their fears passing between them without needing to be voiced.

A commotion from across the terminal caught Jaddi's attention. They stepped out of each other's arms and turned to watch as a figure ran towards them, darting in and out of people, jumping over suitcases and waving his arms in the air.

'Lizzie!' a voice shouted, as a head jumped up above a queue of people next to them.

Lizzie gasped as the athletic frame of her younger brother sprinted into view. 'Aaron, what on earth are you doing here?'

'I couldn't let you go without saying goodbye,' he said, gulping in long mouthfuls of air. 'My train was delayed. I thought I'd missed you.'

Without a word, Ben unzipped his shoulder bag and pulled out a camera the size of two shoe boxes. He pressed a button and lifted it with ease onto his right shoulder, obscuring half of his face as one eye stared down a black scope.

Lizzie pulled her brother towards her and wrapped her arms around him. 'You didn't need to come all this way. We said goodbye last night.' She looked up, her eyes scanning the terminal. 'Are Mum and Dad with you?'

Aaron shook his head. 'They didn't want to make it harder for you. They do understand what you're doing. I know it doesn't seem that way, but they do. We all do.'

Tears filled Lizzie's eyes as she continued to hold onto Aaron.

'How are you going to get home?' Lizzie asked him, stepping away and tilting her head up a fraction to meet his gaze.

Aaron laughed. 'Oh, you know, I thought I'd hitchhike back to Aldeburgh. There's bound to be some lorries heading that way.'

'Hey, doofus –' Lizzie punched him on the arm '– I was being serious.'

Aaron sighed and ran a hand through the short waves of his brown hair. 'I'm not eight-years-old anymore. I'm more than capable of using public transport, you know?'

Lizzie smiled. 'I know, I know. but you'll always be my little brother, no matter how old you are.'

It took another few minutes before the watch-tapping prompts from the man behind the check-in desk became too frequent to ignore.

As Aaron turned to leave he touched Jaddi's arm and leaned closer. 'Look after her.'

He had the same piercing blue eyes as Lizzie. They stared into hers with a fierceness she'd have expected from Lizzie's father, not a cute eighteen-year-old with nothing but a bright future ahead of him.

'You know I will.' She smiled through the pang of guilt radiating out from the pit of her stomach. For the first time since she'd created the website, Jaddi wondered how much of what she'd done was for Lizzie, and how much of it was for herself.

CHAPTER 5

Lizzie

Lizzie shifted position in the narrow chair, banging her elbow against the armrest and causing a sharp pain to shoot up her arm. She scrunched up the muscles in her face, rubbed her hand over her funny bone, or ulnar nerve, whatever it was, and wished she hadn't accepted the window seat when Samantha and Jaddi had offered it to her.

She was also regretting her insistence that they travel economy. Her left foot had begun to tingle. Caroline had offered to book them First Class, but Lizzie had said no. She'd wanted to be like any other ordinary backpacker, squashed into cattle class seats and sleeping in shared rooms at cheap hostels. It was part of the experience. Lizzie wiggled her toes inside the red flight socks her mum had insisted she pack. The appeal of being ordinary was quickly wearing thin and they were only six hours into their journey.

Samantha and Jaddi slept motionless in the seats next to her, trapping her in her seat. She poked her head up and cast her eyes around the dim cabin of the aeroplane. She could see rows of heads slumped to one side, some with inflated cushions around their necks, others wearing headphones. Air stewards moved without a sound around the galley in the middle of the aircraft.

Lizzie reached for her travel bag, stashed under the seat in front of her. She pulled out the camera Ben had given her and opened the flap. The small screen glowed white in the darkness. A second later her face appeared.

What would they do if she didn't bother with the diaries? Cancel the documentary? Cut her trip short? It seemed so personal – an intrusion into her thoughts, which she supposed was the point. Lizzie sighed and glanced around her. What difference did it make if she did it? It wasn't as if she would ever have to watch them.

Lizzie held down the record button until a red dot appeared in the corner of the screen.

'Hi,' she whispered, looking into her own hollow eyes, staring back at her from the screen. She looked pale and gaunt in the illuminating glow from the camera. She tried a smile, but it only added to the ghost-like effect. 'This is my first video diary. We're currently on a night flight to Thailand. The time in the UK right now is almost three in the morning. Everyone is asleep.' Lizzie smirked and turned the screen towards Samantha and Jaddi. 'Including these two. Maybe I'd be asleep too if I'd had half a bottle of wine at take-off. Luckily for the viewers, and my parents, I can't drink because of the anti-seizure medication I'm taking. So you will be spared any drunkenness. From me anyway.

'I'm supposed to tell you how I feel. Well, I feel excited, and a little nervous. I'm not sure I really believe it's happening yet. We're finally going. First Thailand, then Cambodia, Vietnam, then onto Australia before we finish up in America. It's a shorter trip than we first planned in our second year at uni, but I'm just so excited that we're finally doing it. I can't thank everyone enough who has helped me get here. I guess the countdown begins now: welcome to day one; eighty-nine to go.'

Lizzie stopped herself. She'd meant it to sound peppy, but the words that left her mouth rang of remorse. What else should she say?

Lizzie stared into the camera screen, her mind blank.

Then she smiled. 'I'm OK, Mum. Truly I am, so no tears. That goes for you too, Dad. I'm with two amazing girls who I love so much, and with the exception of the tumour in my brainstem, I'm healthy. I feel great, in fact, and I can't wait for this plane to land.'

Lizzie sensed a movement next to her, and closed the camera before dropping it back into her bag.

'Are you really all right?' Samantha sat up and stretched her arms up above her head. Tears glistened in her eyes.

'Of course I am. We're finally fulfilling our dream.'

'Liz,' Samantha said, shifting in her seat so that her body faced Lizzie, 'it's just me now. There are no cameras on. Jaddi is still out for the count. You can talk to me, Liz, about your tumour, I mean. You haven't spoken about it; do you know that? Every time I bring it up, we always seem to end up talking about how I feel, or you change the subject.'

Lizzie closed her eyes as a sadness engulfed her. It was as much a sadness for Samantha's pain as her own. 'I know,' Lizzie said, trying to find the words, 'but when I think about what will happen at the end of this trip, I feel like I'm being crushed. It's like Jaddi said, we have to live in the here and now. Make every moment together count. In fact, maybe I should wake up sleeping beauty over there.' Lizzie grinned, wishing it wasn't just part of the truth she was sharing with Samantha … wishing the plane would hurry up and land so they could start the here and now.

Samantha narrowed her eyes. 'You're doing it again, changing the subject on me. You don't have to pretend,' she said, her voice a whisper.

'I'm not pretending.' The tingling across her left foot intensified momentarily before ceasing, as if her foot had simply disconnected itself from her ankle.

Samantha continued to stare into Lizzie's eyes, like a teacher waiting for the truth. What did that word even mean? Truth. A flashback of the dressing room hit Lizzie's thoughts. The suffocating walls, Samantha's face crumbling before her. How close had Lizzie come to telling her the truth then? Too close. Samantha's world was black and white, right and wrong, good and bad. Samantha never saw the grey areas, to her they didn't exist, but Lizzie's life now existed only in the grey areas.

How different would things have been if Samantha had been home the night Lizzie had returned from the hospital, standing behind the rickety ironing board watching back-to-back reruns of *Sex in the City*, ironing her own clothes and any Lizzie and Jaddi added to the pile, instead of staying with David? Would they still be sitting on this aeroplane? Lizzie doubted it.

'My left foot is numb.' Lizzie shrugged, that much was true at least.

'What?' Samantha's eyes dropped to Lizzie's footwell. 'Do you want to get up and move around? How long has it been numb for?'

'A few minutes. I had pins and needles for a while and now I can't feel anything.' Lizzie glanced towards Jaddi and lowered her voice. 'I don't think I can walk on it. What if I don't get any feeling back? I'll have ruined the trip for all of us.'

Saying the words aloud caused a panic to grip Lizzie. They hadn't even landed in a foreign country yet, she hadn't so much as tasted the freedom she'd craved her entire life, and already she could see it ending before it had even begun. The freedom from the waiting, from the treatment, from all the times her parents and her doctors had shaken their heads, creased their foreheads as if it was them in pain, and not her, and said no.

All of a sudden Lizzie could hear her own nine-year-old self, sitting at the kitchen table with her homework splayed out in front of her, and asking the question she'd already known the answer too, but asking it anyway. 'Tracey Sanders has invited me to her birthday party,' she'd said, her eyes focused on the page of her book as if an invitation to a party was an everyday occurrence for her, as if the girls and boys in her class hadn't stared at the tufts of hair growing back on her head and whispered too loudly, *Lizzie Appleton is contagious*, despite the special assembly the entire school had had about her condition. So they'd known, they'd all known. But Tracey Sanders's mum had told Tracey that she'd had to invite the whole class, and that had meant Lizzie too.

'Oh, that was nice of her,' her mum had replied, turning a page in the magazine she'd been reading.

'Can I go?' Lizzie had looked up then, their eyes meeting. Lizzie hadn't been able to help it. Hope had taken hold of her insides, propelling her forwards. She could be normal, she'd thought. She could show them all how normal she could be.

'Umm, I'm not sure, honey. Maybe. It depends when it is. You know, we're back in London the week after next for the follow-up with Dr Habibi.'

A smile had spread across Lizzie's face. Glee. That was the word for it. Her mum had said exactly what Lizzie had expected her to say. The week after next, yes, they were busy, they were in London for another scan, but this weekend, the weekend of Tracey Sanders's party, they were free. 'That's OK,' Lizzie had replied, the hope bursting inside of her like the fizz of sherbet in flying saucers. 'Tracey's party is on Saturday.'

'But that's only two days away.' Her mum had frowned, closing the magazine and pushing it to one side.

'I forgot.' Lizzie had shrugged, wishing her cheeks didn't feel so hot. 'So can I go? It's at half past ten. We're free, I checked the calendar.' Lizzie had leaned forward. Please say yes, please, please, please, she'd thought, but didn't say, because begging would make it harder for her mum, and whilst she had desperately, desperately wanted to go to Tracey Sanders's tenth birthday party, she hadn't wanted to upset her mum. 'It's at the leisure centre. It's a swimming-pool party.' There, she'd said it. The final piece of information had sat on the table between them.

Her mum's face had said it all. The frown contorting, the smile disappearing. She'd started shaking her head before the words had left her mouth, pulverising Lizzie's hope and causing a pain to harden in her throat. Lizzie had tried to swallow, tried to hold back the tears, but they were already falling onto her cheeks.

'Oh, honey, you know you can't go swimming.' Her mum had stood up, shuffling around the table until she'd enveloped Lizzie in a hug that had smelt of kitchen soap and flour. 'Dr Habibi said no swimming, remember, honey? It's your immune system; it's just not up for swimming pools. All those germs in the water.'

'But it's chlorinated.' She'd sniffed, burying her head inside the fold of her mum's jumper. 'I'll keep my mouth shut.'

'They'll get in anyway. Dr Habibi explained that to us. I'm sorry, honey. How about I call Tracey's mum and see if you can come after the swimming bit? They'll probably be going to McDonald's. You can go for that.'

'Pizza Hut,' Lizzie had murmured, wishing she hadn't mentioned the party at all. Wishing she could take it back so she wouldn't have to go to the restaurant and see all of her classmates with their wet hair and shining faces. Them and her. Not normal at all, but different, very different.

'Are you sure you don't want me to have my head shaved too?'

Fresh tears brimmed in Lizzie's eyes, but she'd smiled. 'The only thing worse than being a bald girl is having a mum who's bald too.' Lizzie had tightened her hold on her mum. 'Pizza Hut will be fun,' she'd lied.

'Lizzie?' Samantha's voice broke through her thoughts. 'Should I call one of the air hostesses?' Samantha reached her hand up to the low ceiling and the row of square buttons. 'They might have something that you can take.'

'No, don't.' Lizzie grabbed Samantha's hand, pulling it down. 'Just give it a few minutes and see if it passes.' Lizzie wiggled her toes again. Only her right foot responded. 'Let's change the subject. Maybe it's like watching the toaster. It will take longer if we fixate on it. Tell me, what do you make of the cameraman?'

'He seems OK,' Samantha said. 'Nice-looking in a rugged, unwashed sort of way. He's not said much, but that's not a bad thing. I'd be more worried if he was all chatty and pally with us, like most men are when they catch sight of Jaddi – as if being friends with us will help their chances. At least if he's quiet we might be able to forget about the camera, and it won't get in the way of our time together.'

'I don't know,' Lizzie said, lowering her voice. 'Quiet is one thing, rude is another. Did you see the way he demanded we all wear our microphones twenty-four seven? He's travelling the world and getting paid, did he really need to be so rude to us?'

Just then a beep sounded from the row of seats in front of them. Lizzie glanced up as Ben's face appeared. 'Babysitting you three is not my idea of travelling the world.'

'Have you been filming the whole time?' Lizzie asked, a flush creeping over her cheeks.

'It's my job to capture your life, remember?' Ben replied.

Passengers around them began to stir. A reading light switched on from somewhere behind her.

'What is your problem exactly?' Lizzie whispered.

Ben rolled his eyes. 'I don't have a problem. I have a job to do. I'm not your friend or your travel buddy. This is not one of those reality soaps where you get to do another take and cut whenever it suits you. I might ask the odd question when I'm filming if I think the viewers need more explanation, but that's it. I'm quiet, or rude, or whatever you want to call it, because I'm here to capture your story, not be part of it. And what I just heard was the most real thing that's come out of your mouth so far.'

'Tell it like it is, why don't you,' Lizzie muttered, as her face burnt crimson.

A row of lights along the cabin ceiling flickered on.

The overhead Tannoy crackled above Lizzie's head. 'Ladies and gentleman, we will shortly be serving a light meal,' a man's voice sing-songed. 'We do ask that you move your seats up to the sitting position and have your tray tables down ready. Thank you. You may also wish to set your watches to Bangkok local time, which is ten fifteen am.'

Ben shifted back in his seat and disappeared from view. Lizzie lurched forward, another retort teetered on her lips, but Samantha shook her head in a 'just leave it' gesture and the quip disappeared. Lizzie blew out a puff of air and slumped back in her seat.

'I'm not sure making an enemy out of him will make it any easier,' Samantha whispered, her voice so quiet Lizzie only just heard it.

'Everything he says rubs me up the wrong way.' Lizzie bent her head closer to Samantha.

'Are you sure it's him and not what he represents? The documentary?' Samantha replied with her usual dose of common sense.

'Probably.' Lizzie shrugged. 'I know Jaddi thinks we'll forget about the camera, but I don't see how.'

'Hey, we'll have a good time,' Samantha said with quiver in her voice that sliced into Lizzie's heart.

Lizzie opened her mouth to reply but stopped. A cold seeped over her left foot as if she'd submerged it in a bucket of ice water. She wiggled her toes again. This time both feet responded.

'I've got the feeling in my foot back.' She smiled.

'Phew, that's a relief,' Samantha said. 'Now we won't have to leave you behind at the hostel all day whilst we go exploring.' She grinned.

Jaddi stirred in her seat. 'What did I miss?' she said without opening her eyes.

'Nothing,' Lizzie said before Samantha could reply.

CHAPTER 6

Samantha

A deep yawn spread through Samantha as she watched her blue backpack trundle along the conveyer belt towards her. The large chrome-framed clock on the wall read three-thirty. If it weren't for the harsh brightness of the afternoon sun streaming through the glass ceiling above her, she could easily have believed that it was the early hours of the morning, which to her body at least, she supposed it was.

A few metres away Jaddi and Lizzie fell into a cascade of giggles. Their voices, high with excitement, carried through the baggage-claim area. Samantha turned her head to watch them, and just for a moment two strangers stood where her friends should be. It was an alien feeling, one that sent an unease winding through her. Why was she the only one that felt it – the foreboding? It wasn't as if she'd expected Lizzie to lie down on her death bed and wait for the tumour to get her, but this – the documentary, the cameraman – it didn't feel right, and it wasn't just her loathing of cameras, but something else, just out of reach in her mind, a rotting that she could almost smell, almost taste, but couldn't see. If only they'd been able to afford the trip without the help from Channel 6, Samantha thought, then it might have been different.

Samantha glanced at Lizzie. Her pale face, lit from the sun, shone with excitement. Samantha pushed the unease away. Lizzie deserved to see the world. If they had to have their every movement captured on film for three months to make that happen, then so be it. Lizzie and Jaddi were her family. They weren't *like* her family, as Jaddi had said, however many hours ago it had been that they'd stood in the dressing room at Channel 6 together. They *were* Samantha's family. The only family she had.

Did her mother even know she was travelling the world? Would someone on the estate have told her? Would she watch the documentary? Samantha doubted it.

'Don't expect your room to be free for holidays or visits or nothing,' her mum had said to her on the day Samantha had wheeled her one large suitcase out of her bedroom and into the gloom of the living room. 9am in the morning, curtains drawn, the screeching voices from a talk show on the TV, the air stinking of body odour and stale cigarettes. 'When you're gone, you're gone,' her mum had said, glancing away from the screen long enough to appraise Samantha. 'I got no money to help you. You're on your own at university.' Her mother had swished her head and used her mocking posh voice, but it hadn't masked the North London lilt or the disdain she clearly had for her daughter's desire to make something more of her life.

Samantha hadn't expected money, she hadn't expected her mum to be proud of her, or sad to see her leave, but the words she'd used had still cut deep. It was the last time they'd spoken. In the summers at uni she'd picked up the part-time jobs off campus that the other students had left to return home, or stayed with Jaddi and helped wash cars for Jaddi's dad. And Christmases and Easters since she'd spent with Lizzie's family on the Suffolk coast.

Lizzie and Jaddi were her family in every sense of the word. They told each other everything. Almost everything, Samantha corrected.

As her backpack moved into reach, Samantha scooped it up and hoisted it onto her back. The movement caused a pain to grip the top of her arms and images of David's 'game' clouded her thoughts. Goosebumps raged across her skin, her breath caught in her throat. She closed her eyes and the smell of his aftershaves filled her senses. She screwed her eyes tight against the images rearing up, before shaking them away. What she needed now was a hot shower and food that hadn't been processed, shrink-wrapped and shipped thirty thousand feet in the air.

'All set?' Jaddi called out to her.

'Sure.' Samantha said with a nod, falling into pace behind the others and fixing her gaze on her feet, avoiding Ben and his camera, taking long, backwards strides a metre in front of them.

'This place is amazing,' Jaddi said as they strolled along a glass atrium lined with dark-green trees in large white pots.

Lizzie laughed. 'It's just Bangkok airport.'

'OK, fine, but how many airports have you been to that have things like that?' Jaddi said, pointing across the terminal and forcing Samantha to lift her eyes from the floor and stare open-mouthed at a three-headed serpent, glistening with gold and jewels, looming over them. Its long body was coiled around a rock and being pulled in two directions by life-sized colourful men wearing pointy gold hats.

The detail of the men, their expressions, their straining muscles, the look of anguish in the eyes of the serpent, it was as exquisite as it was unexpected.

For one minute the unease cloaking Samantha lifted. She forgot about Ben and the camera, David and his game, Lizzie's prognosis. Staring at the three heads of the creature, the gold spikes on its head shimmering in the sun's rays, she could almost hear its harrowing screech.

'Churning of the milk ocean,' Samantha said, reading the English translation on the plaque below the serpent.

The three of them stared at the statue as if mesmerised by its presence. Maybe Jaddi was right, Samantha thought. If a statue in an airport could make her forget about Lizzie's prognosis and the documentary for even a moment, then surely the sights outside the airport would do the same tenfold. Samantha turned to Jaddi and Lizzie, a smile stretching across her face. 'Shall we go and discover Thailand then?'

'I just need to …' Lizzie shook her head as she spun around. 'I'm going—' She darted towards the toilet sign.

'I'll go too,' Samantha said. 'I could really do with brushing my teeth.'

'Good idea.' Jaddi fell into step beside her as Lizzie rushed ahead.

'What is it about women and toilets?' Ben said. 'I'll just wait here by myself then, shall I?'

'Yep.' Jaddi laughed without turning around.

'Doesn't the camera bother you?' Samantha asked. She risked a glance behind her, relieved to see Ben lowering the camera to his waist and switching it off.

'Not really.' Jaddi shrugged.

'But all those people who'll be watching us. It's a touch voyeuristic, don't you think? People turning on their TVs to watch our every move.'

'It is a bit weird, but you're overthinking it. Forget about the camera, that's what I'm planning to do.

At best, Ben will be like an annoying older brother tagging along,' Jaddi said, throwing a glance over her shoulder and smiling at Ben. 'I know it's not perfect, but don't think about how much better it would be without the camera. It's because of the camera that we're here. I promise you, in a few days it won't even factor in to your thoughts.'

'I'll try, I guess,' she said, the doubt palpable in her voice.

'Hey,' Jaddi said, nudging her elbow against Samantha's side. 'Do you think Lizzie's got Bangkok belly already?'

Samantha laughed as she pushed open the toilet door and stepped into the white, tiled restroom. 'I don't see how, we've only—' Samantha stopped talking, her eyes registering Lizzie's body, slumped on the floor by a row of sinks. 'Lizzie!' Samantha gasped, diving towards her. 'Are you OK?'

Lizzie's eyes fixed on Samantha's. She moved her mouth, causing a gurgling noise to escape from her throat.

Terror exploded inside of Samantha, making every movement feel fumbled and out of sync as she wriggled free of her backpack and skidded onto her knees beside Lizzie.

'What's wrong with her?' Jaddi's voice, loud with fear, ricocheted off the walls.

'Lizzie, can you hear me? What's wrong? What's wrong?' Samantha turned to look over her shoulder at Jaddi. 'Get help!' she half-shrieked at her as hysteria started to tighten around her vocal chords.

Before Jaddi could move, a tremor took hold of Lizzie's body. Lizzie slumped forward onto the tiles as convulsions shuddered through her.

'Oh God,' Jaddi said. 'Oh God, Oh God.'

'Jaddi, snap out of it and get some help!' Samantha shouted again.

Jaddi pulled her eyes away from Lizzie's shaking body and stared at Samantha before jumping to her feet and dashing for the door.

Samantha watched her go, wanting to scream after her, *I told you this would happen. I told you. This is your fault.* Instead, she clenched her teeth together and turned back to Lizzie's still-convulsing body.

CHAPTER 7

Samantha

Lizzie's body continued to shudder and shake in disjointed movements as Jaddi flew back into the restroom. It seemed to Samantha, helplessly watching Lizzie – elbows bolted to her side, her hands twisted into deformed fists – as though a demon had found its way into Lizzie's body and was fighting with all its might to get out.

'I said get help!' Samantha shouted, the hysteria, a cyclone in her throat. 'Where's the help?'

'I got Ben,' Jaddi half panted, dropping down beside Lizzie and avoiding Samantha's gaze. As Jaddi spoke, Ben stepped through the door, camera on shoulder. The same fluid movements from the terminal now shortened in the small rectangular restroom, but still slow, still even. *I'm here to capture the story, not be part of it*, that's what he'd told them on the plane. Why had Jaddi thought he'd help? Why had she not run across the airport, screaming for help until an army of people rushed to her side? All of a sudden the space around them closed in. What now? Samantha didn't want to leave Lizzie's side, but what choice did she have?

'Shit, her lips are turning blue,' Jaddi said. 'We have to do something.' A sob left her mouth as she reached her arms out towards Lizzie's juddering legs.

'Don't touch her,' Ben said from behind them, his voice calm and in control, slicing through the panic swarming through Samantha. She turned her face towards him. In one move, Ben placed the camera onto the floor and hopped over to Jaddi, pulling her up and away from Lizzie.

'What are you doing?' Jaddi cried out, shrugging off his hands.

'She's having a seizure, you can't hold her,' Ben said, taking Jaddi's place beside Lizzie.

'But she keeps banging her shoulder on the tiles,' Jaddi said. 'It must be hurting her. I can help.'

'No, you can't. You'd do a lot more damage by holding her.' Ben pulled off his jumper and slid it under Lizzie's head as a current continued to shake her body. 'All we can do is cushion her head.'

'How do you know?' Samantha asked, not bothering to hide the accusation in her tone.

'My brother has epilepsy,' he said before leaning closer to Lizzie. 'Lizzie, you're having a seizure. It's OK. It'll be over in a minute. Hang in there. You're going to be fine.'

'Can she hear us?' Jaddi asked from behind them.

'I don't know. My brother always says he can, but every seizure is different, and it affects people differently.'

Something in Ben's tone loosened the fear gripping Samantha. She pulled in a breath and watched Lizzie's jerking movements begin to slow. 'I think it's stopping,' she said.

'Let's give it a minute and wait for her to come around before we alert the airport staff,' Ben said, as if reading the question in Samantha's head before she'd had a chance to ask it. 'That way she won't come out of it to a bathroom full of people. There's nothing a doctor can do for her right now.'

Time passed. A minute, then two. No one spoke. Samantha could hear her heartbeat drumming in her ears. She glanced at Ben's camera, still in its position on the floor, the light on the side glowing red. It was still recording, she realised, fighting the urge to stand up and step out of the way. Whether she liked it or not, she was part of this documentary, and nothing would make her leave Lizzie's side.

'She's opening her eyes.' Jaddi leaned in and placed a hand on Lizzie's shoulder. 'Lizzie, can you hear me?'

Lizzie's pupils narrowed into focus as she stared between the three of them, her eyes wide with fear and uncertainty. It was the same look Samantha had seen on Lizzie's face the morning of her first radiotherapy treatment last autumn.

'You're all right, Lizzie. You had a seizure,' Ben said.

Lizzie's face softened, tears formed a wall of water over her pupils but she continued to stare at them in turn.

'I'll get her some water,' Jaddi said, scrambling to her feet.

'She needs to speak first, before you can give it to her,' Ben called after her. 'In case she's still seizing and we don't know it. If she is, the water could go straight into her lungs and choke her,' he explained as he stood up.

'Oh, right.' Jaddi knelt back down and ran a hand over Lizzie's hair. 'Can you hear me, Liz? Please say something.'

'Umm.' Lizzie blinked and touched her hand to the back of her head. 'What happened?'

'You had a seizure.' Samantha swallowed the lump in her throat but could do nothing to stop the tears from rolling down her cheeks and dropping onto the sleeve of Lizzie's top. 'We found you on the floor in the toilets.'

Samantha lifted her head to Jaddi and Ben. 'I'll go and get help,' she said, her voice no more than a whisper.

'No, I'll go,' Jaddi said, already springing to her feet again.

'I don't need any help,' Lizzie mumbled as the door to the bathroom swung shut.

'You do, I'm afraid.' Ben stepped towards the doorway. 'You need to be seen by a doctor.'

Horror printed on Lizzie's face. 'Don't make me go to hospital.' Her eyes shot to Samantha. 'Please.' Her voice, croaky from the seizure, broke at the end, so it came out 'plea'.

Out of the corner of her eye, Samantha sensed Ben stepping back, his movements fluid once more, hoisting the camera into the air and resting it back onto his shoulder. At that moment Samantha didn't care about the camera, or the thousands of people that would see her kneeling on the floor of an airport toilets crying her eyes out. All she cared about was getting Lizzie to a hospital, whether Lizzie wanted to go or not.

CHAPTER 8

Lizzie

'How did you forget?' Samantha asked for the fifth time in as many minutes. She paced the hospital room, throwing her hands about as she spoke.

'I'm sorry, I really am. I don't know how I forgot, I just did.' A layer of treacle covered Lizzie's thoughts. She tried to explain through the pain radiating across her temples. Every millimetre of her head hurt. The innermost part of her brain pounded rhythmically outwards, whilst the outside of her skull, neck and shoulders ached, she guessed from hitting the floor. 'I lost track of time on the flight. I meant to take them when we landed, but then it was too late.'

Lizzie didn't mention to Samantha that the medication took her on a merry-go-round, spinning her endlessly around and around. Or the fact that until her face had smacked against the cool tiles of the airport toilets, she'd thought they were an impotent gesture, prescribed by Dr Habibi because he didn't know what else to do for her.

It hadn't crossed her mind that she'd actually have a seizure, and spend the first day of her around-the-world adventure in a hospital bed. A burst of colours filled the room. Red and blue hues floated across her eyes adding to the fog and the pain.

'Every twelve hours, Lizzie,' Samantha said. 'Not fourteen hours. Not eighteen. You could have been seriously hurt. What if you'd been standing up and cracked your head open on the sink? What if—'

'I know,' Lizzie cut in, wincing as the sound of her voice sent a fresh wave of pain through her head. 'I'm sorry I worried you, but I'm fine.'

'Okaaay.' The doctor who'd taken her blood pressure returned to the room, dragging out the 'a' sound for a few beats. 'How are you feeling, Miss Appleton?'

'Good.' She nodded, forcing herself to smile through the nausea that sprung up from her head movement. 'Really good.'

'I am pleased to hear it. All of your vitals are also good, but we would like to keep you in overnight for observation, and send you for an MRI scan in the morning. This is to make sure nothing has changed, based on what you've said about your tumour. Depending on the results of the scan, we may also need to do a lumbar puncture and an EEG.'

He spoke English with a clipped accuracy, pronouncing every syllable with a slight American twang. It made her think of Dr Habibi, her neurologist in London. In the twenty-six years he'd been her doctor, his Persian accent hadn't softened at all.

'No.' Lizzie sat up in bed, and the movement caused the pain in her head to resonate through her body. The colourful blotches turned black, casting the room into shadow. She resisted the urge to scrunch her eyes shut and flop back onto the pillow. Staying overnight in hospital was not an option, and an MRI was out of the question. 'I really just want to go to our hostel. I forgot to take my anti-seizure medication. It won't happen again.'

'Too right it won't,' Samantha chided from beside the bed.

If every single one of her muscles didn't hurt, Lizzie would have reached over to Samantha and squeezed her hand. Samantha's mothering tone was her way of coping, of regaining control. However hard the seizure had been to go through – conscious but unable to focus, aware but unable to control – it would've been just as hard for Samantha and Jaddi to watch.

'Still,' the doctor, whose name she'd already forgotten, began, 'seizures put a lot of stress on the body. Postictal symptoms of a seizure can develop up to forty-eight hours afterwards. You may develop drowsiness, become confused, nauseous, or have another seizure. It would be better if you stayed here so that we can monitor your condition. If you still feel well after your MRI tomorrow, then you can go.'

Lizzie turned her head to Jaddi, who was sitting bolt upright in a chair on the other side of the bed. She looked pale, her features strained. Lizzie hoped her eyes conveyed her silent plea to Jaddi for help, but her movements felt sluggish, as if she was commanding her body to do things through a faulty connection.

'Excuse me, Doctor Chang … sun … en.' Jaddi smiled and stood up, stepping towards the doctor and smoothing out the creases in her vest top.

He returned the smile and nodded, before correcting her pronunciation: 'Chang-sung-noen.'

'Doctor Chang-sung-noen, it's taken so much for us to travel to your beautiful country. I'm sure you can understand why Lizzie doesn't want to stay cooped up in a hospital bed. We'll take care of her. We'll make sure she rests for a couple of days. If there's even the slightest hint that she is unwell, we'll bring her straight back.'

'No late-night parties?' he said.

'Absolutely not.'

'Okaaay. It's your choice. I will start the process. Bear with me, please.' He clasped his hands behind his back and strode away.

The blotches disappeared from Lizzie's vision. She sighed and looked around her. Her surroundings were just like every other hospital room she'd stayed in – plain walls, polished floors, monitors on tripods with wheels – but when she closed her eyes she could hear Bangkok City buzzing around outside: the high-pitched whir of motorbike engines; horns honking in urgent beeps. She craved to be among the noise.

Lizzie opened her eyes, her gaze falling to Ben, leaning against the wall in the corner. He'd moved his camera down and held it just above the belt of his combat trousers. She couldn't tell if he was filming them or watching footage he'd filmed earlier. Her seizure, no doubt.

He looked up and met her stare, the corners of his mouth moving into a slight smile. It softened his features, and for the first time, Lizzie noticed a concern in his brown eyes, amplified by the thick rims of his glasses.

She wanted to be angry at him for filming her seizure. Did the man have no decency? But the anger wasn't there. Only his voice was there, in her head. Deep and calm. *Hang in there. You're going to be fine.* Was it a coincidence that the seizure had loosened its grip on her the moment he'd spoken? Or had his words penetrated through the seizure, freeing her from its depths?

When she'd first registered his presence, kneeling on the floor beside her, she'd tried to respond. The question had formed in her mind, but had lost its way, so she hadn't asked him, *How do you know?*

'Holy cow,' Jaddi said, weaving around a flatbed filled with large sacks of rice. 'I don't think I've ever sweated this much in my life.'

'You're kidding, right?' Samantha muttered from the other side of Lizzie.

'No.' Jaddi shook her head. 'Seriously, this heat is crazy. Look at me! I'm sweltering.'

'How dare you say that to us?!' Samantha narrowed her eyes as Jaddi tied the bottom of her top into a knot, exposing a toned stomach. 'You, I will admit, are glowing somewhat in the heat, but us on the other hand –' Samantha waved a finger between herself and Lizzie, and smiled '– look as if we've been swimming. My hair is dripping.'

'Thanks for the compliment, Sam.' Lizzie laughed, grateful, for once, for her cropped hair, as the excitement of their trip wound its way back through her. 'Hopefully we'll acclimatise tomorrow.'

Against the protests from Samantha and Jaddi, Lizzie had insisted that they walk the fifteen minutes to their hostel. She'd needed to absorb something that wasn't white tiles, toilets, taxis, or hospital rooms. And seeing Bangkok, alive with lights and people in the early evening was exactly what she'd had in mind.

The oppressive humidity had hit them the moment they'd stepped out of the hospital, as if they'd walked fully clothed, backpacks on, into a sauna, the dense air and sweat soaking them in minutes. The humidity had been a shock, but it was nothing compared to the city streets. Four lanes of cars, buses and motorbikes crawled in both directions, the gritty petrol smell of exhaust fumes adding to the stifling air. Noise bombarded them from every direction: the hum of the engines; the clattering of the old buses; the pip pop of the motorbikes;

music blaring from radios; car horns; people shouting; shop owners heckling. And yet, through the noise, the throbbing of her headache lessened with every step.

'Er, hello?' Jaddi laughed. 'My hair has quadrupled in size.' Jaddi lifted a lock of hair up and frowned.

'That's true.' Samantha grinned. 'Shame the camera's not on to film it.' Samantha shot a glance back towards Ben, walking a pace behind them.

When they'd cut down a side road, Ben's camera had gained him an entourage of young teenage boys, appearing from nowhere, keen to learn what he was doing in their broken English, keener still to touch the lens and try to hold the camera. Ben had been forced to stow the camera away in his bag, something Samantha had delighted in.

'Hey look, there's a street market,' Jaddi said, pointing into a narrow street crammed with stalls and colourful merchandise stretching for as far as they could see and lit by startling neon lights. 'Wow, it looks amazing! We have to come back tomorrow for a look around.'

'Why wait?' Lizzie grinned, already moving towards the crowds and stepping into the street, her eyes feasting on the vast colours and quantity of items now surrounding them. The energy of the city was seeping through her skin and igniting inside her. She sensed Jaddi and Samantha beside her, absorbing the buzzing market that seemed to be enticing them into its depths. The air simmered with whiffs of spices and meats that made Lizzie's stomach gurgle.

'Are you sure you're up for this?' Samantha touched Lizzie's arm.

Lizzie glanced back at Ben.

He heaved the strap of his camera bag further onto his shoulder – so that it rested on the cushioned strap of his rucksack – and scowled.

Lizzie nodded, her smile widening. 'Absolutely. Come on.' All at once she felt like any other traveller. No one knew her history or her future. She had her best friends and she had the world to explore. 'We can grab something to eat too. I'm starving.'

'I don't need to be told twice,' Jaddi said. 'Look at all these clothes. I'm in heaven.'

As they moved further into the market and the crowds, Samantha dove towards a table crammed with sunglasses and bags.

'Oooo,' Samantha squealed. 'I want them all. Look at that red one.' She pointed to a large, dark-red holdall. 'Tell me that isn't exactly the same as the Michael Kors I've had my eye on for the last year.'

'You might have to wait.' Lizzie tugged Samantha's arm and glanced at the unfamiliar bodies budging at their sides and trying to get closer to the stall. 'We've lost Jaddi already.'

Samantha turned and surveyed the street. 'No, look –' she pointed ahead '– there she is.'

Lizzie stood on her tiptoes and watched Jaddi dash in zigzags between the stalls.

'Come on.' Lizzie laughed. 'We'd better grab her.'

'Good point,' Samantha said. 'That girl can burn through spending money as quickly as you burn through a pack of jaffa cakes.'

'Oi!' Lizzie grinned, following behind as Samantha weaved through the jostling crowd. 'You know as well as I do that you can never have just two jaffa cakes.'

'Two? Surely you mean a packet?'

Lizzie laughed as they rushed to catch up with Jaddi.

An hour later, they stepped out of the market and onto a quiet street lined with scooters and motorbikes.

'Can you believe this place?' Lizzie said, her words lost amidst the heckles from the stall owners.

'Where you from?' a man called to them from a doorway which led through to a shop filled with more clothes.

'I'm beginning to think,' Samantha said, turning back to stare at the market, 'that, "Where you from?" roughly translates as, "What currency should I try to sell you things in?"'

Lizzie grinned and followed Samantha's gaze to Ben, camera on his shoulder, pushing through a group of women gesticulating widely over a reel of fabric. She hadn't realised he'd been in the market or filming them. Despite the heat and the sweat cloaking her body she still felt the rush of blood to her cheeks as the lens followed her movements.

'I have no idea how I'm going to fit this stuff in my backpack,' Jaddi said, grinning and lifting four bulging carrier bags – the thin kind with the handles already stretched and ready to snap.

'I'll help you,' Samantha said, taking two of Jaddi's bags for her. 'I bet you haven't even Swiss rolled your clothes in your backpack.'

'Swiss rolled? What are you on about?'

Sam shook her head and smiled. 'I'll show you later.'

'I'm just glad we've eaten,' Lizzie said. 'That noodle dish was lush, I want to eat it every day.'

'I bet you won't be saying that by the end of a whole month in Southeast Asia,' Jaddi said.

A sudden silence fell over them. Jaddi's comment hung in the air. *A whole month*. One month. One third of their trip. Would it be enough? Lizzie wondered, dropping a few paces behind Samantha and Jaddi as they traipsed in the direction of their hostel. Only then did she notice the weight of her backpack on her back and the pain of the straps digging into her shoulders.

'Here,' Ben said, zipping his camera back into its case and falling into step beside Lizzie, 'I got you this—' He pulled a black watch out of his pocket. 'It's not very pretty, but it works.'

'You got me a watch? Why?' she asked, turning the square plastic object over in her hands and pressing a tiny black button on one side.

In one swift movement Ben snatched the watch out of her hands. 'Don't press that,' he snapped.

'Oh.' Lizzie shrugged. 'Look, thanks and all that, but I'm not really a watch person.' She shook her head and picked up her pace. On the bathroom floor at the airport, and again in the hospital, she'd thought she'd glimpsed another side to the cameraman. One that wasn't quite so rude and obnoxious. But clearly she'd been wrong. Why buy her a crappy plastic watch only to snatch it back again?

'Just wear it, please.' Ben frowned, handing her the watch again. 'I've set the alarm for eight in the morning and eight at night. Every twelve hours. So you know when to take your medication.'

'You think I'd forget again? Thanks for the vote of confidence.' She shoved the watch into her pocket and dropped her eyes to the pavement. The brief feeling of normal she'd felt in the market disappeared.

'Once we leave Bangkok, getting to a hospital is going to become a lot harder.'

'Fine.' The smooth confidence of his voice carried in her head once more. *Hang in there. You're going to be fine.* She shook it away. What did he know?

'Hey, there's our hostel,' Jaddi said, pointing at a two-storey yellow building on the opposite side of the road, its colour like a beacon against the backdrop of grey structures that surrounded it.

'Lizzie,' Ben said, drawing her gaze back to him, 'when we get into our rooms, I'm going to get a quick bit of footage of the three of you in your dorm, and then I'm going to need to do some editing and send everything from today back to the studio, so it can go into the first episode on Saturday.'

'Oh.' She squeezed through a gap between two parked scooters, her mind racing through the events of the afternoon. Ben had asked her in the hospital if she'd wanted to watch the footage from the restroom, and she'd said no. She didn't want to see it, but she didn't want anyone else to see it either. She wished she had a little more, or any, of Jaddi's guile when it came to getting what she wanted from the opposite sex.

'And before you ask,' Ben said, 'the answer's no. I send it all. No special cuts.'

'I wasn't …'

He narrowed his eyes. 'Yes, you were. And don't even think about sending Jaddi to sweet talk me. I saw the full force of her charms with the doctor, and they won't work on me.'

'Jaddi's charms work on all men.'

'Not me.' He shook his head. 'But look, there's something you can do.'

'What?' Lizzie asked, the throbbing returning to the back of her head.

'Do tonight's video diary as soon as we get into the hostel. Explain what happened. Reassure the viewers that you're OK.'

Lizzie's energy levels dipped as they crossed the busy road to the hostel. So much for normal, she thought again. Then she pictured her parents, settling down on their floral sofa to watch the first episode; her dad on the left with a glass of his home-brewed beer and a packet of smoky bacon crisps, and her mum beside him with a glass of wine or a Horlicks, depending on her mood. How would they feel when they saw their daughter collapsed on the floor? A rush of guilt accompanied the image. She'd put them through enough.

'OK,' she mumbled, picking up her pace and catching Jaddi and Samantha as they stepped into their home for the next four nights.

'You all right, hon?' Jaddi asked. 'I'd hug you, but I'm too sweaty, and frankly, so are you.'

Lizzie nodded. 'Ben wants me to do a video diary the minute we get into our dorm room.'

Jaddi nodded. 'That's a good idea, so everyone knows you're fine.'

'That's what he said, but ...' Lizzie's voice trailed off. She couldn't find the words to voice her frustration.

'But what?'

'I don't know.' Lizzie shrugged. 'I tried doing one on the plane and it was all right, but it was weird too, you know? I can't decide if I should think about it as talking to my mum and dad, or like I'm talking to you guys, or at the however many people watching.' Lizzie sighed as they stepped into the yellow-walled foyer of the hostel. She wasn't making any sense.

'It's called a diary,' Jaddi said. 'Maybe the easiest thing to do is forget everyone else and talk about your day like you're talking to yourself.'

Lizzie nodded. 'Maybe.'

'If you run out of things to say, then I can jump in, or better yet, just video Samantha meticulously unpacking her backpack. That alone will get some laughs.'

'Hey!' Samantha leant over Lizzie and shoved Jaddi. 'Our backpacks are our snail shells. Our home away from home. It doesn't cost anything to be organised.'

'Of course not.' Jaddi laughed.

Lizzie smiled and tried to laugh, but the burst of energy she'd felt stepping into the market had drained away, leaving the aftermath of the seizure tainting her thoughts. A desire to sleep overwhelmed her along with relief at having dodged an MRI. Day one, and she was clinging to their dream with a spider's thread. At this rate they wouldn't make it to day five, let alone ninety.

CHAPTER 9

Day 4

Samantha

Fifty-one ... fifty-two ... fifty-three. Samantha counted each step as she made her way slowly up the narrow stone steps of the Temple of Dawn. She'd covered the first twenty steps with ease as her eyes had absorbed the detail on the temple walls on each side of the staircase. Tiny seashells, fragments of glass and coloured porcelain placed into spiralling flowers and intricate patterns stretched across every inch of the walls surrounding the temple. Stone sculptures of ancient Chinese soldiers and mythical tiger-like beasts stood in rows around the centre of the vast stone structure.

It was like nothing she'd ever seen before, although she'd had the same thought yesterday when they'd wandered the grounds of the Grand Palace, and again in the evening when they'd entered the ramshackle streets of China Town, the only part of the city that hadn't succumbed to modernisation.

She'd always loved London's old white-stone buildings mixed in with the sleek glass of modern architecture, but now it seemed stuffy and dull compared to the dazzling colour and creativity of Bangkok's history.

A group negotiating their way down the steps bustled past. Samantha shuffled closer to the railing and stopped, relieved to have a momentary break from the burning pain shooting out from her knees and up her thighs. It didn't help that each stone step was at least three times the height of a normal step, making it feel more like climbing a very long ladder.

Her eyes followed the group as they continued down towards the river, lapping at the edges of the temple, now far below, and she wasn't even halfway. Samantha forced her legs to begin climbing again and focused her gaze towards the top of the central prang, where Lizzie, Jaddi and Ben continued up, eager to reach the viewing platform before the sun began its descent.

Sweat cloaked Samantha's skin under her long-sleeved T-shirt, one of the only garments from her backpack she hadn't thrown away. All of the cotton vests and shorts she'd packed in England now felt thick and uncomfortable in the heat. Replacing them with the lighter clothes, sold in the markets for next to nothing, had helped with adjusting to Bangkok's humidity over the past three days. Except when they visited the temples, and had to adhere to dress codes that required the majority of their skin to be covered.

As Samantha continued to ascend, the air began to clear. A breeze blew over her face and neck. It was the first hint of cool she'd felt since leaving the temperature-controlled room in the hospital. Lizzie had bounced back from her seizure almost instantly. The only reminder that it had happened at all were the purple bruises on Lizzie's shoulders and legs. That, and Samantha's memory of it, which played on loop in her mind the moment her head hit the pillow each night. Neither Lizzie nor Jaddi had spoken about it since, and Lizzie had been quick to brush Samantha's concerns away whenever she'd asked. Lizzie hated to be treated any differently because of her illness, and yet it was a struggle not to. She had to try harder though, Samantha thought. The cloud hovering over them was dark enough without Samantha adding to it.

Samantha pulled in a long breath and caught a whiff of musky incense burning from somewhere inside the temple walls. She wondered how much the burning incense was for the monks' rituals and how much was to mask the stench of sewage and rotting vegetables rising from the Chao Phraya River below.

'It's so majestic here. The energy is so peaceful,' a woman with a Scottish accent said from five steps below her. Samantha glanced at the woman, and the boyfriend she'd spoken to, then back at the temple walls. The original china pattern on the porcelain was still visible on some of the larger pieces.

Samantha tried to assimilate the temple's peaceful energy as she neared the top of the spire. It didn't work. The architecture was beautiful, the craftsmanship magnificent, but the energy? She couldn't feel it. What she could feel was the vibration of her phone from the bag around her waist. Samantha resisted the urge to unzip the pocket and read David's latest text message. Whipping out a mobile phone in an ancient, sacred temple seemed somewhat crass, even in a city mobbed by selfie sticks.

Besides, she knew what David wanted to know. The same thing he'd asked yesterday, and the day before that. Where was she? What was she doing? Who had she met?

She understood his need to stay in contact. She was on an adventure in a faraway land, and he wanted to be part of her journey. She just wished he'd give her some space and some time to process what had happened between them. A frown creased Samantha's forehead. David and space were not two words that went together. Even before Lizzie's prognosis and their plans to travel,

David had hated sharing her. She could spend all day working by his side and all evening in his flat, and he'd still want more.

It was one of his worst qualities. She'd loved him for it once, maybe she still did, but it was getting harder to ignore the childishness of it. She still remembered the time when she'd rescheduled their quiet night in to catch a West End show with Lizzie and her parents, and he hadn't spoken to her for two days.

Part of her understood his game. The reason for his timings. He'd wanted to do something to ruin her trip, to ensure that he was never far from her thoughts. But why couldn't he have proposed instead? After all, her belongings were neatly boxed in the corner of the living room, ready to be moved to his flat when she returned. More than that, she loved him. David was everything she wasn't: suave, sophisticated, romantic and good-looking. It was easy to ignore his slightly short stature; easy to thank the waiters herself when he placed their orders without a polite word.

Samantha's legs buckled for a second as she stepped onto the platform at the top of the central prang, tugging her thoughts back to the present. For the first time, she looked around properly – the view over the city was breathtakingly beautiful. She felt Lizzie's arm loop through hers, Jaddi standing on the other side of her. Her heart started to race. How many years had they talked about this and now here they were. Their dream of seeing the world together was coming true. For the first time, she managed to forget the camera lens and all those people at home watching her.

CHAPTER 10

Samantha

Twenty minutes later, the blue sky had turned lilac and the pain in Samantha's legs had dulled to a throbbing ache. Impatience niggled in Samantha's thoughts. It was time to start the descent, to get back to the hostel and change before heading back out into the bustling city for cold beers and noodles. Samantha turned to ask Lizzie how much longer but the question died on her lips. The look on Lizzie's face, mesmerised by the panoramic view, was enough for Samantha to keep the question in her head. Her friend wasn't ready to leave.

Samantha thought of the rooftop bar the previous evening and Lizzie's stricken face when the heavy grey clouds of a thunderstorm had rolled across the sky. She thought she knew everything about Lizzie, but Samantha didn't know why sunsets seemed so important all of a sudden, or why Lizzie seemed to be scrutinising the view as if she was scanning a group of people, looking for a familiar face. Samantha opened her mouth to ask, but closed it again. Lizzie would tell them when she was ready.

'Why do you like to watch the sunsets?' Ben asked, mirroring Samantha's thoughts. Ben sat down beside Samantha, and with his back to the view he leant outwards, angling the camera at Lizzie's face.

Samantha looked at Ben for a moment. Despite his harsh words on the plane, he was growing on her a little. He'd helped with Lizzie's seizure, and he'd never barged into their room at the hostel without knocking first and giving them fair warning. She'd caught him smiling at their jokes a few times too.

But Ben wasn't smiling now. Despite the camera pointing at Lizzie, his eyes had moved to the drop beyond the ledge. His eyes widened, his forehead creased. He swallowed hard; she could tell by the way his Adam's apple lifted up then dropped back down. Was he scared of heights?

'It's beautiful,' Lizzie whispered.

Samantha waited for Ben to ask another question, but instead he waited, the camera fixed on Lizzie's face. It reminded Samantha of a police interview technique she'd read about once. Three sentences in a hundred-page policy briefing document. Samantha couldn't remember what the report had been about, or any other information within in, but for some reason those three sentences had stuck in her mind. Silence was an unnatural state for human beings. If a question was left hanging, then more often than not, the other person felt obliged to speak. A useful technique for police interrogations, and documentary makers it turned out.

'I want to find the place in the world with the most beautiful sunset,' Lizzie added.

'Do you think this is it?' Jaddi asked, looping her arm around Lizzie as Ben zoomed in on their faces, then turned, traversing the shadowed buildings of Bangkok as the tip of the sun disappeared from view, leaving behind a spectacle of pink and purple.

'It could be.' Lizzie smiled. 'Ask me again on day ninety.'

Samantha's throat tightened. Day ninety. Samantha had never deluded herself. Ninety days, it wasn't long. But now they were here, the days were disappearing like grains of sand slipping through the gap in a timer. Samantha desperately wanted to slow it down, but she knew she couldn't. In the blink of an eye they'd be at day twenty, sixty, ninety. She reached for Lizzie's hand and felt it tighten around her own.

As if on cue, light poured out of the temple around them, basking every inch of the walls in a soft orange glow. Lizzie sighed and stood up. 'Come on, let's go back. I'm famished.'

Samantha looked up from her steaming plate of market food and watched Jaddi, head bent over her mobile and scrolling furiously. Couldn't she ever just relax and enjoy the lights, the buzz, the smells of this vibrant city?

'Oh my God.' Jaddi's voice rang with excitement as she drew her phone closer to her face. 'You're not going to believe this.' Jaddi pulled her eyes away from her mobile and glanced at Lizzie and Samantha.

'What?' Lizzie asked.

'I've just checked our Facebook page and there are thousands of comments from people wishing us good luck.'

'That's nice,' Lizzie said, nodding, her eyes already veering back to her half-eaten plate of noodles.

'No, no, hang on, that's not the amazing bit. One comment got half a million likes, so I read it and it's from …' Jaddi paused, her grin widening. 'You won't believe this when I say it … Guy Rawson.'

'No way,' Lizzie said, reaching towards the phone in Jaddi's hand.

'Yes!' Jaddi giggled, pulling her mobile closer to her body and out of reach. 'It says: Lizzie, caught your interview on *Channel 6 Breakfast*. You're awesome. Hope you can make it to my concert in Los Angeles next month. VIP passes waiting for you and your friends at the gate.'

'It's a con.' Samantha shook her head. 'It's probably one of those fake accounts, created by a diehard fan.'

'I checked. It's definitely the official Guy Rawson.'

'But he's a megastar,' Samantha said, her tone still tinged with scepticism despite the exhilaration now coursing through her veins. 'I mean … I grew up with posters of him modelling swimwear on my walls. We listen to his albums all the time. He must be one of the most famous men on the planet.'

'Oh, come on, he's not just one of, he *is* the most famous man on the planet.' Jaddi squeaked. 'Do you remember that time we stayed up half the night, waiting for his concert tickets at Wembley to go on sale.'

'Remember?' Samantha smirked. 'I've still not forgiven Lizzie for that one.'

'Hang on.' Lizzie laughed. 'I will fess up to getting the time they went on sale wrong, but it wasn't me who forgot to set the phone alarm.' She grinned, waving her finger at Jaddi.

'Well, this makes up for it.' Jaddi jumped up and down, twisting the screen of her phone to face them. 'VIP tickets means front-row seats.'

Lizzie opened her mouth to say something, but stopped as her eyes scanned the screen of Jaddi's mobile. 'What's that comment next to it?' She grabbed Jaddi's arm and pulled it towards her, bringing the mobile with it. 'Does that say Harrison?'

'I don't know.' Jaddi shrugged. 'I've not had a chance to read through them all.'

'It does.' Lizzie's forehead furrowed. 'It's from Harrison.'

Ben adjusted the lens and stepped closer. 'Who's Harrison?'

After a pause, Jaddi spoke. 'Harrison is a guy Lizzie dated for a few weeks in London last year.'

'Not just dated.' Samantha grinned, swept along in the excitement of Guy Rawson's message. 'He was Lizzie's *one that got away*.'

Jaddi nodded, flashing a smile into the camera lens. 'Harrison moved back home to Australia before anything could get going between them and—'

'I thought he was from America,' Samantha said.

'Anyway,' Jaddi said, 'he's put a message on the comment board, which says: Can't wait to show you around Sydney. Message me when you get here.'

'Can you message back through that page?' Lizzie asked.

'To Guy Rawson?' Jaddi asked. 'I definitely want those VIP tickets.'

'No –' Lizzie shook her head '– to Harrison.'

Samantha snorted. 'A world-famous, incredibly gorgeous and talented singer invites you to front row seats at his concert, and you're asking about a boy you went out with a few times?'

Lizzie shrugged. 'Well, can you?'

Jaddi tapped a button on her screen before handing her phone to Lizzie. 'Just type what you want to say there.'

'What do I say?' A spark of excitement lit Lizzie's face as she looked between Jaddi and Samantha.

Samantha leant forward, peering over Lizzie's shoulder. 'Say: That would be lovely, kiss kiss.'

Jaddi laughed. 'No, that's too mushy. She hasn't spoken to him since last summer. He could be seeing someone. Just put, great, see you in a few weeks, then put a smiley face.'

Lizzie tapped at the screen for a minute before handing the phone back to Jaddi.

'We'd better go,' Samantha said. 'Long day tomorrow.' Samantha closed her eyes for a moment as a yawn overtook her body. Tomorrow they would leave the city and spend eleven hours on a bus to Cambodia.

At least it would be more relaxing than climbing a hundred steps in a million-degree heat, Samantha thought.

CHAPTER 11

Day 5

Lizzie

'I can't hear myself think,' Jaddi shouted over the thumping beat of a Gloria Estefan song carrying from one of the bars at the edge of the market.

'I know,' Lizzie said, glancing at the three Thai women in bright-pink bikinis and high heels dancing and swaying, beckoning passing men to join them inside the bar. It wasn't even midday yet.

'We really need to get to the bus station now, Lizzie.' Jaddi wiped away beads of moisture on her watch. 'The bus for Cambodia leaves in an hour.'

Lizzie ran her hand over the row of sunglasses, plucked out a pair with white rims and slid them onto her face. She turned to Jaddi and pointed at her face. 'I thought you said buses never leave on time here. What do you think of these? Too retro?'

'They're nice,' Jaddi replied. 'And I did say that, but we should be there waiting just in case. They'll have markets in Phnom Penh too, you know. Where's Samantha?'

Lizzie pulled the sunglasses away and turned them over in her hands as someone elbowed her in the ribs. She didn't bother turning in search of the culprit. Everywhere in Bangkok had been the same – jostling crowds all looking for or at the same thing. She'd loved every moment of their time in the city, but four days of relentless humidity, people, dance music, and noise was enough. She'd begun to crave fresh air and silence.

'I think she went to get some water and snacks for the bus journey,' Lizzie replied. 'She said she'd see us on the street in five. Which ones –' Lizzie turned to Jaddi '– the white or the diamanté?'

'The white ones.'

'Good choice.' Lizzie reached into her pocket for the money.

'Woah woah woah, Liz.' Jaddi leant closer and stopped Lizzie before she could hand over the money. Ben stepped closer too, pointing the lens at the sunglasses before focusing on their faces. 'What are you doing?' Jaddi asked.

'Paying for these.' Lizzie laughed and shrugged at the same time.

'You don't pay the price on the ticket.' Jaddi rolled her eyes and winked at Ben and the camera. 'This isn't H&M; it's Bangkok. That's the starting price. Here, let me show you.' She took the sunglasses from Lizzie and spun towards the man behind the stall.

Lizzie watched in awe as Jaddi dipped her head and pulled back her shoulders. A half-smile lit her face as she giggled and chatted with the man on the other side of the stall. Every movement part of a perfected routine Lizzie had seen many times before. It reminded Lizzie of Aaron's twists and spins on the vault and the way he transferred his weight from one hand to the other as if it was as effortless as walking. They made it look so easy, but Jaddi and Aaron's skills, however different, were both worlds away from Lizzie's.

With a twinge of guilt she realised it was the first time she'd thought of her brother in days. It seemed the more time that passed, the more immersed she felt in their journey, and the less she thought about home or her future. *Live in the here and now*, Jaddi had said at the start of all this. And that's exactly what she was doing.

Two minutes later Jaddi turned away from the stall and handed the sunglasses to Lizzie.

'Thanks. How much did you pay?' Lizzie asked, slipping them onto her face as they weaved through the market.

Jaddi grinned. 'Less than half.'

'Your talents are wasted in PR.' Lizzie laughed.

'Tell me about it. Now, can we please find Samantha and get to the bus station?'

'Look there she is.' Lizzie pointed across the road to Samantha, leaning against a dark-red car with a small Thai man in faded, blue jeans and a loose, blue shirt.

Samantha waved and motioned them over.

'I got us a ride to Cambodia,' she called as they darted between the traffic.

'What ride?' Jaddi shook her head. 'I told you, we're getting the bus. It's leaving in an hour.'

'I know that was the plan –' Samantha smiled '– but this is Tic. He's a taxi driver. He can drive us in his air-conditioned car to Phnom Penh for the same price as our bus tickets. I've already paid.'

Lizzie watched Jaddi's face as she processed Samantha's change of plans. It always amazed Lizzie how two people so different could live so harmoniously together. It wasn't often that Jaddi's need to be the driving force of their plans, or her daredevil side, clashed with Samantha's common sense organisation, but when it did an argument was sure to follow. That was unless Lizzie could smooth the way.

'You OK with this, Liz?' Samantha asked, a note of hesitation in her voice.

'Absolutely.' Lizzie nodded. 'It's a great idea. Come on, Jaddi, where's your sense of adventure?'

'But …' Jaddi stared between them again. 'But sitting in a car is not exactly an authentic experience. Besides, it's also dangerous. We don't know this guy. What if he's an axe murderer?' Jaddi nodded her head towards the driver.

The three of them turned to look at the skinny body of Tic. He grinned widely at them before opening the boot of his car.

'He doesn't look much like an axe murderer.' Lizzie frowned, shrugging off her backpack and passing it to Tic.

Jaddi shrugged, adding her backpack to the boot. 'Fine, let's do it.'

CHAPTER 12

Jaddi

'Welcome to day five.' Lizzie smirked into the handheld camera. 'We are currently stranded on a dirt road somewhere in Cambodia, although we have no idea where. It's five pm and still sweltering. The taxi that was supposed to take us all the way to Phnom Penh, the capital of Cambodia, drove off about an hour ago.' Lizzie laughed at her own words. 'So it looks like we'll be spending the night here.'

A gust of hot wind blew against Jaddi's neck. She half expected to find someone standing behind her with a hairdryer. For the past hour she'd perched awkwardly on her backpack, elbows on knees, head in hands, as frustration had seared through her, while Ben watched and filmed with his 'I'm here to capture your story, not be part of it' attitude. Damn him! How could they have been so stupid? Alone on a deserted road in the middle of nowhere with only half a packet of crackers and a few bottles of water between them. What did Lizzie find so funny about that?

Jaddi stood up and stretched her arms above her head. She blew out a loud puff of air and glanced towards Samantha, sat in a similar position beside her. 'I told you this would happen,' Jaddi muttered before stumbling down a bank of hardened dirt and into the dense, avocado-green undergrowth, and instantly regretting the spite in her remark.

'No, you didn't,' Samantha said, following Jaddi down the slope.

Jaddi twisted her head in a sharp movement and glared at Samantha. She jabbed her finger in Samantha's direction, powerless to stop the irritation from boiling out of her. 'I was the only one who said we should get the bus, like we'd planned to do in the first place,' she snapped.

'Yes,' Samantha nodded, raising her eyebrows, her tone just as hard as Jaddi's, 'until you'd sat in the air-conditioned car for two minutes. I don't remember you arguing for the bus then. In fact, I think your exact words were, "Who cares about authentic? This is the way to travel."'

'It's not exactly worked out though, has it?' A pressure swelled in Jaddi's bladder.

Warm sunlight dropped like torch beams through gaps in the tree canopies. An outburst of high-pitched bird chatter screeched from the treetops above.

Jaddi weaved further into undergrowth and kicked at the shrubs covering the ground around their feet. 'Let's see, shall we? It hasn't cost the same amount really, because our happy little driver, Tic, demanded we pay him two thousand Baht if we wanted him to keep driving us to Cambodia. Then, when we said no, he threw our backpacks out of the boot of his car, forcing us to get out with them.'

She threw a glance behind her in case Ben had followed. He hadn't.

'You were the one that refused to pay,' Samantha hissed, also throwing a furtive glance back to the road.

'Because he would've driven us to another remote destination before repeating the same thing all over again.'

'He might not have done, but since you refused to let us pay, I guess we'll never know.'

Jaddi rolled her eyes before kicking again at the ground.

'What are you looking for?' Samantha asked.

'Somewhere to have a pee,' she muttered.

'Oh.' Samantha glanced towards the road again. 'I'll block you from view,' she said, turning her back on Jaddi.

Jaddi unzipped her shorts and crouched into a squat.

'How long do you think it will be before another vehicle passes us?' Samantha asked.

As Jaddi opened her mouth to reply something brushed against her ankle. She yelped and wobbled before jumping up and kicking the bushes again. No creature emerged.

'Are you all right?' Samantha asked, without turning around.

'Fine.' Jaddi squatted back to the ground a few paces back from her original position. The frustration and the pain eased as she relaxed the tight hold on her bladder. Perhaps she'd been a little hasty refusing to pay Tic. It wasn't the money so much as the principle of it. But what was the point of principles if you were stranded on a deserted track with nothing but trees in every direction?

'How long—'

'Who knows,' Jaddi cut in. They'd passed a three-wheeled truck pootling along a few hours ago, but it could have turned off on any number of side tracks since. Jaddi briefly considered whether they should try to trek back to the shack they'd stopped at hours ago for a lunch of soggy rice and either very hardboiled eggs or a meat of some kind. Or did they gamble and continue in the direction they were heading in before Tic pulled over? Neither appealed.

She glanced back to the road. Lizzie had stopped filming her video diary and appeared to be arguing with Ben about something. She'd better hurry up and get over there before it escalated.

Jaddi sighed. Everything that had happened since the day Lizzie had walked through their front door on that blustery October night had been Jaddi's idea, and like it or not, she was responsible. She hadn't fully appreciated how draining that responsibility would be. Lizzie's happiness, her health, their rapport with Ben, how much fun they were having, Samantha's worries for Lizzie, and how much the camera bothered them, all fell on Jaddi's shoulders, weighing her down more than any backpack could do.

The burden had been made all the worse by Lizzie's seizure and the uncertainty it had triggered in Jaddi. All Jaddi had wanted to do was give Lizzie the best last three months imaginable, but it was harder than she'd imagined to stand by as the days slipped away. Were they making a mistake?

Just then, Lizzie leant forward and punched Ben on the arm, causing a laughter to break out between them. The tension snaking Jaddi's shoulders eased. Maybe they weren't bickering after all.

Ben had relaxed around them over the past few days, or maybe they'd relaxed around him. Either way, he'd lost the abruptness to his voice and he smiled more. Not much, but more. Although, they'd yet to convince him to have a beer with them when the camera was off.

A moment later, Jaddi stood and zipped up her shorts.

'What's going on with you today?' Samantha asked. 'You've been weird since you got back last night. Don't tell me you struck out with those blokes? Or are you still peeved about changing plans?'

Jaddi paused and considered Samantha's question. Why was she being such a moody cow?

The drinks she'd had with the two shaggy, well-travelled Americans the previous evening had been fun at first, but the exhaustion from climbing the temple, along with the formidable humidity, had given her an instant hangover.

She'd left her new friends and walked the streets alone for a while. Her flirtatious banter with the Americans had reminded her of Suk and how much she missed their weekly clandestine meetings in back-street pubs and restaurants in remote parts of London.

Jaddi had meant what she'd said at the airport – she wasn't ready to get married – but there was more. Jaddi liked the secrecy. Her relationship with Suk belonged only to her, and she belonged only to Suk. She didn't want everything to change by getting married, and she wasn't prepared to lose her family by not getting married. Then again, everything would change when they returned anyway, Jaddi reminded herself.

Jaddi pulled in a long breath of stifling air and stepped alongside Samantha. 'I'm sorry. I didn't mean to lash out at you. I'm tired and letting the heat get to me, that's all.'

'Really?' Samantha tilted her head to one side.

Jaddi shrugged. 'It's nothing. You wouldn't understand.'

'Try me.'

'I think I might be a bit homesick,' Jaddi said in a low voice, feeling the last of her frustration slip away.

'You're what?' A curious smile spread across Samantha's face.

'I'm homesick, OK? I know it's stupid but I miss my
life in London—' Samantha's cackling laugh stopped
Jaddi from saying more.

'How can *you,* of all people, be homesick? All you've
ever talked about since the day I met you is how much
you want to travel the world.'

'I know,' Jaddi muttered, 'I'm as surprised as you are.'

Samantha snorted and threw her arm around Jaddi.
'It'll be all right. You'll feel better when we get to
Cambodia.'

'*If* we get to Cambodia.' Jaddi wished she could laugh
too. It was ludicrous to even comprehend being homesick.
After everything she'd done to get them here. Maybe it
wasn't homesickness, but the growing realisation that she
was never going home to the life she'd had before.

A flash of colour on the road caught Jaddi's attention.

'Hey look, a car's coming,' Lizzie shouted.

'What do we do?' Samantha hopped over the bushes
before scrambling up the ditch to the road.

'Wave it down,' Jaddi said, a few steps behind
Samantha.

The three of them jumped into the centre of the road
and waved their arms in the air until the maroon car
pulled over and wound down its window. The familiar
smiling face of Tic popped out. 'One thousand Baht.
Phnom Penh. Yes?'

The three girls glanced at one another for a moment.

'Yes,' Jaddi said, the others nodding.

Tic smiled and bounced out of the car. Despite his small
frame and skinny arms, he collected their backpacks with
ease, and returned them to the boot of his car.

'Maybe we should try and haggle the price down a bit
more,' Lizzie whispered as they slid back into the cool
interior of the car.

'Or maybe we should just thank our lucky stars that he came back, and hope he takes us to Cambodia rather than selling us to pirates,' Samantha said.

'Good point.' Jaddi breathed a sigh of relief as a blast of cold hair tickled her skin. 'Right now, I'd pay ten thousand baht for five minutes sitting in this car.'

'Shhh,' Samantha hissed. 'Don't say that or Tic will start charging us for the air con.'

'By the way, Ben,' Lizzie said, leaning forward as Ben climbed into the front passenger seat with his camera bag, 'thanks for being such a great help back there. The way you stayed silent as Tic threw out our backpacks was almost as good as your lack of input into a way out of our predicament.'

'Anytime.' He grinned, not appearing to notice Lizzie's jibing tone, or more likely, ignoring it, and causing Lizzie to throw back her head and laugh.

Jaddi glanced at the smiling face of her friend and felt her own sour mood lift. Lizzie was happy; they were finally on the adventure they'd always dreamed of. It was time to take her own advice and start living in the moment.

CHAPTER 13

Jaddi

Jaddi watched Tic's car disappear around the corner and surveyed the empty street. She checked her watch – nine pm. Not late by anyone's standards, but after the journey they'd had it felt more like midnight. Hunger, thirst, and exhaustion battled for first place in her list of needs. Not to mention a shower. By the looks of Lizzie, Samantha, and Ben, they felt the same way.

She stared at the archway leading to their hostel and wished she'd booked the more expensive hotel, much closer to the city centre, with the air conditioning, the pool and the restaurant, rather than the shell of a building staring back at her, promising them nothing but a bed and the most basic of facilities.

'Won't a pool be fun though, Jaddi?' Caroline had asked her when they'd poured over Jaddi's plans in the Channel 6 boardroom two weeks before Christmas. 'After all the time on a bus, won't a swim be nice?'

With the blue-and-white Christmas lights blinking on the tree in the corner of the boardroom, and the rain, running in sheets down the windows, it had been impossible to imagine the heat and the tiredness they would feel. 'We'll have a much better experience in this one,' she'd replied, tapping her finger on the print out of her plans. 'This isn't a holiday to us. We want to see the real life of the places we visit, not stay in some high-walled four-star resort.'

Looking up at the hostel, Jaddi shook her head at her principles. Right now, she'd happily trade real for a chance to jump in a cold pool, or sleep in a comfortable bed.

'This looks … authentic.' Samantha said.

Jaddi looked between Samantha and Lizzie, their bemused exhausted faces causing her to laugh out loud. A second later Samantha and Lizzie joined in.

'OK, OK.' Jaddi held up her hands. 'I might've got a bit carried away booking us into the cheapest accommodations. We can upgrade tomorrow. How about a drink before we go in?' She nodded to a bar next door. It was empty apart from a young man slouched on a stool by the bar. A neon-blue light above the door flashed *24Hours*.

'You're on.' Samantha scooped up her backpack. 'First round's on me. After the day we've had I owe you that much.'

Lizzie hooked her arm through Samantha's. 'We're here now, and anyway, you don't get much more authentic that being abandoned by the side of the road in the middle of nowhere.'

'Second round's on me then,' Jaddi called after them. 'And I'm getting Sambuca if they have it.'

Samantha shot her a look and laughed.

'What's the joke with Sambuca?' Ben asked from beside her.

Jaddi glanced at the small area of Ben's face not covered by the camera. 'Shall I tell him, Sam, or do you want to?'

Samantha stepped into the bar, dropped her backpack at the nearest table and spun around. 'I will tell him, thank you very much. I don't need you 'two blowing it out of proportion.' She turned to Ben and shook her head. 'Years and years ago I had a few too many Sambuca shots and ended up in a karaoke bar singing Dolly Parton at the top of my voice. And these two won't let me forget it.'

'Er ...' Lizzie giggled, stepping into the camera shot. 'You forgot to mention the fact that it wasn't karaoke night; it was quiz night, but you strong-armed the barmen into switching the machine on just for you.'

'And,' Jaddi added, feeling a burst of renewed energy, 'completely derailed the quiz. The team set to win were fuming.'

'Well, I don't remember that bit so I'm disputing that it actually happened that way.' Samantha dropped into her chair and retied her hair into a tight ponytail. It had already turned a shade blonder in the sun and looked almost white under the dull orange lights of the bar.

'If you haven't figured it out yet,' Jaddi said, turning to Ben, 'Samantha is the sensible one. Miss Common Sense. She hardly ever, and I mean *ever*, has too many drinks, makes an idiot of herself, forgets to set her alarm, over sleeps—'

'Unless she has Sambuca,' Lizzie chipped in, sliding into the chair beside Sam. 'Isn't that right, Sambuca Sam?'

Jaddi turned to Samantha and watched her cheeks burn crimson despite the smile stretched across her face. Even Jaddi couldn't have predicted how well Lizzie and Samantha would adapt to a camera in their faces, but she didn't want to push Samantha too far. 'I'll get the drinks in.' Jaddi laughed. 'Fancy a beer, Ben?'

Ben hesitated for a moment too long.

'I'll take that as a yes.' She grinned just as Ben shook his head.

'Yeah, come on, Ben,' Samantha said. 'Turn that thing off for a bit and have a drink with us. You deserve it too after the day we've had.'

'You know what they say.' Lizzie smiled. 'All filming and no play makes Ben a very grumpy cameraman.'

Ben lifted the camera from his shoulder, scowled at each of them in turn, before shrugging and pulling up a chair. 'One beer,' he said. 'Then this goes back on.'

'Absolutely,' Lizzie grinned.

Jaddi leant her weight against the bar and turned to watch as Lizzie moved closer to Samantha and whispered something in her ear. A moment later, Samantha's laugh filled the narrow room. It bounced off the walls, hit Jaddi in the chest and made her snigger. Samantha had two laughs. Her work laugh, as Jaddi had come to think of it – the yes-I-agree-that-is-very-amusing controlled chuckle, which Jaddi had heard more and more of over the past few years; and her goofy, loud, belly laugh that always ended in a snort, sending them all off on another round of giggles. The laugh coming out of Samantha now was the second kind and it was more contagious than the common cold.

A sense of peace washed over Jaddi. She'd promised them the trip of a lifetime and that was exactly what they were having. She might be responsible for this trip and all its adventures – occasional abandonment by the side of the road notwithstanding – but seeing Samantha loosen up and Lizzie enjoying herself was worth it.

'Was I the only one who thought the Emerald Buddha in the Grand Palace looked like he was made of plasticine?' Lizzie asked, as Jaddi moved back to the table with a tray of drinks.

'Completely.' Ben nodded. 'Didn't you just want to poke it and see if your finger disappeared?'

'Are you two off your heads?' Samantha frowned. 'The Emerald Buddha is one of Bangkok's most precious statutes. It's clothed in gold, for goodness' sake. Nobody even knows when it was made, or who made it. Legend has it, it was made in India by Hindu gods in forty-three BC.'

Lizzie and Ben looked at each other and laughed. A second later the smile dropped from Ben's face. He sat back and looked between the girls, an observer once more. Jaddi didn't mind. At least he'd let his guard down for a minute. She was sure it wouldn't be the last time she'd see him relax.

'You're such a guidebook geek, Sam.' Lizzie laughed. 'Although, that's one of the reasons we love you.'

'I'm going to take that as a compliment,' Samantha said.

'Here we go.' Jaddi slid the tray onto the table. 'A beer for you, Ben.' She handed him the bottle.

'Thanks.' He fiddled with the label for a moment before taking two long gulps.

'Coke for you, Lizzie.'

'Rock and roll.' Lizzie grinned.

'And—'

'And,' Samantha cut in, 'what on earth is that?' She pointed to a yellow beach bucket with a giant cocktail umbrella and two straws sticking out the top.

'It's a beach-bucket cocktail.'

'What's in it?' Samantha asked, eying the red liquid.

'I have no idea, but according to Jim, over there –' Jaddi twisted around and waved at the barman '– it's what all the backpackers drink in Cambodia.'

Jaddi leant forward and took a long sip of fruity liquid. A second later the scorch of spirits burnt her throat. 'Wow.'

'Yikes!' Samantha laughed, before glancing around the bar. 'I hope they haven't got karaoke here. This is way worse than Sambuca. Hey, does it feel weird to anyone that the first episode of the documentary was on TV last night?'

'Was it?' Lizzie said. 'I've completely lost track of days of the week.'

Samantha shrugged. 'I'm sure hardly anyone watched it.'

'Humf,' Ben said, his gaze suddenly focused on the bottle of beer in his hands.

'What?' Lizzie asked.

'Do you really want to know?' He raised his eyebrows and looked between them.

Jaddi gave a short shake of her head. She knew what was coming. She'd seen the number of likes on their Facebook page skyrocket overnight. She knew the documentary had been aired and the advertising Caroline had done in the build up to it had paid off. But she'd hoped to shield that side of things from Lizzie.

'I don't know.' Lizzie smiled. 'Do I?'

He shrugged.

'Tell us,' Samantha answered for Lizzie, leaning closer to the table for another slurp from the bucket. Jaddi thought about protesting, but she could tell by the glint of interest in Lizzie's eye that it was too late.

Ben sat up, rubbed a hand against the bristle of his beard before retrieving a tablet from the side pocket of his bag. He pressed several buttons before passing it to Lizzie. 'I downloaded this from *The Sun*'s website before we left Bangkok.'

'Oh.' Lizzie handed the tablet to Samantha as Jaddi leaned over to look.

Lovely Lizzie Steals the Nation's Heart
The Girl with Three Months to Live highest-rated TV show on Saturday night

If viewing figures are anything to go by, then there wasn't a dry eye in the nation last night as 17.1 million people tuned in to watch Channel 6's *The Girl with Three Months to Live*, making it the most-watched show on Saturday night TV since last summer's final of *So You Think You Can Sing?*.

The documentary follows Lizzie Appleton (29) and her two friends Jaddi Patel (28) and Samantha Jeffrey (29) as they embark on a whirlwind, backpacking trip around the world, after Lizzie was diagnosed with an incurable brain tumour and given only three months to live.

Girl-next-door Lizzie's touching and funny video diaries were by far the highlight of last night's episode. 'There is something so inspiring about Lizzie,' explains Channel 6 producer, Caroline Wilks. 'This could've been a harrowing countdown to her death, but instead, Lizzie and the girls' strong bond and playful personalities have made this an unmissable show.'

Can't wait for next week's episode of *The Girl With Three Months to Live*? Following last night's record-breaking ratings, Channel 6 will now be uploading extra footage, including excerpts from Lizzie's video diaries, to their website every day. We certainly can't get enough of hunky cameraman, Ben Holmes. Let's hope his appearance in front of the camera last night wasn't a one-off.

Trepidation sucked away the colour from Jaddi's face as her eyes scanned the article. This wasn't just popular; this was insane. Seventeen point one million people had just upped the stakes of their trip. Seventeen million. The thought made the inside of her cheeks throb.

Jaddi flicked her gaze to Lizzie. Their eyes met. Lizzie's expression, the mirror image of her own. Jaddi could almost see the same thought racing through Lizzie's mind.

'Wow,' Samantha said. 'Seventeen million? Surely that's a typo?'

'Seventeen point one,' Ben said, tucking the tablet back into his bag. 'Caroline emailed me this morning with the news. She's thrilled, of course. She also wants more video diaries, Lizzie, if you're up for it?'

'I guess.' Lizzie shrugged. 'Although knowing seventeen million people will be watching me might make it even more weird.'

'Are you all right, Lizzie?' Ben asked, his eyes watching her face. 'You've gone a funny colour.'

'She's in shock.' Jaddi forced a grin. 'More alarming than the viewing figures is their description of you, Ben. Hunky? Seriously?'

CHAPTER 14

Day 6

Lizzie

Lizzie nodded her thanks to the night clerk and knocked gently on Ben's door, now unlocked by the manager and swinging open.

'Wakey-wakey, Ben,' she said.

Her words, like a cattle prod, jolted Ben to life, his body springing upwards as his eyes shot open. 'Huh?'

'And he's awake,' Lizzie said into the handheld camera, as she stepped further into the room. The light from the hallway behind her illuminated Ben's single-occupancy room, which seemed substantially larger than their four-person room further down the corridor, and the walls were white rather than lime-green.

Ben stared at Lizzie before flopping back onto his mattress and fumbling his hand on the floor until he found his glasses.

'Good morning,' Lizzie said with a wide grin. 'Welcome to day six. I'm here in Ben's room at the Cosy Backpackers Youth Hostel in Phnom Penh, Cambodia. Ben doesn't know it yet, but he's about to be dragged out of bed to spend four hours travelling further north to Siem Reap and to the Buddhist temple of Angkor Wat.'

Lizzie stared at her reflection in the screen of the camera. Her skin and hair shone from the shower she'd had ten minutes earlier. She looked healthier than she had in months. She felt it too, Lizzie thought, with a zing of excitement for her unscheduled trip across Cambodia.

'What time is it?' Ben said in a croaky voice, reaching for a bottle of water. 'My body clock is screwed. It feels like four in the morning.'

Lizzie fiddled with the camera in her hands so that the lens focused on Ben. 'Just before three,' she replied, enjoying the anguish scrunching on Ben's face.

'Three. You've got to be kidding.' Ben sat up, swinging his long legs out of the bed and pulling the bed sheet along with him, keeping the lower half of his torso and groin covered.

'Poor cameraman Ben, getting a taste of his own medicine this morning.' Lizzie grinned, trying not to stare at the sprinkling of dark hair across his broad chest. 'How does it feel to be woken up with a camera in your face? Here's a little known fact about Ben. He hates cameras.'

'I'm a cameraman,' Ben said, rubbing the palms of his hands across his face. 'Of course I don't hate cameras.'

'Being behind them maybe, but in front of them, you're worse than Samantha at dodging the lens during my video diaries.'

Ben shrugged, took another swig of water from the bottle, and as if proving a point, lifted his hand in a wave. 'Hello, viewers,' he said with a sideways smirk. He turned his gaze on Lizzie and frowned. 'What's this about a road trip?'

'As per your instructions, I'm letting you know my whereabouts. I'm leaving in five minutes to travel to Siem Reap to watch the sun rise over the Angkor Wat temple.'

'I thought it was sunsets you were interested in,' he said.

'Both. Anyway, the night manager's brother has agreed to take me for twenty dollars. Come if you want to, or sleep in and meet me back here later today. We're catching the bus to Mondulkiri at ten this evening.'

'Wouldn't it make more sense to travel up at a more reasonable time of day and watch the sun rise tomorrow morning?'

She nodded. 'Probably, but we're already booked on a bus up to the Mondulkiri Project. It's a flying visit. We have to be back in Phnom Penh by the evening to catch the bus by ten pm.'

'The Mondu-what?'

'The Mondulkiri Project. It's an elephant sanctuary in the Cambodian jungle. We're booked in for a week-long retreat before heading on to Vietnam.'

'But you haven't even seen Phnom Penh yet. When did you decide all this?'

'About two hours ago.' She laughed. 'We all agreed that we've had enough of sightseeing temples and historical places. The only caveat was the sunrise over Angkor Wat, so here I am, or here we are, if you're coming?'

Ben pulled off his glasses and rubbed his eyes. 'I'm coming,' he said with another groan.

'Good, because I promised Jaddi and Samantha I wouldn't go by myself.'

'How do Jaddi and Samantha feel about you leaving them?'

'It took some convincing.' Lizzie pulled a face. She loved her friends, and couldn't imagine the next few months without them by her side, but since her seizure, Jaddi and Samantha hadn't let her out of their sights, and she was starting to feel suffocated. Besides, Angkor Wat was somewhere she needed to see on her own. Just her, the sunrise, a cameraman, and seventeen million people watching. Lizzie shook the thought away. She couldn't dwell on the popularity of the documentary. She'd almost lost it in the bar thinking of the millions of people switching on their TVs to watch her. If it hadn't been for Jaddi grabbing her hand under the table, she probably would have done.

Lizzie flipped the screen back towards her. 'This is going to be one spectacular sunrise,' she said, before flicking the off switch. 'See you out front in a few minutes,' she called over her shoulder to Ben.

Lizzie clicked the straps of her backpack in place and stepped out of the hostel. She could hear the sound of traffic from somewhere else in the capital, but here the streets were still, and pitch-black.

After the muggy heat inside the hostel, the night air felt cold against her face. Lizzie was glad she'd thought to throw on her hoody for the journey. She stared out into the silent street and wondered briefly if her night trip to Siem Reap would be worth it. If they hit traffic or got dumped on the side of the road again, then she'd miss the sunrise and the trip would be wasted.

Just then, Ben trudged out of the hostel doors, looking half asleep and dishevelled with his backpack slung over one shoulder and his camera bag over the other. 'Where's the ride then?' he said in a voice still husky from sleep.

Right on cue, a white pickup truck with an open flatbed turned into the road and pulled up alongside them. 'Here.' She grinned. The smiled dropped from her face as she saw the open compartment at the back. No roof, no shelter. They were in for a long, cold and uncomfortable journey.

'Please tell me we're riding in the front,' Ben said.

'Er … no. He's taking his wife and child with him. I didn't quite understand all of the night manager's English, but I think they have family up there and are using the trip for a visit.'

'You realise we'll freeze?' He raised his eyebrows and stared at her.

'He got out of bed in the middle of the night and agreed to take us all the way to the temple so we shouldn't really complain.'

'No, you're right, you shouldn't complain. This was your crazy-arse plan. But I might complain some more anyway.' He sighed, making Lizzie laugh.

A stocky figure appeared from the cabin of the truck. 'Come.' He motioned to Ben and Lizzie. The man unlatched the metal flap on the flatbed and nodded at them before walking back to the driver's door. Lizzie hoisted her backpack onto the truck and without thinking she rested her hand on Ben's forearm, using his body for leverage as she climbed onto the hard metal.

'Thanks.' She smiled, shifting away from the edge so that Ben could climb on.

'At least there's cushions,' Lizzie said, scurrying towards the front and resting her back against the glass window of the driver's cabin. The base underneath her clanged and bowed slightly as Ben moved across the truck.

'And a blanket,' Ben said in mock cheer, sitting beside Lizzie and holding up a wiry sack which had been cut along the seam and sown in large looping stitches to another sack.

'This is just like when I was little and my mum used to wake me up at four in the morning for the annual sunrise service at our local church. I used to be half asleep until the sun started coming in through the stained-glass windows, and then suddenly I was wide awake. We'd go home afterwards and my dad would have a fry-up waiting for us: eggs, sausages, bacon, toast – the whole works.'

Lizzie smiled at the memory and shook her head. Why had she told him that?

Ben shrugged. 'This will be my first sunrise.'

'You what? How can you have *never* seen a sunrise? How old are you?'

'Thirty-three.' He turned to look at her; the whites of his eyes were bright against the darkness of the night.

'And you've never watched a sunrise?' Lizzie shook her head again. 'How is that even possible?'

'I don't know, I just haven't.'

'But what about after a night out? When we were at university, we'd have these crazy nights, which always ended in the early hours of the morning with a portion of chips covered in chip spice, and me, Jaddi and Samantha, sitting on a park bench talking about our evening until the sun came up.'

'What's chip spice?'

'What's chip spice?' Lizzie laughed. 'Are you even human, Ben?'

'I didn't go to university. I did a college course in filming and a few apprenticeships. I guess I was more of a beers-on-the-sofa kind of guy.'

'Was?'

Ben smiled. 'Good point. I *am* a beers-on-the-sofa kind of guy.'

'Well, you're in for a treat this morning.'

'I bloody hope so, after the journey we're about to go through.'

Lizzie laughed again, suddenly glad for the company, even if it came in the form of a grumpy cameraman.

She sat up as the engine roared into life. 'I've just realised I know next to nothing about you.'

'What do you want to know?'

'Well, we've got five hours to kill. Maybe you could tell me where you live for starters.'

The truck turned sharply in the road, performing a U-turn and sending Lizzie flying into Ben's body. 'Sorry.' She smiled, shuffling over and repositioning herself against the window of the cabin.

They sat in silence for a moment as the clattering engine jutted and vibrated beneath them. The noise and the motion reverberated in her ears.

'I live in Balham in South London,' Ben said, raising his voice to be heard over the engine.

'Oh.' She nodded. 'With flatmates?'

He shook his head. 'Just me.'

'That sounds very grown up. I can't imagine living by myself.'

'I had a girlfriend and a cat living with me for a while –' he shrugged '– but she didn't like the length of times I was away for. This job is an all-or-nothing kind of thing.'

'Couldn't you have done studio filming?'

Ben raised his eyebrows as if she'd said something stupid.

She smirked. 'I just thought that a studio might suit you better because of your … er … people skills.'

'Hey, what's wrong with my people skills?'

Lizzie smiled. '"I'm not your friend or your travel buddy,"' she, said mimicking his voice.

'Ah.' Ben laughed. It was deep and loud even with the motor roaring around them. 'Sorry about that. I guess I was kind of rude.' Ben rubbed his hand over the short stubble of his hair. 'It was partly because I'm not a good flyer. Actually, I'm not good with heights full stop, so I'd be grateful if we can avoid climbing ancient crumbling steps a hundred metres above sea level today.'

'Don't worry, I want to watch the sunrise over the spires of Angkor Wat, so we won't be doing any climbing, today at least.'

They sat in silence again. After a few miles, the city streets gave way to a scattering of shacks, then fields and forests, she guessed, as she stared out into the dark. Occasional flashes of light from the headlights of passing vehicles gave the only opportunity to view anything more than half a metre in front of her face.

The cushions they'd been grateful for had quickly become useless against the harsh oscillating metal beneath them.

'What was the other part?' she said, resting her head against the glass and feeling the vibrations against her skull.

'Oh, I guess I'm always pretty grouchy on the first few days of filming. I wanted to film wildlife, not people. Big cats especially.'

'So why don't you?'

He shrugged. 'It's a hard business to catch a break in. I'd filmed a few music videos for free, to get some experience. The musician liked me and put my name forward for the documentary about her. I was grateful for the work at the time, but now I can't get any wildlife jobs.'

'You must be good at it though, to keep getting the work.'

He smirked. 'No need to sound so surprised. It's the entourage bullshit. A lot of people who work as part of a film crew for celebrities get sucked into the life. They forget they're not working for the celebrity. They let them do retakes and set ups. It's how these reality soaps were created. All that stuff doesn't interest me. I just want to film the truth. It's how I got the nickname Sherlock.'

'So, Sherlock, aren't you going to collect any footage?' she said.

Ben glanced around them before shaking his head. 'The noise and the motion would make anything I collect useless. Anyway, I'm already filming more than I can process.'

'I thought you sent everything back to London for editing.'

'Almost everything.' He smiled, lifting his shoulders. 'The editing suite in London will try and make the footage seem more exciting or dramatic than it really is. There's nothing I can do about that, but I'm the one that's here with you, getting to know you all. So I try not to give them too much ammo of any one thing, like Jaddi's flirtatious side, or Samantha's scathing remarks about herself. If you take them out of the context of their friendship with you, their protectiveness over you, and how funny they are, then it paints a very different picture.'

'So what part of me do you cut?' Lizzie asked. 'Oh no, hang on. Let me guess – my sarcasm. Caroline mentioned it once or twice.'

He laughed. 'Got it in one. Caroline's not all bad. She's an incredibly dedicated producer.'

'I'm sure.' Lizzie smiled. 'But I'm glad she's not here,' she said, thinking of Caroline's constant feedback. Lizzie moved onto her side, resting her head against the window again. Her bottom had started to numb against the cold metal of the flatbed.

She closed her eyes and felt herself drift into a light sleep.

CHAPTER 15

Lizzie

Lizzie jolted awake and all at once became aware of four things: the warmth of Ben's chest where her head seemed to be resting; the griping pain stretching down her spine; the stillness of the truck, no longer juddering into her buttocks and thighs; and the persistent darkness of the night.

Lizzie sat bolt upright, her eyes fixing on the creased area of Ben's T-shirt before dragging them up to his face.

'Are we here?' she murmured, grateful for the darkness masking the flush creeping across her face. The last thing she remembered was resting against the glass behind their backs and closing her eyes. So, how had her body found its way so close to Ben's? And how had her head found its way to his chest?

Ben nodded and shuffled along the flatbed to unhook the latch.

'I'd better go say thank you to the driver,' she said, sliding their backpacks to the ledge without looking at him.

Lizzie scrambled down from the truck and had a sudden longing for the bitter black coffee from the vending machines that sat in the corridors at every hospital she'd ever been to, and she'd been to a lot. She never thought that she'd miss anything about hospitals, but now, in the darkness, she craved that coffee.

Ten minutes later, they'd purchased their tickets into the temple grounds and had followed a crowd of people to a wide stone wall.

Lizzie and Ben positioned themselves with their legs dangling over the edge, facing into the darkness. Lizzie's muscles cried out in protest as she sat on yet another cold hard surface. At least this one didn't vibrate, she conceded.

Ben pulled out his camera, seating it on his lap with the lens facing into the nothingness of night. Lizzie felt the presence of other people nearby, yet no one spoke. The anticipation floated in the air around them.

The first glow of light could have been a handheld torch, almost out of batteries, being held up by someone a few hundred metres away. After a few minutes, Lizzie began to wonder if maybe that's what it had been, but then, even without the presence of the sun on the horizon, the sky around them began to lighten. The three cone spires of the central temple were now visible on the other side of a large moat, which looked more like a lake, stretching across from the outer wall where they sat, all the way to the temple.

Lizzie glanced at Ben and the red light glowing on his camera, and when she looked up again time had jumped forward. Within the blink of an eye the infinitesimal light had morphed into a spectacle of colours. Behind the black outline of the temple a splodge of dark orange glowed, spreading out into a vibrant fuchsia, then deep purples and dark blues.

She stared, transfixed by its beauty. Lizzie had never seen such colours in the sky before. The entire scene reflected back at them in the crystal-clear mirror image from the moat, as if they were watching two sunrises at the same time. It was everything she'd hoped it would be, she thought with both joy and sadness.

'What are you looking for when you look at the sky?' he asked.

She pulled her eyes away from the horizon, glancing first into his eyes before her gaze dropped to the camera now pointed towards her. She could feel herself preparing to answer, feel the emotion welling to the surface, but not yet.

With every minute that ticked by, the sky before them transformed. The dark blues lightened, the pinks faded and the orange glow took on its spherical form. Eventually, the other visitors began to move away.

Only when the full circle of the sun peaked above the highest tower of the temple did she feel ready to answer. 'When I was nine, I spent a lot of time at Great Ormond Street Hospital, in London. There was a boy in the bed next to me, Ethan.' Saying his name out loud felt like picking off a deep scab and feeling the pain of the wound all over again.

'He had Acute lymphoblastic leukaemia so he was in for the long haul like me,' she said. 'I ignored him for a few days, probably because he was a boy and I was at that age when boys were the enemy, but it's hard to ignore someone when you've heard them throwing up a metre away from your bed all night.

'One time he spent the entire night dry retching. It was horrible to listen to, but I knew it was worse for him. You've got no idea how exhausting it is to be sick like that. I guess I felt sorry for him, because I walked up to his bed with a deck of cards behind my back, and he said, "What you looking at, baldy?" and I said, "You, baldy. Can you keep the noise down when you're chundering, please? Some of us are trying to sleep." It wasn't very funny but suddenly we couldn't stop laughing and we were best friends from that point on.'

She tilted her face to the sun and felt the first warmth of its rays. It felt right to tell this story here and now with the sky transforming above them.

Lizzie pulled in a long breath before she continued. 'It must have been around the time that Ethan had started to get better because I don't remember him being sick after that. But the ward was never peaceful at night. There was always someone crying, or a machine beeping, nurses coming in and out, or worst of all, a parent snoring.

'One of us would sneak into the other's bed and we'd play our own version of rummy we'd made up because we only had three quarters of a deck of cards. It never occurred to either of us to ask our parents to bring a full deck in. After a while we'd get tired of playing and just lie there whispering about normal things nine-year-olds talk about. I remember we spent an entire night talking about whether Father Christmas was real.

'We spoke about death a lot too, which I guess wasn't very normal for children of our age, but it was hard to ignore it. A girl across from us, Becky, I think her name was, had been moved to a different ward. We overheard the nurses talking about her. She'd gone to intensive care, but had died a day later.'

Lizzie paused, pushing back the mound clogging her airway.

'Ethan talked a lot about heaven. He used to say that there was this point at every sunrise and sunset when you can see the gates of heaven opening to let people in. I used to tease him about it all the time, but he just smiled as if he knew something I didn't.'

A single tear slid down her cheek. Then another.

'One night I sneaked inside the curtain around his bed and went to climb in alongside him, but before

I got to him I could feel this heat radiating off him. They did everything they could. Pumped him with antibiotics and a cocktail of other drugs, but it didn't make any difference … he didn't make it to morning.'

Lizzie reached into her bag and pulled out a bottle of water. She took three long gulps, wiped the tears from her face, and pushed the emotions away. If she broke down now, then she'd never stop. 'I think about Ethan all the time. Mostly, I wonder what he'd be doing now if he hadn't died that night. Would we still be friends? Would he be a doctor and a goalkeeper for Tottenham Hotspur like he'd planned? I'd forgotten all about the whole sunset thing, until a few weeks ago, when it popped into my head completely out of the blue.

'So, to answer your question, when I'm staring at the sunrise or sunset, I'm trying to figure out if heaven exists.' She tried to say it matter-of-fact, but the quiver of emotion in her voice gave her away. Lizzie dropped her eyes to the water bottle in her hand and fiddled with the cap.

They fell silent. Ben flicked off the switch on his camera and closed the digital screen

'I'm sorry about your friend,' he said.

She shrugged. 'Thanks. It was a long time ago.'

'I'm sorry about your tumour too. It can't be easy knowing you're about to die.'

Lizzie drew in a sharp breath, her head jerking to look at him. Her vision blurred. The colours of the sunrise now dancing across her eyes like an abstract replay.

She nodded and stood up, scrunching her eyes shut for a second. 'So what did you think of your first sunrise?' she asked, hoping to guide the conversation back to safe territory before Ben saw the fear lurking beneath the surface of her skin. She'd seen what she'd come for. A sunrise so spectacular there weren't the words to describe it, so why did she feel suddenly deflated? The high of the previous night was gone. Another night gone.

'It was spectacular, I'll give you that,' Ben said. 'But I'm not sure it was worth the hours in the back of that truck.'

'Just as I suspected.' She forced herself to smile. 'Not human at all. Now, how about breakfast?'

'Definitely,' he said. 'I could murder a fry-up, or some cereal or a croissant. Some toast would do. Anything really that isn't noodles or rice. What are the chances, do you suppose?'

'Slim to none, I'd guess.' She smiled, her mood lifting.

'Me too.' He smirked. 'Noodles it is then. Oh, and by the way, don't go thinking you can use me as a human pillow again on the journey back.'

Lizzie snorted as she looked at Ben and the mischief glinting in his eyes.

'And there I was thinking it was you using me for warmth.'

They laughed and fell into an easy stroll out of the temple grounds.

CHAPTER 16

Day 7

Samantha

The sky above the clearing was grey. Not the dark, mottled grey of the two elephants strolling across the land ten metres in front of them, but a light grey, the colour of the washed-out, cement, tower block Samantha had grown up in.

Despite the cloud, or maybe because of it, the heat of the morning was bearing down on them as they waited to meet the owner of the Mondulkiri Project. Samantha fanned her hat towards her face, but it did nothing to cool the slick layer of moisture forming on her forehead.

The trance-like exhaustion Samantha had felt when she'd scrambled down from the night bus and slid into an equally hot, equally loud, military-style old Land Rover two hours ago, had vanished. She had no doubt her fatigue would return soon enough, but for now her body raced with the nervous excitement of being in close proximity to such magnificent animals.

The larger of the elephants turned in a slow arc and ambled towards them, her trunk swinging and snuffling against the grass. As she drew closer, her ears flapped back and forth, waving a greeting, or so it seemed to Samantha.

Samantha reached for Lizzie's hand, wrapping it in her own as the elephant drew closer. A smile touched

Lizzie's face before she looped her own free hand into Jaddi's.

'This … is … amazing,' Lizzie whispered. 'I'm so glad we're here.'

'Me too,' Jaddi said.

They stayed like that, their hands entwined, silent and waiting. It was a moment Samantha would remember forever.

It wasn't just the first elephant Samantha had been close too, but the first one she'd ever seen in real life, and they were so much larger than she'd imagined. All the years she'd lived in London, all the times she'd promised herself, *this summer, this year, I'll visit the zoo*. And she never had. 'Children go to the zoo,' David had mocked when she'd asked him to take her as a birthday gift last year. 'All those families and pushchairs, no thanks. Let's enjoy a day with the papers on the riverbank somewhere, save the zoo for when we've got kids of our own.'

In fairness, she hadn't told him that she'd never been to a zoo, never seen the animals she knew only from television and books. Tigers, monkeys, penguins and so many more. It had been too ridiculous to voice; it still was. A twenty-nine-year-old woman living a tube ride away from one of the best zoos in the world and she'd never gone.

When she was younger there'd been no thought on her mother's part to take Samantha or her two older brothers to see animals, or anything else for that matter. There'd been no money for it, even if her mother had been struck by the idea. Samantha had been to plenty of farms though, tiptoeing around pens of cows and sheep with a clipboard and pencil, trying to avoid the squelchiest areas of mud because she didn't own a pair of wellies. Some initiative with inner-city schools and forging a connection with rural life, because inner-city school children needed to see cows and sheep, it seemed, but not elephants. By the time Samantha had been old enough to have her own bank account and earn her own money from a weekend job at New Look, she'd been too hell-bent on saving for her A level books, university and escape to think about spending her wages on a day out to the zoo. Her mother had frittered every penny of her money away on nothing. Samantha hadn't been about to risk making the same mistake.

The smell was the same as the farm though, she thought, as the elephant stopped a metre in front of them, her ears still flapping but her trunk now still, and her black eyes watching them. One elephant was emitting the same musky manure odour as an entire field of cattle.

'Hey there,' Samantha cooed, holding out her empty palm as the huge bulk of the creature towered over them. Up close the elephant was as much dusty-orange as it was grey. The skin around her legs, trunk and eyes was ringed with lines, but the top of her head and back were smooth. The elephant lifted her trunk up and brushed its prickly nostrils against Samantha's hand, covering it in warm slimy liquid. 'Nice to meet you too.' She laughed.

'Hello, my Mondulkiri family friends,' a short, dark-haired man said, stepping close to the elephant and rubbing the side of her face. 'I am Chris, owner of Mondulkiri Elephant project. This is my son, Narith.' Chris motioned to the teenage boy who'd collected them in the Land Rover from the nearby town. He was the same height as his father, with the same small nose and dimpled chin. 'He will take you on trek today.

He is your brother this week. Help him with his English, please, he is learning. In return he will show you how to care for our elephants.'

The elephant began to nudge the end of her trunk against Chris's body. He batted her away but pulled out a banana from a pocket in his trousers. The elephant circled it in her trunk before swinging it into her upturned mouth.

'Thank you for agreeing to spending your next. six days with us,' Chris continued, his English accented with the same Southeast Asian tones she'd heard from the Cambodian natives they'd met. 'There is lot of work to do this time of year. Today you will go on trek with two of our elephants, bond and clean them, see some of Cambodia's beautiful jungle. Rest of week, lots of jobs to do. Fences to build. We have many more space for elephants. Ten more. Twenty. But no money. Elephants are big tourist business. We must pay for business if we want owners to give us their animals. Elephants are not free. Maybe people in your country watching this, maybe they like our Mondulkiri elephants. They give us money to buy more elephants.' Chris smiled into Ben's camera as he spoke. He had two teeth missing from the top row but his smile was wide and genuine.

'Today you will take Happy –' he patted the elephant's neck '– and her friend Comvine for walk in jungle. Comvine is our youngest elephant. She is thirty years old. And Happy, she is our newest elephant. She has been with us only six months.' Chris shook his head, his smile disappearing. 'You see, her scars.' Chris pointed to an area of deep, black grooves on the bottom of Happy's front legs.

Samantha's stomach flipped as she stared at Happy's injuries. How could someone harm such amazing creatures?

'Happy came to us from Siem Reap. She worked giving tourists rides. All day, up and down. No water. She was very ill when she came here. One more day, maybe two, she dead. So you see, she is happy.' Chris smiled, scratching an area behind Happy's ear. 'So I say bye bye now, and I see you in huts for dinner.' Chris stepped over to his son and spoke in a fast Khmer dialect. Narith nodded before beckoning them to follow him.

'Bath time.' He turned and grinned at them.

They followed Narith and the two elephants into an area with trees so dense that at first it seemed impossible to Samantha that humans could find a way through, let alone two wide elephants. But soon enough, they saw well-trodden elephant tracks leading them down a long slope.

Birds called from the treetops above them. The sound was like the yelping city foxes Samantha could hear at night from their east London flat, but louder and with a pitch that pierced her eardrums. Twice Samantha looked up into the canopies and saw flashes of brown fur moving through the trees, keeping pace with them.

They heard the water before they saw it. The pounding splatter of a waterfall and crickets so loud and in abundance that it sounded like a car alarm.

Happy and Comvine picked up their pace as they reached the water, their legs thundering the ground as they broke into a trot, marching straight into the water, Happy veering to the left and Comvine to the right. They sunk down until only the top of their heads and backs were visible.

'We clean like this,' Narith said, wading into the water in his T-shirt and shorts and rubbing his hands against

Comvine. She responded with a loud short trump. 'You come.' He beckoned to them.

They dropped their packs, slid off their shoes, unhooked their microphones and stepped across the smooth slippery stones. Ankles, shins, knees, thighs, they waded into the cold water, then hesitated, lifting onto their tiptoes as the water skimmed their belly buttons.

'We should just drop in,' Jaddi said. 'It won't feel so cold after that.'

'You're right,' Samantha said, 'you first.'

Just then Comvine blew her trunk again, shooting a spray of water into the air, and soaking the tops of their heads.

'Ah.' Lizzie laughed. 'Might as well dunk now,' she said before dropping into the water.

Samantha did the same and swam the rest of the way to Happy, lying still and peaceful in the water.

'Hey, Happy,' she whispered, her feet finding the stony waterbed. Samantha's hand quivered as she ran her fingers over Happy's rough wet skin.

Narith waded across to her and placed his hand over her fingers. 'Like this,' he said, pushing her hand harder against Happy's body. 'She likes it.' He turned to the shore and waved at Ben. 'I ...' Narith pointed at Ben's camera and nodded.

'He wants to hold the camera, Ben,' Jaddi called out, 'so you can come and join us. Stop being a cameraman for five minutes. This is a once-in-a-lifetime thing.'

'Come on, Ben,' Lizzie called, 'you have to do this!'

Ben smiled and moved the camera to Narith's shoulder. 'It's heavy, isn't it?'

'Heavy, yes.' Narith nodded, moving the camera up and down with him. 'Very heavy.'

'Thank you,' Ben said, then dove below the surface, only reappearing when he reached Lizzie's side.

Jaddi grinned. 'I can't believe they just lie here for us.'

'Like getting a massage, I guess,' Ben said.

Comvine curled her trunk over her head, showering herself with water, along with Ben, Lizzie and Jaddi in the process.

Ben and Lizzie burst out laughing.

'Hey, cut that out!' Lizzie exclaimed.

'Ben –' Jaddi wiped the water from her face '– I don't think I've ever seen you smile so much.'

He laughed. 'It's like you said. It's once in a lifetime.'

Samantha smiled at Comvine's antics, but she was glad to have Happy all to herself as she worked her hands over the elephant's body. It was the rip across Happy's ear that broke her concentration, and stopped her dead.

All at once, David intruded into her peace. She squeezed her eyes shut and felt his hand pressing the tape over her mouth, forcing it on hard, too hard. The iron bed creaking as he moved over her naked body, tugging at each of the restraints holding her spread-eagled to the bed … the beep of the video recorder and the sick feeling knotting in her stomach and the bile rising in her throat.

Something brushed her shoulder, jolting her backwards, her eyes shooting open. She staggered before realising it was Happy's trunk.

As her eyes drew to the gashes and grooves that told the tragic story of Happy's life, Samantha felt an inexplicable connection to the elephant, as if Happy could see the mental scars inside Samantha just as easily as Samantha could see Happy's. As if Happy understood all too well the memories bombarding her head. Samantha ran her fingers over the jagged edges of the rip in the elephant's ear and felt the pain as her own.

Just like that, the veil dropped. She'd spent the past two weeks trying to convince herself that the man she loved, the man she'd planned to marry one day, wasn't the same man that had treated her like that in his bedroom the day she'd left, but he was. And standing in the water, running her hands over the scars of the most magnificent animal Samantha had ever seen, she saw David, the real David, with a clarity that chilled her to the bone.

The sing-song voice he used to sugar-coat the belittling remarks that chipped away at her. All of her. *Is that really what you want to wear? Are you sure you want to eat all that? She'll have the Caesar salad, won't you, darling?* It wasn't just her looks or her body, but her mind and her friendship with Lizzie and Jaddi too. *Doesn't it bother you that Lizzie and Jaddi do so many things without you? Applying for a promotion? Really? Well, if you're sure.*

How could she ever have loved someone who could hurt her in so many unspeakable ways?

The realisation of what David had done, like a fist in her abdomen, forced the air right out of her lungs. Samantha spun away from Happy, the nausea building. She gagged and choked gasping to breathe.

'Sam?' Jaddi shouted. 'Are you OK?'

'Sam?' Lizzie called, their voices drawing closer.

Samantha heard the sound of water splashing as her friends moved towards her. She had to compose herself. She wasn't ready to tell them. Not yet. Maybe not ever.

'What happened?' Jaddi asked, touching Samantha's back.

'I'm OK.' Samantha swallowed hard as she spoke. 'A bug flew into my mouth. I choked on it.'

Jaddi laughed. 'Is that all?'

Samantha pulled herself upright, forcing away another wave of sickness.

'Are you sure that's all?' Lizzie frowned. 'You don't look well.'

'It was a big bug,' she said with a meek smile.

'We go now,' Narith called from the edge.

Samantha looked up, surprised to see Happy and Comvine already out of the water and Ben holding his camera once more. She waded to the edge and back to dry land, shivering, but not from cold. She looked down at her shorts and T-shirt, already starting to dry, misshapen and clinging to her skin.

Samantha slipped on her shoes and pulled out her phone from her bag. One unread message blinked on her home screen: David: What are you up to today baby? Missing you xx

With shaking hands she tapped out a reply: It's over between us. I'm blocking your number. Don't try to contact me.

A red 'message failed' icon appeared on the screen. *No signal. Damn!*

Samantha found David's number in her contacts and pressed block. She deleted all the messages in her inbox and stuffed her phone back into her bag. As soon as they reached a place with signal again, David would get the message.

The rose-tinted glasses, the veil – whatever it was that had clouded her judgement about David – had gone, and it was never coming back.

Just then, Samantha felt a movement above her head. She looked up to find the long wrinkled trunk of Happy sniffing her hair before bringing her trunk down and running it over Samantha's cheek. A sense of peace travelled over her.

'She like you.' Narith laughed as Samantha smiled and wiped away the slime from her face.

'I like you too, Happy,' she said, patting the elephant's neck and pushing thoughts of David away. She knew she couldn't ignore him forever, in her head, or in reality, but she wanted to try, for Lizzie and for herself. This was the trip of a lifetime for all of them and she wouldn't let him take that away from her.

CHAPTER 17

Lizzie

Lizzie steadied her feet, leant forward and stared over the rock edge. Then a smile stretched across her face. The water below was dark blue, almost black.

'There has to be some kind of mistake,' Samantha whispered, her eyes darting to the edge of the rock and to Narith. 'Didn't Chris say his son was still learning English? Surely he's muddled his words and means we should look over the edge.'

'You jump,' Narith said for the second time, smiling the same wide smile as his father, but teeth intact, and pointing into the water. 'It safe.' Lizzie glanced over the edge one more time. The drop, twenty metres, maybe a little less, hadn't seemed that far down as they'd followed the path along the cliff edge to the top. That was, until Narith had told them to jump off. Now it seemed like a very long way down. A buzz of excitement coursed through her body.

She looked at Ben, positioned well back from the edge. His face behind the scope was one of amusement. She turned to the others and lowered her voice so as not to offend Narith. 'Do you think he's got his English in a muddle?'

'Absolutely.' Samantha nodded at the exact same moment Jaddi shook her head.

'It's cliff jumping.' Jaddi grinned. 'We have to do it. You heard him, it's safe.'

Samantha turned to Narith. 'We,' she said, pointing to herself and the others, 'jump –' she made a dive signal with her hands '– into the water.'

Narith smiled. 'Yes. Everyone jumps.'

'Including you?' Samantha frowned.

Narith chuckled, his slim frame shaking up and down. 'Elephant no jump. I walk with elephants down there.' He pointed to the path ahead of them, leading into the undergrowth.

'We –' Samantha pointed to each of them in turn '– could walk down with you.'

He stared back at her for a moment, his face struck with a bewilderment that transcended the language and cultural barriers between them. 'You don't want jump?' he asked. The tone of his words, just so, that he might as well have asked: 'You don't want to have this amazing, life-altering experience?'

Lizzie looked at Jaddi. An excited anticipation sparked in her friend's eyes and she hopped from foot to foot. Then there was Samantha, her forehead wrinkled with concern, her eyes wide and flitting.

'I have to do this,' Lizzie said.

'Great.' Jaddi grabbed her hand. 'Let's do it. Samantha?'

Samantha backed away from the edge. 'No. Absolutely not. Do you know how many people break their legs and their backs doing stupid things like this?'

'He said it was safe, Sam,' Jaddi said. 'Everyone does it.'

Samantha shook her head and stared at Lizzie. 'Do you remember, in the dressing room at Channel 6, when I said, I'd follow you anywhere, except off a cliff? This is a cliff.'

'You don't have to do it, it's OK.' Lizzie smiled. 'We can meet you at the bottom.'

'But you're still going to do it?' The crease in Samantha's forehead deepened.

Lizzie smirked. 'Why not?'

'Come on, Samantha,' Jaddi coaxed. 'We went to jump out of an aeroplane that time for the charity parachute thing, remember? You were willing to do that.'

'You tricked me into that one,' Samantha replied, taking another step away from the edge. 'You got me drunk and made me sign the consent form.'

'Yes, but you came with us.'

'I never would've done it.'

Jaddi nodded. 'Yes, you would have. If that fog hadn't come in and it hadn't been called off, you would have. We all would've. This is our chance for redemption.'

Samantha stared open-mouthed at them. Lizzie could almost see the risk assessment running through Samantha's head.

'Sam,' Lizzie said, 'ignore Jaddi, you don't—'

'Come on then.' Samantha sighed, stepping alongside Lizzie and gripping her other hand. 'If we're doing this, we might as well do it together.'

They unhooked their microphones, stripped off their packs and shoes, and placed them in an empty rice sack Narith handed to them. 'I take.' He nodded.

Lizzie looked one more time at Ben and the camera, flashed a smile and stepped, in one long stride, to the ledge. Adrenaline pulsed through her body, throbbing around her like a chiming church bell.

'On the count of three,' Jaddi said. 'One.'

Lizzie stepped closer, the soles of her feet scraping the rough surface of the rock.

'Two.'

Her toes found the edge. She pulled in a breath, keeping her head high.

Lizzie bent her knees and launched herself from the cliff. If Jaddi had said three, Lizzie didn't hear it, all she heard was the shhh of the air around her as she lifted her feet from the rock and pushed herself forwards, releasing her hands from Jaddi and Samantha.

Cold and darkness surrounded her body as she plummeted into the water, stripping her of the excitement she'd felt moments earlier. The water gurgled in her ears and forced its way up her nose and into the back of her throat. Lizzie flapped her arms and kicked with her legs until the water began to lighten and she broke through to the surface.

'Oh my God!' Jaddi shouted. 'That was the most exhilarating thing I've ever done in my life.'

'The most stupid,' Samantha said, swimming closer. 'It's a miracle we're all alive.'

'Ben!!!' Jaddi shouted, staring up to the ledge. 'Stop being a wimp and jump!!' She laughed and turned to Lizzie. 'I am seriously going to take the piss out of him for missing this.'

'Liz,' Samantha said, 'what do you say, exhilarating or stupid?'

'Both.' Lizzie coughed, squinting in the sunlight and staring up at the ledge they'd just dropped from.

'Hey,' Samantha said. 'You OK, hon?'

Lizzie stared back at them. Was she OK?

All of a sudden the water around her closed in, pressing against her chest and crushing her lungs. She couldn't breathe, she realised, fighting to draw in one ragged breath after another as she swam to the edge.

'Lizzie, wait up!' Samantha shouted.

Lizzie held up her hand. 'I'm OK,' she said. 'Give me a minute.'

Lizzie clawed her arms across the water until her fingers reached the bank and she scrambled upwards. Leaves and twigs slapped and scraped at her body as she plunged into the undergrowth, only stopping when all she could see was dense foliage. Only then did she allow the panic to take over.

This is it, I'm going to die. Lizzie dropped down onto the log of a fallen tree, her shoulders shaking as sobs wracked her body.

A minute passed, then another. Her tears stopped, leaving a rawness inside her.

'Lizzie?'

Lizzie lifted her head from her hands. 'Hi,' she said, wiping her fingers across her cheeks as Ben stepped alongside her. His camera was nowhere in sight.

'Jaddi and Samantha are looking for you,' he said. 'We all are. It's time to go back to camp.'

She nodded and stood up. 'Sorry, I needed a minute alone.'

'Are you feeling ill?'

She shook her head. 'That was the craziest thing I've ever done.'

'I bet.' Ben rubbed his hand over his beard and continued to look into her eyes. 'Although you wouldn't catch me doing it.'

'I'll remember it forever.' She choked, turning her back to Ben as the tears streamed once more down her cheeks.

'Hey,' Ben said, 'what's going on?'

'I'm sorry. I hate feeling like this,' she whispered. 'I want to be happy, but there are times when it feels like it's crushing me. All this fuss over me. This ... this ridiculous documentary. All the people watching. What difference does it make? I'm dying. In a few months, I won't exist. What difference will I have made? I'm … I'm no one. I'm utterly insignificant to the world—' she broke off, her shoulders heaving.

She closed her eyes and allowed her body to sink to the ground. The earth was clammy and warm and all she could think about was Ethan, the one person she knew who had gone through all of this before. She hadn't understood it then, but she did now.

'Have you ever felt like you're dying?' Ethan had whispered once, climbing into her bed. Sometimes they'd talked about heaven and sometimes they'd talked about the kids in their classes who annoyed them. That's how it was in hospital. One minute they were normal kids in a bad situation, the next they were different.

'I dunno.' She'd shrugged, shifting herself around to look at him. 'I'm still here, aren't I, so I guess not.' The light in the corridor had shone through the gap in the curtain and bounced off his head. Two beds away a machine had started to beep, signalling an empty IV bag. They didn't have long, she'd thought. One of the nurses would be in soon. She'd hoped it was Maggie. Maggie was younger than the other nurses and had freckles just like Lizzie's. Maggie had tried to be stern and always told them to get back to their own beds, but she'd always said it with a smile, and they knew she'd let them keep talking for a little while more.

'What colour hair did you have?' Lizzie had asked. 'Sometimes I think you were blonde, like your mum and your brother, but then other times I think maybe more gingery.' She'd given him a wicked grin and readied herself for a teasing match.

Instead, Ethan had rolled his eyes. She'd known she was being stupid but she didn't want to talk about death tonight.

'What do you think dying feels like?' he'd asked. 'I think it feels like this.' Tears had built in his eyes.

A sharp pain had hit her chest, right in the middle, and all of a sudden the backs of her eyes had started to swell as if she was going to cry too.

'I mean it,' he'd said, gripping her hand suddenly. 'I think I'm dying.'

'You know what the docs say, Ethan. Chemotherapy is the worst, but it means you're getting better.'

He'd shaken his head but hadn't replied.

Lizzie had flopped her head onto her pillow. 'I'm tired. We should go to sleep.' Ethan would feel better in the morning, she'd thought, then they'd go back to being normal again.

Ethan had slipped out of her bed but didn't leave. 'Lizzie?'

'Yeah?'

'Do you ever think, like, if I die today, then I haven't done anything? That all we've done is made our mums and dads be upset the whole time.'

'Shut up.' She'd tried to snigger but it had come out a cough. 'Look, if one of us dies and the other one lives, then the one who lives has to promise to do something amazing with their life. Really amazing, OK?'

'Like fly a hot air balloon around the world?' he'd said with a smile.

'Yeah, and help loads of people who need help.'

'Like my teacher, Mrs Briggs.' He'd nodded. 'She helps tonnes of people.'

'See. It'll be fine. Everything will feel better in the morning.' That's what her dad always said, anyway, whenever she'd had a bad dream or was sick.

Laurie Ellingham

Ethan had smiled at her. 'Goodnight, Lizzie.'

An hour or two later she'd awoken with a start. She'd thought someone had cried out, but the ward was eerily quiet for a change. She'd dropped her feet to the cool floor and, checking the coast was clear, had scurried to Ethan's bed.

'Ethan?' she'd whispered, fiddling with the curtain until she'd found the gap and her way inside. His eyes had been closed but his face was scrunched up and gleamed with moisture. She'd stepped closer and reached her hand out. A second later she'd lurched back with a yelp. Ethan was hot. Burning hot. Like touching a saucepan boiling on the hob. She'd leapt to the other side of the bed and stabbed at the nurse call button. 'Ethan, Ethan, talk to me, please, Ethan!'

He never did answer her.

'Lizzie.' Ben's voice cut through her thoughts.

He gripped her arms and pulled her upright, drawing her into his body until her head rested on his chest. She didn't pull away.

A second later she felt his chin rest on the top of her head.

Confusion and something else, something oh-so-distracting, whipped around her body. She pulled her face back and stared into the depths of his brown eyes. They drew her in, his eyes, pulling her closer, like a tug of war that she was losing, but didn't care. Her mind cleared, the memory of Ethan stopped. Everything stopped.

Slowly, very slowly, she moved closer. She could smell his skin and his breath, warm and sweet. A final wrench and her lips pressed against his and they were kissing. All at once fire crackers popped inside of her. She was eighteen again and on a rotating dance floor, spinning her head around and around, whilst her stomach dropped like the dip of a rollercoaster.

It was Ben that broke the spell. He moved, just a fraction, destroying the hold he'd had on her. Lizzie leapt back, stumbling a little as her feet landed on a stick that wobbled under her feet.

'I ... I'm so sorry.' She shook her head. Her entire face flamed with embarrassment. What had she just done? 'I shouldn't have done that.' She continued to step backwards whilst Ben remained rooted, his mouth open, staring back at her.

'Forget it ever happened.' She waved her hands in the air as if she could erase the last minute like erasing the writing on a whiteboard. 'I was having a moment. Dying girl and all that.' She tried to laugh but it sounded wrong, more like a 'ha'.

'Liz ...'

'Like I said, I'm sorry, forget it happened. Please, let's not speak about it again.' She spun around and dove into the undergrowth. He said something else, she was sure of it, but she didn't hear him, she didn't want to hear him. They were barely even friends. She was meeting Harrison in a few weeks' time. It was just the distraction she'd been drawn to. A moment of forgetting that she'd clung to with both hands.

Lizzie fought her way back to the path and the others.

Jaddi raised her eyebrows and smiled at her. 'You look like you've seen a ghost.'

'Sorry.' She shook her head. 'I just needed a moment to collect my thoughts. I'm fine. Come on, let's go back to camp.' She glanced back as Ben joined the group.

'Oh, Ben,' Jaddi said, 'there you are. At last! I can't believe you were too scared to jump.'

Ben mumbled a reply, but Lizzie didn't hear it. Whatever it was, it wasn't enough to stop Jaddi continue her teasing.

Lizzie felt Samantha move alongside her. Samantha dipped her head close before she spoke, 'Are you really all right?'

Lizzie's cheeks were still glowing, she was sure of it, but she nodded. 'Totally.' What else could she say? There was no point in telling Samantha and Jaddi what an idiot she'd been. Even if they found a minute without the microphones, without Ben, she couldn't tell them. Jaddi and Samantha would read something into it when there was nothing to read. Nothing at all. It was a blip, an insane moment caused by the exhilaration of the jump and the need to escape from her own thoughts. It wouldn't happen again.

PART II

CHAPTER 18

Day 17

The Sun, TV Picks
The Girl with Three Months to Live, Saturday 8pm
Make sure you have your popcorn and tissues ready for another emotional instalment from Lizzie, Jaddi and Samantha this Saturday. The Channel 6 documentary, which topped the ratings for two weeks running, has been moved to the earlier slot of 8pm to take Saturday's prime-time spot.

In tomorrow night's episode, the girls will be leaving the elephant sanctuary and heading by boat to Vietnam. Hopefully they won't find themselves stranded by any roadsides (or riverbanks) this week! But the question on everyone's lips this week has to be – are there romantic rumblings going on between Lizzie and cameraman Ben?

Day 25

The Mirror, TV Picks
Columnist Jo Herrington talks about her TV choices for the weekend
There is only one show I'll be watching this weekend, and that's the show everyone is talking about – episode 4 of *The Girl with Three Months to Live*! It seems everywhere I go people are chatting to me about Lizzie and the girls, and for good reason. This show is seriously

addictive viewing. I'll admit to being on the fence about *The Girl with Three Months to Live* when it first aired in January, but after watching Lizzie tell her heartbreaking story of losing her best friend, Ethan, aged 9, (episode 2), I was hooked. If the sneak peeks from Channel 6 are anything to go by, then this week we'll be watching Lizzie, Samantha and Jaddi's last week in Southeast Asia. I can't wait to see what's been happening with Ben and Lizzie. Even from Ben's position behind the camera there are some serious sparks flying between that pair. Join me on Twitter tonight to share your thoughts about the show. #TGWTMTL

Day 28

The Daily Star
The Girl with 2 months to Live
One month has already flown by for Lizzie Appleton – the star of Channel 6's *The Girl With Three Months to Live* – who was diagnosed with an untreatable brain tumour and given just three months to live. Lizzie and her friends, Samantha Jeffrey and Jaddi Patel, will now travel from Southeast Asia to Australia for the next leg of their journey.

It was a rocky start to their travels with Lizzie collapsing from a seizure in episode 1, and the girls being stranded by the roadside in episode 2. But things have calmed down in the last two episodes as the girls spent a week working at an elephant sanctuary in the Cambodian jungle, trekking the Ho Chi Minh trail in Vietnam, and snorkelling off the coast of Thailand. Far from seeing a dip in viewing figures, the show's popularity has continued to climb ahead of their time in Australia and Lizzie's plans to meet with old flame, Harrison Kelly.

CHAPTER 19

Day 30

Lizzie

'Welcome to day thirty. We're just about to touch down in Sydney, Australia, and if you look out the window right now –' Lizzie turned the screen of the camera and aimed it over Samantha and Jaddi to the oval-shaped window '– you'll see Sydney Harbour Bridge in the distance.'

Lizzie angled the lens back to her sun-kissed reflection and tried to remember what else she needed to say. For a fleeting moment, she thought about the millions of people watching at home, and the insanity of it all – the popularity of the documentary, what they were doing. Her head began to throb. Blobs of red and orange floated lazily across her eyes like the gloopy stuff in a lava lamp. They'd disappeared for a while – the colours, and the churning in the pit of her stomach that accompanied them. The experiences, the fun they'd had, the sheer exhaustion of their long days, had made it easy to forget what they were doing, the millions of eyes on her, but nine hours sitting on an aeroplane had allowed it all to creep back again.

Lizzie blinked several times until the colours disappeared and forced her hi-mum-hi-dad smile. Forgetting would be just as easy in Australia. It had to be.

'For those counting, namely Caroline and Ben, you'll notice that I've skipped a day of my video diaries.

I meant to do this last night during the flight, but after weeks of sleeping on camping mats and in beds with springs digging into my ribs it's amazing how comfortable an aeroplane seat can feel.' She smirked as Ben tutted from the seat in front.

'Thank you to everyone who has posted suggestions on our Facebook page of where to stay and things to do in Sydney. We're reading them when we can. We met so many lovely Australian travellers in our final week island hopping around southern Thailand. It's so nice to know we'll be spending the next part of our trip in such good company.'

Jaddi snorted from beside her before leaning over and whispering something in Samantha's ear, sending them both into a fit of giggles.

'Oh, we're just about to hit the tarmac,' Lizzie said. 'I'd better go.'

Lizzie turned off the camera and jabbed Jaddi in the ribs. 'What did you just say?'

'Just that I know one friendly Australian you'll be keen to see.'

Lizzie rolled her eyes as the aeroplane wheels bumped and skidded on the runway, lifting up into the air for a second before juddering harder onto the ground. Lizzie hardly noticed the jerking movements of the plane as the force of the breaks lurched her forward in her seat.

Her mind had already drifted to Harrison.

They'd met on a Saturday afternoon last April before the tips of her fingers had started to tingle and her hands had started dropping things for no reason. She remembered a time in August when her Oyster card had fallen out of her hand onto the tube platform at Leicester Square, and been kicked onto the tracks by a scurry of feet. Of course, it was the day she'd forgotten her purse and had had to traipse back up the broken escalator to the ticket office and plead for a ticket so she could get home. Another time, a cup of tea had slipped from her grip in the kitchen one morning and scalded Samantha's feet.

Harrison had been the only Australian in a heaving sports bar overlooking the Thames. He'd tapped her on the shoulder and dropped to one knee as she'd turned around. 'Will you marry me?' he'd said, causing raucous laughter to erupt from the group of drinkers behind him.

She'd grinned. 'How about buying me a beer first?'

So he had.

'I'm being deported!' he shouted over the noise of the rugby match on the big screen and the cheers from a nearby table. He pouted as he handed her a tall, cold glass of lager, pushing his lips out and turning the corners of his mouth down.

Without thinking about anything but the buzz of alcohol already cloaking her head, without questioning why someone as drop-dead gorgeous as Harrison with his blonde floppy hair and perfect face would be talking to her, Lizzie had leant forward and planted a kiss on his lips.

She drew away, laughing at herself, her cheeks colouring. But one of Harrison's hands touched the back of her head, guiding her back towards him until they were kissing. Properly kissing, right there on a Saturday afternoon in a pub that served cheap beer and soggy chips. It was the best kiss she'd ever had.

'I did try to appeal and change it to a working visa,' he'd told her much later as they'd strolled hand in hand along the river. 'But I'm done for. Last I heard, the deportation letter is in the post.'

The uncertainty of it all had drawn her in. Hook, line and sinker. She'd spent so much of her life shrouded in equivocalness; surviving three brain tumours, not to mention the countless check-ups and hospital visits, did that to a person. For all of the days she'd woken up filled with a sense of empowerment, desperate to seize the day, embrace life and enjoy herself, there were as many days she woke up imprisoned by an invisible wall of foreboding, as if her life was one big visa application about to be denied.

They'd dived into a relationship head first, jumping straight over the awkward first dates and getting to know each other stage, and straight into the love-sick teenager phase. They'd taken day trips to all the places Harrison still hadn't seen. One day they were riding the pier train at Southend-on-Sea, the next they were climbing Mount Snowdon.

For two weeks they spent every moment they could together. And then, just like that, he left.

She'd cried for a day and moped for a week, but eventually she'd stopped thinking about him. Even when Caroline and Jaddi had booked their flights to Sydney it hadn't crossed Lizzie's mind that she might see Harrison again. It was only when his name appeared on the message stream that it had all flooded back. They'd been pinging messages back and forth ever since, catching up on the time they'd spent apart. She'd told him how exciting it had been to quit her data admin job and start a teacher-training qualification, and the first MRI scan two weeks into her course. Then a CT and a PET scan. Endless tests while all the time knowing they'd find another tumour.

Harrison had told her about adjusting to life back in Australia, training to be a recruitment consultant, which he hated. The sights he couldn't wait to show her, the friends he wanted her to meet. Each message ebbing away from friendly reminiscence and closer to something more intimate.

Lizzie fiddled with the ends of her hair, which had finally grown over the tops of her ears. Harrison had loved her swishy ponytail. Now what would he think? Lizzie dropped her hand and shook the thought away. Whether he liked her hair or not was a tad trivial compared to the reason she was on this trip in the first place. Somehow, in all of their messages, her prognosis and the documentary had never come up. What did that mean? And was she ready to pick up where they'd left off, even if it meant millions of people would be watching?

'All set?' Jaddi nudged Lizzie's elbow.

Lizzie looked up, surprised to hear the clanging metal of unclipping seatbelts sound across the aircraft and the hatch door ahead of them swing open. They'd arrived. Nerves popped in the pit of her stomach. It was the good kind for a change, the kind she'd felt before jumping off the rock in Cambodia, rather than the kind she felt anytime she allowed herself to think about her future.

'Yep.' Lizzie smiled.

CHAPTER 20

Samantha

Harsh morning sunlight burnt at the back of Samantha's retinas as she stepped out of the aeroplane and clonked down the metal air stairs. Her body craved a Coca-Cola or sweets, or anything in fact that contained a strong hit of sugar. Oh, and a shower. She was pretty sure the tangy whiffs affronting her nose were emanating from her armpits and the damp area of her T-shirt, growing by the second in the heat.

Samantha understood the appeal of night flights – go to sleep in one country, sleep all night, and wake up in another country without wasting a day travelling – but it never worked out like that, or at least it didn't for her. Sleep just wasn't the same. The quality, the depth, the length of time before the ache in her neck forced her to wake and change position. She ducked her head and stared at her feet as Ben stepped in front of them, already on the runway filming their descent. There were times when Ben and his camera were nothing more than a blip on their horizon, but there were also times, like now, when the reflection of the black lens made her cheeks flush red and her stomach cringe.

Samantha glanced at Jaddi and Lizzie as they stepped through the glass doors and into the baggage-claim area. There was no mistaking the excitement at a new destination hovering between them, but it was tinged with something else. Something unspoken. The gut-wrenching reality that one month and one part of their trip was behind them. She could see it in the crease of Jaddi's forehead and the way she kept glancing behind her, left and right, as if waiting for something bad to happen. Samantha felt it too.

Time had slowed on the Thai islands as they'd lounged in the sun, taken boat trips to remote coves, and snorkelled in an ocean as clear as tap water. A grey fog of exhaustion had clouded Samantha's head in Vietnam, blocking out the sights of the trails. Only David was clear. His voice, his touch, it was all there, running on repeat inside her head, as if seeing Happy's injuries had unleashed the memories from somewhere hidden inside her head, and she'd been stuck reliving them over and over.

Only during their weeks on the islands had the exhaustion released its hold on her. As if submerging herself into the depths of the turquoise ocean had cleansed her of the shock and anger from her final afternoon with David.

'You OK, hon?' Lizzie touched Samantha's arm.

Samantha jumped back, startled by the touch. She mustered a short laugh. 'Yes, sorry, I was miles away.'

'You've been doing that a lot, you know.' Lizzie frowned, her eyes scanning Samantha's face. 'Are you sure there's nothing wrong?'

Samantha shook her head. 'It's tiredness, that's all. I didn't sleep properly on the plane.' A heaviness spread over Samantha's chest for the lie she'd told. But however much it hurt, upsetting Lizzie wouldn't change what had happened.

CHAPTER 21

Jaddi

Jaddi shrugged off her backpack and dropped it to the floor. There didn't seem much point carrying it when they weren't moving.

'I never realised how nice orderly queues could be,' Samantha said, oblivious to the tedium circling Jaddi as they joined the back of the line that would take them through Australian customs.

If it was up to Jaddi, she'd barge to the front and play the can-we-cut-in-front-of-you-because-my-best-friend-only-has-sixty-days-left-on-earth card. Instead Jaddi sighed and scooped her hair up into a messy bun. It wasn't up to her, it was up to Lizzie, and drawing attention to themselves didn't exactly fit with Lizzie's desire to be like every other traveller, something they'd done well with so far, considering the growing media attention back in the UK and online.

Despite the dozens of tabloid stories, the trending Twitter hashtags, and the millions of followers on their Facebook page, they'd existed within in their own bubble in Southeast Asia. But would it last? From the number of comments posted by Australians on Facebook, it was clear that the documentary's reach had expanded outside of the UK.

Jaddi glanced over her shoulder, half expecting to see a group of well-meaning fans rushing towards them.

She smirked to herself and discarded the thought. Fans? Who was she kidding? Australia was a huge country with just as many remote places as Southeast Asia. Nothing would pop the bubble. She wouldn't let it.

As the passengers in front of them began to move, Jaddi hoisted her bag from the floor and stepped forward two paces. 'I kind of liked the mosh pit of travellers trying to get into Vietnam,' she said. 'All those men zipping around offering to bribe border control and get us through in minutes for a small fee. It was fun.'

'I've always thought there was something strange about you, Jaddi.' Samantha shook her head. 'Well, your idea of fun anyway. We were at that border for two hours. I must have sweated my entire body weight whilst watching coach loads of people walk straight past our so-called line and to the front. What is the point of organising visas in advance if that's how they're going to manage it? Call that fun?'

'Maybe fun is not the right word. It was definitely an—'

'Authentic experience,' Lizzie and Samantha chorused before falling into a fit of giggles.

'Well, it was.' Jaddi laughed, pulling out her mobile and turning it on.

'Will you put your phone away for five minutes?' Samantha flicked Jaddi's phone with her finger. 'It's been glued to your hand for the past week.'

Jaddi grinned. 'Sorry. I'm just confirming the Segway booking for tomorrow.'

'Oh God, I know that smile.' Samantha shook her head. 'What are you getting us into now?'

Jaddi laughed. 'It's just an off-road Segway ride through Newington Park.'

Samantha shook her head. 'So why are you smiling your mischief-making smile? The one you had last summer when you talked me into doing that mud-wrestling event in Regent's Park.'

'Hey, that was hilarious,' Jaddi said, grinning, 'and you know it. And it was for charity. Don't worry, the Segways will be fun, I promise.'

'Plus –' Lizzie winked at Jaddi '– don't you want to see Ben trying to drive a Segway and film at the same time.'

'I'm standing right here, you know?' he said from behind the camera.

Lizzie laughed. 'Sorry.'

'No, you're not,' he said with a smirk.

'You're right, I'm not.' She grinned at him.

Ben poked his head out from the camera and shot them a look. It didn't last. His face relaxed and the bemused smile Jaddi had seen more and more of appeared.

A movement caught Jaddi's eye. 'Er, Ben?' She raised her eyebrows as a man in a pale-blue uniform strode purposefully towards them.

The officer tapped Ben twice on the shoulder before positioning himself in front of them. The officer's legs stretched into an upside-down V, one hand on the black baton on his hip, the other on the radio receiver attached to his breast pocket. 'I'm going to need you to pack your equipment away, sir.' The officer's head barely reached Ben's shoulder, but the man had a presence about him. The tanned muscles bulging out his shirt sleeves added to the effect.

'I'm a cameraman,' Ben said, pulling a plastic identification card from the side pocket of his khaki trousers. 'I'm filming a UK documentary.'

'Sir, turn it off.'

'No problem.' Ben smiled a cooperative smile and zipped his camera into its bag whilst the officer continued to stare. The line ahead moved three paces without them.

'Ben got told off,' Jaddi sing-songed once the officer was out of earshot.

Ben shook his head before hoisting his bags onto his back.

'Don't be mean, Jaddi,' Samantha sniggered. 'Poor Benny is upset enough as it is.'

'All right, all right.' Ben glared between them. 'I know it was very funny, but the line is moving.' He nodded towards the white screen and three more uniformed officers.

Jaddi patted Ben on the shoulder and stepped forward. 'Sydney, here we come.'

'You coming, Liz?' Samantha smiled.

'Er …' Lizzie dropped her eyes to her clothes and ran a finger over a stain on her top. 'Go on without me. I think I'll freshen up quickly.'

'Oh, yeah.' Jaddi grinned. 'Lover boy is waiting.'

Lizzie swiped Jaddi on the arm. 'I'll be five minutes,' she called as she turned towards the toilet sign.

Samantha stared after her. 'Shall we wait for her?'

'You guys go,' Ben said. 'I'll wait for Lizzie and hold our place in the queue,' he added, pointing towards a new wave of passengers trundling out of baggage claim towards them. 'Get us some coffees, OK?'

'Done.' Jaddi nudged Samantha's arm. 'Let's go.'

CHAPTER 22

Jaddi

It was the little boy who dropped his panda that saved them. The bear slipped out of his chubby hands smack bang between the automatic doors, stopping the family in their tracks for several seconds as the boy wailed and wriggled in his mother's arms, and the dad let go of his daughter to retrieve the teddy and return it to the boy's clutches. All the while the automatic doors remained open, giving Jaddi a clear view of what awaited them.

On the other side of the waist-high plastic barrier, separating those arriving from those waiting, a swelling crowd of friends, family and loved ones craned their necks, searching for the first glimpse of the next people to walk through. And boxing them in were a dozen men and women with notebooks and cameras. Lots of cameras. Even from the other side of the doors, Jaddi could feel the anticipation crackling in the air. Then, just as the family ahead of them moved through, just as the doors began to close, Jaddi saw him. Front and centre to it all, in a bright, lime-green T-shirt, was Harrison.

Jaddi gasped and grabbed Samantha's elbow, dragging her to one side. So much for being like any other traveller. So much for obscurity. Panicked questions raced through Jaddi's head. How was Lizzie going to react? She'd be pissed, that's for sure. Hurt too? Frustrated? Sad? All of the above? Something sank deep down inside of her. Their bubble had well and truly burst.

'What are you doing?' Sam asked, staring around her as the doors closed.

'Right,' Jaddi said, dropping Samantha's arm. 'Don't panic, but there are some reporters out there.'

'Oh.' Samantha raised her eyebrows, peeking her head over Jaddi's as the doors closed again. 'Do you think there was someone famous on our flight?'

Jaddi shook her head. 'They're here for us, Sam. For Lizzie.'

'Oh, shit. We have to warn Lizzie.'

'It's too late; we're through customs already. We can't go back now.'

A woman from customs started to wave them through and Jaddi made a step to the doors, but Samantha stood rooted to the spot. 'What do we do? No way am I going out there.'

'Yes, you are.' Jaddi took Sam's hand. 'Stay this side of me. Smile, wave and keep walking.'

'But—'

'Harrison's out there. They're waiting for Lizzie, not us. Best thing we can do is get through and wait for Lizzie there.'

Samantha nodded. 'OK.'

As the automatic doors opened for them, Jaddi whispered into Samantha's ear, 'Look normal.'

'What does that mean?'

'I don't really know. I just thought it would look more normal if we were talking. Here we go,' she added as they stepped into clear view of the arrivals hall. Jaddi raised her head and grinned, waiting for the flashing of cameras and shouts from the paparazzi.

Nothing happened. Nothing changed. The journalists continued to jostle and crane their necks. Some talked on phones, others fiddled with their cameras.

'Ha,' Samantha said with a giddy sigh as she surveyed the reporters from a spot out the way. 'They're so busy looking for Lizzie that they didn't even see us. Guess we're not the famous ones,' she grinned, nudging an elbow into Jaddi's side.

'I guess not,' Jaddi said, frowning at the crowd. It wasn't as if she cared about being famous, or recognised – not really anyway – but she cared about protecting Lizzie and had hoped to draw some of the attention away from her friend. Jaddi's chest tightened.

For the briefest of moments Jaddi wondered, if she could go back to that night in October – when Lizzie had walked like an empty shell into their flat, when she'd fought so hard to swallow back the tears, and failed … when Jaddi had stared at the blank webpage on her laptop and pondered all of their futures – would she still have gone through with it, knowing how big the can of worms would become? The question left a mawkish tingle in her mouth.

CHAPTER 23

Lizzie

Lizzie stared at the mascara stick waving frantically back and forth in her left hand. 'It's just the excitement,' she said to her reflection. 'Excitement and hunger and exhaustion from the night flight. Get a grip.' She pulled a face but her hand continued to shake and dance in front of her. What was it with airport toilets? Lizzie watched the colour drain from her face as the foggy memory of Bangkok airport filled her head. She didn't remember the seizure, not really, but she remembered the smell and the fuzzy out-of-body feeling of watching herself slide to the floor.

Lizzie swallowed hard and swapped hands before swiping the brush over her lashes. This was different. It would pass, just like it always did. She leant forward and surveyed the results. Her right eye looked fine, but the lashes on her left eye had stuck together like spider legs.

She sighed and added an extra swipe to her right eye to match.

Lizzie snapped the straps of her backpack together and surveyed her reflection one more time. She'd dug out the loose brown and orange tunic dress her mum had bought her for Christmas. It was the nicest outfit she had with her.

'I saw it in the summer sales and thought it would be perfect for you. It's lightweight and will fold really small,' her mum had said in a giddy voice amidst the mountain of red and green wrapping paper surrounding the living room. Her mum lived for Christmas. Wherever Lizzie was on the first of December she always thought of her mum, unpacking the umpteen boxes of decorations from the loft and beginning the day-long task of transforming the house. Most of all, though, her mum loved spoiling them all. Christmas was her season.

Later, Lizzie had found her crying in the kitchen. Deep wrenching sobs had heaved through her mum's body causing tears to form in Lizzie's own eyes. She'd gone to her mum and wrapped her in a tight hug.

'I've ruined the turkey pan,' her mum had said in a shuddering whisper. 'That's why I'm crying. It was a wedding gift from my mother. We've had it for donkey's years.'

Lizzie had rubbed her mum's back and hugged her tighter. They'd both known it had had nothing to do with the turkey pan.

Fresh tears welled in Lizzie's eyes thinking of that last Christmas with her family. She blinked them back and yanked open the restroom door. She had to get moving before any more of her past caught up with her. Or did she mean her future? Lizzie wasn't sure.

Ben stood waiting for her where she'd left him. The sharpness of his buzz cut had started to grow out. He really wasn't the same guy who'd snapped at her on the aeroplane at the start of their trip. Perhaps that was just because she knew him better now. She knew he was grumpy first thing in the morning, or all day if there wasn't any coffee going. She knew how he preferred vegetables to meat because of a time when he was six and choked on a mouthful of chicken, and how the taste still reminded him of the feeling of choking. She knew that behind the serious cameraman was an intuitive person who had an uncanny knack for sensing when to switch off the camera and step away, allowing them time alone together. In the same way, he seemed to know just the moment to turn it on, like when they'd been snorkelling near the Phi Phi Islands and three blacktip reef sharks had swam right up to them. One moment Ben had been swimming, the next he was back on the boat with his camera out capturing the whole thing.

'Where are the others?' she said, keeping her left arm close to her side. The juddering had eased to a tremor but she didn't want Ben or the others to see it. The last thing she needed was for Jaddi and Samantha to start worrying about her again.

'I told them to go through and get us some coffees.'

'Good thinking.'

'Ready?' he asked.

'I guess,' she said, staring ahead. Her eagerness to get moving faltered. A pressure closed in around her, squeezing her tight. Once they stepped through into the arrivals hall, they'd be on the second part of their journey. One month down, two to go. There wasn't enough time.

'Why are you nervous?' Ben asked.

Her eyes shot to his face. His tone was direct, as if his camera was on his shoulder, but it was just him.

Ben returned her stare, the rich brown of his eyes, flecked with green, willing her to move closer just like they had in Cambodia.

'I'm not nervous,' she lied, bouncing forwards.

Their arms brushed against each other as they rounded the corner into the arrivals terminal. The dipping rollercoaster of their kiss filled her head and whipped around her body. Why, after weeks of successfully ignoring it, why, when she was just about to meet Harrison again, someone she really liked, was she thinking about that insane kiss with Ben? Before she could consider the answer, a burst of camera flashes dazzled her eyes. A dozen voices fired at her from behind a barrier.

'Lizzie, how does it feel to be in Australia?'

'Lizzie, how are you feeling?'

'What will you be doing on your stay?'

'Lizzie, over here, give us a smile.'

The shock was a brick wall and she'd slammed right into it. Who were these people? Why were they here? Even as her mind asked the questions, even as she sidestepped into the crook of Ben's arm, even as he caught her hand in his, pulling her back and stepping in front of her like a human shield, she knew the answer – they were for here for *The Girl with Three Months to Live*. They were here for her.

'Lizzie, Lizzie, Lizzie!' a familiar voice rang out over the questions.

Her eyes roamed the crowd until she saw him. She stepped out from Ben's protective grasp. All of a sudden she didn't care about the Australian media, or anything else for that matter.

'Harrison.'

He ducked under the barrier, ran the two paces towards her and scooped her into his arms, spinning her around before pulling her close and kissing her right on the lips. In the background, the crowd cheered.

CHAPTER 24

Samantha

'Well, I'm just going to say it,' Samantha murmured, watching from outside the terminal, 'that was quick.'

Jaddi nodded, her eyes fixed on Harrison and Lizzie wrapped in each other's arms. 'Just a bit.'

Samantha waved Ben over.

'Are you all right?' Samantha asked as Ben dropped his backpack to the floor and repositioned his camera bag across one of his shoulders.

'Yep.' Ben pressed his index finger and thumb on his forehead as if he was trying to smooth away the furrows that had formed there since Samantha had seen him last.

'Did Channel 6 arrange this?' Samantha pointed at the media gaggle.

Ben shrugged. 'If they did, then they didn't tell me.'

'Would you expect them to?'

'Caroline's been emailing me details of our America leg already, so if she'd planned anything here, then, yes, I'm sure she would've told me.'

Eventually the press gathered their belongings and left in a mass exodus.

Even though Jaddi had mentioned the astronomical number of fans growing daily on their Facebook page and Twitter account, it still seemed unbelievable, disturbing even, to see their reach on the other side of the world.

'Hey,' Lizzie said, striding towards them. 'Sorry about the delay. Are you guys OK?'

Harrison lingered a few paces behind, his face bent forwards as his fingers danced across the keypad of his mobile. He looked up, catching Samantha's eye and stepping forward.

'Jaddi, Sally.' He flashed a row of perfectly straight teeth. 'Great to see you.'

'It's Samantha.' She smiled.

'Oops, sorry, Sammy,' he said, in a stronger Australian accent than Samantha remembered from the few times she'd met him in London. She was sure he'd had an American edge to his voice when they'd met him last. Either way, he was still just as gorgeous.

He was a poster boy for the young carefree-surfer look and seemed to know it. The subtle blond highlights from the sun or a bottle (the latter, Samantha suspected, based on their too-perfect scattering) swept into a just-rolled-out-of-bed look, that probably took an hour to perfect based on the way his fringe sat just so on his forehead.

He wasn't particularly tall, under six foot, she guessed, but he was toned and athletic, and had a bounce to his gait which made him seem bigger.

'Are you OK with all this?' Samantha asked Lizzie as Ben repositioned his camera bag with a stern pull, reminding her they needed to get going.

'You mean the media circus? Sure.' She smiled as she spoke but Samantha thought she detected more than a hint of sarcasm in the way Lizzie clipped the final letter of each word. Harrison dropped an arm around Lizzie's shoulder and kissed her cheek.

Ben held out a hand to Harrison. 'I'm Ben Holmes, the cameraman.' He turned his gaze to Lizzie.

'Oh, sorry.' Lizzie smiled. 'Ben, this is Harrison, Harrison, this is Ben.'

Harrison fell half a foot shorter than Ben, but if he felt uncomfortable by Ben's height as he bounced forward then he didn't show it. 'G'day, mate. Welcome to Sydney.'

'Thanks.' Ben unzipped a pocket in his camera bag, riffled inside it for a moment before pulling out a sheet of paper. 'I'm guessing that you'll be joining us for some of the trip, in which case, you're going to need to sign this waiver.' He handed the document to Harrison. 'It basically says that you're fine for me to film you for the purposes of this documentary and that you won't be receiving any payment for doing so.'

Harrison grinned. 'No worries. Gotta pen?'

Samantha raised her eyebrows at Jaddi as Harrison signed the form, but Jaddi's eyes were watching Lizzie. Jaddi's forehead was creased, her mouth a thin, straight line as if she was trying to figure something out in her head.

'I gotta shoot into work,' Harrison said a moment later, handing back the sheet of paper to Ben and turning to face Lizzie. 'The boss wants me to do a quick handover before my hols.'

'Holiday?' Lizzie said. 'Are you going somewhere?'

Harrison leant forward and kissed Lizzie on the lips. 'I'm going wherever you're going. I've got this whole week off to spend with you. I'll be your very own tour guide. Starting with snags on the beach tonight in your honour.' He turned and addressed them all. 'We'll give you a proper Aussie welcome.'

Lizzie smiled. 'Sounds good.'

'Where ya staying?' he asked, his eyes lingering on Jaddi.

'A youth hostel just by the harbour,' Jaddi replied.

'Oh, yeah, I know it. The Rocks. Just hop onto one of the red and white Captain Cook ferries from Darling Harbour and head to Watsons Bay for around seven. You can get a bus but the ferry is way cooler. I'll make sure there are enough spare seats in cars to get you back afterwards.'

Harrison collected Lizzie in his arms and spun her around a final time before bouncing off towards the exit, leaving a silence that none of them seemed to know how to fill.

Eventually Samantha spoke. 'Shall we go find our hostel and dump our bags then?'

Jaddi nodded, but Lizzie stared off into the distance wearing an amused expression.

'Lizzie?' Jaddi said.

'Yeah.'

'Ready to go?'

'Definitely. But can we make a detour before the hostel? I don't know about you, but I'm in need of a fry-up.'

'Actually, I was just thinking I could go for some noodles right about now,' Ben said, making them all laugh and restoring the equilibrium to their foursome.

'By the way,' Jaddi said, 'anyone know what a snag is?'

Lizzie laughed. 'Not a clue, Sam?' She pushed Samantha's arm. 'You must know. Surely you've done your usual boffin research on culture and language?'

'Sausages, I think,' Samantha said as Ben unzipped his holdall and pulled out his camera.

'Oh,' Jaddi said, 'that makes sense.'

Ben strode three paces ahead of them and hoisted his camera onto his shoulder, and as they strolled out into the warm Australian sunshine, Samantha tried not to dwell on the potential trouble that the Australian media, and Harrison – with his all-too-perfect smile – might bring to the group, and especially to Lizzie.

CHAPTER 25

Lizzie

Lizzie dropped into a black plastic seat on the top deck of the ferry and pulled her hands inside the sleeves of her hoody. Despite the heat of the day, the evening breeze had an English feel to it.

A moment later, Jaddi and Samantha settled down beside her and the ferry engine roared into life.

'So, I'm *really* pleased I bothered to blow-dry my hair.' Samantha shook her head as a gust of wind lifted her hair and blew it into her face. She scooped it up and tied it into a high ponytail. 'I thought escaping the humidity would mean at least one good-hair day.'

'Who cares.' Jaddi grinned. 'Look at this view. What a place to see the sunset from, eh, Lizzie?' Jaddi rifled in her satchel. 'And look what I found in that supermarket,' she said, holding up a miniature bottle of Prosecco and ripping off the foil wrapper.

Lizzie smiled and nodded as the ferry dipped and rose, bouncing over the waves made by a large boat heading into the harbour, and rocking them in their seats.

'I'd shoot the cork into the water,' Jaddi said, twisting the bottle in her hands with a pop, 'but the city is so clean I think I might get arrested, or something. I don't think I've seen a single piece of litter today.'

As the ferry turned out of the harbour, the vast black metal of Sydney Harbour Bridge came into view.

'Hey, look up there,' Samantha said, pointing towards the top of the bridge where people were walking up.

'Wow,' Jaddi said, offering the bottle to Samantha, 'we have to do that.'

'Definitely,' Lizzie said. 'I'll have cheeky swig,' she added, plucking the bottle out of Samantha's hands and filling her mouth with cold, fizzing bubbles.

She passed the bottle to Jaddi and laughed at the expression darkening their faces. 'It was one sip, guys. Relax. I'm sure it won't kill me.' The bubbles of alcohol danced alongside the excitement jumping in her stomach. She'd known for weeks that she'd be seeing Harrison again. And from the flirty tone of his messages she'd have to have been a complete idiot not to realise that things between them would be more than platonic, but it had always seemed distant, like a dream she could push to the back of her mind and forget. Harrison's sudden appearance had literally and figuratively swept her off her feet.

'There's our hostel,' Jaddi said, pointing at a four-storey building that stretched the length of the street. It was a dark-red modern structure with two thick strips of black bricks running through its centre.

The hostel was, they'd discovered after wandering the clean streets of the city, eating a huge fry-up and drinking copious cups of coffee, well-equipped compared to the places they'd stayed in Southeast Asia. It had a cafe and a large rooftop area with tables and chairs overlooking Sydney's two most iconic sights – the distinctive white peaks of the Opera House, which reminded Lizzie of a shiver of shark fins like they'd seen off the Thai islands, and the Harbour Bridge. Despite the spectacular view, it was the communal kitchen they'd spent the most time cooing over. Lizzie didn't miss cooking dinners, and she suspected Samantha and Jaddi didn't miss it either, considering the number of times she'd managed to serve undercooked chicken with overcooked vegetables. But Lizzie did miss breakfast. Being able to eat a bowl of cereal whenever it suited her was a strangely thrilling prospect.

'Ah!' Jaddi cried out as a gust of wind carried droplets of cold sea water, hitting their faces. 'Maybe we should have got the bus after all. I'm getting soaked sitting here.'

Lizzie turned her face to the sun, enjoying its last rays of warmth as it began to inch lower in the sky.

'Are we in the right outfits?' Samantha asked, touching her shorts. 'I'm starting to think, maybe we should have gone dressier?'

'It's a beach party, Sam,' Jaddi said, 'and it's going to be dark. Don't worry.'

Jaddi was right. Samantha needn't have worried. Harrison and his friends had also chosen similar outfits – baggy multi-coloured board shorts with oversized jumpers – with the exception of one waif-like girl in a floral ankle-length dress.

As Harrison introduced them around his friends, Lizzie found her eyes drawing back to the girl. Every one of her features appeared angular, from her jutting elbow bones, to the pointed tip of her nose and deadly straight blonde hair. She seemed to know Harrison and his friends, but, at the same time, stood on the outskirts like an observer.

There was something intriguing about her, and alluring, Lizzie assumed, based on the way Harrison's male friends would periodically drift over to her. She chatted amicably for a time, but her face remained impassive. Lizzie envisaged a gust of coastal wind blowing through the bay, catching the billows of the dress and carrying the girl up into the air and out to sea.

'Who's the blonde?' Lizzie asked Harrison after the introductions to Teddy, Jimbo, Lance, Tessie, Gill, Sally, and two couples whose names Lizzie had already forgotten, had been made and the angular girl missed out.

Harrison's eyes moved across the group until they settled on the waif, who glanced back before finding a spot in the distance to focus on. 'Oh, her. That's Cress.'

'Why didn't you introduce us?'

He shrugged. 'Dunno. I don't know her that well, I guess. And she's pretty moody most of the time.'

'Oh, I see.' Although she didn't. Why would they be friends with her if she was such a grump?

Without warning, Harrison pulled Lizzie towards him, scooping her into his arms and charging towards the crashing waves of the black ocean, sparkling with flecks of orange from the reflection of the bonfire.

'Hey!' she shrieked, excitement racing through her veins. 'Put me down.'

'No way, it's time for your swim. You've been on Aussie soil for eight hours and still haven't been swimming in the sea, and that is a capital offence.'

She squealed as he entered the sea, only drawing to a stop when the water reached his knees. 'You wouldn't dare,' she gasped as droplets of cool water splashed onto her bare feet.

'Wouldn't I?' he laughed, allowing her body to slip a few inches lower.

'Harrison, you're crazy. My microphone will break.' Lizzie clung harder to his neck.

'The only thing I'm crazy about,' he said as he led her feet to the soft squidgy sand of the ocean floor, and drew her towards him so that it seemed every part of their bodies were touching, 'is you.'

The cold water lapped against the bottom of her shorts, sending goose bumps across her body, or maybe that was the feel of Harrison's toned body against hers. Whatever was going on between them it was happening quickly. Too quickly for her to process what it meant and whether she was prepared to drag someone else into this. But was that a bad thing?

'You don't need to look so surprised.' He smiled. 'I thought you knew.'

'It's not that. I ... I just thought after last summer, when you left and I didn't hear from you, that it was just a fling, which was fine. I mean, we live on opposite sides of the world and I completely understood; it's not as if I was heart-broken or anything.' Lizzie couldn't stop the words from tumbling out of her mouth. A nervous energy fluttered around her as Harrison's arms tightened their hold on her.

He leant his head towards her until the softness of his lips brushed against hers. Like a strong current, Lizzie allowed herself to be swept away.

CHAPTER 26

Lizzie

Sometime later, although Lizzie had no idea how long – seconds, minutes – they drew apart, leaving her suddenly aware of the numbing chill of her legs in the water, and how wet the bottom of her shorts had become.

'I'm totally crazy about you.' He spoke in a husky voice full of desire and intent. 'I didn't contact you after I left England because I thought that's what we'd agreed. That it would make it harder if we tried to stay in touch. I wanted to call you so many times, you know?'

Had they agreed that? Lizzie couldn't recall a conversation along those lines, but at that moment all her brain seemed capable of remembering was the feel of Harrison's body next to hers and the parts of their brief relationship that, up until that moment, she'd forgotten; like the soft groan he'd emitted when she ran her hands down his bare back, and the way her skin tingled from his touch.

'Anyway,' he said as he pulled her into the crook of his arm and guided them back towards the shore. 'I have something else a little crazy to tell you, which I hope you'll be OK with.'

'What?' She grinned. After the intensity of their kiss, Harrison could suggest skinny-dipping and she'd agree.

'Well, when I got back to the office today my boss was in fits. He accused me of wagging, even though

I'd cleared it with him ages ago to have this week off. Then he said, because of my "casual relationship with timekeeping" –' Harrison raised his voice, Lizzie guessed to mimic that of his boss '– my holiday request for the next week has been denied.'

'Oh, that's all right, we'll work around it. We can always see each other in the evenings.'

'No way. No way am I missing out on spending time with you. Which is exactly what I told him. Which is when he said, "If you don't show up for work tomorrow, don't bother coming in any other time, either." So I was like, "Bonza!" because now it means that I can spend more than just your week in Sydney with you. I can come to the East Coast, too.'

'Wow, I'd love that, but what are you going to do when we leave? Will you be able to find another job?'

'I reckon. I've got some irons in the fire, as you Poms say.'

As her toes touched the dry sand, Lizzie looked up, her eyes finding the angular waif before anyone else. She was standing on her own in the orange flickering glow of the bonfire, staring right at them. Lizzie smiled but the girl had already spun around and was gliding off in the opposite direction. With the glow of the flames on her features, Lizzie thought for a moment that she saw anger etched onto the girl's sharp face. Before she could think any more of it, Jaddi and Samantha strolled towards her, both holding cans of lager and laughing about something. Just beyond them stood Ben, his face obscured by the camera.

Lizzie tried to ignore the heat burning in her cheeks as her conversation and kiss with Harrison replayed in her mind, just as it would be replayed on millions of television screens the following week. She wanted to call Ben over and coax the camera away for a little bit, but she didn't. Why was she suddenly lost for words to say to him? Lizzie pulled in her bottom lip. She wouldn't let Ben or the documentary change her behaviour or her relationship with Harrison. The thought of a relationship sent a warmth radiating through her.

'I'm just going to catch up with Lance for a mo,' Harrison said as Jaddi and Samantha reached them. He planted a kiss on her cheek before striding away.

'How was your ... swim?' Samantha asked, her voice giddy with alcohol and mischief.

'It was good.' Lizzie laughed.

Jaddi stepped forward. 'What's going on then? You two seem to have hit it off quickly.'

'Just like the last time then, I guess.' Lizzie smiled. 'He says he's crazy about me. And he wants to spend time with me whilst we're in Australia.' She paused as a thought struck her. 'Is that OK with you two? Sorry, I should've checked first.'

'What do you think, Sam?' Jaddi said, looping an arm around Samantha.

Samantha shook her head. 'I'm not sure.'

'Me neither,' Jaddi said. 'It's just, you look so ... so happy, and as your very best friends, we have to put a stop to that.'

'Absolutely.' Samantha nodded.

'Very funny,' Lizzie said, grinning. 'Seriously, are you all right with this? I know it's not what we planned.'

'Definitely.' Jaddi laughed. 'Stop worrying.'

Lizzie smiled until her cheeks ached. They'd skipped a few steps again, just as they'd done the first time, but it felt right. Yes, it was ridiculously fast, and she couldn't begin to contemplate what saying goodbye to Harrison again would feel like when they left for America, but at that moment she didn't care. Her future would be full of goodbyes.

CHAPTER 27

Day 35

Samantha

A gust of wind buffeted against Samantha's blue and silver climb suit. She tightened her grip on the cable, which held her to the railing of the vast steel structure, and concentrated on keeping pace with their climb leader, Chloe. Why they couldn't have watched the sunset from the rooftop of the hostel rather than climbing 1,332 steps to the very top of the bridge frame, she didn't know.

When they'd first entered the climb facilities at the base of Sydney Harbour Bridge, the late-afternoon sun had been bearing down on them. It had seemed ridiculous that they would need another layer, especially one in the same stifling material as a wet suit, and especially one so unflattering, on her at least. Jaddi and Lizzie's climb suits had clung to their bodies, accentuating Jaddi's lithe figure and Lizzie's petite frame. Samantha, on the other hand, was pretty sure she'd been given a man's suit, given how it bulged and sagged in all of the wrong places.

So instead of basking in the sinking sun, spreading its egg-yolk-orange glow across the harbour, and the city beyond, she was focusing the majority of her attention on keeping as many steps ahead of Harrison as she could, so that his own views didn't include a close-up of her bottom.

As they reached the summit and stood in the centre of the archway, Samantha turned back to face the way they'd come. Her eyes scanned the ground, now far below, for the distinctive silhouette of Ben and his camera. With part of the harbour now obscured in shadow, nothing but ant-like specs could be distinguished. Even the traffic crossing the bridge looked no bigger than the toys in a Kinder Egg.

'OK, climbers,' Chloe called out, 'gather round for your group photo.'

Jaddi sidled next to her, wrapping one arm around Samantha's shoulders and linking her other arm with Harrison.

'Smile,' Chloe said.

Samantha pulled her lips back into what she hoped would pass for a smile and wished the experience would end.

'I can't believe you've done this three times,' Lizzie said, gazing at Harrison.

'Are you kidding? I'd do this every week if it didn't cost so much moolah.'

Lucky you didn't have to pay then, Samantha thought, biting back the comment before it could leave her mouth.

It turned out that she wasn't OK with Harrison's sudden and constant appearance in their group, arriving when they were still in their pyjamas and groggy with sleep, and only leaving when one of them (usually her) told him to go.

There had been an amusing moment on their second day in Sydney when Harrison had suggested to Ben that he 'bunk down' in Ben's dorm room to save himself the journey back and forth to 'the rellies' every day. Ben had replied in a deadpan tone, 'That's never going to happen, mate.' He'd accentuated the word 'mate' just enough to leave Samantha wondering if she wasn't the only one vexed by the new addition to their group.

Then there was his constant use of slang words which none of them understood. In all of their conversations with other Australians, whether from Sydney, or visiting from another part of the country, no one had used a single slang word, so why did Harrison drop them into every sentence? What was he trying to prove? It would be like Samantha highlighting the fact that she was from London by conversing in cockney-rhyming slang.

'I think once will be enough for me,' Lizzie said, turning slowly around and gazing at the view.

'It's a shame Ben's missing this,' Jaddi said.

'I don't think Ben was particularly disappointed.' Lizzie smiled. 'Did you see his face when they said he couldn't bring his camera? I'd say he was relieved to be keeping his feet on the ground.'

'He could've come anyway,' Jaddi said. 'I'm sure Caroline wouldn't have minded if he'd have stopped filming. This is too spectacular to miss.'

'It's totally different up here at sunset, that's for sure,' Harrison said, pulling Lizzie towards him and drawing her into another kiss.

Samantha hated how he'd inserted himself among them; an interloper in surfer's clothing hijacking their trip, and worst of all hijacking Lizzie. It was this last thought which made Samantha loathe herself to her very core. Her very best friend, the reason she was on this trip in the first place, was happy, and if anyone deserved to be happy it was Lizzie. If anyone deserved to fall head over heels in love with a hunky Australian, it was Lizzie. So why did it irk Samantha so much? Was it as simple and pathetic as jealousy?

'I'll be sad to leave Sydney,' Jaddi said. 'It's such an amazing place, especially with our very own tour guide.' She winked at Harrison.

'Gotta try surfing though, and the Gold Coast is the place to do it. Not so many shark attacks.'

Lizzie frowned. 'I'd prefer it if you said "no shark attacks".'

'Babe, I'll be there to punch the suckers on the nose if they come near us.'

'Umm,' Samantha nodded. 'Punch them on the nose, that sounds like a foolproof plan for fending off a shark attack.'

'Don't knock it, Sammy, I've seen it work.'

'Really?' Lizzie asked without any hint of sarcasm. Samantha was starting to miss Lizzie's abrasive comments.

'Yep.' Harrison grinned. 'I was with Jimbo and Lance …'

Samantha stepped to the other side of the arch, and out of earshot of Harrison's story. Her eyes focused on the soft afternoon sunlight casting long stretching shadows of the bridge on the river.

She ground her teeth together, her head reeling from his comment. Sammy? Since when was that a name? It was no better than when he'd called her Sally. She was a Samantha, and very occasionally, and only to Jaddi and Lizzie, she was Sam. Never ever was she Sammy.

CHAPTER 28

Jaddi

'Hey,' Jaddi whispered in Samantha's ear. 'You OK, Sammy?'

Samantha blew out a puff of air. 'Watch it. We're a long way up, and the next person who calls me Sammy is going in the water. I just hope it's him.' She nodded her head towards Harrison.

'He's not that bad, and he's making Lizzie happy.' Jaddi followed Samantha's gaze and smiled at Harrison.

'I know. I'm sorry.' Samantha sighed. 'I didn't mean to grumble. I'm being pathetic. It's just hard. This is our time together, not his. The days are flying by and we don't have time to be sharing Lizzie with him.' Samantha scrunched up her face.

'We're still all together. You've never minded about Ben being with us.'

'It's not the same, and you know it. Ben's different.'

'Talking of Ben …' Jaddi smiled, desperate to cheer Samantha up. 'Do you think he likes Lizzie?'

'I don't know. Why?'

'Oh, come on. All those little sideways smiles he gives her when he's not filming.'

'And the bottles of water. He's like her personal water assistant.'

'I know.' Jaddi nodded. 'Sometimes I want to wave my hands in the air and say, hey, look at me, I'm thirsty too.'

Samantha laughed. 'Do you think Lizzie knows?'

'I don't think so. She's always been a bit oblivious to men liking her.'

'Should we tell her?'

Jaddi scrunched up her nose. 'Nah. She's pretty wrapped up in Harrison right now. It's hard to see how telling her that Ben fancies the pants off her will help. It could end up making things really awkward between them.'

'That's true,' Samantha said. 'I don't want to rock the boat with the filming. At least Ben gives us space to be just us, unlike someone else.' Samantha nodded towards Harrison. 'I can't explain it, but things have been different since Harrison showed up. Lizzie's been different.'

'I know Lizzie has been focused on Harrison this week, but it will calm down soon enough, I'm sure,' Jaddi said. 'How about I engineer some time for just the three of us once we get to the Gold Coast. No Harrison, no Ben, no microphones.'

'How?'

'Let me worry about that. You just try a little harder to be happy and not to hate Harrison so much—'

'Is it that obvious?'

'Only to me. I'm sure the others are oblivious.'

Samantha sighed. 'I just wish I could be more like you, but I can't sweep it all to one side and bounce around as if everything is fine. Everything is not fine. It's an effort every day not to cry, or shout about the injustice of it all. She's twenty-nine. How is that fair?'

'It's not.' Jaddi swallowed back the lump forming in her throat. 'But Lizzie doesn't want us to be sad.' She threw a glance to Lizzie, still enthralled in Harrison's story.

'We have to be happy for her. I'm not thinking about what will happen at the end of all this, I'm just trying to live in the moment, enjoy every bit of our time together before it all ends.' Jaddi was lying; of course she was thinking about the end. It had always been the three of them. How were they supposed to go back to their old lives without Lizzie there completing the trio?

Just then, Chloe cleared her throat. 'Time to get moving, climbers, whilst that sun is still setting.'

Jaddi idled for another moment. It wasn't the burnt-orange sky, now turning a dusky purple, that Jaddi was thinking about, but Samantha's words echoing in her head. *I can't sweep it all to one side and bounce around as if everything is fine.* Is that what she was doing? Sweeping reality under the rug just like her parents. Jaddi's upbringing, her entire family for that matter, had always been about skirting around truths and glossing over difficult subjects. Like her Uncle Prem's unexplained disappearance. Not a single word had been spoken about it in fifteen years. She hadn't gone to the funeral. She hadn't known there'd been a funeral, or even been told he'd died, let alone how. If she hadn't found the note he'd left when she'd been rummaging in her father's study for a pen, she might still have believed he was off enjoying himself in some remote corner of the world.

Jaddi had adored Prem – his exaggerated gestures, his multitude of brightly coloured turbans, the way he seemed to know her thoughts before she'd voiced them, and the fact that he hadn't succumbed to his parent's pressures to make his marriage to some horrid woman, whose name Jaddi couldn't remember, work.

It had been years later before she'd realised why.

It was another reason Jaddi loved Suk, she realised with a sudden ache in her chest, as she clipped her safety cable to the railing and began the descent. They had a shared acceptance of the maddening ways in which their families acted. They didn't always agree on how to handle them, but they understood.

CHAPTER 29

Day 36

Lizzie

'... and this is the kitchen-living room with a pretty spectacular view of Coolangatta Beach, when it's not pitch-black outside, anyway.' Lizzie held the camera out and turned slowly around the apartment. 'Thank you, Caroline and Channel 6, for moving our booking at the hostel to this fabulous apartment.'

Lizzie wasn't stupid. She knew someone at Channel 6, probably Caroline, had decided that the viewers at home had seen enough of dorm rooms, and that an apartment, especially one with Harrison in, would make for more interesting footage. Nevertheless, the three-bedroomed apartment on the ground floor of a twelve-story apartment complex, with its balcony overlooking the ocean, and its own private access to a long stretch of sandy beach, was a welcome change.

She hadn't realised how much of a blind eye she'd turned to the dirt and wear in the places they'd stayed so far, until she'd noticed the sheen of the white toilet and crisp bed sheets. Every surface in the kitchen gleamed. They could take their shoes off and walk barefoot without fear of stepping on a shard of glass or picking up a fungal infection.

'I'm not sure how we'll go back to sleeping in hostels after this,' Lizzie said, 'let alone the outdoor hammocks at our next destination. Although, I'm a bit surprised

Jaddi hasn't complained about the disruption to our authentic travelling experience yet.'

'Hey!' Jaddi shouted from the bedroom. She poked her head out of the door wearing a towel wrapped around her hair, and not much else based on the bare skin of her shoulders visible from the doorway. 'Who am I to complain? This is authentic Gold Coast-living, after all.'

Lizzie laughed before turning back to the camera.

'As you'll see from some of the footage –' Lizzie stopped talking as she stepped out on to the balcony. She knew it was ridiculous to want privacy – after all, millions of people would be watching her diary in a couple of days – but she pulled the sliding door closed behind her anyway '– Harrison has joined the group. He's come with us to the Gold Coast and is going to join us on our O'Reilly rainforest trek. It's funny, when you start putting a list together of the things you haven't seen or done, you have to think: do I actually want to do it? I haven't piloted my own aeroplane or base jumped off of a building, but those are things I would never have done, even if I was going to live to a hundred.

'Falling in love, though, if I could've put it on a list, I would've done. It's a stupid one because you can't actually control it. You can't put it on a "things to do this week" list. And when we first set out planning this trip, it wasn't something that I'd thought would happen. But here I am, happier than I could ever have hoped to be. Harrison is sweet and considerate. He's so much fun and knows all the best places to go, and even though we'll be saying goodbye in a few weeks, having him here right now, is just perfect. It's more than I could have dreamed of.'

Lizzie paused and listened to the crashing roar of the waves as they hit the wet sand, followed by the rhythmic shush as the sea drew the wave back into its depths.

A flood of nervous energy cascaded through her. Soon it would be time to go to bed, or pretend to go to bed at least. The plan was simple – feign a few yawns, say goodnight to Ben, turn off the lights and then climb out of the bedroom window. Harrison was doing the same from his room, and Jaddi and Samantha were set to distract Ben if necessary.

She didn't like sneaking around, or deceiving Ben, but she didn't want this part of her relationship with Harrison to be on the documentary either. Harrison had been the one to suggest a late-night walk on the beach. 'It will give us some time alone,' he'd said, holding her against him in a way that left no room for misunderstanding.

A sudden piercing scream broke through Lizzie's thoughts. She reached to switch off the camera, but as the scream took on a comical yelping tone, Lizzie smiled. 'Sounds like Jaddi might have got herself into a spot of bother.'

Lizzie faced the camera screen outwards and followed the sound of the shrieks, resonating from their bedroom. She reached the door at the same time as Ben, also carrying his camera.

'Cockroach!' Jaddi shrieked, pointing towards her rucksack. 'In my wash kit. A giant, red cockroach.' Jaddi jumped up and down, flinging her hands in the air and almost losing the towel wrapped around her body. 'It crawled across my hand when I reached in to get my moisturiser.'

Harrison joined them in the doorway. 'I thought you might 'av found a redback or something. Now, that's worth shrieking over,' he said.

He winked at Lizzie as he stepped into the room. 'I'll get rid of the little pest for ya.'

'There is nothing little about that creature,' Jaddi said, shaking her hands in the air again. Her voice sounded ludicrously clipped and very British next to Harrison's easy cadence.

'You'll get used to them,' he said.

'That's never going to happen.'

'Oh, come on, Jaddi,' Samantha shouted from behind the bathroom door. 'Surely you've seen enough *cock*-roaches in London.'

'Oh, ha ha,' Jaddi said, readjusting her towel. 'Thank you Harrison, you're my hero.'

'At your service.' He grinned, giving a mock bow before scooping the insect into his hands and walking towards the balcony.

Lizzie scanned the darkness of the deserted beach. 'Are you sure we're alone?'

'I'm sure.' He slipped his hand through hers and pulled her gently towards a row of sunloungers. 'Let's sit on one of these.' He smiled. 'It'll be less sandy.'

There was no moon in the sky, just a dim light cast from the nearby apartments. The only noise was the hush of the waves lapping the shoreline a few metres away.

As she sat down, Lizzie buried her bare feet underneath the soft cool sand. A sudden nervousness swarmed in her stomach as Harrison dropped down beside her. They'd had sex countless times during their weeks together in London, so why did it feel different now? Was it just the sneaking around and lying to Ben that made it seem wrong?

Then Harrison's lips found hers and her head emptied of thoughts. His hands ran over her body in the darkness, causing a desperation to crash through her like the waves of the sea.

CHAPTER 30

Lizzie

'Harrison?' Lizzie said, pulling away as his hands slid under her skirt.

'Mmm.'

She grappled to gain control of her thoughts as his fingers ran up the length of her thighs. 'Have you got protection?'

'Huh?' He sat up and stared at her.

The light from the apartments was enough to illuminate the desire on his face. Part of her longed to continue, but there was too much at stake. 'You know ... a condom?'

His expression hardened. 'Shit, babe, I didn't think.'

'Oh.'

'I could run to the store?' he said, scrunching his face and shaking his head.

Despite the offer, he didn't draw away or stand. Instead he leant forward, kissing Lizzie with renewed intensity. A moment later, she felt his weight against her, willing her to lay back.

'Harrison,' she said, pressing her hands against his chest.

He groaned. It wasn't a sound of pleasure, but of frustration. 'Lizzie, babe. Come on. You don't know what you're doing to me here.'

'I'm sorry. It's not that I don't want to, but ... I'm not on the pill. My doctor thought it might interfere with my anti-seizure medication.' She was killing the mood now, but what else could she do? 'So we *really* can't have sex without protection.'

'What difference does it make? Aren't you going to be dead before it matters?'

Lizzie heard his words like a punch to the chest. Another time and she could easily have laughed. It was the same sentiment as Caroline had expressed not so long ago, but instead, her heart pounded with an intensity that made her head spin.

'That's ... that's not the point.' Lizzie stood up and turned in the direction of the apartment.

'Lizzie, wait. I'm sorry,' he called after her. 'I got caught up in the moment. I was being a dick. Please, don't go.'

'It's fine. Don't worry about it,' she said over her shoulder as she continued to stride away from him.

She knew it was childish to leave him on the beach, but a burning rage had taken hold, and even as it fogged her thoughts, she knew it had little to do with Harrison. Her pace increased as she continued onwards past their apartment building. Frustration gnawed at her insides. She was running out of time.

The days were hurtling by like someone had pressed the fast forward button on her life. Three months. She'd thought it would be enough time, but it wasn't. Not even close. There was so much she would never get to see or do. How was this fair? Lizzie clenched her teeth together and kept walking until all she could feel was exhaustion. Only then did she turn on her heels and walk back to their apartment.

'Hi,' Ben said, as she reached the top of the steps.

'Oh, hi,' Lizzie spluttered, realising her mistake. She'd forgotten to sneak back in through her window. Even so, she hadn't expected to find Ben sitting on the balcony.

'Couldn't sleep?' Ben frowned.

'No. I thought a walk on the beach might help. I know I'm supposed to wake you and all that, but I was only planning to go out for a few minutes—'

'Did it help?'

'Maybe.' She shrugged as she opened the glass door. 'Goodnight.'

'Lizzie?'

She turned to face him. An image from Mondulkiri, the kiss they had shared and the intimacy she'd felt towards him in the jungle, played in her head. Lizzie thought of the strange force that had drawn her towards him.

'Never mind,' he said. 'I hope you sleep better now.'

'Thanks, you too.'

As Lizzie slipped beneath the crisp cool bed sheets, she thought about Ben. Calm, watchful Ben.

It had been his voice that had dragged her from the depths of the seizure in Bangkok, and it had been Ben who'd shielded her from the strobing camera flashes at the airport. But he couldn't protect her from what was going to happen to her. No one could do that.

With that final thought, she fell into a fitful sleep.

CHAPTER 31

Day 37

Lizzie

'This is the life,' Jaddi said, tilting her face towards the midday sun. 'Chilling out on a surfboard, just the three of us.'

'Do you think we should practise some actual surfing, though?' Samantha asked. 'I think our teacher has given up on us.'

'Nah,' Lizzie said.

Lizzie scanned the beach for their instructor, Damien – an extremely tanned, wiry man in his early twenties – who'd spent more of their one-hour lesson flirting with Jaddi than teaching them any practical skills.

The long stretch of golden sand was scattered with people and surfboards standing upright in the sand. Beyond the beach sat the wetsuit hire shop and a collection of outlet stores selling all manner of brightly coloured beachwear and surf equipment.

'I'm so glad you said that.' Samantha laughed. 'I couldn't do that standing-up move on the sand, let alone out here. But maybe that has something to do with our instructor's wandering focus.' She narrowed her eyes at Jaddi.

'Hey.' Jaddi raised her hands in protest. 'It wasn't like I enjoyed being singled out for every demonstration. I had to do twice as much work as you two. Did you see how many take-offs Damien made me do?'

'My heart bleeds,' Samantha said, rolling her eyes.

Lizzie smiled and pulled at the cord on the back of her wetsuit until she felt the zip come apart. Wriggling her arms free she rolled it down to her waist, revealing a simple black bikini top. There didn't seem much point sweltering in a wet suit if she wasn't in the water.

She closed her eyes and listened to the sound of water sloshing gently against their boards. The scent of coconut sun lotion mingled with salt and sea filled her senses.

She'd been looking forward to learning to surf, riding the wave with the force of the sea propelling her to the shore. It had taken several failed attempts at balancing on the board and several more mouthfuls of sea water that made her stomach gurgle with nausea, before she'd discovered a more enjoyable side to surfing – waiting for the wave. It turned out that sitting on their boards, just beyond the break, bobbing up and down on a hot summer's day was her kind of surfing.

'I've pretty much got used to wearing a microphone and having Ben with us everywhere we go,' Lizzie said, 'but it's nice to have a break from having every word we say recorded.' She squinted against the sun and watched Ben's figure on the beach. He was easy to spot. The brown shorts and plain white T-shirt looked out of place against the flamboyant colours of the other beach goers. 'Although I don't think Ben's best pleased that we're staying out here.' Even from a distance she could tell by his skulking walk that he was annoyed.

The sun bore into her eyes as she watched Ben, causing flashes of red and white to streak across her vision. She dropped her head and shielded her face.

'He'll get over it,' Jaddi said.

'Um, I not so sure,' Lizzie said, thinking of the set of Ben's face on the balcony. 'I'm pretty sure he didn't buy my midnight walk excuse last night. He looked as if he'd been sitting out there for a while, like he was waiting for me.' Ben had been about to tell her something last night and changed his mind. What? Had he been about to tell her off for sneaking off? It hadn't seemed like it, but then what else could it have been?

'Where's Harrison gone off to this morning?' Samantha asked.

'I'm not sure,' Lizzie said, rubbing her eyes as the colours continued to blur her vision. 'We haven't exactly spoken properly after last night. I think he's got some job applications to do.'

'You two seemed fine at breakfast,' Jaddi said.

'Yeah, I think we are. It's difficult in front of the camera. Ben hasn't let up at all since we got here. I thought spending some time alone with Harrison would be nice, but now it feels like it's done more harm than good.'

Lizzie hadn't known what to expect from Harrison when she'd finally emerged from her bedroom that morning. Would he be annoyed with her for ruining their one moment of privacy, or grovelling and apologetic for his cruel comment? The more she'd thought about it, the more she'd begun to question which one of them had been in the wrong. Why hadn't she brought protection with her? After all, she'd guessed they would have sex, and it seemed unfair to have expected Harrison to bring a condom when she hadn't asked him to.

But what she hadn't expected from him was normal. She hadn't expected him to kiss her on the cheek as if the previous night hadn't happened. She hadn't expected him to lean across the breakfast bar and take her hand in a moment of intimacy whilst explaining the different types of surfboards to Jaddi. What did that mean?

'He's probably organising some grand romantic gesture,' Jaddi said.

'Or off buying condoms,' Samantha smirked, making them all laugh.

They fell into silence for a minute. Lizzie drew in a deep breath, and with her eyes closed she turned so that the sun fell onto the back of her neck. The burn of the rays tingled her skin just as the radiotherapy had done.

'Maybe we should try water boarding tomorrow,' Samantha said, tilting her face towards the cloudless blue sky.

'Water boarding, as in the torture?' Jaddi asked.

'Oh.' Samantha laughed. 'No, I meant the thing you always see the celebrities doing on their holidays. Standing on a surfboard with a stick.'

'I think you mean paddle boarding,' Jaddi said.

'Yes, that's the one.' Samantha nodded. 'That looks easy.'

'I thought surfing looked pretty easy,' Lizzie said, 'until I tried it. I always imagine I'll be better at these things than I actually am.'

'I think I need to go in,' Jaddi said. 'I'm busting for a wee.'

'Just slip into the water and go,' Samantha said. 'It's the sea. You're supposed to wee in it.'

Lizzie lifted her head and glanced at Samantha. Even with the sun still hurting her eyes she could see the mischief on Samantha's face.

'But what about the wet suit?' Jaddi asked, shooting a questioning look at Samantha.

'It just goes right out. You're supposed to wee in it. I thought everyone knew that,' Samantha said, winking at Lizzie on the sly.

'Oh, OK then.'

Jaddi slipped off her surfboard and into the water. A moment later, she yelped. 'It's not going out. Ewwwwe!'

Lizzie and Samantha burst into a fit of giggles just as the hump of a wave moved underneath them. Lizzie let out a shriek, unable to stop the board moving one way and her body moving the other. A second later, she toppled into the cold water.

Lizzie scrunched her eyes shut from the sting of the salt water and kicked her legs up until her head emerged.

'… was going to happen?' Lizzie heard Jaddi say as Lizzie grabbed hold of her surfboard and pulled in a long gasping breath.

'I thought it might.' Samantha grinned.

'You cow.' Jaddi laughed. 'I can't believe I've just wet myself. I'm going in search of a shower.'

'Hold up,' Samantha said. 'I need the toilet after all that laughing.' She let out a shaky sigh, before turning to Lizzie. 'You coming, Liz?'

'I'll catch up in a minute,' Lizzie replied, pulling herself back onto her surfboard. 'I just need to get the water out of my eyes.'

'Doesn't look like you'll be alone for long,' Samantha said. 'Ben's commandeered a kayak.'

Lizzie rubbed her eyes with both hands as the sounds of Samantha and Jaddi's laughter drifted further away.

'Do you know how difficult it is,' Ben said from beside her, 'to balance a camera on your lap whilst steering a kayak over waves?'

She opened her eyes and felt the sting of the salty water and the glare of the sun on her irises. Lizzie waited a beat for her vision to focus. Then another second passed. And another.

A slow realisation began to dawn on her, sending a shiver of panic racing down her spine.

CHAPTER 32

Lizzie

'Lizzie?'

'Yeah,' she said, trying to keep the panic out of her voice as she stared into what she assumed was the distance. The world had disappeared. One minute it was there, the next it was gone. Replaced with bright shining white. She could hear the world – the noise of shouting and laughter carrying from the shore – and she could smell it – the sea now drying in salty droplets on her skin – but all she could see was bright white.

A lightness spun in her head from the furious beating of her heart. She pulled in a faltering breath, fighting to gain control of her thoughts before she fainted and flopped back into the sea.

Her vision would be just like the numbness in her foot, and the shaking in her hand. It would pass, wouldn't it?

'I said,' Ben began, 'do you know how difficult it is— oh, never mind. Lions are so much easier.'

'What's that?'

'Nothing.' He sighed.

'Sorry we were out here so long,' Lizzie said, closing her eyes and covering them with her hands. Maybe it was the sun. Maybe if she rested her eyes for long enough, then the brightness would fade and the world would reappear.

They floated in silence for a moment.

'It's getting pretty hot out here,' Ben said. 'Your shoulders are starting to turn pink.'

Lizzie moved her hands and opened her eyes again. The brightness was still there, the world was not. She was blind. An army of goosebumps marched along her body.

'Here,' Ben said, 'have some water.'

Lizzie imagined Ben holding the bottle out to her, but she didn't try to reach for it. She couldn't risk unbalancing herself and falling into the sea again.

'Lizzie,' Ben said. She could hear the concern ringing in his tone. Was that the blindness heightening her hearing? 'Lizzie, what is it? Talk to me.'

Without waiting for a reply she heard the splash of Ben's paddle blade in the water and the change in the motion of the board as he manoeuvred the kayak alongside of her.

'I can't see,' she whispered, unable to stop the tears from falling.

'What?'

'I can't see anything. My eyes went blurry about twenty minutes ago. I thought I'd got some water in them, but it's been a while now, and I can't see.'

'Nothing at all?' Ben asked.

'I know where the sun is,' she said, pointing up to the sky, 'but I don't know if that's because I can see the change in light or because of the heat.' Tear drops continued to run down her cheeks. She didn't wipe them away.

A second later she felt the edges of his fingers brush her leg as his hand gripped her board, guiding her closer.

'Try not to worry,' he said, 'you're going to be fine.' He clasped his hand in hers. Her grip tightened around his fingers. 'We need to get you back to the beach and to hospital.'

She nodded, but didn't reply. A new layer of dread added to the mounting panic.

'Can you slide into the water next to me and lean over the board to kick with your legs?' Ben asked. 'It'll be safer than sitting when we go over the waves, and that way I can push the tip of the board over the front of my kayak, and we'll go in together.'

She nodded. A shivering gripped her body as she slid into the water and began to kick.

It seemed to take a long time to reach the beach. Long enough for Lizzie's legs to grow tired and her mouth to dry. 'How much further?' she asked.

'You should be able to stand up,' he said, his voice strong and calm against her panicked whispers.

She stopped kicking and dropped her legs into the ocean. 'Yes, I can.' Adrenaline continued to pump through her veins as she felt Ben's body slide into the ocean next to her.

'Keep holding the surfboard,' he said. 'I'm going to push it.'

As the sea lapped against Lizzie's knees, she sensed Ben move away a fraction. She let go of the surfboard and gripped his arm. 'Don't go anywhere,' she said.

'I won't,' he replied. 'People are moving towards us. What do you want me to say?'

Voices grew louder. She recognised the peppy voice of Damien, their surf instructor, shouting to them. 'Everything OK there, Lizzie?'

'Don't tell them.' Lizzie tightened her hold on Ben. 'Just get me out of here.'

'Er, right. Any change?'

She shook her head, biting back a sob.

'Everything OK, mate?' Damien asked as they reached dry sand.

'Yep,' Ben said. 'Lizzie just felt a bit sick, so I thought I'd help her in.'

She imagined Damien's eyes on her, waiting to see if she'd elaborate, but she kept her head down and her eyes closed. She didn't need a crowd of well-meaning helpers; all she needed at that moment was Ben's arm and to get the hell off the beach.

'Let me get that board for you,' Damien said, undoing the tie on Lizzie's ankle. 'I'll take your kayak too, mate.'

'Thanks,' Ben said.

A moment later, she felt him pull away, but, before she could protest, his arm reached around her, pulling her into the warmth of his body.

'I'm sorry about your clothes,' she said as they moved in slow stumbling steps across the sand.

'Do you really think I care about getting my clothes wet, Liz? All I care about is getting you to a hospital.'

CHAPTER 33

Jaddi

This couldn't be happening, Jaddi thought. They were supposed to have another month at least; she wasn't prepared for this yet. She needed more time. The world around Jaddi had started to hum. It wasn't the low rumbling of a car engine or the electrical hum of the hospital equipment. It was high-pitched ... a whine, like mosquitoes trapped in her ear drums, buzzing around in her head whenever there was silence, like now.

'I've got good news and bad news for you, Miss Appleton,' Dr Moss said, stepping into the hospital room and saving Jaddi from the humming. The doctor smiled at each of them in turn before picking up the red folder at the edge of the bed.

She appeared unfazed by Ben's movements as he stepped around her with his camera. Her dark-blonde hair was tied in a neat ponytail at the base of her neck, and she had the freckles and tan of someone who enjoyed the beach.

Dr Moss flicked through the notes in the folder before continuing. 'The good news is that there is no sign of any optic nerve damage or problems with the retina, so we can rule the eyes out as being the cause of your vision loss.'

She placed the folder back in its holder before stepping to the side of the bed. 'The bad news is that we don't know what has caused your sudden onset of vision impairment. It may be a side effect from the anti-seizure medication you're taking, or the tumour itself, or it may be something completely unrelated. Temporary loss to one or several of your senses is a postictal symptom of a seizure, so it may be that you had a very mild seizure without realising.'

She pulled out a small silver torch and waved it in front of Lizzie's eyes. 'How is your sight now?'

'Better.' She looked in the direction of Dr Moss. 'I can make out a few shapes and I can see the torch light.'

'Can you tell me how many fingers I'm holding up?'

'No.' Lizzie shook her head. 'I can't even see your hand.'

'Try not to worry,' Dr Moss said, patting Lizzie's shoulder. 'It's extremely encouraging that your sight has improved in just the few hours you've been here. We're going to keep you overnight and see how your vision is in the morning. Unfortunately, our own neurologist is on holiday at the moment. We only have the one here as we're not a big hospital, but I've sent your MRI scans to your doctor, Dr Habib—'

'Habibi,' Lizzie said, as creases appeared on her forehead.

Jaddi leaned over and took Lizzie's hand. Events were spiralling out of their control, and she didn't need to exchange a look with Lizzie to know that she'd be worried.

Dr Moss nodded. 'And also to a good friend of mine in the states. He's a neurologist, but most importantly, his speciality is brainstems. I've explained your situation and hope to hear from him by tomorrow.'

'Oh.' Lizzie's hand formed a vice around Jaddi's fingers.

'The doctor raised her eyebrows. 'Is there a problem?'

Lizzie closed her eyes and shook her head.

'Well, then, get plenty of rest and sleep. A nurse will check on you every few hours, and I'll see you on my rounds in the morning.'

'Thank you, doctor,' Jaddi said.

There was a moment of silence before Samantha spoke. 'Are you OK, Liz?'

Lizzie nodded. Jaddi could guess the questions running through Lizzie's head: was this it ... had their trip come to an end?

One perfect moment. That's all it had taken for Jaddi to give herself a figurative pat on the back. Just one moment when the three of them had been happy, had laughed in the sunshine, and been themselves.

But now Lizzie had lost her sight, they were stuck in hospital waiting for news, and Harrison, who had yet to check if Lizzie was all right, was standing outside talking to reporters, who'd magically appeared from nowhere again.

'Shall we pop back to the apartment and get you some clothes?' Jaddi asked.

'That would be good, thank you,' Lizzie said. 'Has anyone heard from Harrison? Does he know I'm here?'

Jaddi and Samantha exchanged a look but neither spoke. Anger knotted in Jaddi's stomach. She liked Harrison. If things had been different. If time and distance hadn't been factors for him and Lizzie the first time around, then Jaddi had no doubt that their relationship would have fizzled out. Harrison wasn't a bad person, but he wasn't right for Lizzie. He was too self-centred; he was always looking for the next fun activity. But time was an issue, a huge issue, and Lizzie didn't have time for fizzling, she didn't have time to be hurt or messed about by someone as insignificant as Harrison. If that meant Jaddi had to go down to the steps of the hospital and drag Harrison up to Lizzie's room, then so be it.

Images of Suk played on her mind. She hadn't realised how much she'd miss their time together. Harrison wasn't right for Lizzie, but Suk was right for her. Jaddi had found the one person she wanted to spend the rest of her life with, so why wasn't she ready to commit? It would be so easy to get married and live the life Suk wanted for them, but being easy didn't make it right. Jaddi sighed inwardly and glanced at Lizzie and Samantha. When it came to Suk, or anything else for that matter, Jaddi didn't trust herself to know what was right anymore.

Ben cleared his throat. 'I think I saw him wandering around downstairs. I'll go see if I can find him.' He removed the camera from his shoulder and zipped it away in its case.

'Thanks,' Lizzie said.

'And I'll go back and get your things,' Samantha said.

'Do you want me to come?' Jaddi asked Samantha.

'No,' Lizzie said with an urgency in her voice. 'I need Jaddi to be my eyes.'

'Good idea,' Samantha replied. 'I won't be long. I'll grab some sandwiches for all of us too.'

Jaddi waited until Samantha had left the room, then she peeled her hand away from Lizzie's and stepped over to close the door. She reached around to the microphone pack on her back and flicked the switch to off.

'Liz—'

'Are we alone?'

Jaddi nodded before realising her mistake. 'Yes, and my mic's off.'

'What are we going to do?' Emotion clung to every word so that Lizzie's voice came out rushed and high-pitched.

'Just what thc doctor said. Rest and sleep. We can push the rainforest trip back whilst you recover.'

'If I recover.'

'You will, Liz.'

'You don't know that. No one knows.' Lizzie sat up in bed and crossed her legs under the sheet. 'I can't stay here. Time is running out. I'm not wasting any more of it in a hospital.'

Jaddi stepped back to the bed. She reached out her hand to Lizzie's, but thought better of it. Lizzie didn't want comfort; she wanted answers, and Jaddi didn't have any to give her.

Jaddi perched on the edge of the bed. 'Do you wish we'd stayed at home? Do you wish I'd never set up the website and started this?' she asked, the question appearing from nowhere and yet it seemed to have been resting at the edges of her thoughts for weeks. She glanced back at the door, checking it was still closed.

A silence filled the room. The question hung between them.

'No. Sometimes. I don't know,' Lizzie said, her voice calmer. 'When I lie awake at night turning over what we've done in my mind, I always consider the alternative.'

'We can go back, you know. Any time. Say the word and I'll book us the first flight back to London.'

Lizzie didn't answer for a moment. 'No.' She shook her head. 'For better or worse, I'm sticking with my decision.'

Uncertainty dug into Jaddi's thoughts. Was Lizzie talking about more than just their trip?

Lizzie stretched her arm out and fixed her gaze on her hand. 'Hey.' She smiled. 'I can see my fingers.'

'Really? That's brilliant.' Jaddi breathed a sigh of relief and stood up. 'Get some rest. I'll go and get us a cup of tea and see where Ben and Harrison have got to. At this rate, your sight will be back to normal by the morning.'

'Let's hope so.'

Jaddi stared at Lizzie's face. Beyond the bronze glow of her tan Lizzie's eyes were circled in dark rings. 'If it's not, though, if you're still here tomorrow, it'll be OK.'

Lizzie turned to Jaddi, staring a few inches to the left of her face. 'You know that's not true.'

'What I mean is, your health comes first. Everything else we've done and this trip comes second, OK?'

'It's not that simple, though, is it?' Lizzie closed her eyes. 'I'm not ready for this to end.'

A throbbing hurt stretched across Jaddi's chest. In that moment, Jaddi was glad Lizzie couldn't see the tears dropping from her eyes. She wasn't ready either.

'Jaddi?'

'Yeah?' Jaddi stepped closer to the bed.

Lizzie swallowed and when she spoke the voice that came out was a raspy whisper. 'I'm scared.' A single tear slid down her cheek.

Jaddi shook her head as her own eyes blurred with emotion. What could she say to help Lizzie? Jaddi dropped back onto the bed and wrapped her arms around Lizzie. 'If there was anything I could do to make this ... all go away ...'

Lizzie gave a small laugh and pulled away, wiping her fingers across her face. 'But you can't.' Lizzie finished for her. She gave a watery smile. 'I'll take that cup of tea though.'

Jaddi nodded and stepped towards the door, walking straight into the lens of Ben's camera. She gasped, his sudden presence outside the hospital room catching her off guard.

'Ben, hi.' She forced her megawatt grin. 'I was just coming to look for you and Harrison.'

'Well, I'm here.' Ben raised his eyebrows, his words curt.

'Great.' Jaddi reached her hand to the small of her back and fumbled with her microphone battery pack.

'It's off,' he said, nodding towards her hand. 'If that's what you were wondering.'

Jaddi's mind raced. 'I know, I'm sorry. Lizzie needed a few minutes, just us,' she said, flicking on the battery pack.

'That's not how this works.' Ben shook his head. 'You of all people know that. It stays on all the time, no matter what. I've tried to give you all time to yourselves, when I'm not supposed too, I've tried to be fair, but if you're going to mess me ab—'

'Watch out.' A porter pushing an empty hospital bed veered towards them, forcing Ben and Jaddi to jump away. The gurney took an unexpected turn and seemed to follow their movements, forcing Ben and Jaddi to take another leap backwards until Jaddi's back hit the opposite wall.

Ben turned to Jaddi and opened his mouth to speak.

'It won't happen again,' she said, striding along the corridor as the humming filled her ears again.

CHAPTER 34

Lizzie

Sitting alone in the hospital room was making her jittery. Lizzie fidgeted in the bed and held her hands out in front of her. She could see the milky colour of her skin now, and the blue of the veins running under it. Lizzie reached for the remote control, attached to the bed by a plastic cord. She pressed the green button and the unmistakable sound of an advert jingle filled the room. Lizzie stared into the corner where the sound was coming from. She could see the square screen but nothing else.

'Hey,' Lizzie said, muting the sound as Ben stepped into the room.

'How's your sight?' he asked, tucking his camera under his arm.

'Much better. I can see my hands and about a metre in front of me. I can see you, almost, but beyond that, it's still hazy, like I'm looking through a window that's gone steamy.'

'I'm glad it's coming back,' he replied.

'Thank you for helping me on the beach,' Lizzie said, gnawing at her lip and wishing there was another word that conveyed her gratitude. 'I'm not sure what I would have done without you.'

He nodded. 'Someone would've rescued you.'

'It wasn't just the rescue.' She shook her head. 'If you hadn't helped me off the beach I'd have been swamped by people trying to help. I don't know why my sight went like that. It was so scary.'

'You know what I don't know?' he said, the irritation clear in his voice as he stepped forward. 'I don't know what this is all about.' Ben opened the LED screen on his camera and moved around the bed so that Lizzie could see it.

He pressed several buttons, then, after a short pause, she saw herself on the bed and Jaddi standing next to her. A new wave of fear propelled its way through her thoughts. She knew why Ben had filmed it, and why he was showing it to her. Their faces etched with fear, Jaddi's wide-eyed furtive glances back to the door, even without the sound, it looked suspicious.

'I don't know what you and Jaddi were talking about,' Ben said, 'but I feel like I'm getting to know you pretty well now, Lizzie, so I feel pretty confident that the look on your face when the doctor told you she'd sent your scans to a specialist, was fear. And I'm really starting to get the sense that you're hiding something. Why were you so hell-bent on not having an MRI in Bangkok? What are you scared of?'

Tears filled her eyes but she didn't respond. How could she?

His face softened. 'I know you're sick. Not even the best Hollywood actress could fake a seizure, or blindness. So what is it? You can tell me.'

'You wouldn't understand,' she whispered, staring at the images on the camera screen.

'Try me,' he said. 'I can help you.'

'You want to know what I'm scared of? Fine, I'll tell you,' she said, her voice rising as an anger began to circle her body. 'I'm scared of dying, OK? There. Happy now. If it seems like I'm hiding something, then it's because

I am. I'm trying to hide the fear, from myself and from Jaddi and Samantha, from everyone.' She pointed at the camera.

Ben stared at her for a moment longer, assessing her, trying to decide if she was lying. She bit her lip and tried to look defiant. A second later she tasted the metallic tang of blood followed by a sharp sting. Whether he liked it or not, what she'd told him was the truth.

'I'm not buying it,' Ben said, snapping the camera screen shut and placing his camera into his bag. 'There's something else going on here. I knew something wasn't right within ten minutes of meeting you three, and whether you realise it or not, the cracks are widening. The truth always comes out, Lizzie. So do yourself a favour and tell me what's going on so I can help you.'

Lizzie turned her face to Ben. His forehead was creased with concern, or frustration, or both, Lizzie thought, but his eyes were clear and bore into her with an intensity that made her gasp. The pull returned. The tugging sensation of being drawn forward. But it was more this time. She felt her mouth open, her breath draw in, words forming in her head, lining up, one after the other, ready to flow out into the world, and come what may.

Then a light flashed on the television screen above his head. Lizzie's eyes flicked upwards and the words she'd been ready to speak melted away. 'Is that Harrison on TV?' Lizzie leaned forward, narrowing her eyes. It was Harrison. A Gold Coast Hospital sign was visible in the background as he nodded along to a reporter. She could see it all. She could see.

'Yep,' Ben said, accentuating the final letter as he shook his head and packed his camera into its case.

Lizzie frowned. How did a news reporter know she was here? Could a nurse have tipped them off? She wasn't so famous that a hospital worker would call in her whereabouts, was she? And why was Harrison talking to them? She wished he'd asked her first, or at least come and seen her.

'He's been here the whole time,' Ben said. 'He's been so concerned about you that he hasn't moved from that spot outside the hospital where some reporters, and by the looks of it, a local news crew, have gathered. Love is sweet, ain't it?'

Ben glanced at the TV one more time before striding from the room.

Lizzie stared after him, wishing she could call him back and explain. But what could she say? Lizzie sighed and inspected her hands again. She just wanted to get out of here.

CHAPTER 35

Day 41

Lizzie

Lizzie stretched out her legs, causing her bed to sway back and forth, and wondered again what had possessed them to spend the night in hammocks. She gripped the rope edges and steadied herself. The website blurb had made it sound so appealing: *Drift off to sleep in the tranquillity of the Green Mountains. Star gaze from the comfort of your very own luxury hammock and wake up to the soft melodies of the dawn chorus.*

Chorus? More like a hundred screeching bird calls reverberating through the trees and perforating the otherwise still morning. One yawp-like wail after another, after another. Each more piercing than the last.

Lizzie stared at her watch. It was nearly 5am. Two minutes before their alarms would sound, although she doubted they would hear them over the bird noises.

She yawned, drawing in a deep lungful of cool air. She pulled in another long breath, filling her senses with the clear, sweet freshness of the forest and the scent of musky earth. The hit of oxygen caused her head to spin but did nothing to dent the fog of tiredness.

Lizzie swung her legs over the edge of the hammock, dropped to the forest floor and yawned again. The past three days on the Gold Coast should have been peaceful, but the combination of restlessness, and the resulting frustration, as well as Jaddi, Samantha, and Harrison's changed behaviour, had added an enervating quality to the week. They'd tiptoed and cosseted, asking the same questions in soft voices: Was she OK? Yes. How was her vision? Perfect. Did she need anything? Yes – for everyone to stop acting as if she was about to collapse to the floor at any moment!

She glanced at the other four hammocks, spread around their camp in a wide circle. Only one other was empty – Ben's. It took Lizzie a moment to register the hump of sleeping bag on the floor beneath it. Why hadn't she thought of that? The ground would have been hard and cold, but at least it didn't move.

Ben had kept his distance since his accusations in the hospital room. They hadn't spoken. Not a single word. He seemed content to linger at the back of the room and hide behind the scope of his camera, and she'd found herself missing their friendship.

He'd caught her at a weak moment. She'd been grateful for his help and shaken from losing her sight. She'd wanted desperately to explain to him that she knew he meant well. His promise to help was touching, but in the end what could he do?

Being able to see again had been the only bearable part of the past three days. She'd discovered an appreciation for the reflection of the sun glistening on the ocean, and had spent hours on the balcony of the apartment watching the sea.

In those days on the Gold Coast, the only distraction had been her phone. She'd scrolled through the thousands of well-wishing comments on their Facebook page, and browsed the internet, reading the headlines: Lizzie in Love; Is it Love for Lizzie?; The Girl with Three Months to Live loses sight.

It was impossible to comprehend the media attention surrounding their journey. In Thailand it had been easy to ignore. Facing the photographers at Sydney Airport had changed that. And the more stories, the more Facebook comments, the more interest in her life, in her journey, the more jittery she felt.

She could no longer hide from it. The world was watching. The thought had unleashed an electrical current into her body, pulsing through her veins and forcing her heart into overdrive.

Then Dr Moss had started calling, leaving Lizzie no choice but to switch off her phone. It was stupid of her to think that discharging herself from hospital would be the end of it, but it hadn't crossed Lizzie's mind that Dr Moss would call her, let alone leave half a dozen voicemail messages that she had no intention of listening too.

A movement from one of the hammocks caught Lizzie's gaze.

'Are you sure you're feeling well enough to do this?' Samantha asked, sitting up in her hammock.

Lizzie sighed. 'Good morning to you too.'

'Sorry. I know I sound like a broken record, but I just want to be sure.' She swung out of the hammock in much the same way Lizzie had, and landed unsteadily on her feet. Jaddi repeated the action a moment later and galumphed towards them in her unlaced walking shoes.

'I'm absolutely, one hundred per cent, totally sure,' Lizzie said. 'We've been sitting in the apartment doing nothing for days. My sight is fine, I'm fine,' she said, fighting to keep the frustration out of her voice; Samantha was only trying to help.

Jaddi yawned, rubbing her palm across the back of her neck. 'I thought hammocks were supposed to be comfortable, but I spent the entire night lying with my head to one side, too scared to move in case I fell out.'

'There you go,' Samantha continued. 'Jaddi's exhausted. Yet another reason why we shouldn't embark on a three-day hike through a remote rainforest. Why don't we do a day walk instead, and spend the night in one of the chalets at the retreat? They have hot tubs,' Samantha said, finishing her sentence in a sing-song voice as if talking to a child.

Lizzie sighed again and looked to Jaddi. 'Do you want to tell her, or shall I?'

'Go ahead.' Jaddi smiled.

Lizzie turned back to Samantha. 'We are here for an authentic experience in the wilderness. Not some gentle stroll around the campsite.'

'Yes, but it's *three* full days of walking, plus camping out. We'll be miles from anywhere. If anything should go—'

'It won't. Please, Samantha, I want to do this. A day walk won't take us nearly far enough. I want to see the ancient volcano and the areas of rainforest untouched by humans.'

'Fine. I give up.' Samantha threw her hands in the air, but smiled as she spoke. 'Just promise me if you start to feel—'

'I'll say something,' Lizzie cut in, grabbing Samantha's arm. 'Now, come on, I'm starving and I smell bacon. Let's leave the boys and get some breakfast from the resort.'

As Jaddi laced up her shoes, Lizzie glanced at Harrison. He seemed to be sleeping peacefully in the hammock, oblivious to the noise of the forest. A dull ache spread across her chest. The last time they'd spent time alone together had been on the beach in Coolangatta, the night before she'd lost her sight.

She had so many questions she wanted to ask him, like why he'd stood on the hospital steps talking to a reporter instead of coming to see her? Was he still upset about their night on the beach? So much had happened since then. And where had he been disappearing to whilst she'd been cooped up in the apartment?

Doubt niggled at her thoughts. Harrison wasn't solely to blame. She hadn't tried very hard to initiate a meaningful conversation or broach the questions on the tip of her tongue. Asking the questions was simple enough; it was the answers Lizzie wasn't ready for.

CHAPTER 36

Lizzie

Thirty minutes later, they returned to camp and packed up their belongings. The, bacon, eggs and fresh orange had revived them, it seemed. An eagerness hung in the air.

Harrison and Ben followed a few minutes behind them and reached their camp just as a wide burly man in beige shorts and a matching shirt marched towards them.

'Which one of you lads is the chap I spoke to on the phone?' he said, flicking his gaze between Harrison and Ben.

'That would be me, sir.' Ben stepped forward and held out his hand to the man. 'Ben Holmes.'

The man's arm muscles bulged out of his shirt sleeves like sausages trying to escape their skin as he shook Ben's hand. His face reminded Lizzie of a cinder block, large and square, with tuffs of thick white hair protruding from underneath a wide-brimmed bush hat.

'Good to meet you in person, Ben.' He stepped back and surveyed the four of them before turning back to Ben. 'Ready to get started?'

'Yes, sir.' Ben nodded and hoisted his camera onto his shoulder. He stepped away from them and signalled a thumbs up to the man, who nodded and turned to face them.

'My name is Al Tuckerman, of Al's Rainforest Treks. Welcome to the start of what many believe is the most picturesque part of Australia. In about ten minutes' time, we'll begin day one of the Gold Coast Hinterland Great Walk.' Al removed a faded map, laminated in plastic and splattered with dried mud, from his back pocket as he spoke. 'Today we'll be walking from the Green Mountains, here –' he stabbed his index finger on the map '– to Binna Bura, here.' He moved his finger along a wiggly yellow line. 'Today is the longest distance of all three days. Twenty-one point four kilometres, most of which is up hill, so keep your layers close to hand. This is a subtropical rainforest. With changing altitudes we'll see a changing rainforest, but also a big drop in temperature.

'There'll be a lot of wildlife to look at as we go along, which I'll be pointing out. Platypus, bandicoots, wallabies, pademelon, pygmy possums and a whole lot of birds. Lamington National Park, which is the area we're in right now, is also host to many endangered species of frogs. Look at where you put your feet and if you see a frog, don't pick it up.

'We'll be walking at a steady pace with regular breaks. In the twenty years I've been a bushwalking guide I've always got my group to the campsite before dark, and I intend to keep it that way. Understand?'

They nodded as his eyes scrutinised each of them in turn. Lizzie sensed a movement behind her and looked up to find Harrison grinning down at her. He dropped an arm around her shoulder, causing warmth and excitement to fizz out from his touch.

'Good. Now, as part of Al's Rainforest Treks, all of the camping equipment is provided. This means that when you reach the campsite there will be safari-style tents set up for you, and your food will be cooked by me. We'll be eating traditional bush tucker for the first two nights and at the end of the great walk, you'll be invited to take a dip in Warringa Pool, as well as have a traditional barbeque and hog roast. Any questions so far?'

Lizzie shook her head.

'What about going to the toilet?' Jaddi asked.

'There are toilets at the campsites. If you need to go for a crap at any other time, then you take this shovel, and this bag from me,' he said, lifting up a small rusty shovel attached to a dark-green canvas bag, and find a spot behind a tree. Any more questions?'

No one spoke.

'Time to partner up, so listen closely, because this is the single most important part of trekking in this rainforest. Your partner is your responsibility,' Al said, slowing his voice so that each word had a pause before the next. 'I'll say it again – your partner is *your* responsibility. You look out for them, and they look out for you. If your partner stops, you stop. Never leave your partner.

'Ben, you'll partner with me; that way I can be your eyes when you're filming. Pretty boy,' he said, pointing at Harrison, 'step away from your girlfriend and move over to pretty girl number two over there. You two are partners.'

'But—' Lizzie started.

'No buts. I've been trekking this forest for twenty years and I can tell you right now that nearly all of the accidents that happen, happen to couples. They start bickering or acting all lovey-dovey and stop looking where they're going. So your boy is with this pretty lady here, and you two –' he pointed to Samantha and Lizzie '– can be partners.'

Disappointment weighed down on Lizzie. She'd been looking forward to walking arm in arm with Harrison through the rainforest, and shaking the loneliness of the past week. It was the same feeling of isolation she'd felt during her treatments. Never alone, but distanced from those around her by their well-meaning concerns.

'Now, you're all dressed pretty much OK.' His eyes fell to Harrison's trainers. He raised his eyebrows. 'With the exception of pretty boy's plimsolls, that is. Does everyone have a hat?'

Lizzie nodded along with the rest of the group.

'Your hat will protect you from the sun and the rain, as well as bird droppings. So keep it on your head. Each pair gets one of these packs.' He held up a small red bag. 'It's got clips to attach to your rucksack or your belt. Keep it safe and keep it accessible. Inside, you'll find a basic first-aid kit, a topographical map of the route, a compass, and most importantly for this time of year – leach repellent. Slap it on now, and at every rest stop, or those suckers will be on you in a heartbeat. That just about covers everything. Before we go, does anyone have any alcohol with them? Anyone got a hip flask stashed away?'

No one spoke up.

'Good. Because there is no alcohol on Al's Rainforest Treks. I don't deal with drunks and I don't stop for hangovers.'

'Anyone have any illnesses they need to tell me about?'

Lizzie felt all eyes, along with Ben's camera lens, bore into her, but she kept her head down and her mouth closed.

'Good. Then let's get moving. We've got seven hours of walking to get through today, and it gets dark early in the forest.'

CHAPTER 37

Jaddi

'Wow,' Samantha said.

Lizzie stepped up beside Samantha. 'Very wow.'

'Breathtaking, isn't it?' Al said.

'Just a bit.' Jaddi grinned, moving next to Sam with the giddiness of feeling utterly awestruck. From the viewing platform in front of them her eyes absorbed the endless undulating hills, tree-covered cliffs, and the rich green of the rainforest for as far as they could see.

It was a relief to stop. The small of her back had started to ache with the uphill climb on the narrow footpath, although the pain was easier to ignore than Harrison's incessant moaning. First, it was his hair, becoming messy under the bush hat; then it was his denim shorts, chaffing the inside of his thighs. Finally, and for the last few hours since they'd crossed the shallow creek, it was his wet trainers, rubbing on the heels of his feet.

The forest had transformed with every kilometre they'd trekked. Tarzan-like swinging vines, as thick as rope, hung from the canopies overhead and looped over the treetops. Large birds with flashes of cobalt-blue and yellow perched on branches, their black shining eyes watching them from above.

The trees grew taller, wider and more elaborate the further into the rainforest they travelled. During a brief rain shower, they'd eaten their lunch in the cavern of a hollowed-out tree. Despite the gaping hole, the tree above was full of crisp green leaves, and was very much alive.

'We're making good time,' Al said, checking his watch as Ben stepped around them, spinning in a slow circle to capture first their expressions, followed by a panoramic view of the rainforest stretching before them. 'There's just over three kilometres to go, so have some water, and let's get moving.'

Harrison groaned and pulled off his hat, before raking his fingers through his hair and sweeping his fringe to one side.

Jaddi considered saying something peppy – *We're almost there, you can do it* – but she stopped herself. Anything she said would be met with more huffing and griping. Silence seemed the better option as they fell into a steady walk behind the others, and quickly began to lag.

Besides, Jaddi had her own problems to worry about, and they far outweighed Harrison's blisters. Just as she'd hoped, their journey so far had brought the three of them closer. Especially to Samantha. Samantha had spent the last couple of years working long hours and had spent most of her weekends with David. The days of the three of them lounging on the sofa, watching the *Corrie* omnibus were long gone. But with their renewed closeness came a sickening pressure to release the secrets she'd been keeping. All of them. The pressure was exhausting. She woke up every morning more tired than she'd felt the night before. How much longer could she carry on feeling like this before one or all of the secrets slipped out? Jaddi didn't know the answer, and that only added to her angst.

'I've gotta slow down,' Harrison called out to her, his feet dragging and scuffing on the track.

'We've only just started walking again.' Jaddi sighed, watching the others stride ahead around a bend.

'Hey, let's cut through here.' Harrison limped over to a path leading off to the left. 'It's a shortcut for sure. We can catch up by skipping that bend up ahead.'

'No way.' Jaddi raised her eyebrows and shook her head. 'Al said we need to stick to the path.'

'No, he didn't. He said, "Your partner is your responsibility."' Harrison mimicked the deep voice of the walk leader. 'And I'm your partner, and I'm going this way so you have to come.'

Jaddi sighed and glanced back up the main path. There was no sign of Al, or Lizzie, Ben or Samantha. 'Fine,' she said, striding ahead. 'Let's catch up with them then.'

'Hang on, hang on, I gotta stop first.' Harrison groaned, shrugging off his backpack and dropping onto a log. 'It's these blisters. It would've been fine if we hadn't gone through that river.'

'It was a creek. And my feet didn't get wet.'

'Well, I don't have any special shoes, do I? No one said we'd be going through water, and now I've got, like, a gazillion blisters.' Harrison kicked off his trainers and peeled away a damp, white sock, revealing a tanned foot with tuffs of dark fuzz and circles of raw pink skin.

'How bad are they?' Jaddi asked, placing her hands on her hips and fighting to keep the distain from her voice.

Harrison scrunched his face and closed his eyes. 'Bad.'

Jaddi summoned her remaining energy and looked at Harrison. 'Where's the pack Al gave us?'

'Here.' Harrison unclipped it from his belt and held it out for her to take.

Jaddi sighed again. 'I don't want it. It's for you. Get the plasters out of the first-aid kit and put them on your blisters. Do you have any dry socks?'

Harrison shook his head. 'I've used them already.'

'Right, just plasters then.'

Harrison stared at the bag in his hands for a moment longer before unzipping it. With infuriating slowness, he unpeeled the packaging of one plaster after another, before moving his focus onto his other foot.

Jaddi sat down on the far side of the log and tried to remember the Harrison who'd rescued her from the cockroach, rather than the Harrison drivelling over a couple of blisters.

'Is that really as fast as you can go?' Jaddi fought the desire to grab Harrison's arm and drag him along.

She moved the light of the torch over her watch. They'd been walking, or hobbling in Harrison's case, for over an hour, with no sign of the rest of the group or the campsite. Jaddi wasn't even sure they'd turned back onto the main path after the shortcut Harrison had dragged her into.

'Are you sure it's this way?' he asked, hopping beside her.

'No, I'm not sure. Let me check the map and take a look at the compass. Oh no, that's right, we can't because you left it back at the log, along with the rest of Al's pack,' Jaddi replied. She made no effort to hide the mordant tone from her voice as heat pulsed through her.

'I said I was sorry.'

Jaddi groaned and bit back the comment on the tip of her tongue. They'd had the same exchange of words an hour ago and it hadn't gotten them anywhere then. Why did it seem that she was destined to repeat the same squabbles over and over again? She thought of

Suk. How they would laugh about this little episode one day. If they ever found their way to the campsite, that was.

The problem was the light, or lack of it. She'd hardly paid attention to Al's comment at the start of their day – *it gets dark early in the forest* – until the light had started to fade. At first the sun's rays had danced through the leaves, casting intricate patterns on the path before them. Then it was gone and they were left with an eerie twilight, which had quickly given way to darkness.

She couldn't see the trees on either side of her, or Harrison, or her feet for that matter. Only the orange circle of light from the torch kept them on the path, or from walking off a cliff edge.

'Can you slow down a bit? You've got the torch, remember. I almost fell flat on my face back there.'

'Can you speed up a bit?'

'What's the point?'

'Pardon?' She spun around, shining the torch at him.

'Seriously, what's the point of speeding up when we have no idea where we are, or if we're going in the right direction. Surely the best approach would be to bunker down and wait to be rescued.' Harrison's voice shifted as he spoke. The whining, which she'd been subjected to for the duration of the day, morphed into a teasing suggestive tone.

'We are not stopping,' she said, with what she hoped was enough authority to shake Harrison into moving. 'We've followed the path. The campsite is just around this corner, now come on.'

He smirked, shielding his face from the torchlight and taking a step towards her. 'You've been saying that for the past hour. Come on, admit it, we're lost, and it's kind of funny.'

'What are you on about? Nothing about this is funny. Do you know how many acres of rainforest there are here?' She angled the torch at the ground and stepped back.

'No,' he said, with a shrug.

'Neither do I, but I'm sure it's enough for two people to get lost in and never be found.'

'Relax. We're on a footpath. They'll find us in the morning.'

'Morning? I'm not spending the night out here.'

'I'm not sure we have a choice. I really can't walk any further. I have to rest.' Harrison continued towards her, forcing her to inch backwards until the coarse bark of a tree dug into her back. He brushed the back of his fingers down her cheek.

'Harrison, whatever you're thinking of doing, don't.'

'You've been flirting with me since the moment you saw me at the airport,' he said in a low voice. 'Don't bother pretending you haven't. I'm surprised Lizzie hasn't noticed. All those sly smiles and little winks you give me when nobody's looking.'

'Don't kid yourself,' she said as unease wound its way through her, speeding up the beating of her heart. 'I'm like that with everyone.'

'You can stop pretending,' he said, gripping her arms in his hands. 'I'm not going to tell Lizzie.'

'Harrison, GET OFF ME.' She shrugged him away, before striding back onto the path. The angle of the torch threw looming shadows on the ground in front of her.

A moment later, she heard his footfalls a pace behind her. 'Fucking dyke.'

Her stomach reeled as his tone and his words cut through her.

'You're despicable,' she said. 'The second I see Lizzie, you're finished.'

The sound of his laugh rung out beyond the trees. All of a sudden the flapping of wings filled the night as a flock of birds took flight from directly above them.

'And you think she'll believe your version over mine?' he said when the noise had died. 'You were the one that took my hand. You were the one that brushed up against me. You were the one that whispered in my ear, "No one has to know."'

Jaddi drew in a sharp intake of breath. 'Try it, go on. She won't believe you.'

'Oh, really.' Jaddi didn't need to point the torch at his face again to know he was grinning. 'Well, according to Lizzie, you sleep with any bloke with a pulse. So, actually, I think she will believe me.'

Jaddi faltered. Hurt and uncertainty battled for space in her thoughts. Did Lizzie think that way about her? How could her best friend get it so wrong?

No, Jaddi decided. Lizzie may not know everything about her, but she wouldn't have made such a crass comment to Harrison. He was trying to cajole her into keeping silent, and there was no way she was falling for it.

'I'll take my chances,' she said.

They fell silence for a minute.

'Hey, come on, Jaddi, I was only messing with you,' Harrison said.

'Right.' She nodded. 'Just messing.' She shook her head but continued moving. Anger pulsed through her body, but she had to focus. The vulnerability she'd felt from Harrison's advance had renewed her urgency to find the campsite.

'Come on, Jaddi,' Harrison said. 'Lizzie knows the score.'

'And what score would that be?'

He paused for a moment. 'Never mind.'

Jaddi's mind ran through their time in Sydney. Harrison's instantaneous declaration of love, the easy manner with which he'd inserted himself into the group of reporters at the airport. The sudden appearance of the same news crew at the hospital, and Harrison there again, front and centre, harping on about his love for Lizzie and concern for her wellbeing, without actually bothering to go in and see her.

'Is that all it means to you – fame?' she asked.

Harrison didn't answer.

'So that's it then.' Jaddi nodded.

'And, so what if it is? Lizzie's happy. She's in love with me. So what if at the end of all this I make a name for myself? I'm not cut out for office work. Just look at me. I'm meant for greatness. What's so wrong with that? Lizzie won't care, she'll be dead.'

'There's so much you don't understand.' Jaddi clenched her fists until her nails dug into her palms. Just then she heard a clattering noise. She shone the torch further ahead and noticed the widening of the path. Another clang. The unmistakable sound of a saucepan.

CHAPTER 38

Samantha

Samantha shifted on the log bench, moving closer to the warmth of the fire and hugged her arms to her chest. She glanced at Ben, one ear covered by a headset, the concentration on his face scowl-like in the flicking orange firelight.

'How long before Al calls—'

'Shh,' Ben cut her off, twisting away from the fire and staring into the darkness.

She jumped up and followed the direction of his gaze. 'Have you seen something?'

Ben shook his head. 'No, but I've picked up Jaddi's microphone so they must be close.'

Samantha spun towards him, noticing the red dot glowing on the camera. 'What are they say—'

'Shh,' he said again.

A minute passed but she continued to stand, scanning the darkness.

'There.' She pointed. 'I can see a torch. It has to be them.'

A moment later, the torchlight grew brighter and the forms of two hikers walked towards them.

Samantha ran across the grass clearing, relief carrying her forward, her aching legs forgotten. 'Jaddi.' She pulled her friend into a tight embrace. 'I'm so glad you're OK. What happened to you guys? I was beginning to think something terrible had happened.'

'You can't get rid of me that easily.' Jaddi walked over to the collection of logs and sat down with a long sigh.

'We were just considering calling the Park Rangers and forming a search team,' Al said, stepping out from one of the nearby tents. 'Grub's over there by the fire.' He pointed to a red picnic box beside Ben.

'Bonza,' Harrison said, limping in the direction of the camp.

'Seems to me, you veered to the left at some point,' Al said, 'if you ended up coming in from that direction. Probably added an extra couple of kilometres onto your day, but, hey, you're here now. So have some food and get some rest. We're setting off at seven tomorrow. I'll be ringing the breakfast bell at six-thirty.' With that, Al turned and strolled in the direction of his tent.

'Where's Lizzie?' Jaddi asked.

'She's gone to lie down,' Samantha said, sitting back onto the log. 'She won't admit it, but the hike has really taken it out of her. She practically fell asleep eating her dinner.'

'Oh.' Jaddi scanned the tents before glancing at Harrison, already barefoot and halfway through a plate of sausages and jacket potatoes. 'I need to talk to her,' she said, pulling herself up to standing. She pressed her hands against her lower back as she moved.

'Jaddi, just leave it,' Harrison mumbled through a mouth full of food.

Samantha's eyes narrowed on Jaddi. 'Leave what? What happened?'

Neither of them spoke.

'Jaddi,' Samantha said, 'what happened?'

'I'll tell you later. I need to speak to Lizzie first,' Jaddi replied.

'No!' Samantha snapped. 'Tell me now. What have you done? Please tell me you haven't—' She watched the guilt crease Harrison's face and shook her head, unable to finish her question. 'I can't believe you would do that.'

'Sam,' Jaddi spluttered, 'I didn't, but I need to speak to Lizzie. Which tent is she in?'

'Why do you need to see her so badly if you've done nothing wrong?' Samantha jumped up and stepped in front of Jaddi.

'Yeah, come on, Jad,' Harrison said, pausing to swallow a mouthful of food. 'Nothing happened. You tried it on, I said no. I'm with Samantha on this, let's move on. Telling Lizzie is only going to hurt her.'

'What?' Jaddi's mouth dropped open.

CHAPTER 39

Jaddi

The humming had started again. Outrage, hurt and fury rooted Jaddi to the spot. After everything she'd done for Lizzie and Samantha, after everything she'd done to get them here, did her friends not know her at all?

'Noooo.' Samantha shook her head again and covered her mouth with her hands. 'You wouldn't.' Despite the words, there was doubt in Samantha's tone.

Jaddi felt like she was going to explode – something tight within her finally snapped. 'Not that it's any of your business,' she half shouted, glaring at Harrison, 'and beside from the fact that Lizzie is one of my best friends, I'm in a committed relationship. Actually, do you know what, I'm in love, and I have been for years, and there's no way I'd risk losing that for someone like you.'

'What?' Samantha dropped her hands. Confusion crossed her face. 'No, you're not.'

'Yes, I am,' Jaddi said.

The creaking of insects and the hooting call of a nearby animal filled the silence.

'How can you be?' Samantha's tone softened. 'Why have you never said anything before?'

'I'm saying something now,' Jaddi said, wishing already that she hadn't. At least the camera was off, she conceded.

'What's his name?'

Jaddi didn't reply.

'Ja—'

'Suk,' Jaddi cut in.

'I … I can't believe you've never said anything.' Samantha threw up her arms and dropped down next to Jaddi on the log. 'We just assumed you were off with other guys. You let us assume.'

'It's difficult with … our parents,' Jaddi replied, her stomach turning a little at Samantha's comment and choosing her own words carefully. 'We thought it would be better to keep it quiet until we were sure.'

'But …' Samantha shook her head. 'How long have you been seeing each other? I still can't believe I didn't know.'

Jaddi dropped her gaze to her hands and felt the hole she'd dug for herself deepen. 'Quite a while.'

'You're not going to believe her, are ya?' Harrison said. 'She's lying. She's making up some mystery guy to disguise the fact that she made a pass at me.'

Ben cleared his throat. He twisted the camera towards them and unplugged the headphone cable. A second later, Harrison's muffled voice carried in the air.

'*You can stop pretending. I'm not going to tell Lizzie.*'

'*Harrison, GET OFF ME.*'

'This is my favourite bit,' Ben said, skipping the footage forward.

'*Is that all it means to you – fame? So that's it then.*'

'*And, so what if it is? Lizzie's happy. She's in love with me. So what if at the end of all this I make a name for myself? I'm not cut out for office work. Just look at me. I'm meant for greatness. What's so wrong with that? Lizzie won't care, she'll be dead.*'

Harrison jumped up. 'What the …? Mate?' Harrison's eyes widened as his gaze moved from the camera to Ben. 'I'll tell Lizzie you cut it to sound different. She'll still believe me.'

Just then a torch flicked on and a figure stepped out of the darkness. 'Are you sure about that?' Lizzie asked.

'Lizzie! I … I can explain,' Harrison spluttered, dropping his plate to the ground.

'Go on then,' she replied, stepping over to Jaddi and sitting next to her. 'I'm glad you're OK, but why on earth didn't you tell us about your boyfriend?'

'Sorry,' Jaddi said, guilt and relief curdling together inside her. 'It's difficult to talk about. It's not something we've shared with our families.'

'Lizzie.' Harrison limped towards her.

'I thought you wanted to explain,' Lizzie said, putting an arm around Jaddi. 'We're waiting.'

'Can we go somewhere private?' He mumbled, glancing between them.

Lizzie sighed and stood up. She turned back to Jaddi. 'Have something to eat, OK?'

Jaddi nodded.

Lizzie strode away to a nearby clearing, with Harrison limping after her.

Ben waited a moment before standing up. He nodded towards the darkness. 'I'd better go and film this.'

'Thank you, Ben,' Jaddi said.

'Any time,' he said with a shrug.

'Will you get in trouble for letting us hear it?' she asked.

'If someone feels the need to tell Caroline, then, yes, I probably will get in trouble. Anyone feel that need?' He looked between Samantha and Jaddi and waited a beat before he spoke again. 'Didn't think so.'

'Why did you?' Jaddi asked.

'Because I didn't want there to be a rift between you three over someone like him.'

Jaddi smiled. 'And you like Lizzie.'

'Er ...' Ben's gaze flicked to Samantha and back to Jaddi. 'I like all of you. And, more importantly, we've still got another six weeks together, and I don't want to be filming a load of stony silences. I need to film this though –' he nodded his head in the direction of Lizzie and Harrison again '– or I will be in trouble.'

Ben tucked the camera under his arm and stepped into the darkness.

'He totally likes her,' Jaddi said, hoping to smooth over the awkwardness hovering between her and Samantha.

'Jaddi, I'm—'

'It's fine.' Jaddi stepped over to the hamper. Hunger was the last thing on her mind, but she knew she had to eat.

'I'm sorry,' Samantha said, touching Jaddi's arm and stopping her in her tracks. 'I shouldn't have doubted you.'

'You didn't.'

Samantha nodded and scrunched up her face. 'I did a bit.'

'Honestly, it's fine.' Jaddi shrugged, pushing away the sting of Samantha's doubt. After everything Jaddi had done what right did she have to feel hurt? Jaddi pulled Samantha close and hugged her tight. 'I know how I come across. I know I'm a massive flirt. It doesn't mean anything though.'

'I'm still sorry.'

'In the grand scheme of things, it really doesn't matter. You were worried about Lizzie, I understand that.' Jaddi sighed, reaching for her plate of food.

They huddled in silence by the dying fire watching the glow of Lizzie's torch across the campsite. 'Should we go and make sure Lizzie is all right?'

'No.' Jaddi shook her head and swallowed a mouthful of warm potato. 'Lizzie didn't exactly look cut up, did she? She'll give us a shout if she needs us.'

CHAPTER 40

Lizzie

Lizzie balanced the torch upright on the ground, casting ghostly shadows on Harrison's face. A memory of trick-or-treating, and of Aaron holding her hand, toddling along in a skeleton outfit, flashed in her mind. She felt a sudden longing for home. She didn't want to jump on an aeroplane and go back; she wanted to be a child again, sitting at the kitchen table with a bowl of soggy cornflakes, the smell of burnt toast and coffee in the air, and the sound of her mum's tinkling laugh over the babbling of the radio.

'Look, Lizzie,' Harrison said, taking her hand and drawing her thoughts back to the campsite, 'I'm sorry about what happened back there. Let's put it behind us. It doesn't have to change anything.'

Repulsion crawled up her arm. Embers of fury burnt inside of her. But underneath the anger, a dull ache began to settle on her chest, like a niggling pulled muscle that refused to heal. She drew her hand out of his reach and sat down on one of the logs. 'I thought you were going to explain why you felt the need to try it on with my best friend?' She knew he had no explanation, and if he did, it wouldn't make a difference, but after what he'd done to Jaddi, he deserved to squirm for a little bit.

He dropped to his knees in front of her. 'I'm completely crazy about you and I want to marry you.'

'Harrison.' Lizzie gritted her teeth, exasperation and frustration coursed through her. 'What planet are you on, exactly? We've been together, what, a fortnight, and you want to get married? Even by our standards, that's insane.'

'But think about it. You want a big white wedding, don't you? I mean, that's what all women want. We'll get a magazine to pay for all of it, or maybe Channel 6 will. I spoke to Caroline last week and she's—'

'You spoke to Caroline? When? why?' Hurt and anger warred for space in her thoughts.

'I wasn't going behind your back or anything.' He looked up from the ground and reached for her hand again.

She moved it out of reach and stood up, increasing the distance between them.

'It was just about me being part of the trip. Where I was going to stay, who was going to pay for it. That kind of thing. It wasn't worth bothering you about. She was really excited about a wedding, she even—'

'Harrison, stop talking. Just stop talking and listen for a moment. No one is getting married, especially not us.'

'But ...?

'Listen,' Lizzie said, 'I had a great time in Sydney with you. And it really was romantic being swept off my feet and being showered with attention.' She smiled.

'Exact—'

'SHUT UP!' Lizzie drew in a deep breath before she continued. 'But we haven't had a single real conversation. Not one. Everything has been about how much we like each other, and isn't it great. But that's not a basis for a relationship. I don't know anything about you. I don't know the names of your parents, or what your favourite foods are, or a million other things I should know.' An image of Ben sprang into her head as she realised she knew him better than she knew Harrison.

'Please, Lizzie, I need this.' He elongated the words, coating them with pity.

'Why?'

'I do like you a lot, and everything you've said is right, but does it matter? Can't we just pretend it's for real and carry on like we have been? You said yourself, it's been fun.'

'It really is all about the fame, isn't it?' She sighed, the air leaving her body and draining her of energy.

'I just want to be someone. You get that, don't you? My life was so boring. The same thing every day. A crap job, a crap life. I know I might be deluded, but not everyone is supposed to have that life. I've been taking acting classes. I want to be a TV presenter. My teacher says I've got what it takes. I just need a break.'

Lizzie closed her eyes, shutting out the image of his pleading puppy-eyed gaze. 'You tried it on with my best friend, and then you lied and made out as if Jaddi had been in the wrong. Even if we ignore everything else, I can't ignore that.'

'Liz—'

'Harrison, it's over. Go back to your beautiful girlfriend in Sydney, if she'll take you back, and get on with your life.

'What girlfriend?'

'Come off it. The girl at the beach party on our first night? I knew something was strange about the way she was looking at me, but I couldn't see it, or I didn't want to. Even if you hadn't tried it on with Jaddi, we'd still be having this conversation.'

'Cress understands.' Harrison stood up from the ground and slumped onto the log.

'Well, you deserve each other then.'

'What about the rest of the hike?' he said.

'There's a group going back to Green Mountain in the morning, you can tag along with them.'

'Back the way we came? But that's like twenty kilometres.'

Lizzie stood up. 'You'll live.'

CHAPTER 41

Day 43

Lizzie

'Right,' Ben said, drawing to a stop and titling his head out from behind the camera, 'I'm not sure how much more silence I can film. So here's what we're going to do: you're going to start walking again, and I'm going to start filming, and you three are going to start chatting. OK?'

Another moment of silence dragged on. Lizzie's gaze followed the cascading water, sprouting out of the cliff above and falling in a dozen individual waterfalls down the rocky cliff, before ending in a brook running parallel to their path.

'OK?' Ben said again.

Lizzie turned to Ben. It was the first time she'd seen his face unobscured by the camera all day. He held her gaze for a split second, before ducking back behind the scope. She wanted to help him, but she really did not feel like talking right now. The hurt from her break-up with Harrison had eased quickly, but left in its place was an emptiness she couldn't begin to articulate.

'It was the length of time he took over his hair in the morning,' Jaddi said finally, nudging Lizzie's arm and smiling. 'And how he kept touching it every few minutes. Seriously, what was that all about? It always looked the same to me.'

'The hair I could live with,' Samantha said, stepping up beside them and nudging Lizzie's other side, 'it was the constant boasting about things his mates had done. Punching a shark on the nose? Really, Harrison? Really?'

Lizzie smiled despite the warmth invading her cheeks.

'Too soon for the ex analysis, Liz?' Jaddi asked, looping her arm through Lizzie's.

'A bit.' Lizzie scrunched her face. 'Didn't we impose a forty-eight-hour cooling-off period?'

'That was only because you broke up with that guy at your office, and we started listing all of the things we didn't like about him, only for you to get back together the following day.'

Lizzie smiled. 'Poor Ian.'

They fell into silence again.

'It had to be the picking me up and spinning me round,' Lizzie said. 'Oh, and the head patting. He would pat my head any time I sat down. I swear there were a few times I almost barked at him.'

'Are we talking about Harrison now or Ian?' Jaddi asked.

'Harrison,' Lizzie said. 'Not much point in a cooling-off period, is there?'

They shared a look and burst into a fit of giggles.

'And his constant use of slang words,' Samantha said. 'It was like he'd been given one of those novelty loo rolls for Christmas with Australian slang words printed on it. And his arrogance! He thought he was God's gift to the world.'

'I'm starting to get the impression that you didn't like him much,' Lizzie said, raising her eyebrows at Samantha.

Jaddi threw her head back and laughed. 'Not much, ah Sammy?'

'And that was another thing. He couldn't get my name right. First I was Sally, then I was Sammy. How difficult is it to remember someone's name?'

'I think Sammy quite suits you.' Jaddi winked at Lizzie.

'Me too.' Lizzie grinned. 'I think we'll all start using it. Hey, Sammy, can you pass me the map?'

'Right, that's it. Back to silence now, please.' Samantha glared at Lizzie and Jaddi, as a smile tugged on her lips.

'I do feel a bit sorry for him though,' Lizzie said.

'What?' Jaddi cried out.

'I know he was an idiot, but we left yesterday morning without even checking on him. What if the other hiking group went without him? We just left him in the middle of nowhere.'

'He'd get what he deserved then,' Samantha said.

Al cleared his throat from a few paces ahead of them. 'One of my team was at the campsite soon after we left. He made sure your boy got out with the other group.'

'Thanks, Al,' Lizzie said. 'So come on then, Jaddi.' Lizzie nudged her friend back. 'Tell us about your boyfriend then? What's he like? Where did you meet him? When will we get to meet him? What was his name?'

Samantha opened her mouth to speak. 'It was Su—'

'Hey,' Jaddi half shouted, 'there's the Warringa Pool. We've finished.'

'Really?' Samantha asked.

Al drew to a stop and turned to address them. 'Yep. Welcome to Warringa Pool, which is considered by most of us to be the best swimming hole on the mountain, and just up that path is the Settlement Campground. You can follow me up to the campground and have a rest, or you can head straight into the pool for a swim. I'll be getting the hog roast set up with one of my team. Well done.' Al clasped a large hand on Ben's shoulder and strode away.

'What do you two want to do?' Samantha asked.

'Swim,' Jaddi and Lizzie said in unison.

Lizzie dangled her legs over the rock and dipped them into the clear water. A shiver ran up her legs and continued over her body. The water had definitely felt a lot warmer earlier in the afternoon, when they'd thrown off their backpacks, kicked off their shoes and jumped into the clear water, surrounded by rocks and forest.

Lizzie lent back on her elbows and stared up. Above the tree tops to her left she could see the sky, and clouds that looked like they had captured a ray of sun, the colour of vanilla ice cream. On the other side of the pool, the forest had already began to darken. Bright stars glowed next to a sliver of moon, so that it seemed to Lizzie as if day and night were places and she was smack down in the middle, halfway between the two.

They'd been in Australia only a few weeks and yet it felt as if their time was already drawing to a close. Tomorrow they would travel to Ayers Rock for a week, and then Alice Springs, before flying to America. Her stomach flipped suddenly as if she'd dropped several metres without knowing it. The time was slipping by so fast.

'Hey,' Ben said, dropping to a squat beside her.

'Hi. How did you know I was here?' Lizzie asked, their eyes connecting for a moment.

'Just a hunch. It's beautiful, isn't it?'

'Amazing.'

'It feels strange to see the sun set whilst the stars are out,' he said.

'That's just what I was thinking.'

A dozen thoughts bombarded her head as Ben dropped down into a sitting position beside her. His arm brushed against hers. An apology lingered on her lips, and she desperately wanted to say it aloud. Was there an expiration date on apologies? It felt as if too much time had passed since the hospital; besides he was here now and speaking to her. She'd missed their talks; she'd missed him.

'Where's your camera?' she asked, eying his empty hands.

'The battery packs are running a bit low, and I've still got editing and tomorrow morning to film before we find an electrical point. So I thought I'd check how you were doing instead. You did a good job putting a brave face on the whole Harrison thing today.'

'Thanks,' she replied as a flush of red glowed on her cheeks.

'Was it just a brave face or are you really doing all right?'

'I'm good,' she nodded, fixing her eyes on the miniature waterfall at the far end of the pool. 'I've been sitting here trying to figure out what to say for my video diary. I feel like such a fool.'

'Give it to me.' Ben reached for the camera beside Lizzie. 'You don't have to say anything. You don't owe anyone an explanation. So what if it didn't work out with Harrison? Relationships end all the time.'

'Yes, but most relationships aren't built on a fame-hungry sleazebag trying to make a career out of a dying girl.'

'True.' Ben nodded. 'But it could be worse. He could've been a fame-hungry sleazebag who succeeded in making a career out of a dying girl.'

'Good point.' She smiled. 'Still, I can't help thinking about all of the millions of people watching this who are going to see me gushing over Harrison and all of the romantic things he did in one episode –' Lizzie sighed as a cringe rippled through her '– and then in the next, they'll see Harrison throwing himself at Jaddi, and me breaking up with him.' Lizzie paused for a minute. 'It sounds more like a soap opera than a documentary.'

'I wouldn't worry too much,' Ben said. 'I've been doing, let's say, some strategic editing, over the past few weeks, to give a … balanced view of Harrison.'

'You haven't?' Lizzie grinned and glanced at Ben. Relief sparked inside her. She didn't know if it was for what Ben had said, or the fact that he was talking to her again.

'Come on, that guy was only in it to get his face on television. I could see it a mile off. The way that cheesy smile plastered on his face the second I pulled my camera out. I've seen it a hundred times before. When people are like that, I make sure to get some footage when they don't think anyone's watching.'

'Do I want to see it?' Lizzie laughed.

'Probably best you don't.'

'So the only one who didn't see Harrison for what he was then, was me. Brilliant.'

'Er, no comment.' Ben smiled.

She pulled her gaze away from the sky and looked at Ben. He gave a rueful smile and rubbed his hand across the stubble spreading over his face. She had a sudden urge to scooch across the small gap between them and fold herself under the crook of his arm. The thought caused another spark to jump inside her.

They fell into an easy silence. From somewhere nearby the deep belches of croaking frogs sang their evening chorus.

'I guess I really should do the diary. At the very least, my mum will want to know I'm not a heartbroken mess.'

Ben said nothing, but opened the screen and handed the camera back to her. 'I'll leave you to it.'

'Stay,' she said without thinking.

He shrugged.

Lizzie switched on the camera. 'Welcome to day ... er—' Her mind blanked.

'Forty-three,' Ben said.

'Thanks, Ben.' She smiled at him before focusing back on the screen. 'We've made it to the end of the great walk. Fifty-four kilometres in three days. The scenery was worth the exhaustion. It was jaw-droppingly beautiful.'

Lizzie paused and drew in a deep breath. 'As you'll probably have seen, we lost Harrison on day one of the walk. Sorry if you were rooting for us. It turned out he ... he wasn't who I thought he was.' A single tear escaped from her left eye and slipped down her cheek. 'It made me realise though that I'm lucky to have this tumour now, rather than later in life. Maybe in five years' time I'd have been thinking about settling down, getting married, having babies. But my head hasn't really got round to that yet. I'm fine about not having a big white wedding, or making a home with someone. I'm sure I would've wanted children at some point. But right now I'm not even thinking about that stuff, so I don't feel like I'm missing out. Aaron will make up for it. He'll marry someone really nice and have four babies at least, that will make my mum happy. No pressure, Aaron.' She smiled.

'But I really, really wanted to fall in love,' Lizzie said as tears caught in her throat. 'I knew it was crazy with Harrison and moving too quickly, but it was fun and I thought ... after what we shared last summer, maybe he could look past the documentary, and all the other stuff, and see *me*. And if I just let myself be swept along with it, then maybe I'd get to see what love feels like.' Lizzie paused, her throat aching with emotion.

'I think most people have been in love by the time they reach thirty. But teenage romances, long-term boyfriends ... it has passed me by. It's not exactly easy to meet people when you spend so much time in hospital waiting rooms.

'So, I'm not sad about Harrison, but I am a little sad about the broken heart I've never had, which is pretty dumb, I guess.' Lizzie turned to Ben and smiled.

Ben frowned. 'Well, it's—'

Samantha's voice spoke from behind them, 'Pretty dumb? That's about as dumb as it gets. I'm not supposed to cry about my best friend dying, but here you are snivelling away about never having a broken heart. Pah. Broken hearts suck. What you had with Harrison wasn't love. Not even close. Love is finding someone who makes your heart soar and brightens your entire world. And for most people the gooey stuff fades and all you're left with is someone who doesn't compare to your best friends, who you love too.'

She plonked down next to Lizzie and wrapped an arm around her shoulder. 'Sorry for cutting you off there, Ben.'

'No, it's fine, you took the words right out of my mouth.' Ben smiled.

'So I should stop feeling sorry for myself, is what you're saying?' Lizzie dropped her head onto Samantha's shoulder.

'Yes. Now, come on, the bush tucker is almost ready and those bat wings look yummy.'

'Bat wings?'

'Or maybe they're very crispy burgers, hard to say.'

Lizzie laughed and switched off the camera.

Samantha looped her arm through Lizzie's as they stepped back towards the campsite.

'Lizzie?'

'Yeah?'

'Despite all the dramas we've had, I'm glad I'm here doing this with you,' Samantha said.

'I couldn't have done this without you, Sam. Remember that, OK?' she said with a pang of guilt. Fresh tears welled in Lizzie's eyes.

'Although,' Samantha said, 'maybe we could have a little less drama from now on.'

'Good thinking,' Lizzie said, pulling Samantha closer.

Part III

CHAPTER 42

Day 47

TV Picks
***The Girl with Three Months to Live*, Saturday 8pm**
If you thought sparks were flying between Harrison and Lizzie in last week's episode then prepare yourself for another exciting instalment of *The Girl with Three Months to Live* this Saturday. If the snippets uploaded to Channel 6's website are anything to go by then, it's not just sparks that will be flying in Saturday's episode, but punches too as Harrison clashes with Jaddi during a three-day rainforest trek.

Day 49

***The Vault* – Your home for all the latest Gymnastics News**
Appleton injured
British Juniors Champion, Aaron Appleton, pulls out of the Men's competition over injury fears. Appleton (18) was due to compete in two events at the British Gymnastics Championship in Birmingham later this month. According to coach, Joel Watson, Appleton has 'a minor wrist injury which will not impact the long and bright future ahead of him'.

'We're playing it safe and resting Aaron's wrist,' adds Watson. 'It's disappointing for everyone, especially Aaron, having missed out on gold in the championship last year, but Aaron has the Olympics to think about, and that's what we're focusing on right now.'

Although after a date and time-stamped training video, showing Appleton performing on the pommel horse without any signs of injury, was uploaded onto YouTube yesterday, there is now speculation that his recent decision to pull out of the Championships has more to do with his sister, Lizzie Appleton, who after being diagnosed with a brain tumour is taking part in a Channel 6 documentary, *The Girl with Three Months to Live.*

Day 56

The Sun
Lizzie: 'I really wanted to fall in love.'
The girl with three months to live admits her one regret is never being in love. In an emotional video diary Lizzie explains that love has passed her by, and with Harrison now out of the picture, love for Lizzie is looking even less likely.

Ratings for the Channel 6 documentary continue to soar as Lizzie, along with friends, Jaddi and Samantha, land in America for the final leg of their journey.

The Channel 6 website even crashed on Monday morning after the documentary production team uploaded a sneak preview of one of Lizzie's video diaries, which went viral within minutes.

Emotions have been running high in recent episodes as Lizzie temporarily lost her sight, and broke up with her Australian boyfriend, Harrison Kelly. Things look set to continue hotting up as the girls begin their US tour in Los Angeles with front row tickets for Guy Rawson's sell-out tour.

CHAPTER 43

Day 58

Lizzie

'I hope this isn't too much drama for you, Sam?' Lizzie shouted, as the crowd roared behind them.

'No way!' Samantha shook her head and laughed.

'This is AWESOME.' Jaddi leaned over the metal barrier and touched the stage. 'I just touched the stage that Guy Rawson is about to sing on!'

Lizzie pulled the camera out from her bag and switched it on. She held it up above her head and twirled around, capturing the giant black stage in front of them and the thousands and thousands of cheering fans behind them.

They were in their own barricaded area, just the three of them, at the very front. Three red, cushioned chairs sat to one side, unused. Instead of a gate or a rope, they had a tall woman dressed head to toe in black, who reminded Lizzie of the customs officer at Sydney airport. She had the same 'don't mess with me' stance.

Lizzie's eyes scanned the crowd for Ben. She caught sight of him five rows back. The only man in a legion of screaming women. Lizzie snorted, recalling Ben's flummoxed expression when they'd been led to the VIP area and he'd not been allowed in.

'But I'm with them,' he'd said.

'Sorry, sir,' the woman in black had replied. 'I've got three names on this list; yours isn't one of them.' She'd said it with an air of authority, but still retained the cheery 'have a nice day' octaves they'd grown accustomed to since landing in Los Angeles. 'Your ticket is for just over there. It's still a very good seat, sir.'

She'd waved the three of them through, before positioning herself across the gap.

'But—'

'Is that a video camera in your bag, sir?' she'd cut in.

'Yes. I'm filming a documentary.'

'There is no professional filming of any kind allowed during the concert.'

'So I'll just go stand over there, by myself then, and watch the concert?'

He'd looked at Lizzie as he'd spoken, but it was the woman who'd replied: 'Thank you.'

Lizzie waved at him. He lifted his hand in acknowledgment and raised his eyebrows as he smiled, as if to say, 'you've got to be kidding me'.

She laughed and without thinking blew him a kiss. Their friendship had settled back into an easy banter. He seemed to have a knack for drawing her out of herself, and sweeping away the darkness that was threatening her more and more.

'Welcome to day fifty-eight!' she shouted. 'I know there'll be people watching this that will think I'm crazy for caring about seeing Guy Rawson in concert, but this is seriously one of the best feelings *ever*. It means a lot to the three of us that we can see him in concert together. We've had his albums on repeat in our flat for years, and we're all huge fans.'

A chant soldiered across the arena. Samantha and Jaddi joined in. 'Guy,' they shouted before clapping three times. 'Guy.'

She angled the camera at the stage as Guy appeared, striding to the centre of the floor in blue jeans and a tight black T-shirt. His arrival caused a frenzy of screaming women to jump up and down, Lizzie included.

'Hey there, Los Angeles,' he said into the microphone, before picking up the guitar beside him and lifting the strap over his head. 'How are you doing tonight?' The deep echo of his voice bounced through her. 'How about those Rocket Boys?' He winked at someone out of sight in the wings of the stage.

The clamour of screams, whistles, stomps and claps pummelled Lizzie from every direction. She turned off the camera and wrapped her arms around Jaddi and Samantha. 'You girls are the best!' she shouted.

'I just saw Guy Rawson wink!' Jaddi shouted. 'THIS IS AWESOME.'

Guy plucked a string on his guitar, and then another. The chords vibrated out of the gigantic speaker next to them and continued reverberating into Lizzie's body.

As Guy launched into his set, Lizzie felt the familiarity of the songs wash over her. The volume of music allowed no room for thought in her head, which suited her just fine.

A dark sadness had clouded her final weeks in Australia. Ayers Rock had been breathtaking, especially the sunsets, but she'd taken to pacing more and more. Up and down, back and forth, in long, deliberate strides whilst gnawing her bottom lip. Any time, day or night, it felt as if she'd had ten cups of coffee pinging around her body.

Landing in Los Angeles had changed that. They'd gained a day in the time difference, leaving in the early afternoon, and arriving in the morning on the same day. The concept of time zones boggled her mind, but it also lifted her spirits. The weeks were flying by, time was running out. To gain an extra day felt like a lottery win. She didn't want to count the days or to think about the world continuing to turn when she was no longer there to see it. She wanted to dance, to sing, to laugh, to forget.

'So, Los Angeles, that's it from me,' Guy said with his famous lopsided smirk. 'You've been a great audience tonight, thank you.'

A tidal wave of protest crashed over the arena.

'What's that?' Guy grinned. 'You want another song?' He picked up a bottle of water and downed it in three quick gulps. 'Well, it just so happens that I've been tinkering with something new over the last few weeks. Perhaps you'd like to be the first to hear it?'

The stadium cheered its agreement.

'I thought you might.' He laughed. 'I wrote this song about someone very special and truly inspirational, and she's here with us tonight. Shall we get her up on stage?'

'Maybe it's Taylor Swift,' Lizzie said to Jaddi.

'I don't think so.' Jaddi nudged her and pointed. 'Look at the big screen.'

'Holy crap.' Samantha gasped.

Lizzie followed Jaddi and Samantha's gaze to one of the large screens on either side of the stage, which up until that moment had mirrored Guy's every movement. She drew in a sharp intake of breath as their startled faces gawked back.

'We love you, Guy!' Samantha shouted, before hiding her face in her hands.

'Now, my manager warned me that it might be a bit embarrassing to get Lizzie up on stage and sing her a song in front of all of you, but I'm going to ask her anyway, so what do you say we give her a big LA welcome. Lizzie, how about coming up here with me?'

A new chant surged through the stadium. 'Lizzie, Lizzie, Lizzie.'

Jaddi took her bag and said something, but all Lizzie could hear was the ferocious beating of her heart drumming in her ears.

The woman in black took her elbow and guided her towards a row of steps. Her feet moved forward as if someone else had gained control of her body. And then Guy Rawson, one of the sexiest men on the planet, stepped towards her and kissed her cheek.

He covered the microphone with his hand. 'Hey.' He smiled.

'Hey,' she heard herself reply.

'Is this OK?'

She racked her brain for a witty retort but drew a blank and found herself nodding like the gimmicky bull dog with the bobbing head in the back of her dad's Volvo.

He moved his hand away from the microphone. 'Lizzie Appleton, everyone.'

Guy dropped his gaze to his guitar and checked the placement of his fingers. 'Hopefully I'll remember the chords,' he said, sending a ripple of laughter over the arena.

Suddenly he began strumming a fast, catchy melody. Guy's gaze found hers as he started to sing.

You set out to see the world, with two best friends
Ninety sunsets, but what happens then?
What happens then?

You're laughing every day, being so brave,
But you can't be saved …
Can't be saved

I wanna buy you some time, have some of mine
But life's just so unkind …
So unkind

When you try and you try but you can't stop the light
When you try and you try but you can't win the fight,
At least we've got tonight
Tonight ... tonight
At least we've got tonight

When you try and you try but you can't stop the light
When you try and you try but you can't win the fight,
At least we've got tonight
Tonight ... tonight
At least we've got tonight

A droplet of water fell onto Lizzie's hand. She looked down at it as another one dripped to the floor. They looked like tear drops. Her tear drops. A dizzying tornado spun around her head. Her fingers reached to her face and found her cheeks wet with tears. She drew in a breath and tried to steady her thoughts.

Her eyes met Guy's. In the intense lights of the stage his pupils looked almost black.

He smiled. 'Let's give Lizzie a round of applause.' He turned to face the cheering crowd. Lizzie's eyes followed his gaze. She expected a sea of faces to be staring back, but all she could see was a darkness as black as the rainforest nights. Camera flashes of light blinkered across the stadium.

Guy leant towards her. The bristle of his stubble grazed her cheek. 'I hope I didn't embarrass you too much, Lizzie,' he said in her ear.

She shook her head and took an unsteady step back. How could she explain? Lizzie spun on her heels and stumbled on shaky legs into the wings of the stage and immediately found herself in a large space, empty apart from a few clusters of people. She recognised the four boys from the warm-up act, sat on a large black box drinking bottled beer. Only then did she realise that she'd gone the wrong way. She should have gone down the steps and rejoined Jaddi and Samantha, not wandered back stage.

A high-pitched whir rang in her ears as she continued forward. A moment later, she entered a long corridor with doors running down it on either side.

'Lizzie,' a voice called from behind her.

She didn't stop or turn to see who the voice belonged too. Instead, her hand reached for the nearest door handle. It opened easily and she tumbled into a windowless dressing room. Empty water bottles and white food cartons littered every surface. A large suitcase sat on the middle of the floor, its contents piled onto a red sofa in one large heap.

The energy drained from her legs as she shut the door. Lizzie slid to the floor. Long gasping sobs took hold of her body. Every line of his song struck like a knife to her chest. *When you try and you try, but you can't win the fight.* The lyric swam in her head but without the strumming of his guitar it had taken on a taunting intonation.

'Are you all right?'

Lizzie yelped as the pile of clothes on the sofa sat up. A woman with messy dark hair smiled at her, before drawing in a deep yawn and stretching her arms above her head. There was something familiar about the woman's face.

The woman squinted at her watch and groaned. 'I've missed the whole concert, haven't I? I only meant to rest my eyes for a few minutes. This bloody jet lag is killing me,' she said in a London accent. Her eyes moved to Lizzie and a spark of recognition crossed her face. 'You're Lizzie Appleton, aren't you?' She didn't wait for a reply. 'I'm guessing that Guy got you up on stage, then? He really doesn't get it. Some people don't want to stand up in front of thousands of people. Oh, I'm Debbie, by the way.'

Lizzie wiped her hands across her face. 'Hi.'

'Do you want a bottle of water?' Debbie stood up and opened a fridge in the corner of the room. She pulled out two bottles and handed one to Lizzie.

'Thanks.' Lizzie sniffed.

'Was it a good concert?'

A smile touched Lizzie's face. 'Fantastic. I … just wasn't expecting to be part of it.'

'Of course you weren't. Which is what I told Guy, but as usual he didn't listen.'

'Are you his manager?' Lizzie asked.

Debbie laughed. 'No, much worse than that; I'm his sister.'

Lizzie saw it then, the reason Debbie looked familiar. She had the same dark eyes and high cheekbones as Guy.

'I'm sorry for barging in here.' Lizzie pulled herself to her feet and straightened her top.

'Thank goodness you did. Otherwise I probably would've slept through the after-party too. Hide out for as long as you need.'

'Thanks, but I'd better find my friends.'

'Stay for a minute. I'll make us a cup of tea. Your friends will come and find you, I'm sure.'

Footsteps sounded from the other side of the door. Lizzie recoiled her hand and sucked her lower lip between her teeth.

Guy's voice continued to sing in her head as loud as if she was still standing on stage with him. A sickness spun in her stomach. *What happens then?*

'Ten minutes,' Debbie said. 'I've even brought my own PG Tips, all the way from London. I'm not sure why, but tea bags in other countries never taste quite right.'

Something mothering in Debbie's voice made Lizzie turn around. 'Thanks.'

'Great.' Debbie smiled. 'Here.' She scooped up the clothes on the sofa and dropped them into the open suitcase, before pulling out a small kettle. 'Never leave home without one of these.' Debbie laughed. 'Gosh, I feel so old saying that.'

CHAPTER 44

Lizzie

'I have to tell you, that as a mother to a little girl,' Debbie said, passing Lizzie a steaming mug of tea, 'I can't imagine how difficult this must be for your parents, as well as for you.'

'I try and focus on the positives,' Lizzie replied, watching the steam rising from her mug. 'They've put so much of their lives on hold to nurse me through my previous tumours. My dad lost his job as an engineer the second time because he had to take so much time off whilst I was in hospital. He was out of work for a long time, and ended up a delivery driver for a supermarket. Their lives would've been so different now if they hadn't made so many sacrifices because of me.

'Now they can focus on themselves, enjoy retirement and be there for Aaron. He needs them too.' A sadness wrapped itself around her. Aaron's face in Dr Habibi's office flashed in her mind. The wide eyes and the trembling lip. The age gap between them should have made them distant, worlds apart, but it hadn't. She'd loved him from the moment she'd held him in her arms. Lizzie had never asked her mum why they'd waited eleven years to have Aaron, probably because she knew the answer. It was Lizzie's fault. Lizzie's tumours putting her parents' lives, their plans, on hold. Well, not anymore.

'I'm sure they don't see it as a sacrifice. Being a parent is your life; it's not something you do for a few years in-between jobs. I would stop at nothing to help my children.'

'How old are they?' Lizzie asked, fighting to keep her voice level as Debbie's words sliced into her.

'Samuel is four, although he'd want me to tell you that he's almost five. And Faith is three. This is the first time I've left them for more than a few hours. I told them the other day I was going …'

A pain began to throb across Lizzie's head. Blobs of white, the same piercing colour as the camera flashes in the stadium, appeared in her vision. She gritted her teeth and struggled to keep the tears from falling. Aaron's voice replayed in her head. *They do understand what you're doing. I know it doesn't seem that way, but they do. We all do.* The more days that passed, the less she knew herself what she was doing on this trip.

'… but they didn't cry. I cried, of course. Sobbed my heart out at the check-in desk, but they just laughed and went with Carl to get a hot chocolate.'

Lizzie blew on her tea again before taking a long sip just as the dressing-room door flew open.

'Debbie, have you seen—' Guy stepped into the room. His eyes moved from Lizzie to Debbie and the half-smile returned. He poked his head out of the room. 'Don, I've found her. Make sure the girls have everything they need in the blue room, and tell them Lizzie is fine.'

He closed the door and stepped into the room. The hot liquid continued to scold the inside of her mouth, but all of a sudden she couldn't swallow.

'Lizzie, I think I owe you an apology,' he said.

Debbie nodded from beside her as Guy cleared some space on the coffee table and sat down opposite them.

'I got a bit carried away with the set. It's just, you've been on my mind for weeks and I just keep thinking, what if it was me, what would I do? And I'm pretty sure that I'd spend the three months holed up in my flat, drinking my sorrows away, crying and yelling at everyone who'd listen about how unfair it all is. But you've said, sod it. You're not feeling sorry for yourself, you're—'

Finally, she swallowed the tea swilling in her mouth. 'A blubbering mess.'

'No, you're so brave. Seriously, I'm in total awe of you.'

A lump ballooned in her throat. 'You're wrong,' she whispered. 'I'm not brave.'

Lizzie saw a look pass between Guy and his sister, but she didn't care.

'I need a clean T-shirt,' Guy said, standing up. 'Those stage lights were like heaters tonight.' He hopped over the suitcase to the other side of the dressing room. 'Made yourself at home a bit here, Debs.'

'Sorry. I got cold and tried to find a jumper. Turns out I forgot to pack one.'

'*You* forgot something? But you're the most organised person I know.' He laughed, pulling his T-shirt over his head and throwing it to the floor. Lizzie's mouth dropped open. She was drinking a cup of English tea backstage at a music concert, and Guy Rawson was standing topless in front of her. The day was getting stranger by the minute, and yet there was something so normal about Guy, now that he wasn't on stage holding a guitar and serenading her, that was. He might be a mega superstar, but he was also someone's little brother, who got carried away and made mistakes, something she could relate to.

'I'm only organised with the kids,' Debbie said. 'When it's just me, it's a different story.'

Lizzie drained the last of her tea and tried not to ogle Guy's bare torso. 'I should probably find Samantha and Jaddi.' She stood up. 'Thanks for the tea, Debbie. It was nice to meet you.'

'And you,' Debbie said, smiling.

'Woah, woah, woah.' Guy pulled a different black T-shirt over his head and looked at Lizzie. 'You don't get away from me that easily. Your friends are in the blue room, chatting to The Rocket Boys, where food and drinks are currently being served. I thought you might like to come along. Plus the fact that if you leave me alone with my sister, then she is going to start nagging me about the state of my personal life.'

'I am not,' Debbie said.

Guy tilted his head and furrowed his forehead as he looked across at Debbie.

She laughed. 'For your information, I was going to wait until breakfast for that.'

'The joys of big sisters.' Guy laughed. 'Come on then, you two, this way.'

Before they could reach the door it swung open and a bald shiny head appeared. 'Guy, sorry to disturb you, but we've got some bloke at the VIP entrance claiming to be with your guests. We've told him to do one, but he says he's not going anywhere until he has seen for himself that Lizzie's all right.'

Guy nodded. 'One of yours?' he asked, smiling at Lizzie.

'Sounds a lot like our cameraman, Ben,' Lizzie said as a flush crept over her cheeks.

Guy turned back to the head in the doorway. 'Thanks, Don. Let him through and show him to the blue room.'

'Gotcha.'

CHAPTER 45

Day 59

Samantha

Samantha clutched her stomach and groaned as she stared at her reflection in the motel-room mirror, and the inch of skin protruding out between the two halves of her nautical-style tankini. For over a month she'd unintentionally cut out refined sugar. She'd eaten rice, noodles and vegetables in Southeast Asia, and mainly fresh fruit and meat in Australia. With the exception of a few Oreos when they'd been miles from anywhere, she'd had a healthy diet, and it showed. Or it had, until she'd landed in LA. Now even the apple she'd eaten at breakfast tasted as if it had been injected with sugar and her stomach was bloating in protest.

Samantha sighed and flopped onto one of the beds, causing the springs to creak in protest. So much for a day lounging by the pool in a bikini.

Her eyes followed the blotchy swirls of yellow and brown on the otherwise white polystyrene ceiling tiles above her head. Their motel room could quite easily have been the film set for any American movie. They had two double beds in a gloomy room with one small window and a small beige shower room.

Deep-fried odours lingered in the air. Samantha imagined the previous occupant digging into a box of crispy fried chicken wings, wiping oily fingers on the olive-green bedspread. The smell reminded her of her grandmother's flat and the deep fat fryer that had been in almost-constant use.

The motel was built in a three-storey L-shape, with the doors all facing a small swimming pool area. They were staying on the second floor, which had led to some confusion when the desk clerk – a bony man with thinning blonde hair and wire-framed glasses – had given them the keys.

'You're halfway down on the second floor. Rooms E and G,' he'd said. 'Any problems, there's someone here twenty-four-seven.'

Her head had spun with jet lag as they'd traipsed up two flights of steps and spent several minutes jiggling their keys in the locks.

'Sorry to bother you again,' Lizzie had said as they'd trundled back into the desk clerk's office, 'but our keys don't work.'

The clerk had removed his glasses and squinted at both the keys. 'You went to the second floor?'

'Yes.' Lizzie had nodded. She'd pointed to a fire exit map with a drawing of the motel building on it. 'One, two.'

The clerk had chuckled, which was about the time that frustrated tears had stung in Samantha's eyes, and she'd considered giving up on a room and curling up on one of the armchairs in the clerk's office. 'One, two, three,' he'd said.

In the end, the clerk had locked the office and showed them to their rooms. It turned out ground floors didn't exist in LA and they'd been on the wrong floor.

Samantha closed her eyes and willed the ringing in her ears to subside. Last night had been such a high. Singing at the top of her voice to every one of Guy's songs. Finding themselves invited back stage. She'd even spoken to Guy. For two surreal minutes, they'd chatted about the weather in Thailand. Although why she'd felt the need to go into such detail about how much she'd sweated was beyond her.

Then there was Kev, the drummer of The Rocket Boys, and the polar opposite of David. Kev was shy to the point of rudeness, with scraggly hair that he'd kept scooping behind his ears, only for it to fall back onto his face a moment later.

He was tall, with clown-like baggy jeans and a faded red T-shirt which had sleeves so long they'd covered half his hands. He wasn't her type. She'd known that just by looking at him. He didn't fit into the 'future husband', mould in her head, but after David, she was happy to break the mould … smash it to smithereens even.

'Do you ever get the impression that everyone else in the room was born with some kind of sociability gene which we didn't get?' he'd asked.

'Or was it taught in school?' she'd replied. 'And we were off sick that day? Somewhere between RE and double maths there was a socialising-at-parties class.'

He'd smiled then, although his focus had remained fixed on peeling the label off his Budweiser bottle.

It turned out that they'd both grown up in tower blocks. Him in Hull, and her in north London. Both had been the only members of their families to want more. Kev had focused on his drumming, and she on her studies. Both had made it out.

'What does your boyfriend think of you lot travelling then?' he'd asked her much later.

'I don't have a boyfriend. I did when we left, but we broke up.'

'Long-distance relationships are tough.'

'Not as tough as relationships with controlling dickheads.'

He'd raised his head and looked into her eyes for the first time. 'At some point, we'll be heading back to England to finish our album. Can I see you?'

There was nothing quixotic about his question. He hadn't asked her on a date. He hadn't tried to kiss her, or so much as brushed his leg against hers, but a miniature tornado had still funnelled in her stomach. 'Sure,' she'd said.

A knock at the door startled Samantha out of the memory.

'Hang on,' she said, wincing at the effort inflicted on her vocal chords. Her voice felt as if it had been dragged through stinging nettles.

She reached the door and pulled it open. Caroline stood in the doorway in an immaculate, navy, trouser suit.

'Oh,' Caroline said.

'Hi, Caroline. I didn't know you were coming,' Samantha said, her voice still hoarse.

Caroline's eyes peered into the room. 'You're not supposed to know. I thought this was Ben's room.' She threw her hands up. 'I've been on the floor above, knocking on the wrong rooms for ten minutes.'

'Really.' Samantha smiled, before pointing to the pool. 'Lizzie and Jaddi are at the pool. I'm sure Ben's with them too.'

'Thanks. Can you head down there? Don't tell them I'm here, and look surprised when you see me.'

'Sure.' Samantha nodded and closed the door. 'Just give me a minute.

Samantha's brain sped into overdrive as she grabbed her sarong and tied it around her cleavage. Something was clearly going on, but no way was she going to obey Caroline's request not to warn Jaddi and Lizzie.

CHAPTER 46

Samantha

The motel swimming pool was a small kidney-shaped area surrounded by plastic sunloungers and a row of wilted palm trees in terracotta pots. Without any other guests using the area, Lizzie, Jaddi and Ben had taken over. Six sunloungers had been dragged together, three in the patchy shade of the trees, and three in the sun. Towels, T-shirts, sun lotion and magazines were strewn across them.

'You're not going to believe this,' Samantha said, shielding her eyes from the sun as she dropped onto the lounger beside Jaddi. Ben climbed out of the pool and joined them.

Jaddi and Lizzie sat up.

'What?' Jaddi asked.

'Caroline's here,' she hissed, glancing around the pool area for any sign of the producer.

'Really? Where?' Lizzie looked behind her.

'In the motel, a second ago. She just knocked on my door looking for Ben.'

'Ah,' Ben said, pulling a face and reaching for his towel.

'What does that mean? "Ah,"' Lizzie mocked. 'Have you been keeping something from us?' she asked, throwing her flip-flop at him.

'Ouch,' he said, before picking up Lizzie's flip-flop and throwing it into the pool.

'Oi!' Lizzie laughed.

'You deserved that.'

'You haven't answered my question. If you know something, you have to tell us.'

Ben laughed and shook his head. 'I'm sworn to secrecy.'

'Hi, girls.' Caroline grinned as she stepped between the plants and stood in front of them.

Two men holding cameras the same as Ben's, and a man holding a microphone, which looked like a dead squirrel on a stick, appeared from the other side of the pool.

'Hey, Caroline.' Jaddi said. 'What brings you to sunny LA?'

'Well …' Caroline paused and looked at Ben. 'We have something very exciting to share with you, don't we, Ben?'

Ben lifted his shoulders in a 'don't look at me' gesture before dropping down beside Lizzie at the end of her sunlounger.

'Channel 6 has arranged a huge surprise for the three of you in … Las Vegas!' Caroline's voice rose and she lifted her hands in the air. 'You'll need to pack your things and be down in reception in twenty minutes, where a limousine is waiting to take us all to a private airfield.'

Caroline deflated like a lilo left in the sun as they stared unfazed by her revelation. Samantha glanced at the others. Las Vegas? It wasn't on their original itinerary. Why did she have the feeling that this wouldn't be good?

Lizzie looked first to the cameramen, then Caroline and finally Ben. 'Why aren't you filming? Have you been fired?'

He opened his mouth to reply but Caroline spoke first. 'Of course not. Ben has been working super hard over the past two months and we wanted to give him a break. He'll still be joining you, and filming the sunsets, but let me introduce you to Sandy, Bill and Will,' she pointed towards the new film crew, 'who'll be filming all of you for the next couple of days. Oh, and more good news for you, I'm sure – you won't need to wear your microphone packs for the weekend, thanks to Bill and his blimp.' She pointed at the dead squirrel.

'Are you OK with this?' Lizzie said, her eyes fixing on Ben.

'A break from lugging the camera around will be nice.' He rubbed his hand against his right shoulder. 'As long as you don't mind me tagging along?'

The frown on Lizzie's face disappeared. 'You're a bit like a bad haircut, Ben. Annoying, but you get used to it.'

'Thanks, Lizzie. You know how to make a guy feel welcome.'

'Any time.' She grinned.

Samantha glanced at Caroline and watched the uncontained glee spread across her face. Why did Samantha get the impression that the new camera crew were here for more than just giving Ben a break? Jaddi had shown Samantha the articles speculating a romance between Ben and Lizzie, and she had to admit, the pair were getting on well, but a relationship? Samantha wasn't so sure. What was Caroline up to?

'That settles it, then.' Caroline clapped her hands together. 'Let's get moving.'

Samantha fought to contain the smirk twitching on her face as they remained seated.

'Did you say twenty minutes?' Lizzie flopped back onto the sunlounger and closed her eyes.

Caroline stood for another moment. 'Right, well, I'll see you out the front then.' She stepped away and walked in the direction of the motel lobby, her heels clicking on the paving stones.

Only when she was out of earshot did Jaddi burst out laughing. 'Lizzie, you're too cruel.'

Lizzie grinned and sat up. 'She makes it so easy though.'

'What if we don't want to go to Las Vegas?' Samantha said. 'It wasn't on our original list.'

'It'll be great,' Jaddi said. 'Plus, I don't think we've got a choice, so we might as well enjoy ourselves.'

Samantha stood up, casting a shadow over Lizzie. 'What do you think, Lizzie?'

'Um, not sure. I feel better knowing that Ben's in on, whatever it is.'

They all turned once again to look at Ben.

Ben stood up and held his hands up in surrender. 'I'm sworn to secrecy, so don't even think about asking me. All I can say is that you'll like it, I promise.'

'Come on then,' Jaddi said. 'I'm sure they've got sunloungers at the motel in Vegas.'

CHAPTER 47

Jaddi

It had taken the white stretch limo longer to negotiate its way through Los Angeles traffic and drop them at the private airfield than it had taken them to fly to Clark County, Nevada. For most of the flight, all they'd seen from their windows was an expanse of orange desert. It stretched for endless miles in every direction. Even as the aeroplane began its descent it seemed as if they were dropping into the middle of nowhere. Finally, the familiar icons of the city had appeared in the distance – a replica Eiffel Tower, a black, glass pyramid and a giant sphinx, and a long strip of road with hotels on either side, each one more impressive than the last.

She'd been wrong. They weren't staying in a motel, but rather a five-star hotel with its own casino, right in the centre of the city. Although, as far as Jaddi could tell, every building was a casino of some kind. Even the corner diners advertised slot machines inside.

The Wynn Hotel was built in a long, slim curve that reminded Jaddi of a flat-screen television that looked like it reached all the way to the sky. The lobby was as big as the entire LA motel complex, and dotted with thick red rugs and an entire garden of indoor flowerbeds, and trees decorated in fairy lights. It was comically extravagant and luxurious in equal measure.

'This way, this way,' Caroline said. There was something childlike about the producer's excitement. It zigzagged in the air and whipped around them all. The three of them grinned at each other as they followed Caroline to a corner of the lobby.

One of the cameramen ran ahead and stopped by a collection of high-backed armchairs.

A buzz danced around Jaddi's body. She loved surprises. For a fleeting moment she wondered if Caroline had arranged for Guy Rawson to spend the weekend with them. That would be a surprise to remember. Then she saw Suk, and the buzz stopped dead, and with it her feet.

She couldn't move. The entire lower portion of her body had frozen in a catatonic state. Questions pelted her mind, but her eyes remained fixed on Suk.

From the periphery of her vision, she saw Lizzie rush forward and dive into the arms of her parents and Aaron. From the other side of her, Samantha moved too. She strode towards David, accepting a rose and a kiss before pulling him away.

Then Ben stepped towards the seating area and started shaking hands with Lizzie's dad. All the while Jaddi remained immobile, studying Suk's face. Her smile, how she'd missed that smile. Suk's long hair, tied in a loose side plait. How she'd missed winding her fingers through that hair. Suk's lips, her perfectly delicious lips.

Jaddi's mind willed her feet to move, to charge forward and taste those lips, yet the reality of Suk's presence had rooted her to the floor. She was out. They both were out.

It wasn't that she'd expected to live a lie for her entire life – that was Suk's plan – or it had been – find two nice Sikh boys to marry, and continue their relationship in secret indefinitely. She just hadn't expected to tell the world in one all-encompassing swoop that she was gay.

She'd planned to tell Lizzie and Samantha, and her parents, when the time was right. That time just hadn't arrived yet. She'd tried once, to test the water with her mum. In hindsight, it hadn't been the best time. They'd been in the kitchen preparing a family dinner with her nan and the usual assortment of aunts, cousins and neighbours.

Her mum had been speculating about a wedding between two Bollywood actors.

'I'm not sure they'll be getting married,' Jaddi had said. 'I read somewhere she was gay.'

A silence had filled the kitchen. It was as if she'd accused the actress of drowning puppies in her spare time. Finally, her nan had tutted and replied in a matter-of-fact way, 'Indian women can't be gay.'

It wasn't a 'can't' because a culture steeped in tradition wouldn't allow it, but rather an impossible 'can't'. Like saying, 'you can't be a dog, because you're a cat.' That had been the end of the conversation, and the end of Jaddi's attempts to broach the topic with her family.

Their images flashed like snapshots through her mind – her parents and her nan, her brother Ravi, and her sister Halima. Nothing would ever be the same again. What had Suk done? Her legs no longer felt frozen, but stuck in a quicksand that she would never free herself from.

Jaddi's breath caught in her throat as her eyes darted to the two cameramen. One was filming Lizzie's reunion with her family. The other had moved over to film Samantha. A brief moment of relief swept through her. How much could her parents possibly know? The footage from today wouldn't be aired for another week. She could speak to Caroline, beg her to keep Suk out of it. Maybe it wasn't too late to salvage her secret.

She glanced back at Suk.

'Hi.' Suk mouthed. A small smile pulled at the corner of Suk's mouth, whilst a lone tear ran down her face, and just like that Jaddi's feet responded to her commands. Whatever happened next, they were in it together.

Jaddi ran the distance between them and pulled Suk into a quick embrace.

'I can't believe you're here,' Jaddi said.

'Me either.' Suk shook her head.

'I have so many questions,' Jaddi said, her eyes darting around them.

Suk's body tensed. 'Me too.'

'Let's get out of here.'

'Really?'

Jaddi frowned and glanced around the lobby. 'Come on.'

CHAPTER 48

Samantha

'Hi, baby.' David stepped forward and kissed her cheek.

Samantha coughed as the scent of his aftershave choked her senses. 'What are you doing here?' she asked, dragging him away from the cameras. Everyone was focused on Lizzie, wrapped in her parents' embrace and chattering away at one hundred miles an hour.

'Channel 6 arranged it.' He grinned. 'Great, huh? You look amazing, by the way.'

'But …' Her eyes scanned the group and the film crew, but no one had followed them. 'What are you really doing here?' she asked again.

'I told you.' He smiled, 'Channel 6 invited me to come. They wanted to surprise all of you by flying in the people you love for a weekend in Las Vegas.'

She shook her head. 'Yes, but …'

'By the way –' he leant towards her and lowered his voice '– you never told me Jaddi was gay.'

'What? She's not.' Samantha shook her head again and shot a glance behind her, noticing for the first time a lone, Indian woman, about their age. She had long black hair tied to one side and wide, startled eyes, but she was smiling. Samantha followed her eye line to Jaddi.

'I'm sure that must be a cousin or someone.'

Even as she spoke, doubt began to gnaw its way into her conceptions of Jaddi. Jaddi's comment in the rainforest ran through her head. *I know I'm a massive flirt. It doesn't mean anything.* Had Jaddi been trying to tell her something?

A movement shattered her thoughts. David's face loomed in front of her, and before she could stop him, his plump lips pressed against hers.

A noise escaped her throat. She pressed her hands against his chest and yanked her head back. 'David, what are you doing?'

'Er … kissing my girlfriend, who've I've not seen for two months.'

'I'm not your girlfriend.' Samantha shook her head.

'What?' A single line creased David's forehead. His eyes searched hers.

'I broke up with you. I sent you a text, I blocked your number.'

'No, you didn't.' David shook his head. 'I never received a text like that. Look, I know I was a being a tad needy for the first few weeks, and I probably shouldn't have been texting you so much, but I never meant to upset you.' Her body tensed as he wrapped his arms around her.

'But I … but we … we haven't spoken for a month,' Samantha said, stepping back. 'What did you think that meant?'

'I thought you just wanted a bit of space or maybe your phone had been stolen. It happens all the time. I certainly never imagined that you broke up with me. I've been watching the documentary. You didn't say anything.'

Tension wound around Samantha's shoulders. 'After what you did, can you really tell me you're surprised?' She coughed, masking a sob that caught in her throat.

'Samantha, if I'd have thought for a single second that you'd wanted to end things between us, would I be here right now?' he asked, ignoring her last comment.

Samantha rubbed the palm of her hand across her forehead. She scrunched her face, her mind suddenly blank.

All of a sudden David shrank back. 'But, we love each other, don't we? At least, we did before you left. You'd all but moved in with me last time I checked. Isn't that the plan? You'll come back to London and we'll live together?'

Her head spun. Since being on the trip she hadn't thought about returning to London, or where she'd live.

David picked up her hand and held it in his. 'Baby, I'm sorry. I've been jealous and rather horrid since the moment you told me about the trip. Please. Don't ruin what we have together because of one stupid mistake.'

She hesitated as confusion wound through her. Was he talking about his game or her decision to end their relationship? She caught a movement from the corner of her eye. One of the cameramen was stepping towards them.

'I'm sorry, David,' she said before dropping her gaze to his hand, entwined in her fingers. 'I'm sorry you've come all this way for nothing, but it's over between us. Being apart has made me realise that we're not good for each other.' She pulled her hand free.

It wasn't the 'Fuck off, you wanker' she'd practised in her head all the times she'd fantasised about seeing him again, but considering their location and the camera aimed at their faces it would have to do.

'Oh,' he said.

She held her breath and waited for his temper to flare.

Instead he nodded. 'I'm sorry too. I'll get my bags and check into a different hotel. See you back in London at some point, I guess.'

He kissed her cheek and spun towards a bay of lifts.

Her body slumped against the pillar as she waited for her heartbeat to return to normal. Despite the hurt and anger she felt, it was relief that overwhelmed her. She'd stood her ground, she'd told him it was over and he'd accepted it. But something wasn't right. The kind of guy that David was just didn't fit with his reaction. Where was the explosive temper? The unreasonable demands? The manipulative behaviour? Was this all for the cameras?

It was over … and yet, at the same time, it wasn't. Would she ever be free of him?

CHAPTER 49

Lizzie

Lizzie hugged her mum tighter as she felt her throat closing around her airway.

'Surprise!' her mum said. Lizzie could feel her mum's shoulders shuddering inside their embrace.

'I can't believe you're here. Aaron.' Lizzie touched her hand to his wrist. 'I thought you were injured. Didn't you have a competition to win this week?'

Aaron rotated his wrists around and grinned. 'If I'd have said I was pulling out of the competition for personal reasons then you might've guessed the surprise. This was way more important than any competition.'

Hot tears burnt at the corners of Lizzie's eyes. 'I've got so much to tell you. You wouldn't believe some of the stuff we've done.'

'We have been watching, you know,' Peter replied with his 'dad chuckle', which made Lizzie's heart swell. It sounded like a mix between a Father Christmas 'ho, ho, ho' and a dog barking, but it was her dad's laugh, and it always made merriment dance through her.

'I forgot.' Lizzie grinned.

'Tell us anyway,' her mum said, dabbing a tissue under her eyes. 'I want to hear it.'

'Oh, Evelyn.' Her dad rolled his eyes. 'She's only watched every episode ten times. She probably knows more about what you've been doing that you do.' Peter stretched an arm around his wife and dropped a kiss on the top of her head.

'And you haven't?' Her mum smiled. 'Which reminds me, where's Ben?' She dropped her voice to a whisper. 'Is he filming? Are we allowed to say hello, or is that not cool?'

Lizzie laughed. 'They can still hear you, Mum, even if you whisper. Ben's not filming this weekend.' She spun around and waved him over.

'Hello, Mr Appleton, Mrs Appleton. It's nice to meet you,' Ben said, shaking their hands, which for some reason made Lizzie laugh again.

'Nice to finally meet you, Ben, and call me Peter,' her dad replied.

'We're so grateful for everything you've done for Lizzie,' Evelyn said, 'and for calling us when you did. It means so much to us to know that Lizzie is being looked after.'

'You've been calling my mum and dad?' She fixed her eyes on him and felt the familiar lurch in her stomach, urging her to move towards him.

Ben furrowed his forehead. 'I was hoping you wouldn't find out. It was just the once, whilst you were in hospital on the Gold Coast.'

'Why?'

'Because that idiot Harrison had called the papers and was standing on the steps of the hospital telling anyone who'd listen that you'd lost your sight. I knew it wouldn't be long before it hit the British media, so I thought your parents would want to know you were OK.'

'Oh.' Lizzie stared at Ben. He smiled at her. 'Thanks, I guess,' she said, her stomach turning in somersaults.

Aaron stretched his hands above his head and opened his mouth in a long yawn. 'Not that it's not great to see you, sis, but I need to close my eyes for a minute, or have a shower or something, if I'm going to be awake for this helicopter ride later.'

'What helicopter ride?'

'Caroline's arranged it,' Ben said. 'For all of us. You'll be watching the sun set over the Grand Canyon from a helicopter tonight.'

'And,' Aaron continued, 'we're all staying in a massive suite on the forty-second floor. It even has a kitchen and a private butler,' Aaron said. 'You can pick up the phone, day or night, and ask him for anything.'

'Wow.' Lizzie cast her eyes around the lobby, searching for Caroline. She needed to say thank you, but the producer had disappeared, along with Jaddi. She caught sight of Samantha and David huddled in the corner.

'I think we'll go for a quick shower and change too,' her mum added. 'We set off for the airport at a ridiculous hour this morning.'

'OK, Mum. Good idea. I'd better just say hi to David, then I'll come up.'

'We had a nice chat with him on the plane. Didn't we, Peter? And Jaddi's friend, Suk; she's very nice too.'

'She?' Lizzie frowned, her mind reeling. Had she missed something?

'That was her name, wasn't it, Aaron? Jaddi's ... er ... friend?'

'Yep.' He nodded.

'See you upstairs in a bit,' Peter said, before kissing her cheek.

Her eyes followed her family across the lobby. Pain gripped her chest. She thought she'd made peace with it – only having three months left. Now though, she wasn't so sure. Seeing her family made the enormity of her situation wash over her again. Maybe she should have stayed at home, soaking up every last minute of her time with them.

'I told you that you'd like it.' Ben's words startled her. A dizzying uncertainty clawed at her thoughts. She felt herself nod and turned in search of Samantha.

'Hey, where's David?' Lizzie said, stepping towards the pillar Samantha was leaning against.

'I … er … we broke up,' Samantha said, her eyes wide and staring.

'What? Just now?'

'Sort of. I've known for a while it was over. Spending time away from him, and with you guys, has made me realise that he wasn't good for me, you know? He came here expecting us to still be fine.' She shrugged as if it was no big deal, but Lizzie could tell by the pale colour of her complexion that Samantha was masking her emotions, or trying to at least.

'Why didn't you say something?' Lizzie stepped forwards and hugged Samantha's rigid body.

'I didn't want to spoil your trip,' Samantha said. 'It's not like you haven't got enough to worry about.'

'Oh, honey,' Lizzie said, throwing an arm around Samantha's shoulder, 'I knew something was wrong in Vietnam. You were so quiet. Anyway, you breaking up with Mr Control Freak isn't bad news.'

'I thought you and Jaddi liked him?'

Lizzie tilted her head and gave a wry smile. 'Probably about as much as you liked Harrison.'

'Oh.' Samantha frowned.

'I've really missed you at the flat, you know. Jaddi never makes me a cup of tea in the morning and leaves it by my bed. When we get back to London, it will be just like it—' Lizzie stopped and bit down on her lower lip.

She dropped her gaze rather than stare at the anguish crumbling on Samantha's face. Nothing would be as it was. There would be no going back.

A silence grew between them.

'I can't think about going back yet,' Samantha said. Fresh tears welled in her eyes.

Hurt jabbed at Lizzie's chest. What could she say to help Samantha, or herself? Nothing.

'Where're your mum and dad?' Samantha asked, drawing in a long breath. 'I haven't said hello yet.'

'They've gone for a shower. Caroline's booked us all on this sunset helicopter thing over the Grand Canyon.'

'She's really pulled out all the stops,' Samantha said.

'Tell me about it. She's even booked us all a suite, according to Aaron.'

'Seriously? You mean I won't have to put up with your night mutterings and Jaddi's snoring for two nights?'

'Looks that way.'

'Talking of Jaddi –' Samantha scanned the lobby '– did you see where she went?'

'I'm not sure. Suk's here. Maybe they went to look around.'

'That was Suk? As in, Jaddi's-secret-relationship Suk?' Samantha's mouth dropped open.

'I think so.' Lizzie nodded. 'My mum said she introduced herself as Suk.'

'Um ... did you know Suk was female?' Samantha asked.

'You mean, did I have any clue that our best friend who we've lived with for nine years was in a relationship with a girl?'

Samantha nodded. 'Yes.'

Lizzie shook her head. 'None whatsoever. You?'

'Nope.' Samantha shook her head. 'Although, for some reason, I'm not surprised. Do you know what I mean?'

'I was thinking the same thing. She's always been kind of protective about her love life. She was forever walking out of the room or the door whenever we tried to get any information out of her.'

'No wonder she was hiding Suk from her family, though. I mean, that's going to be tough on both of them,' Samantha said. 'But what about us? Aren't you just a little hurt that she didn't tell us?'

'I don't think I am,' Lizzie said. Lizzie stared into Samantha's pale-blue eyes when she spoke. 'Sometimes, people keep secrets from the ones they love the most to protect them from being hurt. They start down a road and before long they know there's no going back. But whatever we're feeling right now, we need to put it to one side and look at the bigger picture. Our friend needs our support, now more than ever.' Lizzie paused. 'She'll need your support,' she corrected in a low voice.

Samantha's face fell. She opened her mouth and closed it again before shaking her head and pulling Lizzie in for a hug. Lizzie felt a jolt of guilt as she hugged her back.

'Come on, let's go and meet Suk,' Lizzie said a moment later, taking Samantha's arm.

CHAPTER 50

Jaddi

'I still don't understand how you're here.' Jaddi closed her eyes behind her sunglasses and dropped her bare feet over the edge of the pool. The cool water on her skin was heaven in the burning heat of the day.

They'd found a secluded spot on the far side of one of the four hotel swimming pools. Each pool was connected by a narrow swimming lane, which ran the entire width of the hotel. The pool they'd chosen was furthest away from the càbanas, the casino, and an outside bar – away from the older couples sunbathing, the groups of men and women their age drinking colourful liquids from tall glasses, and those in between, enjoying their holiday.

Suk dropped her gaze to the pool and ran her fingers across the edge of the glistening water. 'I've missed you so much.' Tears teetered on her eyelids before cascading down her face. 'It half killed me to wait until they'd put the episodes on catch-up,' she whispered as the beat of music drifted towards them, 'so I could watch it on my iPad when everyone else was in bed.'

'So your mum and dad haven't seen it?' A spark of hope shot through Jaddi. Maybe it wasn't too late.

A smile touched Suk's lips. 'Are you kidding? You know they won't watch anything unless it has Kamal Haasan in it.'

'Do they even know you're here?' Jaddi asked.

Suk shook her head. 'I've missed you so much,' she said again, placing her hand on top of Jaddi's.

Jaddi yanked her hand free and glanced around the pool, ignoring the burst of warmth that had radiated from Suk's touch. 'Where do they think you are then?'

'I don't know.'

Jaddi drew in a sharp breath and stared at Suk's face from behind her sunglasses. Who was this person? The Suk she'd said goodbye to in London cared about what her parents thought. She cared so much that she would glance over her shoulder every five minutes whenever they were together, no matter how remote their location. Suk cared so much that she'd spent hours fantasising to Jaddi about the two of them marrying brothers, living together in one house, and cementing their secret and their futures forever.

Suk's parents would care too. They cared so much about where Suk was, who she was with, what she was doing, that she'd been forbidden to go to the shopping centre with Jaddi on a Saturday afternoon when they were sixteen, or anywhere in fact, unless she was accompanied by a member of her family.

There were two exceptions to this rule. Suk was allowed to go to work at Jaddi's dad's car company, where she took bookings, dealt with the admin and occasionally drove the cars to the carwash and back.

The other exception was dating. Now that they were in their late twenties both girls were under pressure to marry, Suk more so. Once Suk's mother had exhausted her family and friendship network to find Suk a suitable match, she'd turned to Sikh dating websites. Her mother, pretending to be Suk, had scoured the websites for eligible men, messaged them, and then if she'd liked what she'd read, sent Suk off to meet them.

It seemed illogical to Jaddi that Suk's parents forbade their twenty-eight-year-old daughter from seeing her friends by herself, but they had no problem whatsoever with sending Suk out to meet complete strangers, simply because he ticked the right boxes on a website.

Jaddi had used this information to their advantage half a dozen times in the past year, by signing up to the same dating websites, and creating fake male profiles that she knew would appeal to Suk's mother. After two or sometimes three dates, where Suk and Jaddi had spent precious time alone together, her mother would invite the man to meet Suk's family, at which point Jaddi would either decline and end the relationship, or accept, but in doing so let slip something which would lead Suk's mother to end it instead. It wasn't hard to find something Suk's parents didn't approve of. Any suggestion of Suk becoming more Western had always done the trick.

'What's going on, Suk? Jaddi asked. 'Why are you so relaxed about this? Before I left, you didn't even want me to tell my best friends.'

'Things change,' Suk mumbled.

'What things? Suk, this doesn't make any sense.' Jaddi closed her eyes. She didn't recognise the sound of her own voice.

'I love you,' Suk said. 'I thought you felt the same way.'

'I do, of course I do, but I thought we were on the same page about this. Last time we spoke about coming out, we agreed it wasn't the right thing to do.'

'You didn't want to walk away from your family,' Suk said, her tone suddenly hard.

'Neither did you.' Jaddi shook her head, thinking of the last time she'd seen Uncle Prem. It was a cousin's wedding and he'd worn a magenta pink turban. *Old wine, new labels, Jaddi*. That had been his favourite saying. She must have heard it a hundred times. He'd always said it in the context of current affairs, but she wondered now, was history about to repeat itself? She couldn't let that happen.

'Suk, please tell me what's going on here?' Jaddi asked.

Before Suk could answer a voice shouted from the doorway of the hotel. 'There they are.'

Panic circled Jaddi's head as Lizzie, Samantha, and Ben, followed by the film crew, made their way towards them. Scenarios and explanations raced through her mind whilst her legs ached to jump up and run.

'We wondered where you'd got to,' Samantha said, grinning.

Jaddi attempted a smile, hoping to mask the whirlwind of panic swirling inside of her. 'We just came out to see the pool. Not bad, uh?' Her voice still sounded wrong. It was too high. Too squeaky.

'Um, are you going to introduce us?' Lizzie said.

'Yes, sorry, this is Suk. Suk, this is Lizzie and Samantha.'

'Hi,' Lizzie and Samantha chorused with a wave of their hands.

'It's nice to finally meet you,' Suk said. 'I've heard so much about you both.'

'And we've heard absolutely nothing about you.' Samantha laughed. She turned to Jaddi and raised her eyebrows.

Jaddi shrugged. She wanted so much to explain but the black lens of the camera stopped her. It might as well have been her father standing behind Lizzie.

'So how long have you two been—' Lizzie began.

'My dad does a lot of business for Suk's dad. They're old friends.' The words flew out of Jaddi's mouth before Lizzie could finish her sentence. Jaddi's eyes avoided the camera. 'We've been friends since we could walk, I guess.'

An awkward silence hovered over them.

It was Ben that spoke first, Ben who saved her. He cleared his throat. 'Why don't we get some lunch,' he said, glancing between Lizzie and Samantha. 'I think these guys have a lot of stuff to catch up on.' His eyes darted back and forth between Lizzie and one of the cameramen. Jaddi could have kissed him then.

'Oh, yes … good idea. Let's do that.' Lizzie grabbed Samantha and pulled her away. 'I hope we'll get to meet you properly a bit later on, Suk.'

Suk nodded. 'I'd like that.'

Alone once more, Jaddi kicked at the cool water with her feet, unable to lift her eyes to look at Suk. How many times had she dreamed about the two of them going away together, lounging by a poolside, drinking cocktails, laughing, kissing? Never having to look over their shoulders or sneak around. So why did this feel so wrong?

'My parents are sending me to India,' Suk said.

'Huh?' Jaddi looked up, her head already shaking in disbelief.

'It's the only way that they won't cut me out of their lives. I move to India and marry a man of their choosing. Oh, and I never see you again.'

'That's crazy.'

'Is it?' Suk raised her eyebrows. 'What did you expect them to say?'

'Hang on a minute,' Jaddi said, the tone of her voice rising again. 'I get why Lizzie's family are here, and why Caroline flew David out, but why you? How did Caroline know? Why did you tell them?' Invisible walls closed in around Jaddi.

Anger flashed across Suk's face. 'Because *you* told the world about us,' Suk snapped.

'No, I didn't.' Even as the words left her mouth, Jaddi realised Suk had to be right. She knew Suk as well as she knew herself. Suk had never once talked about coming out to their families. It had always been Jaddi's musings, not Suk's. Suk telling her parents that she was gay and in love with Jaddi seemed as likely as their families welcoming the news with open arms.

'Yes, you did.' Suk threw her hands in the air. 'In Australia. You were all sitting around the campfire and you told Samantha and Lizzie that you were in love with me.' Suk drew in a shaky breath. Tears continued to stream from her eyes. 'My brother was watching.'

'I … I …' Jaddi faltered. The rainforest trek. She'd blurted Suk's name out after Harrison had accused her of hitting on him. She hadn't realised Ben had been filming. 'I said your name, but I … I didn't say you were you; it could just have easily been a bloke. That's what Samantha and Lizzie assumed. I didn't correct them. Surely, you could have denied it?'

'I tried. Don't you think I tried that?' Suk's voice rose, carrying across the deserted pool. 'Tev accused me outright in front of Dad. I tried to deny it, but they pieced it together. You have no idea what I've been through. My dad literally shoved me out of the front door in my dressing gown.' Suk's shoulders heaved as the words tumbled from her mouth. 'I had no clothes, no shoes, no money, no phone. Nothing. I had to hide around the side of the house until they'd left, and plead with my mum to help me. She wouldn't open the front door. I was lucky she even passed me my bag, phone and some clothes out of the window. Someone at Channel 6 tracked me down through your Facebook friends list and invited me here. I thought that after what you said in Australia about us, I should come.'

'I'm ... I'm sorry. I didn't know any of that. I'm so sorry that I did this to you.' Hurt seared through Jaddi as Suk's pain became hers. Jaddi lifted her sunglasses onto her head and looked into Suk's eyes.

'Where have you been staying?'

'At your flat.' Suk hung her head. 'Sorry, I had the keys. It was the only place I could think of to go.'

'Don't say sorry. I'm glad you did. Does my family know?' Jaddi asked.

'I don't know. Have Ravi or Halima been in touch?'

Jaddi shook her head. Water pricked at the edges of her eyes. A dizzying relief spiralled through her mind as if she'd gulped down a cappuccino on an empty stomach. Her family didn't know. There was still time to salvage this.

'I guess no, then,' Suk said. 'Tev phoned me last week to tell me to come home and pack for India or never come back again. I can't see them telling your dad. It would bring them too much shame.'

'It will be the same for me,' Jaddi said.

A noise escaped Suk's mouth. 'Of course it won't,' she said. 'Sure, your parents will make a big song and dance of cutting you out when they find out, but you know they won't. You might not get to go to the weddings and the festivals but you'll still get invited to dinner. Your mum will still call you most days and moan about how much your dad is working.'

Jaddi closed her eyes again. Was Suk right? Would her family find their own way to accept her sexuality? Or was she also facing the possibility of a lifetime of never seeing or hearing from them again? Never seeing her nephews and nieces, or catching the scent of jasmine in her mum's hair when she was near. Was she prepared to take the risk?

CHAPTER 51

Jaddi

It was his laugh that Jaddi had loved most about her Uncle Prem; a booming whole-body occurrence that stopped conversations and drew people towards him. It was infectious too. Jaddi had been standing on the other side of the dance floor at her cousin's wedding reception, nowhere near her uncle. She couldn't even see him, and yet when his laugh had echoed across the marquee it had sent her into a fit of giggles.

But it was impossible not to think about Prem's laugh without thinking of the darkness that followed his suicide. The weeks and months of devastation that hung over her father and their house. There'd been no explanation for it. Jaddi had had no clue as to why. She'd been thirteen and her parents hadn't even told her he'd died. It was only when she'd found Prem's letter in the bottom of her dad's office drawer that it had all clicked into place. Old wine, new labels, Jaddi thought again.

'What do I do now?' Suk asked, pulling Jaddi's thoughts back to her.

'What do you want to do?'

Suk dropped her head into her hands, her shoulders shaking as she spoke. 'Be with you,' she whispered. Suk sat up and grabbed Jaddi's hands. 'Let's do it. Let's start a life together, a proper one.'

'Suk, I ... I can't. I can't do that to my family. I can't walk away from them.'

'But *I* can?' Suk cried out.

'It's different. This is Uncle Prem all over again. I can't do it to them or to myself.'

'But you don't even know what happened with Prem.'

'I read the letter he sent my dad, his ... his suicide note. He was gay. He'd lived the lie, married a woman, who was mean and spiteful, just to please the family. When he finally found the courage to leave her and come out to his family, they cast him out. They acted like he'd never existed. Wouldn't speak to him, even when he begged them. He couldn't live without them. They were his exact words: I can't live without you, my family, your blessing. So I won't live at all.'

Suk tightened her grip on Jaddi's hands. 'But that's exactly why they won't make the same mistake with you. And anyway, you're stronger than him. I know you are. And you have me. Do you think I want to live without my family? Of course I don't. But I don't want to live in India either; I don't want to live without you. We have to make a choice. Tell your family before they find out watching the documentary.'

Jaddi shook her head. 'I'll lie. I'll tell them the producer made a mistake. I'll find a Sikh boy with a name that starts with Suk – Sukhit, Sukhiam, Sukhnam. I know my parents. They'll believe me.'

'So that's it then. This was all for nothing. Our relationship was for nothing. You ruined my life for nothing.' She spat out the final words as she leapt to her feet.

Pain clenched Jaddi's heart. 'Please understand, Suk, I can't walk away from my family. I'm so sorry for saying what I did – I thought the camera was off. If you were in my shoes, wouldn't you do the same?'

Suk's voice softened. 'They'll still be part of your life; I know they will. It's me who won't have a family anymore, not you.'

Jaddi swallowed. 'I can't risk it.'

Suk gasped and broke into a run.

Jaddi watched Suk weave around the pool, her long braid flapping against her back as she darted through a door and disappeared.

'I'm sorry,' Jaddi whispered, allowing the tears to fall.

She needed to find Caroline, Jaddi thought, and beg her not to show Suk in the next episode. She'd thrown Suk to the wolves, destroyed her life and their relationship, and if she was going to live with that choice for the rest of her life, then Jaddi needed to make damn sure it wasn't for nothing. She couldn't risk her family finding out the truth too.

CHAPTER 52

Samantha

Samantha's eyes roamed the surroundings of the hotel as they sat down at an empty table in the terrace restaurant. Exquisite, colourful, glass butterflies hung all over the walls, drawing her attention.

The relief of ending things with David had dissipated leaving an exhaustion clinging to her body. She stifled a yawn.

'Samantha?' Lizzie said.

'Huh?' She shook her head. 'Sorry, I was miles away. Did you say something?'

'I just asked, what you were planning to eat? It's going to have to be the burger for me.'

'Um …' Samantha scanned the list of dishes. 'I don't know, I'm not that hungry.'

A movement beside the table changed her focus.

'Oh, there you are,' Evelyn said. 'Peter,' she called out, 'they're over here.'

'Mum,' Lizzie said with a smile, 'that was a quick shower.'

'Of course it was.' Evelyn leant down and hugged Lizzie. Her hair still glistened with water. 'We only have two days with you, after all. And, Samantha –' she smiled and held out her arms as she moved around the table '– I've not even said hello yet.'

Samantha stood up and allowed herself to be drawn into a tight embrace. The smell of Evelyn's perfume transported her to Christmas Day, and sitting around the dinner table, pulling crackers and laughing at the bad jokes inside. Evelyn had taken Samantha under her wing since their first Christmas break during university. Lizzie had dragged Samantha, against all of her protests, to Aldeburgh to join Lizzie and her family for Christmas dinner. 'I've already told my mum that you're spending Christmas alone,' Lizzie had said. 'If you don't come with me, I'll never hear the end of it.' Samantha had spent Christmas with the Appletons ever since.

'It's so lovely to see you.' Evelyn squeezed Samantha. 'How are you enjoying the trip?'

'It's fantastic, thank you,' Samantha said. 'There have been some ups and downs, but I'm loving our time together.'

'That's so lovely to hear.' Evelyn smiled. 'Shall we get some more seats here?' she asked.

'Have mine,' Samantha replied, stepping out from the wicker chair. 'I'm not that hungry. I might go check out the hotel room and grab a quick shower myself.'

'Are you sure, dear? I didn't mean to scare you off.'

'No, honestly, it's fine.' She turned to Ben. 'Do you know what time we're supposed to leave for the sunset helicopter thing?'

'Three o'clock,' Ben replied, also standing up. 'I'll leave you to it as well,' he said, as Peter and Aaron stepped up behind Lizzie.

'Oh, no, you don't,' Evelyn said, taking his arm. 'Let us buy you lunch. It's the least we can do.'

He glanced at Lizzie.

She shrugged with a smile. 'You might as well sit down. My mum doesn't often take no for an answer.'

'Shall we meet in the same place in the lobby at three?' Samantha asked, already stepping away from the table.

'Make it two-forty-five,' Ben called after her. 'I think Caroline wants to be leaving by three, and we all know how she gets when things don't run on time.'

Samantha nodded as she spun around and walked towards the lifts. She waited a beat before glancing over her shoulder. The two cameramen hadn't stopped filming since they'd left LA, but at least their focus seemed to be centred on Lizzie.

She pressed the call button by a row of lifts and imagined the feel of the soft mattress against her body. Maybe she should have a power nap, she thought as another yawn took hold.

'Jaddi? Caroline?' she called out as she entered the suite. 'Anyone here?'

A corridor ran to her left and right, whilst floor-to-ceiling windows covered one side of the living room in front of her. The view faced out towards the back of the hotel and to an entire city beyond the main strip. White three-storey apartment buildings and houses lined the streets – all the signs of everyday life away from the casinos, the hotels, and the tourist attractions. Just past the city, orange hilltops and empty desert loomed, as if at any moment it might rise up and swallow the city into its sandy depths.

A muffled noise startled her. She heard a movement from somewhere in the suite.

Samantha twisted in the direction of the sound, just as a force struck the side of her head, knocking her to the ground. Her thoughts fell like a broken puzzle. The pieces were still there, but the picture was incoherent.

A shadow passed over her, then pain exploded from the top of her head. A hand grabbed her hair, yanking her head up from the floor. She slapped at the fist clenching her hair as it dragged her across the floor. The prickles of the carpet burnt against her bare legs as she kicked out her feet and tried to stand. Her eyes darted back and forth but all she could see was the floral Artex pattern on the ceiling.

The pain eased as the hand released her hair. Samantha tried to steady herself, but she was still facing upwards and couldn't find her balance. Momentum carried her forwards until she slammed into the wall. The strength drained from her body as she fell in a heap on the floor.

Samantha opened her eyes and for a split second she thought the blow to her head had blurred her vision, but then the warmth of his breath brushed her lips and her pupils focused on David's face, millimetres from her own.

She shrieked.

'Do you think I'm stupid?' He grabbed both of her wrists in one iron grip.

'No,' she said. A quiver ran over her body.

'That's strange, because earlier you acted like I was pretty stupid.'

'I … I didn't. David please, what are you doing? I don't think you're stupid.'

'Of course I knew you'd broken up with me. I knew your bitch friends had been whispering in your ear, telling you I wasn't good enough for you.' He snorted. 'What a joke.'

'Why did you come then?' Samantha whimpered. A sharp fear clutched her heart. It was like nothing she'd ever felt before. Her eyes scanned the bedroom, searching for anything that could help her. A large bed dominated the space. Two ornate cabinets sat either side, each with an oval-shaped lamp sitting on top. Then she saw it – the telephone. She swallowed a mouth full of saliva and struggled to collect her thoughts. She just needed a chance to use it.

David grinned. 'I couldn't let you go without saying a proper goodbye. What a waste that would've been.' He chuckled. 'I have to say the hand-luggage restrictions made things a little awkward at first but, do you know what? It was rather fun improvising. Take this phone,' he said, reaching for the telephone with his free hand and yanking it towards him. Using his knee for leverage, he ripped the wire away from the base unit, taking with it her glint of hope. His eyes, wide and unblinking, continued to stare at her as he spoke. 'Who needs handcuffs when this will do the same job? Here, let me show you.'

He pulled her wrists towards him and began coiling the wire around them.

Samantha gasped as the plastic wound tighter and tighter around her wrists. She couldn't let him do this. She dragged her legs out from under her and bucked them towards David. He grunted and released his grip as her foot impacted with his abdomen. Adrenaline flooded her body. She jumped to her feet and leapt over him.

A second later she felt his hand clamp around her ankle and pull her to the floor. In one swift movement he lurched forward, forcing the air from her lungs as his weight bore down on her body. She coughed and swallowed back a mouthful of vomit. Her heart was beating so fast she thought it might stop dead from the excursion. A lightness drifted through her head, from the oxygen being pumped at speed through her veins, or from the blow in the living room, she didn't know.

'If you don't want me to punch you again, then I'd stop struggling. Me, I'm fine with it either way, but the end result will be the same,' he said, his voice chipper as if he was discussing targets in the weekly team meeting.

Samantha continued to draw in heaving breaths as he wound the wire even tighter around her wrists.

'David.' The side of her head throbbed as she spoke. Her voice sounded muffled as if she was listening to herself from the next room.

'Shh.' He bent over her and placed his index fingers against her lips. She reeled at his touch and scrunched her eyes shut. 'I'll be right back.'

Her eyes shot open as his words filtered through the fog. He was leaving her alone.

'Don't worry, I'm only going to get my camera,' he said, reading her thoughts. 'I left it in the living room. Since you like being filmed so much, I thought we'd make another of our own little documentaries. That way I can watch our farewell anytime I like. I'll send you a copy too, if you want?'

He laughed again and turned as if to leave, but stopped and stood over her. Another explosion of pain hit her stomach as his shoe landed just above her belly button. Seconds passed as she tried and failed to draw breath. For a moment she thought her lungs had collapsed, but then at last she gasped. Her head swam as she pulled her body into the foetal position and vomited.

By the time she was able to look up again, David was back, holding a small video camera on a tripod.

He exhaled a long sigh like an exasperated parent unable to reason with a child. 'Looks like we'll need to move rooms now, doesn't it? I don't want to be smelling that stench whilst we're trying to have our farewell fun.'

She wiped her bound hands against her mouth and used her elbows to push herself up to sitting. A new thought struck her – Lizzie and Ben would expect her to be in the lobby by three, but would they come looking for her when she didn't turn up, or assume she'd decided not to go? How much time had already passed? It felt like hours since she'd stepped over to the window and admired the view, but she knew that was impossible. Minutes seemed more likely.

'Can you walk or do I need to drag you again?'

'Walk.' She coughed, scrambling to her feet. Her legs wobbled but she fought to stay upright.

He looped his arm through hers, just as he'd done hundreds of times in their relationship, and pulled her into the corridor and along to the next bedroom.

As her gaze fell onto the bed, her legs stopped moving. Images of his game flooded her head. If that was what he'd done to her when she'd been a willing participant, what would he do to her now?

She jerked her arm and tried to move away, but his hold was too strong. 'Fine, have it your way,' he said.

David placed the tripod and camera on the floor and turned to face her. In a single movement, he scooped her legs up and threw her onto the bed. She hit the soft springs of the mattress but then kept rolling, colliding with the lamp and the nightstand and dropping to the floor.

CHAPTER 53

Samantha

Samantha flinched as she opened her eyes. A sharp pain resonated from a long cut on her right arm where she'd struck the edge of the nightstand during her fall. Droplets of blood, the colour of the dried ketchup around the rim of the bottle, trickled towards her wrist.

She held her breath and forced herself to listen over the throbbing in her head. Was she hearing things or did a door shut inside the suite? Relief swept through her as a voice called out.

'In here,' David replied.

Samantha's eyes shot to the open doorway as the sound of flip-flops padded along the corridor.

'Ben?' Jaddi said. The sound of her friend's voice sent a chill racing down Samantha's spine.

Samantha gripped the bedside table with both hands and pulled herself up. 'No.' In her head the word had been loud and full of fear and warning, but the noise that came out was barely a whisper. Hot tears welled in Samantha's eyes.

David's face contorted into a manic grin as he stepped out of sight behind the open door.

'Sam?' Jaddi said, taking a step into the room. 'What are you—' Her eyes bulged as her gaze fell to the ligature around Samantha's wrist.

'Run!' Samantha shouted, launching herself across the bed towards them just as the door slammed into Jaddi's body.

David leapt forward and yanked the door open again as Jaddi's body flew back. David dived on top of her as she dropped to the floor. She yelped and writhed her body back and forth.

'Get off me!' Jaddi shouted.

Samantha clambered off the bed. Her only thought was for Jaddi as she jumped onto David's back and hooked her bound hands around his neck. She pulled her arms back, forcing David away from Jaddi.

'Run,' she croaked as she felt David's weight push her backwards to the edge of the bed.

Jaddi pulled herself up, but she didn't run. Instead, she charged at David. He raised his knee up and kicked out, striking Jaddi in the stomach and sending her careening back out of the doorway. At the same time, the force of his elbow struck Samantha's ribs. She groaned, relaxing her hold on him just enough to allow him to drop to the floor and out of her grip. He spun around and pulled something from his pocket. The coiled metal of a corkscrew glinted in the sunlight from the window.

'Another good thing about upmarket hotel rooms,' he said, breathing hard, 'is that they usually have a corkscrew. Pretty handy really, if you think about it. This little thing can cause a lot of damage.'

He knelt to the ground and dropped one knee onto Jaddi's chest, pinning her down as he touched the point of the corkscrew against the skin on her neck. She gasped but didn't try to move.

'Should've listened to Samantha, Jaddi,' he said. 'Should've run whilst you had the chance.' He stared at Samantha, his pupils large and dilated. There was something unnatural about the glaze of his eyes, and she wondered for the first time if he might be on drugs.

'Samantha, be a dear and pass me the wire from that phone, would you please? And remember, try anything stupid and this corkscrew is going into Jaddi's neck.'

Jaddi cried out again as he pierced her skin with the corkscrew. A drop of blood trickled out from the wound.

'Don't hurt her, please, David.' Samantha moved to the far side of the room and pulled the telephone away from the wall. The receiver clattered against the handset from the violent shaking of her hands.

The wire resisted for a moment, pulling taut before giving a small pop and jumping free from the wall.

She dropped the wire into his free hand as her mind raced through scenarios. Her eyes flicked to the doorway and back to David as he focused on tying Jaddi's wrists together. She might be able to jump past him and run to the hotel room door, but would she make it? And what would happen to her if she didn't? Another thought crossed her mind and pained her just as much as the strike from David's fist – what would happen to Jaddi if Samantha did make it? How long would it take her to find help? Two minutes? Five minutes? She couldn't leave Jaddi alone with him, not for a second.

'I'll kill her if you so much as try,' he said, reading her thoughts and sending another shiver down her body. 'Now be a good girl and pop yourself on the bed, that's it, all the way back against the pillows.' He nodded as she shuffled up to the head rest. 'You,' he said, looking at Jaddi, 'have just earned yourself a starring role in our farewell video.' David's tone remained jovial as if he was salesman offering her a good deal on a new car.

'David, please let us go,' Samantha said. 'This has gone too far. You were upset, I understand that, but things have got out of hand. If ...' She paused and racked her brain for the words that would filter through the madness which seemed to have consumed him. 'If you walk out the door right now, I promise you we won't call the police, or tell anyone. Just let us go.'

He threw back his head, cachinnating a sound full of menace and fear in equal measure. 'Oh Samantha, it's far too late for that.'

'You won't get away with this,' Jaddi snarled at him.

David turned to face Jaddi. 'Actually, I will. By now your friends will all have left for a three-hour excursion to the Grand Canyon. By the time they get back, I'll be long gone.' He chuckled.

David fastened the wire around Jaddi's wrists and pulled her up from the floor. 'The only problem with these hotel beds is that they don't have any posts to tie things too. You remember how much fun that was, don't you, Samantha?' He shoved Jaddi onto the bed. 'Looks like we'll need a bit more improvisation. Never mind, we have plenty of time.'

CHAPTER 54

Lizzie

Lizzie watched Ben's fingers drum against the overstuffed armchair and smiled. He was clearly lost without a camera to fiddle with. The lift chimed again, pulling her attention to the shining gold doors as they opened into the bustling lobby. Half a dozen people moved out of the lift; none of them were Jaddi or Samantha. Where were her friends?

All of a sudden a warmth crept over her neck and face. She could feel his eyes on her again.

'Do I have ketchup on my chin, or something?' Lizzie wiped her fingers over her lips and smiled at Ben.

'Are you feeling all right?' he asked, ignoring her question.

She nodded. 'I'm great. Why? Do I look ill?'

'No.' He looked into her eyes. 'You look –' a half-smile stretched across his face, crinkling the skin around his eyes '– fine.'

'So what's wrong? You're doing your frowning face.'

'My what?'

'Your frowning face.' She laughed. 'Like this.' Lizzie scrunched up her forehead, flared her nostrils and pouted her lips, before doubling over in a fit of giggles.

'Hey.' Ben smirked. 'My face doesn't look anything like that.'

'It does; you've just never seen it before because you've always got a hump of plastic in front of it.'

Before Ben had a chance to retort, the lift chimed another arrival and Caroline glided towards them. Her eyes were glued to the screen of her mobile, and yet she weaved around plants and people as if she had a second set of eyes in her forehead.

She smiled a greeting at Ben and Lizzie, before glancing across to the opposite sofa and nodding to Lizzie's family. Aaron lifted a hand in greeting as his mouth stretched into a wide yawn. Like a wave in a football stadium, it passed between them, hitting her dad and then her mum, before moving back to Aaron.

'Where's the rest of you?' Caroline asked.

'It's only just gone quarter to,' Ben said. 'They'll be here in a minute, don't worry. We lost track of time ourselves over lunch.'

It had been fun spending time with her family and with Ben. There had been an initial awkwardness and small talk about the weather and jet lag as her mum and dad had thrown furtive looks at the three members of Caroline's film crew, stepping in a slow perimeter around the table. Then Ben had turned to her mum and asked, 'Has Lizzie always been sarcastic?'

Evelyn had laughed. 'Born with it.'

The rest of their lunch had flown by as her parents had regaled Ben with stories of Lizzie and Aaron's childhood, whilst Lizzie and Aaron had laughed along, hid behind their napkins, and declared their parents outright liars. Like the time she'd tried to dye her hair red one Christmas Eve and had spent the entire holiday hiding her bright orange mop under a hat. Or the dozens of times they'd taken Aaron to A&E because he'd been attempting double summersaults off the top of the sofa and hit his head.

'Have you tried their mobiles?' Caroline asked, tapping her foot against the polished floor.

'Yes, and neither of them are answering,' Lizzie said.

Caroline's eyes fell back to the phone in her hand. Tap, tap, tap, her foot continued.

Ben leaned closer to Lizzie before he spoke. 'How many times have you known Samantha to be late?'

'Samantha?' Lizzie raised her eyebrows. 'Never. Jaddi, though, always.'

'That's what I thought.' He nodded, glancing at his watch.

Caroline pulled her wrist up to her face, looked at her watch again and gave a loud sigh. 'Right, well, we simply can't wait any longer, so we'd best go without them. I've already sent the crew ahead to the launch area to set up.'

'Hang on, Caroline,' Ben said. 'We've still got a few minutes. Let me run up and check the suite. I bet they've fallen asleep and forgotten to set an alarm.'

'Fine, but be quick.'

'I'll come too.' Lizzie sprung from the chair and jogged after Ben. The urgency of his movements caused an unease to worm its way around her.

'Maybe you should wait down here,' he said.

'Why?' she asked. 'What's wrong? Do you know something I don't?'

He paused and stared at her for a moment before answering. 'I'm sure it's nothing.'

Ben jabbed his finger against the button causing a red light to illuminate behind it. He pressed it several more times anyway.

'You know that doesn't make it come any faster, don't you?' Lizzie said.

He shrugged, his gaze fixing on the plain white door next to the lift.

'Don't even think about it,' Lizzie said. 'Waiting a minute for the lift to arrive will be a lot quicker that sprinting up forty-two floors.'

He nodded but didn't speak.

As the lift doors began to open, Ben darted in, almost tripping over a woman and her suitcase. She tutted and gave a shake of her head as she wheeled her luggage out of the way and walked into the lobby. Lizzie stepped in after him.

The key card was in Ben's hand as the lift arrived and the doors slid open. Without a word, he ran into the corridor.

'Ben?' she called, her feet sinking into the plush red carpet as she chased after him. He didn't stop until he reached the door of the suite.

She made it to his side just as he whipped the key card out of the lock. They waited for the small red bulb to illuminate green. It didn't.

'Here,' Lizzie said, brushing his hand aside and feeling the warmth radiate from his body as she stepped closer. 'You're doing it too fast.'

She repeated his action, pulling the plastic card slowly from the lock. A split second later, the bulb flashed green. Ben gripped the handle in his hand and pulled it as far down as it would go before pushing his weight against the door. It opened without a sound. He touched his finger to his lips as they entered the suite.

Lizzie frowned but did as he asked.

They stepped into a living room area with sofas and a glass coffee table. To one side was a small kitchen, but it was the expansive floor-to-ceiling window and the view over Las Vegas that drew Lizzie's eyes, and Ben's, she noticed a moment later, as his body froze beside her.

All of a sudden, Ben's upper body lurched forward, his hands gripping the back of the sofa. It seemed as though his feet were encased in concrete and someone had pushed him.

'Ben,' she said, her voice low as she followed his gaze to the window. 'Speak to me, what's going on?'

With his eyes still fixed on the window, he pushed himself to standing and nodded. 'I forgot we'd travelled up so high. I'm fine.'

Lizzie stepped closer, and placed a hand on his cheek, guiding his gaze away from the window and on to her. 'Focus on me for a second,' she said, staring into the depths of his eyes until she felt the muscles in his body begin to relax. 'Let's find Samantha and Jaddi and get out of he—'

Out of nowhere a scream pierced the air. Lizzie spun towards the corridor and the direction of the noise.

'Please let Jaddi go,' she heard Samantha beg. 'I'll play your game, but please let her go.' The fear in Samantha's voice sent a shiver down her spine.

'Enough!' a man's voice replied.

Lizzie jumped towards the noise, but Ben grabbed her arm and pulled her back towards him.

'Wait,' he mouthed, picking up the phone on the coffee table. A moment later, he spoke into the receiver. 'I need security, now!' he said, his voice a low, urgent whisper.

'Stay behind me,' he said, darting along the corridor.

Another screech rung in the air. The door to the second bedroom was pushed closed but not shut.

As they reached the door, Ben stopped. Panic and frustration gripped Lizzie's body. She wanted to barge into the room but Ben's frame blocked her path. Slowly, Ben pressed his fingers against the door and pushed it open an inch.

Through the gap, Lizzie could see Samantha's face and body. Her right leg and right arm were bound to Jaddi's left, whilst her other hand was pulled out at a right angle to her body and tied to a taut wire. She couldn't see where the wire ended, but she guessed a radiator below the window.

A figure passed in front of the gap. Lizzie's heartbeat began to pound in her ears, and in front of her she felt Ben steady his feet.

'That should do it,' the man said. 'Don't you think, ladies?'

Lizzie knew the voice instantly. David. His back was to the doorway as he waved a small object in the air. Metal glinted in the light from the window. A knife? A blade? Lizzie couldn't tell. This couldn't be happening, she thought over and over.

David placed the object on the edge of the bed and moved his hands to the bottom of his T-shirt. As he pulled it over his head, Ben made his move, rushing into the bedroom and shoving David to the floor. With his arms and his head still immobilised inside the T-shirt, David lashed out with his legs.

As Lizzie dived past them and onto the bed, Ben rolled David onto his front with his face to the floor and sat down hard on the centre of his back. David grunted and tried to buck his body upwards, but it was no use. Ben's hold on him was too tight.

'Oh my God!' Lizzie panted. 'Are you OK?' Her hands shook as she began pulling at the plastic knotted around their hands. Samantha had a long cut on her arm, and Jaddi had a smear of blood on her neck, but they were conscious and nodded their heads.

'Where's Suk? Is she OK?' Jaddi asked, rubbing the wrists of her freed hands.

'I haven't seen her,' Samantha said.

'You don't think he …' Jaddi's eyes widened as she allowed her sentence to trail off.

'I'm not sure, but I don't think so. He didn't say anything,' Samantha replied. Her body began to shake. For a moment Lizzie thought it was the shock hitting her, but then she drew in a wrenching breath. 'I'm so sorry.' Tears streamed down her face.

'It's not your fault,' Jaddi said, placing an arm around Samantha. 'It's that pig down there who should be sorry.'

David kicked against the floor. 'Fucking bitches were asking for it,' he said, his voice muffled behind the T-shirt.

A ball of fire ignited inside Lizzie. Her body moved without thought, spinning towards the figure on the floor. Her fists were clenched so tight she could feel her nails digging into her skin, but she didn't care.

'How dare you hurt my friends,' she hissed, jumping onto the floor and raising her fist.

'Hotel Security,' a man's voice shouted from along the corridor. 'Las Vegas PD are on their way.'

Three men burst into the room.

CHAPTER 55

Lizzie

Lizzie opened the door to her bedroom and waited for her eyes to adjust to the darkness. 'Samantha?' she said.

Objects came into focus: a dresser with a flat-screen television mounted on the wall above it; a night table with a light on top; her backpack resting against an armchair. The room was the mirror image of Samantha's, without the paraphernalia of David's attack – the phone wires, the blood, the broken lamp.

Lizzie's eyes fixed on the bed and the shadowed profile of Samantha, sat bolt upright on the edge, staring at the blank screen of the television as if immersed in a film only she could see.

Lizzie kicked off her sandals and padded bare feet across the carpet.

'How are you doing?' Lizzie asked as she sat down next to Samantha.

'I can't stop shaking,' Samantha said. 'Look.' She released her hands from their position clamped between her thighs and held them up. Even in the darkness it seemed as if an electrical current was running through Samantha's body, causing her hands to judder back and forth, and her teeth to chatter.

'It's the shock. It'll pass.' Lizzie rubbed Samantha's back and tried to formulate the words that would make Samantha all right again, before realising with a stab of pain to her chest that there weren't any. Nothing she could say or do could wipe away the fear and hurt David had caused.

The last few hours had slipped away in a blur of police, crime-scene technicians and paramedics. The police had arrived minutes after the hotel security men had barged into the room. David had been dragged away by two uniformed officers, leaving behind a plain-clothed detective to ask them question after question after question.

Only when they'd each told their part in the event three times, and each been given the all-clear from a paramedic, did the detective leave. Lizzie had guided Samantha through the living room to her own room, before going back to check on Jaddi.

'I'm so sorry, Lizzie.' Samantha dropped forward, burying her face in her hands and unleashing loud, weeping cries.

'It's not your fault, Sam.'

'If I'd have known what David was capable of … I'd never …' she sniffed and sat up. The whites of her eyes shone bright against the darkness as she stared at Lizzie. 'This was supposed to be the trip of a lifetime for you, and I've ruined it. I've ruined your time with your family. I've ruined everything. I'm so sorry.'

'Sam.' Lizzie gripped her friend's shoulders. 'You have to hear me when I say this – this was not your fault. You had no idea David was a whack job, and you had no idea Channel 6 had invited him to Vegas, *and* you had no idea he'd do what he did. You're the victim here. Understand?'

She shook her head, drawing in a shuddering breath. 'I did know. Sort of anyway. In London, the day we left, when Caroline gave us the afternoon off, I saw David.'

Samantha paused for a long time before she continued. 'He called it his game,' she said, emotion rippling through her words. 'God knows how he convinced me to do it—'

'You don't have to tell me now, Sam, if it's too hard.' Lizzie squeezed her hand tighter and wished again that she could take Samantha's pain away.

'It's OK, I want to. It wasn't like this; he didn't attack me or anything. I agreed to it. I let him tie me to the bed and cover my mouth with tape. I let him … I let him hurt me. So I did know some of what he was capable of, and if I'd just said something, anything, they wouldn't have flown him out here and he wouldn't—' The rest of her words morphed into a wailing cry.

'I'll say it again, Sam. It wasn't your fault. Not even a little bit. And you haven't ruined anything, I promise,' Lizzie said in a voice she hoped masked the sudden rage pounding through her. How could he do that to her? Lizzie touched her head against Sam's. 'I would never have agreed to this trip without you, Sam. The only thing you could have done to ruin anything would be to have stayed at home.'

A gentle knock sounded from one of the inside doors. A moment later, it opened and Ben appeared, his profile illuminated from the light in the bedroom behind him.

'Hey,' he said.

'Is that your bedroom? I thought that was a closet,' Lizzie said.

'Adjoining rooms. How are you holding up, Samantha?'

'I'm OK. I can't stop shaking, but I'm OK.'

Ben stepped forward. A moment later, a bedside lamp flicked on. He stepped around the bed and leant against the dresser opposite them. 'Has someone looked at that cut?' He nodded towards the line running from Sam's elbow to her wrist, where it connected with the red bracelet grooves of the ligature marks.

She nodded. 'One of the ambulance guys cleaned it. It's not that bad.'

'How about your head?' Ben asked, glancing at Lizzie and causing a rush of gratitude to wash over her. How different would today have been without Ben? She couldn't begin to formulate the answer.

'Just bumped and bruised. I've got a headache but the paramedics said it wasn't a concussion.' Samantha touched her fingers against the top of her head and scrunched up her eyes. 'Do I need to go to the police station?

Ben shook his head. 'The detective's gone. He has all of our contact details, but considering that David recorded the whole thing, and the statements we've already given, it's more than enough to prosecute him.'

'Will he go to jail?' Samantha lifted her face and stared at Ben.

'Definitely.' Ben nodded. 'I heard the detective talking on the phone. It seems David put up quite a fight getting into the police car. By the sounds of it, he bit a policeman's ear. So even if they didn't have enough evidence for what he did to you and Jaddi, he'd still be going to prison for attacking the officer.'

'Good,' Lizzie said.

'Lizzie, your mum and dad, and Aaron, have gone to bed, by the way,' Ben said. 'They fell asleep on the sofa in the lobby waiting for us to come back.'

'Oh,' Lizzie said. 'The helicopter ride, I completely forgot. We missed it. Is Caroline pissed?'

Ben laughed. 'You're kidding, right? She's already fighting to get her hands on David's video camera, so she can include it with the documentary. Obviously she's glad everyone is OK too.'

Lizzie raised her eyebrows. 'Obviously.' Their eyes connected. For a split second, Lizzie found herself trapped in his gaze, like a piece of metal being pulled towards a magnet. She had a sudden urge to jump up from the bed, step forward and lean her body against him. She held his gaze for a moment more as her stomach flipped and turned inside of her.

'Will they give it to her?' Samantha asked.

Lizzie dropped her eyes to the carpet and tightened her hold on Samantha.

'I can't see how,' Ben said. 'The police are taking a look at the Channel 6 footage from earlier today. Caroline has sent Sandy and Bill down to the police station with them to protect the footage, but since David had nothing to do with the documentary, and considering that his camera didn't belong to Channel 6, there's no reason for the police to give it to Caroline.'

A lone tear escaped one of Samantha's eyes.

'Hey,' Lizzie said, pulling Samantha closer. 'It's OK now. You're safe. We'll stay with you as long as you need. You can sleep with me tonight.'

Samantha nodded. 'Thanks. I think I'd like to have a very hot bath and be by myself for a while.' She stood up and stepped towards the door.

'The maid service are cleaning the rooms now,' Ben said. 'Use my room.' He pointed towards the door he'd come through. 'You could practically fit my entire flat in the bathroom alone.'

'Thanks,' she said, wrapping her arms around herself and shuffling away.

'Shout if you need me,' Lizzie said as the door closed.

CHAPTER 56

Lizzie

'How's Jaddi coping?' Ben asked Lizzie.

'She seems to have shrugged the whole thing off. She washed her face and went down to the lobby to look for Suk. I think they had a fight earlier. Knowing Jaddi, she'll say she's fine for the next few days, then she'll get drunk and cry it out. What about you, are you all right?'

'I think so. My hands are shaking a bit from the adrenaline, but I didn't really do much.'

'Don't say that. If it wasn't for you …' Lizzie's voice trailed off. It was happening again – the magnetic field. The unstoppable force. The desire to stand up and move closer to him. Lizzie swallowed hard and dropped her gaze to her hands. She traced her fingers over the outline of the petals on the floral bedspread, then stopped as a growing awareness of the bed filtered through her. She was alone, in a bedroom, with a man she had a sudden desire to be close to.

Lizzie pushed her hands under her thighs and focused her gaze on her feet. The dregs of adrenaline in her system were mixing up her signals, that was all. This was Ben. Ben, who'd pulled her out of her seizure, and whose voice she still heard in her sleep. Ben, who she'd woken at 3am and dragged halfway across Cambodia, just to watch a sunrise. Ben, who'd guided her in from the water when she'd lost her sight, made her laugh after the whole Harrison thing, and who'd sat through a lunch listening to her mum and dad tell stories from her childhood.

'Are you sure you're all right, Lizzie?' His voice reverberated through her.

She drew in a deep breath and stood up. 'I've been trying to figure out how you knew something was wrong earlier,' she said, taking a step towards him. 'At first I wondered if there were cameras in the suite and you'd seen something, but then I thought, you'd have called security straight away. So now I'm wondering if you're psychic?'

Ben smirked and rubbed his hand against the stubble on his face. He shook his head. 'I'm not psychic. I just had a feeling that something wasn't right. Call it cameraman intuition.'

His eyes stared into her – deep brown with flecks of green, enlarged by the lenses in his glasses. It felt like a dozen ping-pong balls had been unleashed inside of her and were bouncing against the walls of her stomach. Her feet moved another step towards him as if they'd been commanded to do so by an outside force.

'Just an everyday superhero then,' she said, her heartbeat drumming against her chest.

'Something like that.'

'So what's your instinct telling you right now?' Lizzie stepped forward until she could feel the warmth of his body.

Ben continued to stare into her eyes for another moment then drew in a sudden breath as if he'd been underwater for a minute and just resurfaced. 'That maybe I should kiss you right now.' His arms reached around her and pulled her the last few inches into his embrace.

Lizzie pressed her body against him as their lips touched and she felt it again, just like before – the firecrackers inside her, the dipping of a rollercoaster, losing her stomach.

Ben stood up, craning Lizzie's neck back as they continued to kiss. In one fluid movement, he scooped her from the floor and stepped two paces to the bed.

CHAPTER 57

Jaddi

Jaddi's eyes scanned the hotel lobby. Her head pounded as she moved. The impact of each step caused a searing pain to spread across her ribs. The bruise forming on her stomach already had the outlines of a perfect shoe print.

A scuffle of feet sounded from behind her, followed by a clanging crash. Jaddi jumped; an image of David's deranged grin danced before her eyes. With a racing heart, she spun around to find a gold-framed porter's trolley lying on its side and suitcases strewn across the one of the indoor flowerbeds.

She smiled at her own stupidity and shook her head. The movement unleashed a new wave of pounding and a torrent of swear words to rage through her. What he'd done to Samantha, what he'd been about to do, to both of them. A line of sweat prickled the skin along her spine. She tried to shake the images away but events of the afternoon replayed on repeat in her mind.

'Are you OK, miss?' a woman's voice asked from behind her.

She nodded and started walking again. She was fine. It was Suk she needed to focus on. There'd been a flash of realisation when the sole of David's foot had connected with her body and sent her flying through the air, where she'd seen with absolute clarity that Suk meant more to her than anything else in the world, and that included her family.

She loved her parents and Halima, Ravi, and her nieces and nephews. She loved her family home and the playful bickering with Ravi and Halima over who'd set the table for dinner, as if the walls of the home they'd grown up in had the power to rewind the clock and make them squabbling children again. She loved the celebrations and traditions, and Punjab festivals, especially Vaisakhi, but she loved Suk more.

It had taken the impact with the floor to jolt those thoughts away, and replace it with another: had David hurt Suk, or worse?

Once David had been taken away, the hotel security team had searched every corner and every cupboard of the suite and found nothing. The relief had been brief. Where was Suk? Had she left the hotel? Left Vegas? Left Jaddi forever?

Tears began to stream from Jaddi's eyes as her pupils darted in one direction and then another. She wandered into a corridor away from the main lobby. There were doors on either side and a wide set of double doors at the end. Gold plaques with room names sat above the doors – Business Centre, Ball Room, Banqueting Suite, Boulevard Room.

A dizziness begun to swarm her thoughts. She'd lost her. The thought drained the last molecules of energy from her body. Her back scraped against the wall as she sank to the floor.

'Jaddi?'

Jaddi lifted her head, her mouth dropping open. Suk stood in the open doorway to the business centre. Behind her sat a bank of computers and a row of telephones.

'I ... I thought I'd lost you.' Jaddi's voice rose to a squeak as sobs attacked her body.

Suk crouched down alongside her. 'Hey, hey, hey ... what's going on?'

Jaddi nodded and wiped her eyes. 'Sorry, it's been a ... a long afternoon. I've been looking for you.' A burst of love exploded inside Jaddi as Suk reached out and wrapped her hand in hers. 'I'm sorry. I didn't mean what I said. You're right. We should be together. I'll call my mum and dad today. I'll tell them everything. I didn't think I could live without my family, but I was wrong. It's you I can't live without. If they can't accept me for who I am then I'll have to live with that. But you were right, I am strong, *we're* strong, we can do this together, but please forgive me.'

Suk squeezed her hand. 'I forgive you.'

'Really?' Fresh tears ran down Jaddi's face.

Suk smiled. 'If you'll still have me?'

Jaddi laughed. 'Um, let me see – yes.' She dipped her head and touched her lips to Suk's, sending a warmth pulsing through her body. A moment later, Jaddi pulled away. 'You should come with us to South America. Lizzie and Samantha won't mind.'

'I'd love to, but I can't. I need to be on my own for a while. Without my family, and without you. I need some time to think about what it is I want to do.'

'Oh.' Jaddi stared at Suk. A different type of fear wound its way through her.

'I meant career-wise, nothing else.' Suk laughed. 'I'm not going to change my mind about us. Besides, I just sent my mum an email saying goodbye, and one to my brother telling him where he can shove his proposal to ship me away to India. Even without you, I realised it was too late to go back, but it does mean I'm out of a job.'

'I'm so sorry I outed us.'

'Don't be,' Suk said, leaning closer and kissing Jaddi again.

'What will you do?'

Suk smiled. 'I'm not sure. Maybe I'll go back to college. The only good thing about living at home all these years and hardly going out is that I have a pretty decent amount in my savings account.'

'You always said you'd be a vet if you had the choice.'

Suk nodded, her smile spreading. 'I know. Crazy, isn't it? I can't believe I'm doing this. We're doing this,' she corrected. 'I know none of it will be easy, but for the first time in my life I feel excited about something.'

Just then, Suk grabbed her hand and pulled it close to her. 'What's this?' she asked, staring at the raw indentations on Jaddi's wrist.

'It's nothing, I'm fine.' Jaddi pulled her arm free.

'It's not nothing, Jaddi. What happened to you?'

Hot tears scorched the rims of Jaddi's eyes. 'Just a corkscrew-wielding maniac who wanted to rape—' Jaddi's word stopped forming in her mouth as heaving breaths consumed her body.

Suk pulled her closer and held her tight.

Sometime later, when the tears had run dry, Jaddi lifted her face to Suk's. 'I really am fine, it's just the shock.'

'Tell me what happened.'

Jaddi nodded. 'I think I'll need a glass of wine in front of me for that.'

'Done.' Suk stood up, before reaching her hands out to Jaddi and pulling her to her feet.

CHAPTER 58

Day 61

Samantha

Samantha wrapped the blanket tighter around herself and tucked her chin against her knees as a chilly wind blew across the canyon. Her legs were starting to ache from the cold of the rock face they were huddled on, but she wasn't ready to move. They'd found a spot, just the three of them. No other tourists, no Ben, and no cameras. Partly due to a weekend of intense filming, and partly due to her guilt at inviting a maniac to Las Vegas, Caroline had granted them a sunrise alone, just one, and Samantha didn't want it to end yet.

She was OK. Really and truly OK. Shaken, yes. Hurt, a little. But the shock had worn off and in its place was something else, something new. A zinging around her body that she couldn't explain. Up until twenty minutes ago, she'd put it down to some kind of reverse post-traumatic stress. The sudden desire to be back on the ledge in Mondulkiri staring into the dark water below, fearless and wanting to jump again and again. But watching the dusky, orange sky above the black outlines of the canyons she'd realised it was more. She felt awake for the first time in her life.

It was like the childhood buzz from the blue Slush Puppy they'd sold in the cafe her nan had taken her to sometimes. Or the pulsing of her first cup of coffee at sixteen. Samantha had never tried anything stronger, but she imagined it must feel like this. A heightened sense of living that pushed and pushed against her, willing her, no, daring her to live harder, faster, better.

Suddenly, she didn't want to be careful, studious, organised Samantha, too scared to step outside of the rigid lines of the escape plan she'd made when she was just a kid, in case she slipped up somewhere and found herself right back in that council flat sitting alongside her mother and brothers.

Study hard, get a good job, meet a man – someone who'd never set foot on a council estate, let alone grown up on one – get married, have children and maybe a dog too. Be a mother like Evelyn – patient, funny and kind. Break the cycle and undo the damage her own mother had done.

She'd been on course, or she thought she had been, until David's fist had slammed into her head. Now she knew how wrong she'd been about David and about herself. Where in her plan had she allowed herself to live? To question, is this what I want?

'Are you OK, Samantha?' Lizzie asked, breaking her concentration. 'You look, I don't know, angry.'

Samantha blinked and realised the sun had peaked over the canyon, bathing the orange and red rocks in a soft, yellow light. She shook her head. 'Yes, sorry. I was thinking about my mother.'

'Oh,' Lizzie said, glancing at Jaddi. 'You've never really spoken about your mum before.'

Samantha smirked. 'There's not much to say.'

'Do you want to tell us about her? You don't have too, if it's hard.'

'She is a selfish woman who had three children when she'd have been better off having none. She wasn't purposefully cruel; she just wasn't capable of thinking about anyone but herself. She still isn't. One of us would say, "Mum, there's nothing to eat," and she'd say, "Oh, I forgot." No apology, or anything.

'We lived two floors up at my nan's flat when we were very little. She did what she could for us. Taught us to fend for ourselves. She had a stroke and died when I was six so we packed up and moved in with my mum.' Samantha pulled in a breath. She'd never spoken about her past before, not to David, not to Lizzie and Jaddi. No one. Hearing the words aloud, they seemed so blunt, but after so many years Samantha didn't know if she had any feelings left towards her family or her past.

'That must have been really tough,' Jaddi said, taking Samantha's hand.

'I guess it was, but we didn't know any different. A lot of kids in the tower didn't have much in the way of parenting. It was all we knew. Up until I started senior school, I thought it was normal.'

'What about your dad?' Lizzie asked.

'Your guess is as good as mine. I once asked my mum who my dad was. I couldn't have been older than eight, maybe nine. She laughed and said, "Tony-fucking-Blair, honey. He came on a visit to the estate and we fell in love, but you know, he's got a country to run and Cherie at home so I had to move on."' Samantha snorted. 'I believed her too. For years I had this plan to get a job in parliament so he could meet me and take me away from her. Stupid, hey?'

Lizzie and Jaddi remained silent.

'Shit,' Samantha said as the cognisance of her words sunk in.

'What's wrong?' Jaddi asked.

'That's what I did, isn't? I went and got a job in Government. How crazy am I?'

Lizzie rubbed her back. 'You're not crazy. You love your job.'

Samantha shook her head and stood up, stepping closer to the ledge. The sun was well above the peak of the canyons now. The brightness stung her eyes, but she continued to stare. 'No, actually, I don't. It's pretty frustrating and very boring.'

Jaddi and Lizzie scrambled to their feet and followed Samantha's gaze.

'When we get back, I'm going to quit my job and go back to Mondulkiri,' Samantha said, only realising her plan as she heard the words leave her mouth. 'Working with Happy and the other elephants was the best thing I've ever done.'

Lizzie and Jaddi shared a look but Samantha didn't care. It was what she wanted to do, what she was going to do. She was never going to end up back on her mother's sofa, or like her mother, no matter how she decided to live her life. A fresh zinging pulsed through her body. She felt the girls' hands curl into hers and they all stood there for a moment, together, connected, watching the light creep over the sharp formations of the canyon. To Samantha, it felt like an end, and also a beginning.

'Shall we head back for breakfast?' Samantha asked.

'I think I might need to stand under a hot shower for an hour too,' Lizzie said. 'I can't believe it's so cold here.'

'It's the wind.' Jaddi hooked her own blanket further up her body, burying the bottom half of her face in it.

They walked quickly back towards the car park and hotel minibus Caroline had arranged for them.

'Any word from your parents, Jaddi?'

Jaddi shook her head. 'They need some time. My mum didn't hang up on me the minute I told her, which I'm taking as a good sign.'

Samantha wrapped an arm around Jaddi. Watching Jaddi and Suk together for the past few days had made her realise what a relationship should be like. What love should be like. She hoped Jaddi's family would allow themselves the chance to see that too.

'What do you think, Liz?' Jaddi said. 'Sunset from a helicopter or sunrise from the rock?'

'Oh, good question. I liked being with my mum and dad, and Aaron yesterday. It made watching the sunset feel really special, and coming back over the strip and seeing all the lights was amazing, but I felt closer to it sitting with you guys. It's got to be the best one so far.'

A sadness splintered Samantha's buzz. She'd been so busy thinking about living her life, making plans, she'd forgotten that Lizzie couldn't do the same. There had to be another way. There had to be something else they could do. It was a such a simple thought that Samantha wondered how she'd only just come to think of it. There had to be an experimental treatment Lizzie could try. Just because Lizzie had accepted her fate, it didn't mean Samantha had to.

CHAPTER 59

Lizzie

Lizzie closed the door to her bathroom, pulled out her camera and sat down on the tiled ledge surrounding the bathtub. Her image appeared on the camera screen. The left side of her hair was flattened against her head, and had tuffs sticking out at odd angles. The tip of her nose and her cheeks shone pink from where the biting wind of the canyon had chilled her face.

'So last night I said goodbye to my mum and dad, and Aaron. I'm so grateful to Channel 6, and to Caroline, for flying them out to see me. The time we've spent together this weekend has been magical.' Lizzie felt the emotion of last night's goodbye well to the surface. 'When I said goodbye to my mum and dad at the start of all this I knew I wasn't being fair on them, but I had ninety days and the start of our adventure to think about. Spending time with them this weekend has been so amazing, but saying goodbye again was the hardest thing I've ever done.' A loan tear raced down her cheek.

'I thought ...' Lizzie ran through the sentence in her head before forming the words, '... it was OK to be selfish, but now, I don't know. A big part of me just wants to go home and cuddle my mum on the sofa, and eat her leek and potato soup, because right now, I really don't know ...' Lizzie swallowed down the lump growing in her throat.

She drew in a breath and changed the subject before she said something she couldn't take back. 'So tomorrow we're flying back to LA, and the day after that we leave for Brazil.'

'Lizzie,' Ben said, knocking on the door. His voice sparked an explosion of fireworks inside her. 'Breakfast is here, and Caroline wants a word with all of you before she goes.'

'I'll be out in five,' Lizzie replied, powering off the camera and staring at the door for a moment. She could see the shadows of his feet from the gap underneath the door. She had a sudden desire to yank it open and drag him into the shower with her, but she didn't.

They hadn't spoken since he'd lifted her onto the bed. Since they'd ripped off each other's clothes ... since he'd pulled her close so that every part of her naked body was touching his. A burning hunger spread through her.

Lizzie tiptoed to the shower cubicle and started the spray. She glanced back at the sliver of light from the doorway. His feet had gone.

Was he avoiding her? Was she avoiding him? Or had there simply been no time to talk away from the camera crew that had been following her with the assiduity of her own shadow. One thing was for sure, it wasn't just adrenaline or shock that had brought them together. Every time she looked at him, the same yearning pull now grabbed hold of her, willing her to step into his arms.

Lizzie stepped into the shower and immersed herself in the prickles of hot water.

Bright sunlight spilled through the vast expanse of the window and painted rectangles on the soft carpet of the living room as Lizzie made her way to the edge of the sofa and the silver trays of food.

Samantha sat at the end of the L-shaped sofa, her head bent forwards, her face fixed in concentration as she scrolled through something on her phone. A slice of toast sat untouched beside her. Lizzie was glad to see her friend so happy, she just hoped it wasn't masking part of the shock.

Jaddi sat cross-legged next to Samantha, munching on pastries in shorts and a cut-off T-shirt, which displayed not only her flat stomach, but the heel-shaped bruise left by David's shoe print. Her hair was still wet and made wet lines on the back of her T-shirt.

'So did you girls enjoy your surprise trip to Las Vegas?' Caroline turned from the window and beamed at them. Her smile dropped as her gaze fixed on Samantha. 'I meant other than that ...' Caroline laughed her tinkling laugh before fixing her eyes on Lizzie. The thin line of her eyebrows jumped an inch.

'Er ...thank you, Caroline,' Lizzie said, swallowing a mouthful of toast, 'for organising everything and for flying my family here to see me. Seeing them has been amazing.'

'And the helicopter ride over the Grand Canyon that I managed to reschedule for last night ...'

'Was brilliant,' Lizzie said, fidgeting with the cushions behind her back. Beneath its sleek leather finish, the sofa was hard and unforgiving.

'I know it was emotional saying goodbye to your ... er ... loved ones last night.' Caroline flicked a glance at Jaddi before focusing on Samantha. 'I am just so sorry about the David thing. If only I'd known you'd broken-up—'

A sudden heat thrashed inside of Lizzie. 'By thing, I assume you mean the kidnapping and attack of my two best friends by a deranged maniac?'

'Drop it, Liz,' Samantha said, lifting her face from her mobile. 'It's not your fault, Caroline.'

No one spoke. Lizzie sighed and followed the movements of a silver SUV in the distance, negotiating its way through the suburban streets. It reached a line of stationary cars and stopped outside the gated building of a school. Tiny red dots zipped around the playground inside the gates.

'Well.' Caroline clapped her hands together. 'It's almost time for me to catch my flight back to London. So I'll be leaving you once again in Ben's capable hands. But I do have a small favour to ask?

Lizzie glanced to Ben. He'd pulled one of the dining room chairs over to the sofa, and was eating a bowl of cereal with his back to the window. He smiled at Lizzie but gave no indication as to whether he knew what favour Caroline was about to ask. Their eyes remained fixed on each other for a moment too long.

'How would you girls feel about moving your stay in New York from the end of your trip to next on the itinerary?'

Lizzie shrugged and scanned Jaddi and Samantha's faces. Samantha looked up from her phone and focused her attention on Caroline.

'Will we still get to go to South America?' Jaddi asked.

'Absolutely,' Caroline nodded. 'I promise. No more changes to your destinations, just the order.'

Jaddi shrugged. 'Fine by me then, I guess, but why?'

'Neil Mullon of *The Sunday Night Late Show* would like to have you on as special guests tonight. They phoned me last night after the latest episode had aired in the UK and asked if you'd consider it. The videos of you on stage with Guy Rawson are all over the internet, and they have picked us up a huge American following.'

Caroline watched their faces. 'But you don't have to do it. It would be great for Channel 6 and for me personally, but it's by no means compulsory.'

'I don't know,' Lizzie said. She looked at Jaddi and Samantha.

'I don't mind.' Jaddi shrugged again before turning her face to Samantha.

'I'm good with going to New York first, and with leaving here today,' Samantha said, 'but I don't want to do the interview.'

'No, no, of course not,' Caroline said. 'I can put a call into the producer. I'm sure it will be fine for just Lizzie and Jaddi to do it.'

'Let's go to New York then,' Lizzie said.

Caroline grinned. 'Fantastic. Thank you, girls. I'll sort all the flights and accommodation out straight away,' she said, already tapping the screen of her phone. 'There's a flight leaving for New York just before lunch time which will get you in, let me see, with the time difference, it lands at JFK at … six pm. Which gives you two hours to check into the hotel and make your way to the studio.'

With her eyes fixed on the screen of her phone, Caroline stepped towards the door. 'Shoot, Lizzie, I almost forgot.' She spun around. 'Your doctor has been phoning the studio. Dr Hab-i-bi. Am I pronouncing that right? He's trying to get in touch with you. Apparently he's left several messages on your phone?'

Lizzie sucked her bottom lip between her teeth and forced her eyes to remain on Caroline. She could feel Ben's gaze on her, no doubt scrutinising every twitch of her face. 'Oh, my phone's been off. I'll call him in a minute. I'm sure he just wants to check I'm still taking my meds.'

Lizzie leant forward and plucked her last piece of toast from the tray on the coffee table. It lost its crunchy texture the moment it entered her mouth. The sweetness of the jam disappeared too, so that all she was left with was a chewy glob of cardboard. She continued to push her teeth into it whilst fighting to keep her face void of expression, as if she was eating her breakfast without a care in the world, and not spinning into a frenzy of panic at Caroline's comment.

Only when she'd finished every last bite did she stand up. Blobs of red and yellow appeared in her vision again, adding to the dizzying affect.

It was an effort to walk in a straight line across the hotel living room. Lizzie pictured the pink and yellow teacups, on the seafront near her childhood home, and the ride operator, always a teenage boy in a white vest, always moving with purpose and ease between the teacups as if the ride was stationary when in actual fact it was rotating around and around.

CHAPTER 60

Lizzie

Lizzie dove towards her backpack and reached her arm inside. Her fingers prodded through her clothes until she felt the familiar hard plastic of her mobile.

She pressed her finger onto the power symbol. After a pause it lit up and vibrated. It felt as though months had passed since she'd turned it off and left it forgotten at the bottom of her bag. So much had happened since their time on the Gold Coast, it hadn't occurred to her to switch it back on again.

Until now.

Dr Habibi had been her neurologist for twenty-six years. He knew her. He knew everything. If he was contacting her, it could mean only one thing.

Lizzie held her breath as her mobile connected to her messages. A stiff electronic voice announced one new message.

'Hello, my name is Hal Fitzgerald. I'm a neurologist in San Francisco. Perhaps my friend Dr Moss mentioned me to you.' The tones of the man's Californian accent rose at the end of each sentence, so that each one sounded like a question. 'She sent your MRI scans to me, you see, which I've spent some time looking at. I've tried to speak with your own Doctor, Dr Habibi, but it appears he's out of town. Please return this call.

I'm looking at the scans right now, and I'd very much like to talk to you about them.'

Lizzie's mind reeled as the electronic voice spoke again; 'Nine old messages. First old message.'

'Miss Appleton, this is Dr Moss from the Gold Coast University Hospital. Please call me regarding your MRI scan results. You may remember me mentioning a friend of mine in America who is a neurologist and a specialist in brainstems – Dr Fitzgerald – and it's imperative that you call me or him immediately.'

Lizzie skipped through the recordings from Dr Moss. Her tone hardened with each message, and they all ended with the same urgent plea to get in touch.

Another message started to play. 'Lizzie, Dr Habibi here. Please call me as soon as you get this.' His voice sounded muffled as if he was holding the receiver too close to his mouth. She could hear every inhale and exhale of breath. 'A doctor from America is calling me. I need to know what I should say.'

Lizzie slumped into the armchair and stared at the screen of her phone. From the moment she'd been wheeled into the MRI machine in Australia, her hold on the situation had loosened. She'd been unable to stop the edges from unravelling. With Ben's suspicions and the calls from Dr Moss, it had seemed only a matter of time before everything fell apart. Then nothing had happened, and like a fool she'd allowed herself to relax.

Lizzie swallowed and held down the power button on her phone. Her eyes remained fixed on the screen until it transformed into an inanimate object once more.

She knew she should call Dr Habibi, but she couldn't. Time was running out. She could see the end.

Lizzie drew in a sharp intake of air, her eyes widening as another, far more worrying realisation struck her. If this was the first time that she'd switched on her phone in weeks, and the first time that she'd listened to her voicemail, then why weren't all the messages new, instead of just the one from Dr Fitzgerald? Someone else had listened to them, but who? The blotches returned, swarming in front of her eyes until her vision was like looking through a stained-glass window. She replayed the messages in head. How much would someone learn by listening to them?

A scuffling of feet sounded from Ben's room. There was a light knock and then the door opened.

'Did you get through to him?' Ben said from the doorway.

Her mind blanked. 'Huh?'

'Your doctor. You came in here to call him.'

'Oh, yes.' Lizzie dropped to her knees and shoved her phone back to the bottom of her bag. 'He didn't answer.'

'Are you OK? You look really pale.' Ben said, moving towards her.

She stood up and turned to face him. He'd trimmed his beard since they'd kissed, and had his head shaved again. Without his glasses he looked less like the Ben she knew, and more like the faceless cameraman she'd met at the check-in desk at Heathrow Airport. Then she looked into his eyes and the magnetic field drew her in.

Ben reached for her hand, causing a tingling to radiate from his touch.

'I'm sorry we haven't spoken since Friday,' he said. 'I didn't want you to think I was avoiding you, or that I regretted what happened. Now that the film crew have gone, we can talk …'

Lizzie took an unsteady step back and pulled her hand free from his hold. She needed to think, to focus, and Ben wasn't helping. 'Have you been going through my phone?' she snapped.

'What?' Hurt registered on Ben's face.

'Someone's listened to my voicemails. Was it you?' Panic carried in the tone of her of voice.

'No, of course not. Lizzie, what's going on?'

'Nothing.' She shook her head. 'Look, I'm sorry but I can't do this with you. I can't drag you into it.'

Ben threw his hands up and exhaled. 'Can't drag me into it. Into what, Lizzie? I'm already in as deep as I can get. I care about you. I care about what happens to you.'

'You know what's going to happen to me, the whole world knows.'

Lizzie stared into Ben's eyes as the truth caught in her throat. She scooped her backpack from the floor and turned towards the door. 'I'm sorry, I can't do this.'

A solitary tear ran down her cheek as she walked into the living room. It seemed a lifetime ago that she'd stood in the dressing room of the Channel 6 studio. 'It's too late to put the lid back on the can of worms,' Jaddi had said. If it was too late then, she had no hope now.

CHAPTER 61

Samantha

Samantha breathed in the crisp air as a cold wind whipped through her clothes. The smell of fried onions and hotdogs filled her senses, and for the first time in days her stomach rumbled with hunger.

Traffic hummed around them, horns blasted long and loud in the distance, whilst the beat of music drifted out from shop fronts.

New York had been the first place she'd suggested when they'd knelt on the threadbare carpet in the living room of their East London flat and opened up an A3 map of the world. The higgledy-piggledy buildings – different heights, different colours – all set in perfect square blocks across the city, had appealed to her more than the temples and the beaches.

There was something familiar about it: the hot-dog vendors on the street corners; the subway grates on the sidewalks; the dark-haired policemen in crisp blue uniforms; the sea of yellow cabs. It was just as she'd imagined from the hours spent watching reruns of *Friends* and *Sex in the City*.

'Oh crap, it's cold. So cold,' Jaddi said, pulling her jumper up to her mouth. 'Shall we get a taxi?'

'Our first time walking the streets of New York and you want to get a taxi?' Samantha rolled her eyes. 'What happened to your authentic experiences?'

'What could be more authentic than a yellow cab? Besides, my body has forgotten what cold feels like. We've done humid, hot, hot and humid, scorching, warm, and more hot. But not cold. Now I remember why we put New York last on the itinerary. Another month and it'll be spring time here.'

'Well, we're not getting a taxi. This is Times Square. The studio is just across the street.'

All around them, people in winter coats, carrying paper shopping bags, dashed in and out of shops. Tourists with cameras snapped photos of giant electronic billboards rising up the sides of the buildings. Humps of charcoal-coloured snow dotted the edges of the sidewalk. Somewhere above the rooftops the sky was black, but among the shops and the people, and the colourful adverts, it was as bright as day.

Samantha threw a glance at Ben, walking a pace in front of them with his camera balanced on his shoulder, just as he'd done before their trip had been hijacked by Caroline and her film crew, and they'd been dragged to Las Vegas. Before David. Before she'd realised how wrong she'd been about her life.

They drew to a stop by a pedestrian crossing. A small, square screen on the opposite sidewalk displayed a red hand, warning them to wait. A row of people on each side obeyed the command. A smile touched Samantha's lips. In London, pelican crossings were often ignored by pedestrians. In Vietnam, even the cars and motorbikes paid no attention to traffic signals, but in New York, the city that never sleeps, where everyone is in a rush, they waited.

'Has anyone actually watched this show?' Jaddi asked.

Lizzie and Samantha shook their heads.

'I've seen it a few times,' Ben said, moving his eye out of the camera lens. 'He's funny. You'll have a good time.'

'Are you sure you don't mind if I sit this one out?' Samantha scrunched up her face as she looked between Jaddi and Lizzie. She hated the idea of letting them down, but she couldn't face another live TV interview, especially after everything that had happened.

'Of course we don't mind.' Lizzie smiled. 'You can enjoy it from behind the scenes with Ben.'

'Do I have time to stop and get a scarf and a hat, and some gloves?' Jaddi said.

Lizzie laughed. 'No, we'll go shopping tomorrow. That was another reason we wanted to leave New York until last, remember? We'd planned to shop until we drop before—'

A green man flashed on the screen and they found themselves carried forward by the walking crowd. Almost immediately, the light turned red again and a timer ticked down from twenty. They made it to the sidewalk as the timer ran down to three.

Samantha cast a sideways glance to Lizzie and grabbed her arm. 'Liz, before you go in there, can we talk for a second? I need to show you something.'

Lizzie grinned. 'Sure. If it's about Mondulkiri, you know I support you. I just don't want you to rush into a decision about quitting your job. You've worked too hard—'

Samantha shook her head. 'It's not about me. It's about you.' A blast of warmth carried from the heaters of shop. 'Hang on, let's stand here a second.'

Lizzie nodded, wrapping her arms around herself. Jaddi stepped beside Lizzie, the pair waiting for Samantha to speak. She blanked out Ben's movements from the corner of her eye. This was too important.

Samantha drew in a breath. Hope danced in her stomach. 'I've found a clinical trial you have to read about. It's a new radiotherapy treatment for inoperable brain tumours. They haven't published any results so far –' Samantha pulled out her phone from her pocket as she spoke, desperate to get the words out before Lizzie could interrupt '– but the researchers are really positive about it. Look here.' She thrust her phone in front of Lizzie and pulled up the webpage from her browser.

Lizzie shook her head, closing her eyes as if she could block out the information. 'Don't, Sam, please. I know all this stuff. It's not for my tumour.'

'Oh.' The hope hardened to stone inside as she watched her friend. 'But if you just looked at it.'

Lizzie stepped away, her head still shaking from side to side.

Jaddi wrapped an arm around Samantha and gave her shoulder a squeeze. 'Let's talk about this later, OK? We don't want to be late for the interview.'

'Sure,' Samantha said. 'I'm sorry, I just hoped—'

'It's not your fault,' Jaddi said. 'Come on before my fingers drop off from frostbite.'

Samantha trailed a step behind as they continued along the sidewalk. This wasn't over, she thought to herself. The trial she'd found was new. Brand new. Lizzie could be wrong. It could help her. Samantha just had to make her see that.

CHAPTER 62

Lizzie

The producer guided Lizzie onto a small stage. The low hum of voices drifted from the audience. She'd expected a studio with cameras and a crew busy with their tasks, not a stage with a captive audience watching her every move.

'This is you,' he said, pointing to a single white armchair.

Nerves popped like bubbles inside of Lizzie as she sat down and stared out at the sea of faces gawping back at her. A heat crept over her cheeks. She shifted in her seat and watched the show's black and yellow logo zigzag across a large screen, dominating the wall behind a white curved desk and a high-backed leather chair.

'Neil will be out in a minute. Good luck,' the producer said, before walking away and leaving her alone on the stage. Lizzie breathed in a lungful of stuffy air and winced as the bones of the corset dug into her ribcage.

The wardrobe lady – an African American woman in her early thirties, called Natasha, with bright-red lipstick and matching fingernails – had laughed when Lizzie had suggested wearing her own clothes. She'd taken Lizzie by the shoulders and guided her to the long length mirror.

'You want to wear that, honey?' she'd said as she'd pinched the material of Lizzie's shapeless red top – stretched and creased from the weeks of wear and travelling. Lizzie had looked at her own shiny, styled hair and smooth face, and then down at the frays straggling from her top, and had allowed herself to be squeezed into the corset and a pair of skin-tight burgundy jeans.

The lights on the stage flashed twice in quick succession, sending another punch of nerves to hit Lizzie. She scanned the audience in search of Samantha, Jaddi and Ben. Every one of the ten rows of seats was filled. Halfway up, and dead centre, there was a raised platform with a camera on it that made Ben's camera seem dwarfish in comparison. Two other cameras on wheels sat facing her from either side of the stage.

A movement to the far side of the front row caught her eye. Jaddi, Samantha and Ben waved at her. Jaddi pointed at her outfit before signalling a thumbs up. Lizzie wanted to signal a 'I can't breathe in this top' sign, but didn't know where to start. Too many people were watching her.

She had a sudden urge to throttle Caroline for talking them into this. Talking her into it. It wasn't until they'd arrived at the studio and Lizzie had been whisked away from the others, and plonked onto a make-up stool, that she'd realised what was happening. According to the producer the plan had always been for her, and her alone, to talk with Neil. Something Caroline had neglected to mention.

A round of applause erupted from the audience as a man strode onto the stage wearing a mustard-yellow and white floral shirt. He had a mop of white hair and a small beaked nose, which hooked at the end, above a wide, closed mouth smile.

He waved at the crowd before walking over to Lizzie.

'Hi, Lizzie, I'm Neil Mullon. It's a real pleasure to meet you.' He grabbed her hand in a warm grip and pumped it up and down. 'Thank you for changing your schedule to come on the show.'

'Thank you for having me,' she said, willing her voice to stop shaking.

'I love the Brits!' he shouted to the audience.

He turned back to Lizzie with eyes that shone of mischief and merriment. 'Nervous?'

The acrid taste of nausea stung her throat. 'A bit.'

'Don't be.' He smiled. 'America loves you.'

The lights on the stage dimmed and brightened once. 'Oops, that's my cue.'

He sprung onto the desk beside Lizzie and slid across it before dropping haphazardly into his chair.

'Welcome, welcome, welcome to *The Sunday Night Late Show*. I'm your host, Neil Mullon,' he said, grinning into the camera, 'and with me tonight is someone who needs no introductions. It's the beautiful … Lizzie Appleton.' He motioned his hand towards Lizzie before joining the audience in applause.

'We'll get to the travelling and the stupendous popularity of your documentary – *The Girl with Three Months to Live* – later, Lizzie, but I've got to ask this straight off the bat: what was it like having Guy Rawson serenade you with your very own song, on stage, in front of thousands of people?'

'Oh gosh, there aren't the words to describe it.' She smiled, recalling the buzz of the stadium, and standing with her arms stretched around Jaddi and Samantha as Guy had walked onto the stage. 'We've all been huge fans of Guy for so long. Just going to his concert was fantastic. I had no idea he'd written a song about me. It was surreal.'

'Shall we have a quick look at that moment again?' he asked, staring into the camera.

A murmur of agreement spread across the audience.

Neil spun his chair around and pointed at the screen behind his desk. The show's logo disappeared, then a moment later the cheers of the stadium filled the studio.

Guy's voice echoed through her again. 'Lizzie, how about coming up here with me?'

Lizzie had a sudden feeling of detachment as she watched her own face contort with emotion. The lyrics twisting and clawing inside her once more. *Ninety sunsets, but what happens then?*

'I hope he invited you backstage afterwards,' Neil said when the footage had stopped.

Lizzie pulled her eyes away from the screen. 'He certainly did, and I got to meet his sister too.'

'Guy mentions the sunsets in his song. Watching them seems to have been a special focus for you.'

Lizzie nodded, her nervousness abating. 'The trip has had a lot more ups and downs than I think any of us expected, but watching the sunsets brings it all back into perspective.'

'Have you got a favourite sunset?'

'It's so hard to choose.' She frowned and smiled at the same time. 'Every sunset we've watched has been different, and all of them have been spectacular. Yesterday we watched the sunset over the Grand Canyon from a helicopter, which was so different and made even more special because I had my parents and my brother with me. Although, I'm not sure I was supposed to tell you that,' Lizzie said, glancing at the camera and smiling. 'Sorry, Caroline.'

'For me, personally, I thought the sunrise over Angkor Wat in Cambodia looked amazing,' Neil said.

'That was really beautiful.'

'Worth all that time in the truck to get there?'

An image of waking up on the flatbed in the warmth of Ben's embrace sprung into her head, causing a glow to radiate from her cheeks. 'Definitely.' She nodded. 'Although I'm not sure Ben, our cameraman, would agree with me.'

'Talking of Ben.' Neil flicked his eyes to the camera and winked. 'A little bird whispered in my ear that there might be a romance blossoming there.'

'Er …' She shook her head as the glow ignited into flames on her face. 'We've struck up a friendship, that's all. He's a great cameraman, and a really nice guy.'

Neil smiled. 'OK then. I'm not sure I fully believe you there, Lizzie, but as luck would have it, it's time for a short break.' He turned to the face the camera. 'But join us in a few minutes, when we'll be talking to Lizzie about what is was like to lose her sight, and what's next for the girls.'

Neil grinned at the camera for a moment before reaching for a bottle of water underneath the desk and taking a short sip. He swirled the liquid around his mouth before swallowing.

'You're doing great, Lizzie,' he said.

Before she could respond the producer skidded onto the stage. A tablet device was gripped in his outstretched hands. He leant over the desk, blocking Neil from Lizzie's eye line. The two men exchanged a series of hushed words, before the producer glanced at his watch and ran off the stage.

'Is everything OK?' she asked.

Neil nodded but the smile had disappeared and his eyes remained fixed on the tablet.

'Neil?' Fear churned in her stomach. Something was wrong. What had the producer just whispered in Neil's ear? Her eyes darted to the fire exit, glowing like a green beacon to the side of the audience. Her hands pushed against the arms of the chair, lifting her body a few inches from the seat. She had to get to out of here.

'Stay where you are, Lizzie,' Neil said, his tone no longer jovial, but commanding. He faced the camera. 'Welcome back to *The Sunday Night Late show*. I've just been handed some shocking information about my guest tonight, Lizzie Appleton. I think you're going to want to hear it, Lizzie, and I know our audience, and the viewers at home, will too.'

Her heart drummed against the bones of the corset, spreading a chill around her body.

'A British blog called *Inside Scoop* has just this minute posted the following story. The headline reads: Lizzie the Liar. Is *The Girl with Three Months to Live* a hoax?'

Gasps sounded from across the audience. Lizzie had the sudden flailing sensation of falling, as if a trap door on the stage had opened beneath her. She closed her eyes as Neil continued to read.

'For the past eight weeks the story of Lizzie Appleton in the Channel 6 documentary *The Girl with Three Months to Live*, has gripped not just the nation, but the entire world. Now, *Inside Scoop* has evidence to suggest that Lizzie's brain tumour is nothing more than an elaborate hoax concocted by Lizzie and her two friends, Jaddi Patel and Samantha Jeffrey, to travel the world.

'A source close to Lizzie's neurologist has made the following statement: 'Elizabeth Appleton underwent radiotherapy in the autumn of last year to treat a small tumour in her brainstem. As far as I am aware, no further treatment was scheduled, because the radiotherapy was successful.'

'Channel 6 producer of the documentary, Caroline Wilks, was unavailable for comment leaving *Inside*

Scoop to question who else is in on it? Is this an elaborate hoax to boost the ratings of a channel in decline?'

Lizzie opened her eyes and tried to speak, but no words would come out.

'Lizzie, these are some unbelievable allegations, and there really is no other way to ask you this – is it true?'

A silence fell across the theatre. She felt the eyes of the audience drilling into her.

Lizzie's gaze darted to the front row as she searched for Jaddi, but one of the cameras had moved, blocking her view. Lizzie swallowed and stared down at her feet. 'No. It's … it's not how it sounds,' she stammered.

Neil leapt from his chair and strode out from his desk to the front of the stage. 'If it's not how it sounds, then how is it, Lizzie?'

Lizzie pulled her bottom lip between her teeth and bit down. Tears swam in her eyes. She knew she needed to find her voice, to explain what she'd done, but the words wouldn't come.

'Treatment wasn't scheduled because … because …'

Neil spun to face the camera, raising his hands in the air. 'I can't believe it.' He turned to Lizzie. 'How many people are involved, Lizzie?'

She shook her head. Panic threatened to overwhelm her thoughts.

'Is Channel 6 behind it?'

'No.' Lizzie shook her head again. 'It's got nothing to do with them, or with Jaddi and Samantha. It was me, only me. I just wanted a chance to live my life.'

Neil pounced towards her, grasping the arms of her chair in his hands. The smell of gin filled her nose as he leaned his face close to hers. 'So what happened?

Did you want to go on a jolly with your friends paid for by Channel 6 and generous members of the public, and cooked up this scheme to trick us all? Well, bravo, Lizzie, you certainly did that.'

Lizzie reeled back, as much from his sudden presence over her as his words. A spectacle of colours clustered in her sights. A throbbing drum pounded in her head.

'It wasn't a jolly; it's more complicated than that,' she managed. 'I don't know why someone would say that.'

'What was the plan at the end?' Neil started moving again. He paced up and down in front of her, dividing his gaze between her and the camera now positioned in front of them. 'Were you going to fake your own death, or run away to an island somewhere and live off the donations that have been flooding in?'

'It wasn't like that.' She bit back a sob. 'I *am* dying.' The words were lost beneath Neil's rising voice.

'How can I, how can the millions of Americans watching this show, trust a single word that comes out of your mouth. Are you even sorry, Lizzie? My mother, my own mother, donated last week to your website. I told her she didn't need to. Channel 6 have picked up the tab, but it didn't stop my eighty-one-year-old mother, just like it hasn't stopped thousands of innocent people around the world from donating. These are people without much ...'

Lizzie blocked out Neil's words. The inside of her cheeks ached. Her mouth filled with saliva. She tried to breathe, but the corset seemed to be tightening by the second. A pressure began to build inside of her. Her eyes darted again to the fire exit, before moving back to Neil.

'... did you consider that, Lizzie, when you set out to deceive us all? How, for so many ordinary Americans, every dollar counts—'

The pressure exploded. A ticking bomb that had finally gone off.

'I lied.' Her voice echoed across the theatre. Neil stopped in his tracks, his mouth gaping open as his face moved from her, to the camera and back again. Another gasp sounded from the audience, then silence. All of a sudden, her vision cleared, she lifted her head and stared into the lens.

CHAPTER 63

Lizzie

A ragged anger ripped through Lizzie. 'You don't know a thing about me,' she said, sitting forward and digging the tips of her fingers into the soft cushioning of the chair. 'You don't know a thing about what I've been through.'

The stage seemed to shrink around her. The audience and the cameras disappeared from her periphery. It was just her and the presenter. 'Do you know what it's like to wish you were dead?' she ground out the words. 'Do you have any idea how many times I wished my doctor had patted me on the shoulder and said, *Sorry, there's nothing more we can do for you. Go live your life, you've got six months*? Instead of … of all the waiting. That's what my life has been – waiting for the next brain tumour. Waiting for the symptoms to start, because they do, they always do. Waiting for a brain scan; waiting for the result; waiting for the treatments; waiting for agonising side effects; waiting to be sick, to throw up again and again and again and *again*; waiting for more scans, waiting to see if the treatment has worked. It's *never* over. It just starts again. It isn't living.

'Yes, I lied,' Lizzie stared into the camera as she spoke. 'I pretended my wish had come true, that there was nothing else my doctor could do for me, so finally, I could live for a little while. The truth is … the truth is that I *am* dying,' she said again. 'I have a brain tumour in my brainstem. Last year, I had a round of radiotherapy and it failed. Whoever told that gossip site that it worked was wrong. My doctor told me I had only months to live—'

'If that's the truth then what did you lie about?' Neil lifted his hands in confusion, looking between the camera and Lizzie. 'Why—'

'Because I chose it.' Lizzie's voice rang out across the studio.

Neil stepped back and glanced at the camera as a silence fell. He turned to look at her.

'I chose to live what was left of my life instead of spending it hooked up to machines, throwing up, and watching those I love suffer through it with me. I chose death,' she said as a weight pulled down on her shoulders. 'I could have signed up for a clinical trial that currently has no survivors, or one which has left almost every participant in a coma,' she said, staring into the camera, 'but I couldn't do it anymore. Ask yourself, how do *you* feel about those odds? And now imagine that you've been fighting for twenty-nine years, that you've never known a normal life; imagine what it feels like to be tortured by hope and disappointed every time.'

The words were tumbling out now, faster and faster as she tried to make Neil, the audience, the people at home, understand.

'I asked my doctor how long I'd have without any more treatment, and he said six months and I thought, that's six months where I'm not stuck in a hospital bed being injected with every drug imaginable. Six months where I could live my life how I wanted to. Where my family didn't have to sacrifice everything to look after me, worry about me, hope with me. Six months. Well, those six months are nearly up and I'm aware that every single moment could be my last. It's not an exact science – I might go to bed tonight and not wake up. So yes, I could have spent the last few months fighting, and being sick and in pain, and afraid, afraid to hope, afraid to see that hope reflected in the eyes of my friends and family. But instead I have seen the world, I have felt joy and love, and *certainty* about what is coming next. And I can't tell you what a *relief* that has been. I can't tell you because the truth, the truth is just too difficult to talk about – it's too difficult to explain and I was worried that no one would ever understand.'

The roar of the sea rushed through her ears, from the relief of unleashing her secret at last, or the ramifications from it, Lizzie didn't know, but peeling it away left a rawness behind. Tears streamed down her face.

'I'm sorry I lied, truly I am. I'm sorry for the hurt I've caused my friends, my family, and those who've supported me. I never meant to make anyone feel duped. You have all saved my life – each day I had, each moment I now have to treasure. Those memories are not just mine, but my friends', my family's … I didn't want to debate what *inoperable* and *untreatable* mean when it comes to tumours, to be judged for my choices. I just wanted to live a little before I die.'

Neil stepped back to the desk and dropped into his chair. 'And you don't think the American people deserve the chance to choose for themselves? To know the facts before they give—'

She shook her head. 'That's not what I mean,' she said.

'I'm not sure I understand, Lizzie.' He sighed. 'And I sure as hell don't think the American people will either.'

Lizzie fought to control her rising voice. 'Of course you don't understand what it's like to be pinned to a table, unable to move, whilst your body is pumped with poison. That's what the treatment is, you know – poison. Maybe it will destroy some of the tumour, maybe it won't. Either way, it will make you so sick that at some point, I guarantee, you'll wish you were dead anyway. It will fill your head with a fog so thick you'll want to jump off a bridge just to clear it. Puking your guts up, losing the feeling in your arms and legs. Headaches so bad that you have to lie in a pitch-black room for days on end because even the slightest light or movement causes unspeakable pain.

'So of course you don't understand. Only someone who has lived through what I've lived through could understand.'

Lizzie fell silent. She glared at Neil and waited for his next accusation.

Instead the presenter simply nodded and turned to face the camera. 'Well, this hasn't been the show we had planned for you, but that's all we've got time for. Thank you for tuning in to *The Sunday Night Late Show*, and thank you to our guest, Lizzie Appleton.'

A spattering of applause sounded from the audience.

Everywhere she looked people stood in clusters, whispering and shaking their heads as Lizzie navigated her way back to the dressing room. Natasha, the wardrobe lady, handed Lizzie's clothes to her without a word before leaving her alone in the room.

Her fingers shook as she unhooked the clasps of the corset and let it fall to the floor. She drew in a breath, but it didn't feel any easier without the tightness of the corset wrapped around her diaphragm.

Lizzie stumbled out of the dressing room and towards the exit. The anger from the interview had gone, leaving her cold and shivery. It was over. The lie, the trip, the documentary. It was time to go home. She felt only relief at the thought. It wasn't until she'd shouted out the truth that she'd realised how much the lie had weighed like a brick on her every thought. She'd tried to ignore it, she'd tried to pretend, and for a while she had, but the truth had always been there, haunting her.

'Will someone please tell me what's going on?' Lizzie heard Samantha's voice before she saw them. 'Jaddi. You know. I know you know. Tell me.'

Lizzie froze. Horror crawled over her skin. Samantha. She'd forgotten about Samantha.

'Lizzie will be here in a second,' Jaddi said in a quick and hushed voice. 'Let's wait for Lizzie.'

Panic hit, catching her breath in her throat. Lizzie twisted around and stared back into the corridors of the studio, knowing even as she did that she wouldn't run; she wouldn't search for another way out. She owed Samantha the truth, the whole truth, however much it hurt them both.

Lizzie pushed open the door and stepped into a reception area. Jaddi and Samantha stood on the other side of the room by a set of wide glass doors. Beyond the doors, Lizzie could see the black city street. The pattering of rain tapped on the glass. Ben was a few paces away with his back to the wall. She glanced towards him, hoping for something – reassurance, maybe - but his camera was mounted on his shoulder, hiding his face.

'Ben, did you know about this?' Samantha asked.

He shook his head and pointed his free hand at Lizzie.

'Lizzie.' Samantha rushed towards her. 'Why did you say all that stuff about choosing death? It's not true, is it?'

'Sam, I'm so sorry,' she said, fresh tears forming in her eyes. They were no longer tears for herself, but tears for her best friend.

Samantha shook her head. 'I don't understand. You were given the option to have more treatments that could have prolonged your life, or potentially cured you completely, and you said no?' Samantha's voice was low and rang of hurt and confusion in equal measure.

Lizzie sighed. 'It's not like that, Sam. The clinical trials—'

'I … I need some air,' Samantha said, spinning to the doors and fleeing outside.

Lizzie followed, rushing towards her friend as a gust of wind blasted her face. Tiny sharp hailstones hit her cheeks. 'Samantha, please let me explain. I know it's difficult to understand, but that's why we didn't tell you. I wanted so badly to tell you the truth, but I needed you with me, and I knew you'd never come if you knew the truth.' The cold air burnt at the sore rims of her eyes. Something clawed at Lizzie's chest. Desperation? Fear? Regret? She had to make Samantha understand.

'Well, you were right about that. There is no way I would've come on this … this suicide mission if I'd have known for a single second that you could've been having more treatments.' Samantha paused. 'After what I've been through this week, all I can think of is how much I want to live, and here you are throwing your life away. Why couldn't you have tried this one experimental treatment at the very least? Then, if that hadn't worked, said enough is enough.'

'Because it's never enough, Sam. There's always one more and one more. My entire life, there's always been just one more treatment. It's all I've known, Sam, and I don't know what it's all for. Another day, another month, another year, and all full of more treatment, more hospitals, more waiting rooms, more pain and feeling so sick I wish I *were* dead. When do I get to live, Sam? When do I get to actually live?'

'But there was hope—'

'Hope?' A strangled noise escaped Lizzie's throat. 'Hope's the real killer. It creeps in with every new treatment, every scan, every doctor's appointment. No matter how much you try and control it, it's always there building inside of you. It's contagious too. It spreads through family and friends like a disease. Everyone hopes it will be OK, and then, when it's not, the devastation is unbearable.

'I think a part of me has always been waiting for the next tumour. I knew the minute my left hand started dropping things last summer, and after the radiotherapy failed this time, I realised I had a choice. I could choose to really live in the time I had left. There would be no hoping, only certainties. Travel, friendship, love ... and then death.'

'If it had worked though ...' Samantha said.

'If, if, if! Don't you hear yourself? I've been saying if since I learned to talk. I'm tired of if. This is my fourth brain tumour, Sam. I've done it all before. The treatments. Watching the hope on my mum's face, whilst I was poked, prodded and injected with drugs. Then the total devastation in her eyes when it failed. I'm done, Sam. I'm done with if.'

'But the clinical trial ...'

Lizzie shook her head desperate for Samantha to understand. 'The list of side effects with any clinical trial is horrendous. And most are permanent. Blindness, loss of limb function, brain damage. All for something nobody even knows will work? I wanted to *live*, Sam, not spend my last few months in a coma. Please listen to what I'm saying. This is why we didn't tell you, because you'd never have been able to accept that this was my choice to make.'

Samantha stared at Lizzie for another beat before spinning towards Jaddi. 'I can't believe you'd let her do this. How could you let her do—' The final part of Samantha's question was lost by the roar of an exhaust.

'It's Lizzie's decision, Sam,' Jaddi said. Her cheeks shone with tears. 'I was trying to support her.'

Another gust of icy wind blew over them, bringing with it more pellets of hail.

'Support? That's a joke, right?' Samantha's voice rose as she looked between them. 'This is insane. For a minute, I thought, maybe you'd made the whole thing up and lied about it to everyone so we could travel the world. That would've been selfish and cruel, but I could've got my head around it if you were going to live. But just giving up? You're not some seventy-year old grandmother here, Liz.' Samantha stepped forward and gripped Lizzie's arms. 'You're twenty-nine.' Samantha shook Lizzie, gentle at first, then harder until pain stretched along Lizzie's biceps to the top of her shoulders, but Lizzie didn't pull away.

'It's my life,' Lizzie cried out. All of a sudden the anger she'd felt in the interview returned. 'Whether you understand it or not, it's *my* life and *my* body. People get to choose every day how they live their lives and no one bats an eyelid. And I've gone along with it, I've played the dutiful patient my whole life, taking all the drugs I was supposed to take, no matter how bad they made me feel, but I've had enough. Why should death be any different from life? Why shouldn't I get to choose death? Choose how I die and when?'

'Because you're young and beautiful,' Samantha said, releasing her hands. 'You're funny and kind and clever, and you're throwing it all away. Why? Because the treatments are too hard?' She shook her head. 'Do you even believe in heaven? Do you believe there's anything else after this life?'

'I ... I don't know.' A pain crushed Lizzie's chest. Her cheeks were wet with tears.

'*I don't know*,' Samantha repeated the words. 'And that's worth gambling your life on, is it? *I don't know*.'

'I'm so sorry, Sam.'

Samantha stared at Lizzie's face, as if searching for an answer to a question she hadn't asked. 'What about your parents? How can you do this to them? Do you have any idea how lucky you are to have Evelyn and Peter? No, of course you don't, because you don't know any different. Not all parents love their children, Lizzie. Some of them don't give a rat's arse about their children,' Samantha said with a strangled sob.

Lizzie drew in a sharp breath at the mention of her parents. It hurt to think of the crushing grief she would cause them, had already caused them.

Lizzie reached a hand to Samantha's arm. 'I'm sorry.'

Samantha jerked away. 'Stop saying that. It's not me you should be apologising to, it's your parents.' Samantha pulled her mobile out of the pocket of her jacket and thrust it into Lizzie's hands.

Lizzie dropped her eyes, allowing the noise of the passing traffic to fill the silence that followed. She knew what was coming, but she couldn't lie anymore.

'They know, don't they?' Samantha nodded, her voice suddenly calm. 'So, it really was just me, then? Me you didn't tell. Me you tricked into coming on this suicide mission. I can't get my head around it.'

Lizzie opened her mouth to say something, to explain herself, but Samantha raised her hand. 'It doesn't matter what you say or how you've rationalised it in your head, you are choosing to die and I will *never* understand that.' Samantha shook her head and strode away.

'Sam, wait—' Lizzie stepped after her.

'Don't follow me,' Samantha shouted.

'Let her go, Liz.' Jaddi said. 'She'll cool off.'

'Will she?' Lizzie sighed, allowing the hurt and the guilt to wrap itself around her. There was a strange comfort in it – the churning guilt, the regret over lying to Samantha. For so long she'd ignored it, pushed it to one side, hidden it out of sight, but now it was out it wrapped around Lizzie like a blanket.

Ben lifted the camera from his shoulder and packed it into its holdall. 'I need to call Caroline. See if she wants you to make a statement or just let the events play out.'

Lizzie turned slowly towards Ben. She thought of the sea and the beach where she'd grown up. The smooth stones she'd lobbed with all her strength past the waves, changing the movement of the sea as the impact rippled outwards. 'Ben.' Lizzie stared into his eyes trying to read his thoughts. 'I'm sorry. I never meant for you to get caught up in all of this.'

'I know,' he said, 'but I did. We all did.'

Lizzie nodded. Fresh tears scorched hot lines down her cheeks. She had a sudden desire to step into his embrace. She searched his face, but his expression remained impassive.

'Will she pull the plug on the documentary?' Jaddi said.

Lizzie spun towards Jaddi. 'How can you think about that now, after what just happened?'

'It will be alright, Liz. I promise.' Jaddi wrapped an arm around Lizzie. 'We knew it might all come out. It was the only way—'

'Was it?' Lizzie stepped out of Jaddi's hold. 'We should get back to the hotel and wait for Samantha.'

Numbness had swept over her body, like the gloopy white anaesthetic cream the nurses would apply before inserting an IV. The panic, the hurt she'd caused Samantha, the fear of what was still to come, it remained just under the surface, even though she couldn't feel it anymore.

CHAPTER 64

Six months ago

Lizzie

Whenever Lizzie thought about Dr Habibi, she thought of the BFG. A tall man who had a kind way with his patients. When she was seven, she'd asked him: 'Are you actually a giant from an ancient land?' He'd smiled and said in his strong Persian accent: 'You are half right and half wrong, clever Lizzie.' His words were always shorter than hers. It wasn't that he spoke the same words quicker, just that each word he pronounced was shorter somehow, fitting three words into her every one so 'you are' became 'yu a'.

She'd mulled his answer over in her head whilst she played sleeping lions, waiting for the MRI machine to take its pictures, and wondered also if he would be able to see her thinking about him in the photos it took. If she was half right, did that mean he was a giant from this country, or a normal man from an ancient land?

It always surprised her then, when she stepped into his small, square office with its ever-growing wall of colourings and thank-you cards that covered the lifespan of his career, that he wasn't much taller than her. His giant status had been nothing more than a childhood illusion. The knowing doctor who'd towered oh so high over her hospital bed.

'Hello, hello,' Dr Habibi said, ushering them into the four chairs opposite his desk.

Lizzie smiled at Dr Habibi and his energetic hand gesturing. Despite the circumstances of their relationship she liked him. He was thoughtful about the little things, like having four chairs ready instead of three because he'd known her brother was coming with them today. Saving them the awkward few minutes of shuffling and waiting whilst another chair was found and dragged in. They'd waited long enough.

Lizzie swallowed and tried to calm the fluttering of her heart. She'd been willing this day to arrive for weeks, waiting for the news like she'd waited for her exam results at university. Every day growing a little less sure, doubting herself and hoping all in the same breath. But now that they were here she desperately wanted to run far, far away.

'So, how are you feeling, Lizzie?' Dr Habibi asked, sitting down at this desk.

'Better. The effects of the radiotherapy have almost gone.'

'Sleeping pattern?'

'Off and on, I guess.'

'Any more symptoms – shaking limbs, numbness?'

'No,' she said, drawing her bottom lip between her teeth and biting. She should tell him about the colours, the spectrum of reds and yellows that had started to float like drifting balloons across her eyes, but she didn't. The colours weren't important right now. The results of her scans … that was why they were here.

'So, I have looked at your scans.' Dr Habibi's eyes gazed into Lizzie's as he spoke before drifting across to her mum, sitting beside her, then her dad, then Aaron. Lizzie didn't mind that. Her family were in this as much as she was.

Her mum slipped her hand into Lizzie's and gripped it tight. The skin around her mum's fingers was slack around the knuckles, and icy to the touch.

Dr Habibi stood up and flicked on the lamps behind the white display boards, illuminating a dozen pictures of her brain, some sideways on showing the shady profile of her nose and mouth. Others more like an alien image or half a grapefruit. Her eyes fell to the tiny black kidney bean at the bottom of the first scan at the point her brain became her spine. A crushing feeling took hold of her, squeezing and squeezing her body. Lizzie knew what Dr Habibi was going to say before he so much as opened his mouth. It was her response she hadn't planned for.

'Unfortunately, the radiotherapy hasn't been successful. As you can see,' he said, pointing to the brainstem with the nib of his pen, 'your tumour hasn't shrunk in size. However, it hasn't grown either. So, we have options. We can consider a clinical trial. There are some new treatments coming out of America for your type of tumour ...'

Lizzie blocked out the sound of his voice. She couldn't listen anymore. Why had she allowed herself to hope it would be gone? Allowed herself to think forward to the coursework she needed to catch up on, and the school placement she would be able to schedule. To her left, Lizzie felt her mum's shoulders start to shake silently. Why had they all allowed themselves to hope?

The crushing feeling continued, squeezing and squeezing. Lizzie stood up, pulling her hand out from her mum's ever-tightening grip and stepping over to the wall. Her eyes scanned the rows of thank-you cards and drawings, stopping every so often to linger on one then another. Right at the top, the scribbled picture she didn't remember doing. A little girl and a purple dog, or a cat maybe. Someone had written her name and age in neat pencil along the top. Elizabeth Appleton, age 3.

There were pieces of paper pinned on top of other pieces of paper on top of thank-you cards and letters four or five deep on the wall, but hers were always visible. The intricate pencil drawing of a hawk that she'd stencilled from a book. Lizzie Appleton, age 9. Sat beside it was a card with a picture of the Suffolk coast; from her mum and dad, she guessed. More notes, more thank-you cards, from her and from her parents. She even spied a crayon scribbling with Aaron's name on it.

She could have changed doctors numerous times over the years, but she never had. Dr Habibi knew her and her family, and they knew him. Her whole life was on this wall. The thought spun in Lizzie's head. She stepped back and tried to draw in a deep breath, but gasped and coughed instead.

Dr Habibi paused and waited for her to finish before continuing. 'So there you are. It is not the news we hoped for, but we have options.'

She shook her head. The wall before her blurred into smudges of colour. Her whole life, she thought again. Her whole life was on this wall. Year after year. Four tumours and countless scans, innumerable check-ups and tests. A lifetime of not living displayed before her on the wall.

'No.' She heard the word, but it took her a split second to realise she had been the one to say it aloud. Only when it was out there, in the room, did she realise she meant it.

Lizzie turned to Dr Habibi. She felt the wide, watery eyes of her family on her and swallowed through the pain tightening around her windpipe. She couldn't look at them and say what she needed to say, so instead she focused on Dr Habibi. 'If –' she swallowed '– I don't pursue a clinical trial, how long do I have?'

'Lizzie!' her mum cried out. 'What are you saying?'

'It's impossible for me to give any exact numbers,' he said, staring back at Lizzie, both of them ignoring

Evelyn's outburst as if they were alone in his office. 'We don't yet know how quickly the tumour will grow –'

'Best guess?'

'Based on the growth levels I've seen so far, factoring any effect of the radiotherapy, my best guess would be six months. I'm sorry, Lizzie.'

A strangled cry from her mum filled the silence that followed.

'And there's no chance that another course of radiotherapy will do anything?'

Dr Habibi shook his head. 'No, there are no guarantees, but with every treatment we try we get a better feel for what doesn't work, and therefore what might work. With the tumour at its current size, I would like to put you on anti-seizure medication, to reduce the risk of a seizure as the tumour grows. A clinical trial—'

'No more treatment,' Lizzie said, surprised by the confidence in her voice.

Six months.

She knew she should be devastated, and somewhere inside, she probably was, but all she could think about was the wall in front of her. Six months without being stuck in hospital, without throwing up, without sitting in a stuffy waiting room waiting for her turn to be pinned to a table in a dark room whilst radiation was zapped into her body. Six months without having to hope.

A jittery relief gushed through her. She could choose.

'Lizzie.' Her mum stood up and wrapped her in her arms, drawing out a hundred memories from her childhood of being in her mum's arms. Goodnight hugs, hospital hugs, grazed-knee hugs, mean-friends hug, sick hugs. They were all there, unleashed from the nostalgia of her mother's arms, her bosom and her floral perfume. Lizzie's throat tightened again. All of a sudden it seemed as though she'd swallowed a gobstopper whole, and now it was lodged on top of her windpipe.

'You're disappointed,' her mum said. 'We all are. But don't make a decision in the heat of the moment like this, please.' Her final plea came out a whisper.

'Evelyn,' her father said, standing up. 'Let's hear what Lizzie has to say.'

Her mum sniffed and stood back. Four pairs of eyes stared at her. Dr Habibi's were black and narrowed a little, his forehead furrowed with concern. Her mum's, almost grey through the tears, and wide like a wild animal caught in the headlights of a passing car. Aaron, still rooted to his chair, his body twisted. His bottom lip quivered a little until he pulled it between his teeth.

Lizzie looked away. Hugging her mum, looking at Aaron, fractured the wisps of certainty she felt inside her, and she didn't want that. Her dad stepped forwards and rested a large warm hand on her shoulder. She looked up and saw in his eyes the acceptance she needed. He understood. The gobstopper shifted and all at once she could breathe again.

'I don't want to have any more treatment,' she said, turning her gaze back to the wall. 'I've had a lifetime of radiotherapy and chemotherapy, and operations, and scans. And I'm right back where I started. Now, I want to choose. And I'm choosing to live. Six months might not seem like a long time, but it's six months of living in a way I never have before. No more back and forths …'

As Lizzie spoke, the certainty grew and she clung to it. The only certainty in life was death, she thought, wondering where she'd heard that saying. She'd walked into Dr Habibi's office with hope and she was going to walk out with certainty.

CHAPTER 65

Six months ago

Lizzie

At some point on the tube journey home a jittering had taken hold of Lizzie's body. Another symptom or a reaction to the events in Dr Habibi's office? The latter this time, Lizzie thought. The key in her hand danced and scratched against the lock before finding its place and releasing the catch in the door.

The smell of mildew and mould, and Samantha's vanilla air diffuser, greeted Lizzie as she stepped into their dim, one-bedroom flat. When had they stopped complaining to the landlord about the smell? When had they stopped talking about moving somewhere nicer? Cleaner? Bigger? Twelve months, they'd said. Twelve months of rotating which one of them slept on the sofa, whilst the other two shared the double bed, and cold showers two days out of three because there was only enough hot water in the mornings for one person. Twelve months and they would have enough money to go travelling. That had been the plan, anyway. The flat in an apartment block with nine others, nestled in between two high-rise council estate towers in All Saints, east London, had been home now for six years.

Lizzie sighed, the breath leaving her body in broken shudders. She dropped her bag on the floor but didn't bother shrugging off her jacket. The autumn air carried the first hints of winter, and they'd yet to unearth the oil heaters from the back of the hall cupboard.

'Lizzie?' Jaddi's voice carried from the living room.

'Yeah,' Lizzie said, stepping into the room and flicking on the light.

'Oh, that's better, thanks.' Jaddi slid the laptop from her lap and placed it on the floor before standing up. 'How did it go? I thought you were going to text me?'

'Sorry, I forgot.' Lizzie flopped onto the sofa and rubbed her hands over her face.

'What happened?' Jaddi asked.

Lizzie shook her head underneath her hands.

'Oh, honey.' Jaddi stood up and a moment later the sofa cushion shifted and she felt Jaddi's body beside her. 'So does that mean more treatment?'

'I said, no.'

'What?'

'He wanted me to sign up for some clinical trial where they have no idea if what they're pumping into my body will kill me as quickly as the tumour. So I said no.'

'But—'

'Please, Jaddi,' Lizzie snapped, rubbing her hands harder against her face. 'I'm done explaining myself for one night. The rounds of radiotherapy didn't work. The tumour is still there, but I can't go through it again, OK? I'm done.'

'Do you know how long?'

Lizzie dropped her hands from her face and waited for the emotion to overwhelm her. It didn't. She felt nothing. 'Dr Habibi said six months, as a best guess.'

Jaddi didn't reply. She stood up and stepped to the windowless kitchen area behind the sofa. Lizzie listened to the clinking of bottles in the fridge door and a cupboard open then shut.

'I got us some fizz,' Jaddi said, walking back to the sofa with a shrug of her shoulders. 'Just in case, you know? But what the hell, we should have a drink.'

'I thought we said no more Prosecco.' Lizzie pointed to the large world-map poster on the wall, torn and scuffed at the corners from too much blue tack over the years. Next to the map was a line of pink Post-its, each with a number written on it – their savings. The amount had risen steadily at first, as they had tallied what was left from their salaries at the end of every month. Then there had been the wedding of a mutual friend. New outfits, a gift, hotel and travel costs. A month had gone by without a Post-it. Then another, and another. Lizzie couldn't remember the last time they'd put one up. 'We're supposed to be saving again, remember?'

'Does it matter now?' Jaddi asked. 'I'd promise to forgo a couple of cappuccino's next week to make up for it but ...' Jaddi's voice trailed off.

'You can still go without me,' Lizzie said, taking the bottle from Jaddi and twisting the cork until it popped into her hands. 'Next year.' The thought of not travelling the world with Jaddi and Samantha like they'd always planned; the thought of next year – a year she wouldn't see – caused the colours to return to her eyes and a panic to spin and twirl in her stomach. Lizzie blinked until the colours disappeared. She had to focus on living, on the months she had.

'Where's Samantha?' Lizzie asked.

'Working late again. She's staying at David's tonight, so we've got the bed. She thought you might like a decent night's sleep.'

'I'd rather have seen her and slept on the sofa,' Lizzie said, gazing out the window, her eyes following the distant blinking lights of an aeroplane, climbing higher and higher until it disappeared from view.

'David's asked Sam to move in with him.'

'What? When?'

'Last week. She wanted to wait until you'd had the results back before telling you.' Jaddi shrugged again before tipping a long mouthful of Prosecco into her mouth.

'So travelling is out of the question for you guys anyway, then? If we have to split the rent two ways, then one, you'll never have any money left to save.' Lizzie's eyes felt drawn back to the map on the wall, and the red-dot stickers, like an outbreak of chickenpox, that marked the places they wanted to visit.

Lizzie had a sudden urge to rip the map from the wall and scrunch it into a tight ball.

Jaddi topped up her glass. The pale liquid fizzed up and over the lip. Jaddi dipped her head forward and slurped at the foam. 'I'll figure something out.'

Lizzie's head throbbed in rhythm with her heart. Salty tears stung the skin underneath her eyes. 'I'm sorry.'

'Don't be sorry, Lizzie. This isn't your fault.'

'But you really wanted to travel and—'

'So did you, so did Sam,' Jaddi said. 'I wished we'd tried harder to save.'

'We have a little bit of money, don't we? I was thinking on the tube home that we could use it to go somewhere, just the three of us. It wouldn't be all the way around the world, but we could see a little bit of it.'

'A two-week holiday?' Jaddi shook her head.

'I know.' Lizzie dropped her head against the cushion. 'But it's better than nothing.'

An hour later the numbness of alcohol coated Lizzie's thoughts. She had six months. She could spend time with her mum and dad. She could watch Aaron train. She could travel somewhere with Samantha and Jaddi. OK, so it wasn't long enough for her to achieve all the things she wanted, and there was no way that their savings would stretch to all the places she'd wanted to see, but it was enough. Enough to know she wouldn't spend another second in hospital with her head pinned to that table. She wouldn't spend another moment of her life swimming in the foggy after-effects of the treatments. It had to be enough. She'd make it enough.

'I've got it!' Jaddi leapt from the sofa.

'Got what?' Lizzie raised her eyebrows.

'It's perfect.' Jaddi grabbed her laptop and dropped back to the sofa, her fingers dancing over the keyboard. 'I can't believe I didn't think of it before.'

'What?'

'We have to travel. We have to do it. The three of us. Like we'd planned all along. If we go after Christmas then we'll have three months to scrape some money together and three months to travel.'

'Sounds great, but where are we going to get three months worth of travelling money from?' Lizzie drained the last inch of liquid in her glass. The chill and bubbles had gone, leaving a sickly warm tang to burn her throat.

'We'll crowdfund our trip.' Jaddi lifted her head, a smile stretching across her face as she stared at Lizzie. Her eyes sparked with excitement, with hope.

'We'll what?'

'I read this article a few months ago. This couple in America wanted to have a course of IVF but couldn't afford it. The man set up a website and pleaded with people to donate a dollar to help him and his wife. He put up some photos of them together and wrote this heartbreaking story about how long they'd been trying to conceive, and how much they longed for a baby. Then he shared it on social media, and it went viral. They made enough for the treatment and had enough left over to set up a charity for other couples in the same boat. All we need is a website and a good story. I can't believe I've only just thought about it.'

Lizzie shook her head. 'You're kidding? You want to ask strangers to donate a pound for us to go travelling? We'd never get more than the train fare to the airport.'

'We would if it went viral like that American one did. Besides, a pound is just a suggestion, people can give us whatever they want.'

'Yes, but why would anyone give us money? I can see how it worked with the IVF couple, but we can't expect anyone to give us money because we're terrible at saving and now I've chosen not to have any more treatment. It's my choice. People won't understand. They'll say I'm giving up. That I don't deserve it. It's hardly the sympathy vote, is it?'

Jaddi's fingers paused; her eyes fixed on a point in the distance. A moment later she started typing again.

'Jaddi?' Lizzie's heartbeat quickened as she stared at the determination in Jaddi's eyes.

'We'll spin it. It's just like any of the PR campaigns I've worked on. We just have to find a way to hook people.'

'Come again?' Lizzie scooched across the sofa and peered over Jaddi's shoulder. What looked like a pale-blue webpage filled the screen. There were no words, just a selfie of the three of them from a trip to the beach last summer. A large blinking cursor waited for a title.

Jaddi fixed her gaze on Lizzie. 'Who else knows that you're choosing not to have treatment?'

'My parents and Aaron, and Dr Habibi, but, Jaddi, we can't lie.'

'It's not a lie. There is no treatment for your tumour. Everything else is experimental.'

'We'd be defrauding people.'

Jaddi shook her head, 'You said it yourself, there's no way to know if a clinical trial would work. Your tumour *is* untreatable; it's the same thing.'

Lizzie stared at Jaddi and then the blank website and wished she'd not had so much to drink. Her head struggled to keep up with Jaddi's 'act now, think later' mindset at the best of times.

'It's lying, Jaddi,' Lizzie said. 'Let's not pretend it's anything else.'

'But you're not saying no.'

'You know how desperate I am to travel, but not like this.'

'But what harm will it do?'

Lizzie opened her mouth to reply but she had no response to Jaddi's question.

CHAPTER 66

Jaddi

A buzz circled Jaddi's veins. The alcohol had fuelled something inside of her, creating a clarity she'd never have found without it.

'I don't feel right about this,' Lizzie muttered again from the kitchen as she gulped back a glass of water.

Jaddi looked up from her laptop screen and stared at the pale complexion of her friend. The gruelling months of radiotherapy and scans showed in the dark shadows under Lizzie's eyes, and the way her skin sunk in under her cheekbones.

Jaddi clenched her teeth together and squeezed until the hurt passed. She desperately wanted to beg Lizzie not to do this, to grab her by the arm and drag her back to the hospital and sign her up for that trial herself. But she couldn't. This was Lizzie's decision, and however much it hurt, Jaddi had to support her, no matter what.

It had been painful for Jaddi to watch Lizzie's suffering, but more than that, it had gnawed away at Jaddi that there'd been nothing she could do to help. Until now. Now she could offer her friend the support she needed, and no matter what it took, Jaddi would find a way to get them around the world.

Lizzie dropped back onto the sofa and rubbed the back of her neck. 'Even if I did get on board with lying to complete strangers, what about my mum and dad, and Aaron? They know the truth, which means we'll be asking them to lie too. And what about Samantha? She's the most honest person I know. There's no way she'd go along with it. She'd never understand or stop trying to convince me to change my mind.'

'You're right,' Jaddi said. 'We shouldn't tell Sam.'

'Think about what you're saying, Jaddi. Samantha's our best friend, we can't lie to her.'

'I know she'll be pissed afterwards if she finds out we lied, but she'll forgive us when she realises why we did it. She'll see this was the only way for the three of us to travel the world together.'

'And what about my family? I can't ask them to lie. They've been through enough.'

'It's not like we're asking them to be a part of it. It's just one of a million fundraising websites.'

Lizzie's silence ramped up the buzz zigzagging through her. Lizzie was wavering, and that was all the go-ahead she needed. Jaddi returned her focus to the blank web page, her fingers poised on the keys.

'*The Girl with Three Months to Live*,' Jaddi said over the tapping of the keyboard. 'That's what we'll call it.' Jaddi smiled. It was the perfect title. The perfect plan.

'Three?'

'It's just a title. Like I said, we'll need some time to raise the money.'

Lizzie shook her head. 'I can't think about this anymore. I'm going to bed.'

'Good idea.' Jaddi nodded. Without Lizzie's doubts she'd be able to finish the website tonight.

'Jaddi?' Lizzie said as she reached the door.

'Yeah?' she lifted her eyes and smiled at Lizzie.

'Promise me you won't do anything crazy tonight. Can we talk about this tomorrow when I'm sober and we've both had a chance to think about it? What we're talking about is insane. There is no way it will work, and even if it did, it's wrong.'

'Absolutely.' Jaddi nodded. 'Get some sleep, and don't worry about a thing.'

A moment later the bedroom door clicked shut, leaving Jaddi alone with the plans racing around her head. She pulled in a long breath and opened her email account. She found Aaron's email address and began to type. If they had even a chance of getting enough views on their website to make a difference, they'd need Aaron's help. And Lizzie was right, she couldn't ask her parents to lie, but Jaddi could. If Jaddi could get Aaron on board and he explained it to their parents, then surely they wouldn't stand in Lizzie's way.

What harm could it do? Jaddi thought again. Her best friend was dying. This, this wasn't even a lie, more a bending of the truth. Lying to Samantha wouldn't be easy, but Sam would understand eventually, if she found out at all that is. They had to focus on the bigger picture – fulfilling Lizzie's dream, all of their dreams, to travel, whilst they still could. How they made it happen didn't matter.

CHAPTER 67

Samantha

Biting air sliced through Samantha as she strode along the empty street. A row of street lamps cast orange pools of light on the damp sidewalk. Shadows stretched out from the alleyways between buildings, made by the lights from the apartments above. The rain and sleet had stopped, leaving behind a cold, clear night, but Samantha barely noticed.

Her two best friends, her only friends, her family, had lied to her. Did they really believe that a lifetime of experiences could be crammed into three meagre months? The lengths Lizzie and Jaddi had gone to, the number of smaller lies they'd told to mask the big one, the depth of the deceit, it stabbed at her over and over. How could they do this to her?

Car horns honked at her as she zipped across street after street without waiting for the cross signals. Anger continued to pulse through her, driving her forwards.

'It's Lizzie's decision,' Jaddi had said. Was it? Death wasn't a choice.

People get to choose every day how they live their lives and no one bats an eyelid. Why should death be any different?

Because it is, Samantha thought. It is, Lizzie it is, it is.

An ache spread across Samantha's chest but she carried on walking. Then the memories started. A carousel of images spinning in Samantha's thoughts. Lizzie's empty bedroom in their university houseshare. All the times it had been just Samantha and Jaddi, because Lizzie had been in London having check-ups.

Lizzie lying on the sofa last year, her duvet cocooned around her, her body shaking, too tired to watch television or mumble more than a few words. Samantha sitting beside Lizzie at the hairdressers whilst she'd had her lovely brown hair chopped off. Jaddi cracking jokes. Lizzie laughing and crying at the same time.

Samantha gasped. It wasn't the lying that hurt, it was the truth. She could hate what they'd done with every atom in her body, but it didn't change one simple fact – Lizzie was dying. Samantha drew to a stop and closed her eyes, allowing the hot tears to scorch the cold of her face as she wrapped her arms around herself and cried.

Samantha couldn't begin to understand how hard the treatments were on Lizzie and then to find out it had all been for nothing … But did that make Lizzie right? Were six months of living worth more than the pain of the treatments? Samantha just couldn't see how.

Then she remembered a conversation with Lizzie in Las Vegas.

Sometimes people keep secrets from the ones they love … They start down a road and before long they realise they can't go back, so they carry on.

Had Lizzie been trying to tell her something? Did a part of her, however small, want to change her mind? What if she could find a way to make Lizzie see that life was worth fighting for? What if it wasn't too late? There was still hope. Samantha inhaled the cold air and opened her eyes. There had to be way to help Lizzie. Samantha reached for her phone to call Lizzie, before she remembered where it was.

For the first time since she'd left the building in Times Square, Samantha scanned the street names. She was on the corner of 22nd Street and 7th Avenue. Their hotel was on 35th Street. She'd walked too far.

In the distance, the whoop-whoop of a siren blasted. Samantha stepped to the edge of the sidewalk and gazed along 22nd Street. The blare of the sirens grew louder and a flash of red lights peeked out of 8th Avenue and turned onto 22nd Street towards her.

Cars began to swerve to the sides of the road, clearing a path straight down the middle for the emergency vehicle. Samantha jumped to one side as a yellow taxi mounted the sidewalk beside her.

With a clear space, the ambulance accelerated. The shrill of the siren filled the night and pierced Samantha's eardrums.

Her stomach flipped. Could something have happened to Lizzie? Samantha span around to leave, but glanced back as a deafening crunch of scraping metal and wheels screeching on wet tarmac sounded over the siren.

Time slowed. A second stretched into a minute as the flashing of red lights filled her sights and the ambulance lost control, colliding with the yellow taxi and bumping onto the curb. It toppled onto its side but didn't stop moving.

Samantha stared at the whites of the ambulance driver's eyes through the windscreen as the ambulance skidded towards her. He lifted his hands from the wheel and covered his face with his forearms.

Then a brilliant white shone across her vision and she felt her body lift up from the pavement and fly through the air.

CHAPTER 68

Day 62

Lizzie

Lizzie sat down on the smooth face of the rock and stared across the park. The grass glistened with a white, frosty dew. Heavy, white clouds covered the early morning sun. Despite the hour, Central Park was bustling with dog walkers, runners, and men and women in business suits wearing trainers and woollen hats. They glanced in Lizzie's direction as they entered the south side gates, before dropping their heads and choosing one of the dozen different paths winding deeper into the park.

The tips of Lizzie's fingers had begun to numb and she had a sudden longing for a pair of gloves. A hundred metres away Jaddi's feet crunched the frozen grass as she jogged towards Lizzie.

'Any sign of her?' Lizzie said.

'No. I don't think she's here, Liz. I'm sure she just checked into a different hotel. She'll turn up.'

Worry wound through Lizzie. She'd known it had been a long shot coming here so early, but what choice did she have? They had to find Samantha. 'But all of her stuff is still in our room. I don't think she even has a room key.'

'Even more reason why we should be waiting in the hotel then, instead of in this freezing cold park,' Jaddi said, pulling her hands inside the sleeves of her hoody and stamping her feet on the ground.

'I know, but Samantha said yesterday that she wanted to walk through Central Park. It was worth a try.'

'Come on. Let's get some bagels and wait in the hotel lobby. She might already be there.'

'If only she hadn't given me her phone.' Lizzie sighed.

'Lizzie, we'll find her.'

Lizzie nodded and slid off the rock. 'Everyone's looking at me.' Lizzie nodded to a couple walking a dog ten metres away. The couple dropped their heads as Jaddi turned to look. 'They hate me.'

'No, they don't,' Jaddi said. 'I know you don't want to look at the Facebook page, but it's filled with supportive messages. It's all over the internet too. You've sparked a global debate. For every negative remark, there are at least two comments of support.'

Lizzie opened her mouth to say something but Jaddi spoke first. 'We'll fix it with Samantha. I promise.'

A figure in the distance strode towards them as they stepped onto the footpath.

'Is that Ben?' Lizzie narrowed her eyes at the figure. Her spirits lifted. He'd brushed over her apology last night, but she wanted to say it again. Nerves tugged at her insides. Could they find their way back to whatever it was they'd started in Vegas? She hoped so. But she had to find Samantha first.

'I think so.' Jaddi squinted and waved.

The figure waved back as a single snowflake drifted in front of Lizzie's eyes and landed on the tip of her nose.

'Yes,' Jaddi said. 'It's him, and it's snowing. Just what we need.' As the words left her mouth, more flakes appeared around them, floating in slow swaying movements to the ground.

'Hi,' Lizzie said, feeling a sudden awkwardness as he stepped within earshot. What did he think of her? The whole world could hate her, but not Ben.

'Hey,' he replied, his face strained with a sadness Lizzie couldn't read.

'No camera,' Jaddi said. 'Does that mean the documentary's been cancelled?'

Ben shook his head but didn't elaborate.

'How did you know we were here?' Lizzie asked.

'There's a tracking device on the video camera in your bag. In case it gets lost or stolen.'

'And to keep tabs on me.' Lizzie raised her eyebrows as she thought about all the times Ben had found her sitting on her own somewhere.

Ben didn't respond. Flakes of snow landed on his head. A small one caught on his eyelashes before dropping onto the dark-blue smudges circling his eyes.

'You look like you've had about as much sleep we have,' Jaddi said. 'We knocked on your door earlier, but we weren't sure if you were asleep or out. We came to look for Samantha, have you seen her?'

His forehead furrowed as he stepped closer. 'There was an accident last night,' he said. 'An ambulance hit a taxi and lost control. Samantha was there.'

An icy chill spread over Lizzie's skin. Goosebumps prickled her arms. Her throat tightened. 'What?'

Fat puffs of snow swirled around her, moving in every direction. Not just down, but up and around too. A thin layer covered Jaddi's hair, stark white against the loose black strands.

'Is she OK?' Jaddi asked. 'Where is she?'

Ben shook his head. Lizzie watched his Adam's apple jump as he swallowed, and in that millisecond she knew.

'She died at the scene,' he said. 'It was instant. Her head hit the pavement. She wouldn't have felt a thing.'

'No.' Lizzie stumbled back against the rock and shook her head. 'There's been a mistake. It can't be her. You're wrong.'

Ben reached out and pulled her into his arms. 'I'm not wrong.'

'Samantha isn't dead. She can't be. We saw her, what? Eight hours ago. She was so angry with me. She can't be—'

Lizzie felt Ben tighten his hold on her as he spoke. 'The police found her microphone and called the Channel 6 office in London. Caroline called me. I've just come from the morgue. It's her. I'm sorry.'

'No.' Lizzie shook her head against his chest. A chill like nothing she'd ever felt before seeped into her bones. 'You're wrong. You have to be wrong. She can't be dead.'

Pain sliced through Lizzie's chest. Her lungs shrunk so that all she could pull in were short, gasping breaths. It had to be a mistake; it had to be a mistake. Her heart hurt. A raw physical pain that spread all the way to her throat. Samantha couldn't be dead. Her best friend couldn't be dead. Lizzie's weight dropped against Ben's body as a muffled sob escaped her mouth.

CHAPTER 69

Jaddi

'This is on me. This is my fault,' Jaddi said.

In the space of minutes the air had filled with a million flakes of feathery snow. A layer of pure white, the colour of printer paper, covered every surface for as far as she could see. An involuntary shaking had taken hold of her body, and yet she couldn't feel the cold anymore.

'This is on me,' Jaddi said again. Her hands quivered as she lifted them to her face.

'Jaddi?' Lizzie said, stumbling away from Ben and wrapping her arms around her.

'This is my fault.'

'It's not, Jaddi.'

'Yes, it is. I came up with the idea. I created the website. I pushed you into it. I convinced you to lie to Samantha. If I hadn't done those things then she'd still be alive.'

'Then it's on both of us,' Lizzie said.

Jaddi turned her face and stared into Lizzie's eyes. 'I'm sorry.' Jaddi swallowed down a sob; it caught in her throat creating an anguished cry like a wild animal caught in a trap. Jaddi dropped her head onto Lizzie's shoulder. Hot tears poured down her cheeks.

Jaddi dug her fingers into Lizzie's back. She felt Lizzie's shoulders shake as they clung to each other.

'We should go,' Ben said. 'It's really coming down out here.'

Jaddi pulled in a shuddering breath and lifted her head up from Lizzie's shoulder. 'Where?'

'The hotel,' Ben said.

Lizzie shook her head before glancing at Jaddi. 'I need to see her.'

Jaddi wiped her hands across her cheeks and nodded as another sob broke free.

'You don't have to do that,' Ben said. 'I've already done the identification. It's her, Lizzie.'

'I know, but I … I just can't believe you. I have to see her for myself.'

Jaddi swallowed the razor-edged mound in her throat as fresh tears fell from her eyes. 'Me too.'

A porter in a green uniform led them down a long corridor and through two sets of swinging doors with circular porthole windows.

The only noise was the squeak of their shoes on the polished linoleum floor. The porter – a short man in his late fifties with greying-brown hair and a bald spot in the shape of a perfect circle on the back of his head – had raised his eyebrows at their dishevelled, snowy clothes, but hadn't commented or attempted the same chit-chat that they'd endured from the taxi driver on their journey towards the East River.

Jaddi felt a cold droplet of mucus run from her nose and realised she'd been breathing through her mouth, like the times she used public toilets and couldn't bear to breathe through her nose because of the putrid smell of urine and faeces. But this wasn't a public toilet, it was a morgue, and the odour she didn't want to smell was death. Jaddi dabbed the cuff of her jumper against her nose and risked a short sniff. Nothing. No decay or death smells assaulted her nostrils. No zesty cleaning products or redolent air fresheners either.

The porter unlocked the door of a small dark room no larger than a broom cupboard and waved them in. He tapped a switch and a long fluorescent tube flickered to life, revealing two plastic chairs and a window covered with navy curtains drawn across from the other side of the glass.

'It'll just take a few minutes,' he said, nodding towards the window.

'Are you sure you want to do this?' Ben said.

Lizzie gripped her hand and nodded.

Jaddi closed her eyes as her thoughts flitted between willing the curtains to open and wishing that they never would. It could all be a mistake, couldn't it? Ben could have made a mistake? That's what they were about to find out. Someone else's best friend, someone else's life was gone, but not Samantha's. Samantha would be waiting for them in the hotel lobby, furious with them for lying to her, but still alive.

Beside her, Jaddi felt Lizzie's hand tighten around her fingers. Jaddi's eyes shot open as the curtains juddered for a second and then parted to reveal another room similar to their own, empty apart from the steel gurney and the body, covered to the chest by a green sheet the same colour as the porter's uniform.

A wave of elation crashed through Jaddi. It wasn't Samantha. The lifeless body on the gurney was too small. Her blonde hair was wet and brushed back instead of parted down the middle. Her skin was too pale and her face, whilst familiar, was not the face of the best friend who'd stayed up all night to help Jaddi finish her dissertation on time, and had jumped off a cliff with them in Mondulkiri, and had slept in the next room, washed in the same shower, and eaten at the same table as her for the past nine years. It wasn't Samantha.

Lizzie let out an anguished sob from beside her.

'It's not—' The rest of the words caught in her throat as Jaddi's gaze fell to the pink circular marks on the woman's wrists, and the cut stretching along her right arm where Samantha had hit the nightstand in Vegas.

Pain stretched out of her heart. Tears spilled down her face and over her lips until she could taste the salt of them in her mouth. An unbearable energy exploded inside her. She wanted to bang on the glass and shout wake up, wake up, wake up. She wanted to run to the next room and pound her fist against Samantha's chest until her heart started beating again, until Samantha started living again, but Jaddi's feet refused to move, just as her eyes refused to look away.

Ben stepped towards both of them. He wrapped an arm around Lizzie and, a moment later, she felt his hand on her shoulder and allowed herself to be pulled into his embrace. Something warm dripped onto the top of her head. Ben's tears.

Jaddi's legs buckled from beneath her and her body slipped from his hold and onto the hard floor. It was her fault that they were in New York. It was her fault that they'd argued on the street. She was the reason Lizzie hadn't raced after Samantha. This was on her. Samantha was dead because of her. She was the reason that they'd lied to Samantha. She was the one who'd supported Lizzie's decision, helped her hide it too, so Lizzie wouldn't have to explain herself, or be convinced to change her mind.

One of her best friends was lying dead in a morgue because of her, and another would be joining her soon.

All because of her. Jaddi pulled her knees up to her head and covered her face with her hands as tears poured from her eyes.

A moment later the porter returned. 'We have a bereavement room,' he said. 'Perhaps you'd like to use it.'

Jaddi felt Ben's strong arm on hers, pulling her to her feet and guiding her three paces across the corridor and into a larger room with gleaming white walls. Two large canvas prints of the New York skyline hung on the walls.

Loss wound through Jaddi's body. It wrapped itself around her in a cocoon of despair. Samantha would never travel to the top of the Empire State Building and see the New York skyline for herself. She would never get to travel back to Mondulkiri like she'd wanted to and care for the elephants. She wouldn't do anything again, ever.

'There's tea and coffee facilities. Please help yourself, and stay as long as you need,' the porter said, before closing the door.

Lizzie dropped onto the sofa, bent forward and buried her head in hands. Ben moved over to the table and, a moment later, the whirring noise of a kettle boiling filled the room.

The sound made her think of Samantha. Samantha was always the first one up in the morning. Always the first one to flick on the kettle and make three cups of tea, delivering them to Jaddi and Lizzie without a word. How many times had Jaddi joked with Lizzie about that? 'It's the best indicator of how late I'm going to be for work if I've overslept,' Jaddi had always laughed. 'Lukewarm – marginally late; tepid – very late; cold – time to call in sick.'

Ben pushed a steaming mug into her hands before passing another to Lizzie.

'I don't know what to do now.' Jaddi shrugged, looking between Lizzie and Ben. 'Are we supposed to carry on? Because I don't think I can.' Her voice rose and ended in sob.

Lizzie shook her head before turning to Ben. 'What will happen to her now?'

'Channel 6 are arranging to have her body flown back to London. Caroline's contacting her mum.'

'Yesterday was the first time I've ever heard Samantha talk about what it was like for her growing up,' Lizzie said.

Jaddi drew in a sharp breath. Fresh pain sliced through her. Yesterday, Samantha had been talking and laughing and planning her future. Yesterday, she'd been happy to be in New York, and teasing Jaddi about the cold. Today, she was gone.

'I'm not sure she'd have wanted her mum to organise her funeral,' Lizzie said.

'We should do it,' Jaddi nodded.

'I'm not sure she'd want us to do it either,' Lizzie said.

'Liz—'

'We were all she had. We hurt her and we killed her.' Lizzie's cheeks shone wet with tears.

Ben sat down beside Lizzie and touched her knee. 'Lizzie, you can't blame yourself.'

Lizzie let out a howling gasp. 'I don't blame myself. I blame Jaddi.'

Jaddi drew in a breath, her eyes finding Lizzie's. A darkness crossed Lizzie's face. She frowned, holding Jaddi's stare.

'You were right before, in the park,' Lizzie said, 'when you said this is on you. You pushed and pushed, just like you always do. Egging us on, bullying us into things. I'm sure you think you're doing it for us, for me, but it's not.

It never is. It's always about what you want. You wanted to go travelling. You saw a way to make it happen.'

Jaddi recoiled. Her head smarted as if Lizzie had slapped her face. Jaddi had had the same thoughts, she'd blamed herself, but hearing it from Lizzie cut to her core.

Lizzie stood up and stepped towards the door.

'You wanted to know what harm it could do?' Lizzie cast her eyes around the room. Tears fell from her eyes. 'Here's your answer.'

CHAPTER 70

Lizzie

Lizzie's hand trembled as she reached for the door handle. A part of her, a big part, wanted to throw open the door and run far away. But she didn't move. Instead she stood there, facing the door, the handle gripped in her shaking hand. The only sound, Jaddi's wrenching sobs.

Her venomous words hung in the air like a bad aftertaste. Had she meant it? Did she really think Jaddi was to blame? No more than she was. She'd even predicted it.

There will be people out there right now, walking down the street, thinking they've got years ahead of them. When bam, a bus hits them, and it's over. I've been given a chance to live my dreams.

It had been an ambulance, not a bus, but the rest was true. Samantha's dreams, her future, had been stolen from her. There'd been no choice. None whatsoever. One second she'd been walking down the street, angry with both of them for lying, angry with Lizzie for not fighting anymore; the next she was gone.

It wasn't fair. She was the one who'd chosen to die, but it was Samantha who'd been taken. Tears flowed in a steady stream down her face, dripping in perfect circles on the grey floor.

'Lizzie?' Jaddi's voice was hoarse and scratchy.

'I'm sorry.' Lizzie spun around and dived towards Jaddi. 'I didn't mean that. I was hurt and angry and I didn't mean it.' Lizzie buried her head in Jaddi's shoulder and held her tight.

Jaddi sniffed. 'You were right, though. I did push this.'

Lizzie sat down and slid her hand inside Jaddi's. 'We both did.'

'Shall we go home?' Jaddi unleashed a shuddering sigh and rested her head on Lizzie's shoulder.

Lizzie nodded. 'Will you go for me? Arrange something nice for Samantha. Something classy with lots of tulips and cups of tea—' Lizzie's voice broke. 'She'd have liked that.'

'What are you going to do?' Jaddi asked.

Lizzie stared at the photograph on the wall of the city skyline. When she'd said no to Dr Habibi, she'd told herself that six months of living was enough. She convinced herself it would be, that it had to be, but it wasn't. Lizzie didn't know when she'd realised it, or maybe she'd known it all along and hidden it out of reach in her mind, but Samantha's death had thrust it forwards and she could no longer ignore it. She could no longer stare down the path she'd chosen and think it was too late to turn back.

All of a sudden she realised, it wasn't the lie that had weighed so heavy on her thoughts all this time, it was the truth.

'Samantha was right,' Lizzie said as silent tears continued to drop from her eyes. 'I shouldn't have given up. It's on both of us that she's ...' Lizzie shook her head. '*I'm* the one that should be dead. Not her. *I'm* the one that chose it. All she chose to do was to be a good friend. She's dead and I'm alive. I can't let her down now. I have to go to San Francisco and meet this friend of Dr Moss's. He thinks he can help me.'

'Are you sure that's what you want?'

'What I want is to undo it all and be back in our dingy flat. The three of us together.'

Jaddi smiled, fresh tears brimmed in her eyes.

'But since that's not an option, then I need to fight. I thought I was lucky because I was given time, but I've been so stupid. I was lucky to be given the chance to fight. Samantha didn't get a chance so now I have to take mine, for her.'

'I want to come with you. You shouldn't go through it alone,' Jaddi said.

'No.' Lizzie shook her head. Goosebumps spread across her arms. 'I know it might seem silly, but I can't bare the idea of Samantha going home alone. Please, go with her.'

'It's not silly,' Jaddi whispered.

They sat in silence for a moment.

Ben stepped forward and crouched down to the floor beside them. 'I'll come with you, Lizzie.' he said.

Lizzie nodded and reached for Ben's arm, pulling him closer so that the three of them were together on the floor. They stayed like that for a long time.

Jaddi wiped the sleeve of her jumper across her face. 'I can't lose you both—'

'I know,' Lizzie said. She sucked in her bottom lip and allowed hope to spread over her pain. Maybe it was too late, maybe her tumour had grown too much by now, maybe the lie she'd told had become the truth, but she had to try. She had to fight. For Sam.

CHAPTER 71

Day 70

Lizzie

Beyond the blinds drawn shut, and the window that didn't open, the sun was rising. Lizzie thought about lowering the bars of the bed and padding barefoot to the window, peeking through the slats and watching the rays of yellow creep over Golden Gate Park. Or sneaking off the ward in her white hospital gown with its turquoise, teardrop pattern and finding her way onto the roof so she could feel the warmth of those first beams on her skin and smell the sea on the breeze. *Are you up there, Samantha? Did you find your way to the gates all right? I hope so. Wherever you are, I hope you're OK.*

Instead, Lizzie glanced out of the open doorway, past the nurse station to the white clock on the wall. The ward was so quiet at night, the quietest ward she'd ever been on; Lizzie could hear the red second hand of the clock ticking. In a few minutes, the next shift of nurses would begin their day and one of those nurses would be bringing Lizzie the pink chalky liquid she needed to drink before her treatment could start. She couldn't miss the nurse, couldn't delay another day.

In her heart, Lizzie knew that it was more than just her wait for the medicine that kept her rooted to the bed with the blinds shut tight. Watching the horizon transform into a wash of pinks and purples and the land fall into shadow, or rise into the light, signified something Lizzie couldn't quite voice, couldn't quite reach in her mind. But she knew that staring at the sky had been her search for something or somewhere that she'd been journeying towards, and now she'd changed direction.

Lizzie sat up, crossed her legs and switched on the camera in her hands.

'Welcome to day seventy,' Lizzie said, staring into the red-rimmed eyes of her reflection. 'I'm in the Neurology department at UCSF Medical Centre in San Francisco waiting for the first day of my treatment to start. I've been nil by mouth for over twelve hours. I'm hungry, thirsty and terrified that I've left it too late, terrified it won't work.

'Never, when I started on this journey, did I see myself back in a hospital bed waiting for another treatment.' Lizzie pulled in a breath and exhaled. 'Then again. I never thought I'd learn what it is to lose someone I love either. I …' Tears formed in Lizzie's eyes. 'I still have trouble believing Samantha is gone. I wish I'd been able to go to her funeral and say goodbye, but I have a duty now. A duty to fight for my life. Samantha didn't get the chance, she didn't choose any of this, and she certainly didn't choose to die.' Lizzie dry-swallowed.

The grief came in waves. Sometimes, mostly at night, Lizzie felt it wash over her until she was sinking below the surface of it. Other times it was shallow, bearable. Focusing on the details helped. Lizzie looked back at the camera screen and brushed her fingers across her cheeks, wiping away the tears.

'This morning I'm going to be wheeled into the first of many treatments over the course of the next month to see if I can beat this tumour. Dr Fitzgerald is going to insert lots and lots of tiny probes in through the back of my neck and right up to the outer wall of my brainstem.' Lizzie touched the smooth area of skin on the back of her neck where Arianna, a beautiful Puerto Rican nurse with a deep voice and throaty laugh, had shaved it yesterday.

'Then he's going to use microscopic cameras and some kind of blue dye injected into my brainstem to zap minuscule amounts of very strong radiation right at my tumour. The probes are going to stay in place over the next week so that Dr Fitzgerald can do his daily zapping, or whatever the technical term he used for it is, which means I'll have to stay face down on a special bed with a hole in it, like a massage table, and just drink protein shakes. So this is going to be my last video diary for a while, but Ben will be here doing his filming.'

Out of nowhere another wave of emotion flooded Lizzie's body, gripping her throat and causing tears to rise up and drop out of her eyes. It wasn't grief this time, but something else – gratitude? Hope? Love? There wasn't a word for it.

'I ... don't think I could've survived this week without Ben. I've spoken on the phone a hundred times to Jaddi and my mum and dad, but Ben has been the one by my side all the other times.' Lizzie closed her eyes and shook her head.

'Before I go, I wanted to say thank you to Caroline and Channel 6 for their support, especially in the last week, as well as to all the viewers who've continued to support us. I'm sorry we didn't trust you all to have the capacity to support my decision. I never saw it as choosing to die, but choosing to live on my terms. I still believe that, and I still believe that everyone with terminal or chronic illnesses should have the same rights and support that I've had to choose how they wish to spend their lives up to and including their deaths. But after losing Samantha, I know I have to fight, for her and for myself.'

Lizzie smiled for a final time and switched off the camera. She turned the small black object over in her hands and realised she'd miss the video diaries. Jaddi had been right all along. They had been about more than connecting with viewers; they'd been about connecting with herself too.

A flash of red in the doorway caught Lizzie's eye. She turned, the smile widening.

'Hey,' Ben said, stepping into the room. He was wearing his olive-green combat trousers with all the pockets and a new T-shirt, so red that it seemed to glow in the dim of her room.

'Hi.' She grinned. 'How did you get in here so early? Visiting hours don't start for another hour.'

Ben rubbed the palm of his hand against his cheek. She loved it when he did that. 'It's amazing what a large box of donuts can do for a group of hungry nurses. It turns out visiting hours are more of a discretionary thing, so you're stuck with me.'

'Damn,' she said, laughing.

'So.' Ben dropped his gaze to his hands before focusing them back on Lizzie. 'I have two things to tell you. Good news, I think.'

She nodded.

'Your mum, dad and Jaddi have landed at San Francisco International Airport. They should be here before you get wheeled off to the treatment room.'

'And the second thing?'

'Caroline's pulling the plug on the documentary.'

'Oh.' Lizzie opened her mouth to say more, but closed it again. What could she say? A barrage of nerves dropped inside her stomach.

'The last episode will show you here,' Ben continued, sitting on the side of the bed, 'and include your last video diaries. There's talk of follow-up episodes at some point in the future, but I think she's realised there won't be much to see whilst you're in hospital.'

Lizzie bit down on her bottom lip and willed the tears not to fall. Two fat drops raced along her cheeks. Ben reached out a finger and caught one. 'I thought you'd be pleased to have a break from the filming?'

She nodded as a sob broke out of her. 'I am. It's not that.' She closed her eyes, unable to stop her body from shaking. How could she explain? How could she ask him to stay with her when she had no right to?

'Liz? Liz, open your eyes and look at me.'

Lizzie opened her eyes as he tilted her chin upwards with the crook of his finger. 'I'm not going anywhere,' he said.

'It's fine, you don't have to stay.' Lizzie stared into his eyes, feeling the pull of him sweep over her. 'Like you said, I'm going to have a roomful soon enough. You've got a job, a life, and I could be here for months, or I could go to sleep tomorrow and not wake up. I'm sorry I dragged you into this.'

'Lizzie, stop.' Ben smiled and ran a hand across her cheek. 'It may be hard for you to believe, but nothing else matters to me, except being here with you. I'm staying.'

'Oh.' Another sob left her body. The tears falling in fat wet drops onto Ben's arm.

'Anyway, your mum has said she's knitting me a jumper, so I've got to stay for that.'

Lizzie shook her head, laughing and crying at the same time. 'My mum always knits when I'm in hospital. She says it keeps her busy.'

'Good then. I'll see if she can do me one of those cheesy Christmas jumpers.'

'But she can't actually knit. She tries. But the only time she does it is in hospitals so it's always stop and start and she loses the count. Last year, she kitted a jumper for Aaron with one arm hole and two head hole—'

All of sudden Ben leant forward, pressing his lips against hers. He tasted of toothpaste and the salt from her tears and of a future she didn't know she could have.

'I love you,' he whispered, brushing his lips against hers.

She nodded.

'Knock knock.' Alianna smiled from the doorway. Her white uniform glowed with the brightness of a new shift. 'I'm sorry to interrupt, but which one of you ordered the neon liquid for breakfast?' She held up her gloved hand and a small plastic cup.

Lizzie smiled. 'That would be me, thank you.'

'Ready?'

An image of Jaddi in the Channel 6 dressing room sprung into Lizzie's head. Jaddi had asked her the same question. There was no panic this time, no fear, just determination and hope. Lizzie looked into Ben's eyes and smiled. 'Absolutely.'

ACKNOWLEDGEMENTS

My heartfelt thanks goes first to my awesome editor, Victoria, for believing in this story as much as I do, and for helping me to make it what it is today. Thank you, team HQ!

To my beta readers – Pauline Hare, Kathryn Jones, Maggie Ewings, Mel Ewings, Steve Tomlin – I would be lost without your input.

Thank you to the Book Connectors for their wonderful support; especially, Linda Hill – an amazing blogger, who I'm proud to call my friend. Thank you to Tony Ellingham for all that you do, and for the magic refilling drawer of Twix bars.

Finally, to Tommy, Lottie and Andy, who sit beside me on the rollercoaster, and fill every day with laughter and fun. I love you!